HER BEST FRIEND

SARAH WRAY

Published by Bookouture in 2017
An imprint of StoryFire Ltd.
Carmelite House
50 Victoria Embankment
London EC4Y 0DZ
www.bookouture.com

ISBN: 978-1-78681-262-9
eBook ISBN: 978-1-78681-261-2

'Truth is like the sun. You can shut it out for a time, but it ain't going away.'

—*Elvis Presley*

CHAPTER ONE

Summer, 1995

The sun had held out for as long as it could. Thank goodness for that at least, everyone kept saying over and over; a mantra, just to fill the space. But it was getting dark, panic was setting in. She'd been missing for a whole day.

The adults all sat around the kitchen table – Peter and Michael had been out searching for hours along the canal, in the parks. They had come in, everyone's eyes on them straight away. But they shook their heads.

Michael looked grey and he steadied himself, gripping a chair. 'She'll come in any minute,' he said before Judith could ask anything or presume the worst. 'You'll tell her off and in a few days, it will be all forgotten. You'll see. You know what they're like.'

Judith put her head back in her hands.

Sylvie wasn't allowed to stay in the room with them any longer. She had been interrogated all evening – her brain felt scrubbed and numb from it, bleached out. She watched everyone's eyes locking wordlessly as she spoke, but she couldn't decode the messages they were sending each other. She went and sat in the living room, pretending to watch TV, the sound down as low as it would go, ears straining for the murmurs coming from the kitchen, for something she could latch on to.

The brightly coloured balloons from the party the day before still bobbed, ghost-like, around the house, on the gatepost at the end of the garden. Shiny, metallic streamers hung on the doorways and across the ceiling, fluttering of their own accord every now and then. Some had already fallen down and trailed along the carpet. The chairs and furniture were pushed back, the party food drying out, turning rotten on the trestle table Sylvie's dad had once used for wallpaper pasting.

Sylvie shoved a stale yellow party ring into her mouth, swallowing without tasting. Grabbing at the tray, she picked up one of each colour and pushed them in at the same time. Bad luck would ensue if she missed one out, a little voice in her head said.

The buffet was starting to smell – gloopy egg mayonnaise, greasy cocktail sausages, the air thickening with it. No one knew what to do with all the food: inappropriate to spend time clearing it away, grotesque to leave it there. Sylvie glanced back over her shoulder then crammed one thing from each plate into her mouth, breathing heavily through her nose, trying not to be sick. Her jaw was stretched, hardly any space left in her mouth free to chew, and it made her gag. Cold, fatty sausage churned in with gone-off cream. She retched, her eyes straining, then swallowed hard. A big ball of food stuck in her chest, pressing down painfully.

Did they really think she could just switch off and watch *Beverly Hills, 90210* like nothing had happened? Did they think she was stupid enough to believe them just because they said it would all be fine? She sat back on the sofa, hugging a cushion to her distended stomach. All she could hear from the kitchen was mumbles, the words and voices all blurring and running together.

A uniformed police officer waited in the hall. Her radio crackled and the dreaded words squawked out of it, loud and clear.

'Found her. Up at the lake,' the robotic voice said, followed by more interference.

'Got you. Yes, sir,' she heard the officer reply.

Sylvie froze on the sofa. *No, please, no.* She held her breath.

She couldn't make out what the voice said next. The police officer muttered 'Shit' under her breath, missing the 'i' sound out altogether.

Sylvie went to the hall, saw the police officer's back, heard the handle of the door to the kitchen turn. A long silence, then Judith's scream. Sylvie couldn't take it in. She couldn't fathom that Victoria had been here yesterday, right in front of her, here in this house, and now she was gone. She had to see for herself, to believe it was really true, not just a bad dream. She slipped quietly out of the front door.

Alternating between walking and running as much as her breathlessness and the recurring stitch in her side would allow, Sylvie felt like she was floating somehow; sounds were distant. All that food was jiggling around in her stomach. Vomit threatened in the back of her throat. She drifted over the road and a car horn blared but it was remote, removed.

It was still warm, even though it was late, and people sat on doorsteps and in deckchairs in the yards in front of their houses, talking and drinking. Windows were open, people watching TV, folding ironing. Preparing for their holidays maybe. The houses went past as if they were moving and Sylvie was standing still watching them.

Beyond the housing estates, past the school, the road emptied out, becoming just fields, no one around. Two police cars whizzed by, sirens blaring and echoing. Sylvie turned inwards, closed her eyes and clung to the dry-stone wall until they passed.

When she finally reached the lake, she was sweating, wheezy; her chest tight and painful, cheeks burning. But she couldn't stop. Instead of following the road all the way up to the lake, which would have been faster, Sylvie climbed over a gate and approached via the fields. The lake was floodlit – like a stadium. More lights than usual. The police must have brought their own. That wasn't a good sign, Sylvie thought.

Police cars were parked at the road entrance and tape sealed it off. She could see officers mingling around in the distance, like ants. The dry grass came up above Sylvie's knees, scratching her legs, creating criss-crossed red lines that turned to swollen welts. Something had drawn blood. She looked ahead and kept going, as if sleepwalking.

Closer to the lake, the sounds solidified, the blur cleared. Light breeze through the grass, chatter from police radios, birds, the odd shout between the officers. As she got nearer, Sylvie could see they were pulling something from the lake.

Someone, of course.

She imagined herself turning back, running through the grass the way she came, jumping into bed, pulling the covers over her head. But she found she was still powering ahead as they lifted the body out and onto the path at the side of the lake. The police at the lake entrance had become aware of her approaching; they put their hands up to their brows, squinting into the distance to work out who she was. They waved their arms but Sylvie ignored them, woozy, just shapes in the corner of her field of vision.

A female officer ran towards her, holding her hat to prevent it falling off. The policewoman's arms shot out in front of her and she shouted towards the officers at the lakeside. They screwed up their faces, didn't know what she was saying. The officer pointed towards Sylvie, but her running had slowed down. She was too out of breath, she was too late. Sylvie weaved in between two officers by the lakeside, ducking under their arms.

'Oi, you can't be here! Oi!'

Everything stopped. Victoria was there, out on the ground; a strange, grey, waxy quality to her skin. Her red hoody and clothes sodden and sticking to her, rushes in her hair and across her face. Some kind of foam or goo around her mouth and nose. She looked like a crash-test dummy, a shop mannequin.

'Aren't you going to try and revive her?' Sylvie heard herself say, the words swirling in the air around them. 'You need to do mouth-to-mouth. I've seen it on TV.'

'Can you get her out of here, someone, please? Jesus Christ! Is this amateur hour or what?'

Someone grabbed her elbow. The next thing Sylvie knew she was sitting in the back of a police car with a blanket around her. Her teeth wouldn't stop chattering. A disembodied arm passed her some water and her hand shook as she tried to drink it.

'You're Victoria's friend Sylvie, aren't you?' The female officer smiled at her, speaking softly, craning her head round from the front seat of the car.

Sylvie was confused. 'How do you know my name?' She tried the car door but it was locked and they were already moving, the lake and Victoria getting further and further away.

'Officer saw you bolt from your house. Just had her on the radio. We better get you home, sweetheart. You look like you could do with your mum.'

Sylvie put her forehead against the cool glass all the way, watching the grey of the road whizz by.

'She'll have been worried something had happened to you too,' the woman said, a strong Irish accent. 'You shouldn't have your mum worrying as well with all this going on.'

The male police officer in the driver's seat didn't turn at all so Sylvie couldn't see his face.

The female officer eyed him sideways and spoke quietly as if Sylvie couldn't hear, as if she wasn't really there. 'Whole town's going to be on high alert after this, that's for sure,' she said.

Sylvie stared down at her legs, scratched and smeared with bright red blood.

CHAPTER TWO

Sylvie

I clear a spot in the condensation on the window of the café to watch the storm. People gather under the striped canopies and in the doorways of the shops, waiting. Yet more squeeze in, shrieking and scowling at the sudden ferocity of the downpour. The sky is heavy and dark, the rain is falling in sheets.

The café door keeps swinging open and the bell rings, people looking for somewhere to sit to wait it out, shaking umbrellas all over the floor. Each time, the waitress, a teenage girl in a pink cropped mohair sweater, runs over with a mop and metal bucket, wipes most of the grey water up and repositions the yellow caution sign.

Looking through the porthole I've created, it feels like I have my own private view of a film. They have barely changed the shopping centre in the twenty years I have been away. A few different shops, but some of the original ones are still here too. The main shopping area is in a square over two levels, a balcony running right round it. The stonework is even more blackened than I remember it. There's something about the drabness of the shops that makes my stomach feel heavy. Davidson's Family Butchers is directly opposite.

'Family Butchers' always made me think of massacres when I was younger: cannibalism. Dad would shake his head at me. 'I don't know what goes on in there, where you get these ideas from,' he'd say, tapping on the side of my head.

But that image has been replaced by another one now. Seeing the dead meat sitting in the window, some bearing no resemblance to the animal it's from, some gruesomely retaining the shape. A pig's head gaudy on the green felt at the front of the window. I am back in the maternity ward in the stillness after the noise and violence of the birth. The nurse said it was a 'bit of a bloodbath down there, but you'll live', and she sewed me up, chattering about *Strictly Come Dancing* while I stared at the white strip lighting. She might just as well have been doing a cross stitch in front of the TV.

Mother and baby doing well, the word went out.

Outside, a man sticks his hand out under the canopy and looks up at the sky but rushes back in again. It's showing no signs of stopping yet. I force in a mouthful of the iced custard slice. I'm not hungry really, it's too sweet, but comforting too. Me and Mum used to come to this café every Saturday with Grandma. I'd have a prawn mayonnaise sandwich with an ice-cream float, followed by a custard slice. Mum and Grandma would have black coffee, and Mum would smoke and watch me, occasionally stealing the smallest nibble of my food.

'Excuse me. This seat taken?'

I look up and do a double-take at the woman looming over me, her hand still on my shoulder. Her face is blooming into a new expression too: recognition. She narrows her eyes and zooms in.

'Sylvie? Is that you? I never saw you come in.'

Judith looks as neat as ever. Slim, well-fitting clothes. Her bouncy, rollered hair is wilting in the weather. Faint mascara smudges under her eyes.

'Judith! God, I didn't… Please, sit down.'

'Oh, well I need to get home really, but this weather!'

She scrapes a chair out, setting my teeth on edge, and sits down.

'And who is this?' She touches the handle of the pram next to me. 'They've a fine pair of little lungs on 'em, eh? I remember what that's like.' She pushes her lips together and looks out across the shopping centre.

A crack of wind lashes rain against the window so hard it sounds like gravel, setting the whole café chattering. It looks like night-time outside now.

'This will be punishment for the two sunny days we got back in the summer, eh?' Judith says. 'Mind you, even then we got those terrible floods a few days later. It's hardly worth it, is it?'

'I heard that on the news.'

'I didn't know you were back, Sylvie. You should have come to see me or let me know.' She smooths down her coat and tries to rearrange her hair.

'I just got back very recently actually. I need to sort things out at my mum's, you know. I was going to get in touch.'

Judith looks down at the shopping bags of baby things by my feet. I couldn't carry everything with me on the train.

'I'm sorry I didn't go to the funeral, love. I don't do very well with them, I'm afraid. After, well… you know. I sent her my wishes privately.'

Judith taps the side of her head. 'Will you come round to the house?' she says. 'I know Peter would love to see you and it would be so lovely to catch up and hear all your news. You've obviously plenty to tell us all about.'

She's looking at the baby the whole time, as if she's talking to her, not me. People often do.

'OK, I'll come round. You still in the same place or…?'

'Oh yes, same place. That's us now, that house. We'll not move from there. Do come round… I've been trying to contact you, actually. There's something I need to talk to you about.'

'Oh, really? What's that?'

'Can you come tomorrow?' Judith says.

A cry distracts us both. Judith reaches out her hand. 'What's her name, pet? She's absolutely gorgeous.'

I take a swig from what's left of the sugary remnants of my coffee. 'It's Victoria. Her name is Victoria.'

Judith tenses and her eyes start to glitter.

'I'm sorry, Judith... I...'

'Don't be, dear. That's lovely. It's absolutely lovely. It means a lot to me. Really. She's just gorgeous.'

I want to ask Judith again what she wanted to talk to me about, but she's already standing up to leave the café. 'Anyway, the weather looks to be lifting now.' She pulls the belt of her coat tightly around her waist and leaves, clattering into a couple of chairs along the way, accidentally dragging them a short way across the floor.

Outside, it's still pouring with rain.

CHAPTER THREE

Sylvie

The house is finally starting to be inhabitable again. I might be able to think about putting it on the market soon, making a fresh start. I could use the money to go somewhere. Anywhere. All those places I've always said I wanted to see. *With a baby, though?*

Today's dreaded job is to finally clear the fridge out – the warm stench that comes out makes hot vomit squirt up my throat again. Is it even switched on? I throw the kitchen windows open and breathe in the cool air.

On one of the shelves, a rotting tomato is slowly morphing into browny-green sludge; the milk has turned solid and yellow, the bottle bloating out, threatening to explode. A tin of anchovies is peeled open, a thick layer of furry mould gathered on the top.

Anchovies were one of my cravings when I was pregnant with Victoria, although I'm vegetarian and I don't recall ever eating them before. They give me the creeps, little grey hairy things, but I couldn't get enough of them. Anchovies, macaroni cheese and this sour cherry pop drink, and sometimes together. I throw the tin of anchovies into the open bin liner and it releases a fresh cloud of the putrid smell.

I throw the rubbish bag in the bin outside and close the kitchen door. I've spent almost every minute the last week cleaning this place – when I'm not feeding or changing Victoria, or sleeping. My stomach churns when I remember what it was like when I got here. It's not just remembering, though. It's more of a living memory, and it's not the only one.

I experience it again in nauseating detail when I least want to – smell it and taste it even: the dead flies cluttered up against the windowsill, the shellac-like brown sticky coating on everything. Even now, every so often in certain areas of the house I suddenly catch that overpowering, sickly-sweet smell that makes me gag, and then it's gone again.

It's not even so much the disgusting mess itself that turns my stomach. You can wipe that off. More the shame that someone lived like this – my own mother at that. Lived here alone for the last twenty years and died here alone, in her own filth.

I go into the living room, making sure to close the kitchen door, and lift Victoria out of the Moses basket, instinctively pulling her close to me, breathing in the clean, cool smell of her, that gorgeous scent that babies have.

'We'll think of something, won't we, you and me?' I hug her small, soft body close to me and rock her gently from side to side, kissing the top of her head. I concentrate on how warm she feels against me.

I hadn't thought about home, about Victoria and that summer, in a while, when they rang me about Mum, to tell me what had happened, that she'd died. I'd been wrapped up in my own world, my own Victoria.

They said mine was the only name and number in Mum's phone. But I had been thinking about her that week, more than usual. I'd been thinking about how she was, what her life was like now. I'd dreamed about her, vividly. I even thought I'd seen her in the street a couple of times.

I shudder, thinking of Mum found at the bottom of these stairs, in only her nighty, alone. Been there for days. Dying, dead.

Everything downstairs is now much cleaner than it was, but it still looks grubby – dirt ground in; it will never come completely off. Three skips' worth of stuff has already been taken away; the rest stored, crammed into the rooms upstairs. But I still keep finding it... old mobile phones, flip-flops, second-hand board games with bits missing, VHS tapes, bulk-buy toilet rolls to join the family packs already stacked up – things Mum must have ordered on the Internet, all this stuff she could never use, to add to all the other junk.

My phone buzzes and I take it out of my pocket. It's Nathan. I look at the screen and take a deep breath. *Ignore.* It starts up again, insistent. I throw it onto the sofa and it bounces. Eventually, he gives up. I picture our flat in Glasgow. Neat, tidy, white walls, clean lines. Nathan likes it that way; it's 'a designer thing', he says. He couldn't cope with all this clutter. He has a one-in, one-out rule – for books, CDs, kitchen stuff. His desk immaculate in the spare room.

Not long after we met, Nathan came back early and surprised me when he'd been working away. I'd have tidied up if I'd known he was coming. He tried to laugh it off, but his disgust at the state of my flat was obvious; my natural state, when I didn't expect anybody to be looking.

Back in the kitchen, I throw the window open wider to let the fresh air in, and my thoughts about Glasgow and Nathan out. Looking out over the garden, something is off. There are colours that shouldn't be there amongst the long grass and overgrown weeds – solid yellows and bright blues. Something's moving. *Someone.* My insides flutter. The boy with the camera again?

I look closer and bang on the window. A small head pops up, then another, followed by one more. Children, but they make me think of little rabbits.

I tap on the glass again. 'Hey, what are you doing?'

One of them screams and they all run to the gate, barging each other out of the way to be the first out. I didn't mean to scare them away. I wonder then if they used to mock Mum, call her a crazy old lady. And despite how things ended up between us, the idea of her being unhappy still hurts. I pull the window to again and lock it.

In the living room, the corner of something peeps out of one of the open drawers and catches my eye. An old photo album. I pull it out and hold it closed for a long time before forcing myself to open it. It feels like looking at someone else's life, not my own. The photos are neatly glued in; the pages well-thumbed, their corners turned up.

A picture of me in a paddling pool as a baby, food smeared proudly around my face. In my Brownie uniform, scowling. Another in front of the house on roller skates in a hand-knitted cardigan, gaudy colours. It was the day we moved into this house. Dad is in the background, caught unawares, carrying a box up the stairs.

There's one at a theme park. Victoria and me in stupid matching baseball caps. We went with the Prestons, all six of us, just before Dad got ill. We are all smiling in the photo – me, Mum, Dad. Victoria and her parents too.

Mum and Victoria's dad, Peter, wouldn't go on the ride. I sat with Victoria, and Dad sat with Judith and we all dangled our legs and wiggled our feet as we waited in the cars for the ride to get going. Dad didn't want to go on either, at first, but I begged him and eventually his face cracked into a smile and he threw up his hands.

As the ride slowly lifted, the hydraulics spitting and hissing, Mum and Peter were on the ground getting smaller and smaller until I couldn't make them out in the crowd any more. The ride spun and twisted high in the air. Everything was a blur. I kept trying to catch a glimpse of Mum. It made me panic not to be able to see where she was, for some reason. Instead I could only catch distorted flashes of people's faces as their car whizzed in front of ours. Dad's teeth, Judith's cheeks stretched and pushed back, her hair whipping her face… Now, to think of Judith doing something like that is out of place and jarring – she was always so controlled and prim. And I start to question whether the memory is right, if it was in fact Judith on the ground and Mum on the ride. All the time, I could hear Victoria screaming in my ear.

One of the pictures sets a memory playing of a holiday I'd almost forgotten about. We're all sitting outside a caravan – Mum, Judith and Peter, and me and Victoria in matching blonde ponytails. We would have been around ten. Dad must be behind the camera. It was Bridlington. Victoria and I cried on the way home because we didn't want the holiday to be over; no more days splashing in the outdoor pool. Flashes of the week come back to me. Mum and Judith dancing to 'Wig-Wam Bam' with me and Victoria on the dance floor. Dad and Peter taking us to crazy golf. Mum getting pulled up on stage with a magician. Fried egg sandwiches back at the caravan.

I flip further through the album: Flower Fairies dolls peeping out, hidden between the plants in the garden, like the children I saw earlier. Dad helped me recreate the Cottingley Fairies pictures and take the photos. The memory is pastel-coloured. It's soft focus and false-looking. It was to cheer me up because I was upset when I found out the original pictures were faked. I was so angry at the woman for owning up and breaking the magic.

Earlier in the book are pictures of Mum and Dad's wedding: so many bridesmaids. There's a picture of Mum and Judith holding me and Victoria when we were tiny babies. In the photos of Mum when she was younger, she seems like a different person from the one I grew up with: she was thin, even thinner than when I was a child, and her hair was cropped into a pixie cut. People called her Mags then, she said, but it was always Margaret when I was young.

In one of the shots, Mum and Judith sit on the beach in Spain, surrounded by men, Mum in a bright red bikini, the colours bleached out. In the next one they're sitting on a balcony drinking sangria. They grew up together, like me and Victoria.

I slam the book shut, dust clouding out, and shove it back in the drawer, making everything in the cabinet rattle.

I decide to take a bath; it's a good opportunity to make the most of all my cleaning work yesterday. My stomach lurches again to think of the state of the bathroom: the toilet hadn't seen any bleach in years, baked-on mess clinging to the bowl.

The bath is old and ceramic, chipped and rough-looking. I bathed in it many times when I was younger. It's about as clean as it will get for now. I wonder if I will have to replace it in order to sell the house. I don't know how to do any of this: no one tells you. I keep wondering, When you sell a house, do you have to tell people someone died in it? Explain what happened to them?

There's a long strand of grey hair in the tub. I am finding them everywhere and it stops me in my tracks each time. I never saw Mum with grey hair. The mum I remember, my mum, had shoulder-length brown hair that kicked out at the ends, with the help of lots of heated appliances. It's like another different person was here. To think of a living part of her here and yet she is gone... I remember learning at school that hair is actually 'dead matter'.

When I start to fill the bath up, the taps moan and honk like a dying beast. The water has a yellow tinge. I pour in some of the cheap bubble bath that was already here, turning the water bright, holiday-brochure blue. Another thing here that confuses me, trying to make sense of Mum's life since I moved out. Bubble bath, flowers – long dead by the time I arrived, and dried to powder, but once alive – all the ornamental touches and home comforts she had, despite living in such a way. Even tinsel still draped around a mirror. How many Christmases ago?

I turn on the baby monitor in the bedroom. Mine was the only room in the house that was perfectly clean and tidy when I got here. It's almost as if Mum knew I would come and I would need somewhere to stay. It meant that I could keep Victoria in there while I made the other rooms cleaner and safe; we didn't have to get a hotel.

Like everywhere else, the décor is exactly as it was in my room. The moons and stars wallpaper, the Elastica poster faded and cracked, looming over the bed. It's comforting in a way that some things stay the way they were. But it pulls you right back into your old life, too, like one of those cheesy body-swap films. The white fairy lights are still around the headboard, the mirror with the draped pink feather boa, a tiara hooked over the corner – Victoria and I had got into the Manic Street Preachers the year before she died. We'd talked for hours about where Richie might be after he went missing.

The cheap make-up I used to wear is neatly lined up, the garish eyeshadow colours dried out. My yellow Care Bear is on top of the dressing table too, its smile fixed and dumb.

I switch on the lamp. It seems to captivate Victoria now too; it always did me, even when I was too old for it. It casts an array of coloured stars on the wall and they sweep around the room as it spins.

I check the monitor is working properly before sinking into the blue warmth of the bath. My back and arms ache from holding Victoria so much; she's getting heavier now. The water is soothing the pain away; it feels good to stretch out, wallow in the quiet, only the occasional plonk of the taps dripping.

Steam rises. Only my head and feet are above the water, my toes propped against the taps, the turquoise pedicure I had just before Victoria was born almost grown out, chipped off. The rest of my body is a blur under the water, like it isn't a part of the rest of me at all – detached, disappearing.

Something startles me. I must have fallen asleep and I jolt awake, spluttering. Being in the water, my face half-submerged, I can't get the vision of Victoria in the lake out of my head.

The letter box clatters loudly in the wind.

CHAPTER FOUR

Sylvie

Getting out of the house is a military exercise, but if I don't do it now I'll stay here all day. The days whizz by and blur into one another, and yet at the same time they are long. I dwell on things at the moment if I sit still for too long; unwelcome thoughts snarl around my brain like Japanese knotweed.

I seize my moment between feeds. If I move fast enough after the last one, before the next, I can still make it actually worth going somewhere. Coming down the stairs with the bag of Victoria's things – so many things that need to be carried everywhere – I catch the smell again, sweet and sickly. I try to ignore the fact it's close to where they said Mum was found. I stop to see if I can pinpoint it, but then it's gone again. We used to watch *Most Haunted* at uni. Didn't the ghosts sometimes have a distinctive smell? 'Don't be ridiculous, Sylvie.' I realise I've said it out loud.

'Isn't Mummy being silly, Victoria?' I say to the baby instead.

I look out of the window, pulling the discoloured lace curtain back, peering through the filthy glass. It's another blank, sunless day outside. The sky is white, with the slightest tint of grey.

Something catches my attention. A shape, a block of colour; something out of place about it. Then a movement. There's someone there – a man. He's standing halfway up the steps to the house and he's looking directly at the window. He's seen me too. My body jolts. I expect him to run or gesture to me, but he doesn't; he just stands there, fixed, arms by his side. His face is expressionless.

'Can I help you?' I say, opening the door. Seems unlikely, but maybe he knew Mum. He still doesn't react.

He speaks then. 'Are you Sylvie?' He's young, twenties maybe. He's wearing a faux vintage Americana T-shirt depicting a surf café. 'Sylvie Armstrong?' His accent doesn't sound local.

Sometimes I don't even recognise that name any more. It's Reynolds now. Sylvie Armstrong sounds like someone I used to know once but can't quite place the face.

'Sorry, what do you want? Are you looking for my mum… Margaret?'

He doesn't say anything and I instinctively step back into the house and try to get behind the door. He makes one swift move then there's a camera sound then a white flash and another click. The blur clears and I see a camera hanging round his neck, an old-fashioned manual one. He turns and walks down the steps.

'Hey!' I call after him but he's gone across the street. He gets into a car. There are other people inside – two in the front and one in the back. Someone takes another picture with a phone out of the side window. I'm too stunned to move. As the car pulls slowly away, a woman turns in her seat and stares at me out of the back window until the car is out of view.

Why would anyone want a picture of Mum's house? I stand back and look up at it, the half brick, half pebble-dash. I wonder if they heard about her death. About how she had lain there for days before anyone found her. But still, why would they want a photograph? The surface of my skin prickles all over.

I go back inside, gather all the baby luggage, and we set off.

There's a fine, fizzy drizzle in the air, almost imperceptible. After just a few minutes, my hair feels wet and my clothes are starting to stick to me. Walking this so-familiar route to Victoria's house makes my insides tighten.

Maybe I shouldn't have come here again. Perhaps I should have just paid someone to clear out Mum's house and sell it on. Something pulled me back, though, the way your hometown does. Maybe you want to see if it offers any clues as to how you became who you are; see whether you can blame it.

One last time, Conley whispered to me, quiet at first, but then more insistent.

Back then, I'd walk this way to school every day, calling on Victoria along the way. We would always be late for school because she was never ready – she'd be half dressed, one shoe on, eating a bowl of cereal and glued to something on TV. She was like that: a whirlwind through your life. She'd always mess up your plans but usually in a good way.

I'm out of breath when I get halfway up the road, cheeks burning, so I pause and lean on the pram to recover. Victoria is sleeping. I look out over the expanse of open green on the hill between our houses. People call it a park but it isn't a proper one. More a field that's had a few recreational items dropped into it. Masses of green lumps, great for sledging on. There's a concrete football pitch in the middle and a rubber rectangle with rusty swings at the top. It's where we spent most of the summer and even the winter, braving it out, standing around outside just so we could be together, away from our parents. It's empty now, completely still.

After I catch my breath, I carry on. Everything looks the same on Victoria's street, but the colouring or the light is different, somehow, the way it is in old photographs. You can tell straight away they're from a different time. The Prestons' house still stands out as the neatest; it always did. A small, perfectly trimmed lawn, the gleaming car on the driveway, a pristine hanging basket by the door.

He makes me jump when I catch him out of the corner of my eye. Peter is in the garage, the door swung open. He's standing there in his shorts and an old T-shirt, even though it's September. I can't quite tell if he's waving or shielding his eyes from the light. I've been standing here looking at the house for a while, mustering up the courage to knock on the door.

He comes walking out slowly, wiping his hands on an old rag. His face is revealed last of all. He looks at me expressionless for a while before breaking into a craggy smile.

'Bloody hell. Look at you! Look at you two in fact!' He peers into the pram at Victoria. 'Hey, it's smashing to see you. Judith, we've got visitors!' he shouts back through the garage.

Peter and I stand there smiling and nodding; unsure who is going to go first.

'Judith, you'll never believe who's here. Jude!'

'I bumped into Judith in the shopping centre the other day actually.'

'Did you? She never said.' A breeze out of nowhere makes the trees in the street swish loudly.

He looks back through the garage, but Judith appears at the front door. She's wearing neat jeans, a candy-striped pink blouse and pearl stud earrings. She always looked perfectly turned out and dressed up, even in casual clothes.

'Sylvie, love! Thank you so much for coming over.' She reaches out and presses a hard, dry kiss on my cheek. I get a strong whiff of make-up, old-fashioned lipstick, a taste of heavy, sweet perfume.

'You never said you'd seen Sylvie, Jude?' Peter says but she ignores him and he disappears back into the garage, starts wrapping up the cable from something, looping it between his hand and elbow.

'Yes, I did, Pete. It's just that you don't listen.' Her tone is strained but she's smiling at me, gesturing for me to go into the house.

'Come inside, Sylvie love. Do you want a cuppa or something?'

'Yes, that would be lovely, thanks.' I wipe my hand across my forehead, damp with rain.

We go in and Peter appears behind us. Judith falls back and whispers something to him.

'This is Sylvie's daughter, Pete. Isn't she gorgeous?' Judith is on full beam again.

'Hey, she's a bonny little thing, isn't she?'

'Tell him her name, Sylvie.'

The air stiffens. I assumed that she would have already done this, but they are both looking at me expectantly. Peter looks between us, his confusion growing. I send a glance back to Judith, willing her to say it, but she just wears a fixed smile.

'Her name's Victoria. I hope it's not… Sorry, I didn't intend you to find out like… like this.'

Peter takes a big breath, looks winded for a second, but recovers.

'It's an absolutely lovely thing to do, darlin'. We're thrilled, aren't we, Jude? And Victoria would be too.' His voice cracks on that.

The house is silent except for a clock ticking somewhere. Everything so clean and undisturbed. Peter points into the sitting room. Inside it's the same as it always was. Freshly decorated but very similar to the original. Neutral magnolia, tasteful chintz. Three remote controls are perfectly lined up on top of a copy of the *Radio Times*. The house smells of bleach and air freshener.

Peter claps and rubs his hands together. 'Right, you get yourselves sat down in here and I'll get some drinks on the go. What do you fancy? Tea, coffee? Something stronger?' He winks at me.

'Just tea for me, thanks.'

Judith sits with her hands on her knees, prim. The quiet sound of the clock ticking booms around the room. The seconds seem slow. She purses her lips, putting her hand to her chest, flaring her nostrils. 'I'm sorry, Sylvie. Just seeing you here again after everything. It's knocked me for six.'

The last clear memory I have of seeing Judith is at the kitchen table at our house, her hands in her hair. I saw Judith and Peter in the days after, going over and over everything, but they all blur into one. Mum wouldn't let me go to Victoria's funeral. She said I was too young; that it was no place for someone my age.

Judith avoids my eye. 'It's like seeing a ghost, you know?'

She turns her attention to Victoria. I think what it's like for Victoria having a face etched with pain looming in at her. *Does she sense things like that yet? What will she remember?* But she is impassive, tongue lolling adorably.

'The house looks nice,' I say pointlessly. I trail off because I can't think how things should be between Judith and me. I've never known her on an adult footing, not since I was fifteen. Our relationship is trapped in that time, never ageing or progressing.

Judith shifts in her seat, rearranging cushions and primping her hair. She reaches under the spotless glass coffee table and pulls out the local paper, the *Conley News*.

'Did you see this, love?'

I shake my head. *Does she really think I still read it?*

'Have a read. It was in the paper a few weeks ago. I'll go and get some biscuits.'

The paper feels thin, smooth like it's been handled a lot. The article starts on the front page, continued on page seven. There's a picture of Judith taken here in this front room, perched on the end of the sofa, unsmiling, camera tilting downwards at her.

There's an inset picture of Victoria, too, in her red hooded top and green jeans, sitting on the wall outside the house, squinting at the sun. The whole crowd of us used to wear the same stuff – green or red jeans and hooded tops. Matching raincoats from the market too. Walking around like a set of Russian dolls, Dad used to say.

Judith hovers with the biscuits as I read the article. Each time I look up, she is focused on me intently. It has a timeline of Victoria's disappearance and a map of the lake and the local area where she was last seen, the route she took.

'I just have to do something, you know? It's twenty years. *Twenty years.*' She emphasises the words, stretching out the 'years'. 'I ring

the police every year on the day she died. To remind them that
I'm still here. I'm still waiting.'

'Do they have any new leads?'

She bats the question away with her hand. 'Oh, I can't even
understand what they say to me. "It remains open." That's all I get.
Neither this nor that. Fobbed off. They've moved on. They say it's
open but they're not doing anything. I know they wish I would
just go away. But I won't. I won't give up.' Her jaw is set hard.

'Do you have somewhere I could feed Victoria?'

Judith's eyelids flicker at the name again.

'Of course, love. In her old room. You know where it is.'

Victoria's bedroom, where we spent so many hours French-
plaiting each other's hair, listening to tapes, listing our favourite
boys, ranking them into an ever-shifting top ten. I open the door
slowly, bracing myself, but it has been turned into a guest room,
as neutral and ordered as everything else in the house.

Who lives in a house like this? If you were asked, you wouldn't
be able to say.

There's a spare bed and an exercise bike, too. No sign of Victoria
anywhere, except for a picture on the wall from when she was a
bridesmaid – it was that final summer. I remember how excited
she was about wearing the shiny, ice-blue dress and getting her
make-up done by a professional make-up artist. It looks so dated
now – the harsh purples and pinks are ageing.

After I've fed Victoria and sat with her upstairs a little longer
than I need to, I go back downstairs. Judith has put the paper
away now.

Peter is back in the living room, perched on the sofa arm.

'I had to change the room,' Judith says, as if she needs to
apologise. 'It was just too much – seeing all her things every day.
I still have most of it, though. Stored away. People said it was for
the best to redecorate it; that it might help.'

I think of Mum's house, the stink and filth of it.

I make a shape with my mouth but nothing will come out. What could I say?

'So, there was something I wanted to ask you, Sylvie. If you don't mind,' Judith says, a light going back on in her.

I was getting ready to start leaving, but she gestures for me to sit down again.

'It's about Victoria.'

'Oh.'

'My Victoria,' she adds, and my scalp prickles.

'There's a man, a film-maker. He wants to make a documentary about it. Victoria's case.'

Peter tuts loudly, shaking his head. Judith shoots him a glare.

'He's from Wales. He read about the case.' Judith gestures to the newspaper under the table. 'He says it's a good story; there'll be interest in it. We might get new information. Sam is his name. Sam Price. I've a good feeling about him.'

'Good story,' Peter says, a sneer to his voice, his mandible twitching. 'It's not a "story"; it's my daughter's life. And yours. Or it was. And he's turning it into a bloody "story".'

'He doesn't mean it like that, Peter, and you know it.'

'Bloody vultures,' Peter says. 'There's next to nothing they won't make money off of.'

Victoria lets out a sharp cry. 'Will you get involved, Sylvie?' Judith asks.

'Me?'

A loud bang makes me jump in my seat. The glass panes in the door rattle and Peter is gone.

'Ignore him; he's just struggling with it all a bit at the moment. It's bringing it all back.'

'So you've met this Sam?' I say.

'Yes, of course. He's here. In Conley.'

'Oh, really? OK,' I say. 'If you think it's a good idea.'

Judith straightens up. 'Well, don't you? Isn't it worth a try?'

'Of course, of course I do. Sorry, I'm all over the place. I'm just tired and with Mum's house and this one... Sorry... So who's he going to be interviewing?'

'I don't know exactly. He was a bit "journalistic" about it, to be honest. I have to accept it's independent and blah blah blah. But he's going to interview me again, of course. And he wants to talk to you too. You were the closest person to Victoria. Even closer than me, maybe. Well, definitely. Let's face it.' She looks down.

'I just don't know what help I would be, is all. I've already recounted everything I know. Many times now. There's nothing new I could say.'

'Please, Sylvie. Please, for me and Peter. He's never been the same. We're getting old now. We need some closure, Sylvie. We have to know before...' The tendons in her neck tighten and stick out, rock-hard.

'I'll do what I can, OK?'

Judith puts a business card into my hand and squeezes it closed, the corners of the card digging in. 'I'm really hopeful, Sylvie, that this could stir things up – that's what we need. Really jog someone's memory, you know? People move on, things change: that's what Sam said. You just don't know.'

I tilt my head up at her and squeeze her hand back before extricating myself and shoving Sam's business card into my bag.

Judith looks towards the living-room door.

She speaks more quietly. 'I really am sorry, you know. About your mum, and that we lost touch. After Victoria, my head was all over the place. And then your dad... I think we both shut ourselves off for a long time. We should have done the opposite and looked after each other at a time like that. But that's hindsight, isn't it? I guess I just didn't have it in me.'

'I'm sorry too,' I say. 'That I didn't keep in touch when I moved away.'

Judith brushes it off. 'You were a kid. And you were better off away from this place.' She was always a good pal to me, your mother, you know.'

'You were to her, too.'

Victoria starts to wriggle.

'I better go.'

Judith and I hug lightly before I leave. Or at least we mime one; our bodies hardly touch.

Outside, Peter is clattering in the garage. The concrete floor is swept perfectly clean. Various tools are hung up on the wall, cords neatly wrapped away.

I hover in the entrance. 'I'm going to get off, Peter. Great to see you.'

Peter jumps, turning to face me. 'Christ, you gave me a scare. OK, love. I'm sorry about before.' He gives me a strange, long look, a slight grimace to his face, and then he breaks out of it. 'Ignore me. It's just you've such a look of your mother. It's uncanny from certain angles.'

I feel myself flush.

'Anyway, grand to see you. Pop by again, won't you? And don't mind Judith – if you don't want to get involved with this Sam, you've no need to.'

When I have walked halfway down the street, I turn back and Peter is at the end of the driveway, waving and watching us.

CHAPTER FIVE

Sam

Sam stares out across the lake. The water looks like thick black tar, the reflections from the sun scattered pieces of tinfoil. He throws a stone in and rings spread out around it, then they are quickly gone again, healed over. He takes a sweeping video shot across the landscape. The mounds of grass in the fields that surround the lake give it a strange, otherworldly feeling; a set for a film that takes place on another planet.

Midges mingle above the water and rushes, invisible until they get caught in a beam of sunlight. Sam drags his sleeves over his hands and pulls his jumper up around his face. Insects are attracted to him; they always eat him alive.

He dips his hand into the freezing water. It feels thick, full of floating things. His fingers come back out dirty, black blobs of slime, green strings collecting along them. Every so often a breeze makes the water wrinkle up like fabric then smooth itself out again.

'A local beauty spot,' some described it as, when Sam looked the lake up on the Internet earlier, visited it on Google Earth before the drive to Conley.

There's something about it but it's desolate too, only the occasional car whooshing past.

Filming another semicircle around the lake, in the viewfinder Sam now sees someone sitting on the bench at the picnic table, where there had been no one before. It must be Dean, who he has arranged to meet, although he hadn't seen anyone arrive. He looks around and there are no cars anywhere. He gets a shot of the man looking over the lake. He hasn't noticed Sam yet.

It takes Sam longer than he anticipated to walk round to the picnic table, as if he's on a slow travellator. The lake is bigger than it looks. 'Dean?' he says when he reaches him, and the man jumps, twisting his body round. 'Sorry, mate, didn't mean to scare you.'

They shake hands but Dean doesn't meet his eye.

'I'm Sam. We spoke about the documentary I'm doing. Cheers for agreeing to meet me.'

'No bother,' Dean says, rubbing at his nose, skittish.

'I didn't see you turn up?' Sam looks back at the road.

Dean points. 'I just walked across the fields.'

'OK. Well, unless you've any questions, we'll get going, if it's alright with you,' Sam says, positioning the camera.

Dean's face freezes for a second. 'Can you just remind me again where this is going to be on?'

'I don't know for sure yet. I'm just doing the research, getting some preliminary footage together, then pitching it out.'

This seems to make Dean relax a bit. Assuming the footage will never see the light of day, no doubt. A fair assumption, Sam thinks.

'I wasn't sure about doing this, you know,' Dean says. 'I'm still not. It's just 'cos I saw her mother in the paper again. That's why I agreed.'

Sam fiddles behind the camera, zooming in then out until there's just the right balance of the lake behind Dean.

Dean expels air. 'Listen, can we just get it over with? I feel like I'm at the dentist or something here.' His legs are jiggling under the table. He arranges his hair, scraping greasy, grey strands back off his face.

'Look at me, not the camera. It's more natural,' Sam says.

Dean nods, his hands stuffed between his knees.

'So, you found the body?'

Dean looks up, shoulders narrowed. He has the head of an older man on the body of a skinny teenager, Sam thinks.

'Yeah, it was a Sunday and I used to walk my dog, Jessie, every night. She's gone now, bless her, but she was an energetic little thing then. Sheep dog so she needed to be walked twice a day.'

'Did you always walk her at the lake?' Sam asks.

Dean shifts in his seat and pauses to think before answering. 'Not always. In the morning I'd walk her closer to my house, because I needed to get to work. But in the summer, I liked to bring her up to the lake. It cleared my head up here.'

'How old were you at the time?'

Dean considers for a few seconds again. 'I was twenty-one then. I was still doing an apprenticeship – just finishing. To be a joiner.'

'Was there anything unusual or remarkable about that Sunday?' Sam says, reminding Dean to look at him and not straight into the camera. His eyes keep flicking towards it anyway.

'No, I wouldn't say so.' Dean's hands are fidgeting in his lap under the table. 'I had a bit of a hangover, if I'm honest. I'd been out in the town the night before. I wasn't feeling too clever that day. So I went up to the lake for that reason, too. Try and blow the cobwebs off a little bit.'

'What time was it?' Sam asks.

Dean answers with certainty this time. 'It was nine, nine thirty. I liked the light at that time of the evening in the summer.'

'And you always drove up here to the lake?'

'Usually I walked, like today. But you know, the hangover. So I took the car. It was my dad's car. The weather was nice, I remember that. But it had turned nasty so quickly the day before and I didn't want to get caught out in that. Not on a Sunday night up here so, yes, I brought the car.'

Dean keeps glancing at the camera as if it's a person fixing their stare on him.

Sam softens his voice as much as he can. 'Can you talk about what happened, then, that night? It's OK, you can take your time.'

Dean looks at his watch repeatedly, a kind of tic. 'Well, it was Jessie. She was usually pretty good. She did as she was told. But I threw a stick for her and she didn't come back. She was agitated. You know, wagging her tail and everything. And she was looking at something in the water and barking.'

Dean glances over now towards the lake, and Sam makes a mental note to cut in a shot of the water, the midges fizzing on the surface.

Dean bites at his lip and carries on. 'Honestly? I thought she'd seen a wasp or something or that she might have been barking at her own reflection. Because she did that sometimes in mirrors.'

Sam lets Dean go on.

'Yeah, so I went over to her, to Jessie, to tell her to chill out and check if she was OK and I saw it, this…' Dean rubs his hand over the top of his hair, ruffling it. 'I saw a hand on the water. In the water.' He swallows hard. 'It was near some rushes. I thought it was severed at first. But when I looked closer I could tell it was a body. A woman. Well, a girl.'

'What was your reaction?' Sam says.

Dean's eyebrows shoot up and he runs his hands across the curve of his head again. 'I just couldn't believe it, you know? Never in a million years would I have thought I'd see something like that. And not up here.' Dean shakes his head. He needs less prompting now. 'I got a stick and I tried to move the rushes a bit just to be sure. And I saw her properly then, saw her face. I physically staggered backwards, I remember now. I fell to the ground'

'And you went to get the police straight away?' Sam asks.

'Yes,' Dean says. 'Well, not straight away, because I remember thinking I didn't want to go; I didn't want to leave her there on her own. I didn't know whether to pull her out or leave her. But mostly I remember thinking that someone should stay with her. We didn't all have mobile phones or nothing then, of course. So I had to get in the car, and I drove and stopped at the first house I saw. I could hardly drive, I was shaking that much. It seemed to take so long to get to it. And then I came back up here and waited with her while the police came. Me and Jessie waited.'

'Thanks, Dean.' Sam reaches out to adjust the camera, but Dean puts his hand out for him not to, thinking he's about to switch it off.

Dean looks back into the camera then at Sam. 'They didn't keep me up to date or nothing, the police, you know. I asked them to and they said they would. I never heard nothing. I used to ring up myself, but in the end I just gave up and read the papers like everybody else. And then it stopped being in there anyway.'

Sam forces himself to ask the question on his mind. 'Were you worried? That they'd think it was you? Because you found her?'

Dean's face twitches and his eyes fix on Sam's. 'Yes,' he says.

Sam had expected him to say no.

'But I didn't do it, did I, so why should I care what they think? It isn't about that. It's about finding out who did kill her. Today, this is the first time I've been up here in years. I hate it up here now. That water is more polluted than ever,' Dean says, jabbing his finger.

His attention has drifted over Sam's shoulder and Sam senses it's not just the camera distracting him. He turns to see a man standing behind him. The man and Dean exchange small nods.

Dean climbs out from the picnic-table bench. 'Let me know if you need anything else. And keep me posted,' he says to Sam, and then shrugs. 'Doubt you will.'

They shake hands and Dean walks around the lake towards the field, hands shoved in his pockets. Sam watches him go. On the other side of the lake, Dean climbs over the wire fence and walks across the field, the grass coming up to his knees. Sam films him as he gets further and further away.

'Very arty,' a voice says, and Sam is surprised to see the man who had been standing behind him is still there, now leaning against the picnic table.

'Martin,' the man says, offering a handshake.

'Sam,' he says, automatically taking it.

'Do you two know each other?' Sam asks, gesturing in the direction of where Dean walked.

'Not really. Know of,' Martin says. 'I've seen him around. Everyone mostly knows everyone round here. Filming something for the local news?'

'No,' Sam says, feeling himself involuntarily puff up a little. 'I'm making a documentary.'

'Oh?' Martin says, scowling.

'About Victoria Preston.'

'Ohhhhh,' Martin's face opens up in recognition.

'You walk up here a lot?' Sam asks.

'Me? Yes – a fair bit. Been coming up here for years. A lot of people stopped after what happened. You don't get so many picnickers and things now. Puts you off your lunch somewhat, I suppose. But I still like the air up here. Don't you?'

Sam takes a breath in through his nose.

'The Victorians used to come up here,' Martin says. 'Because it's high above Conley they could get away from the smog of the factories. They'd swim up here in the summer. You wouldn't do that now, that's for sure. And there were boats too. And in the winter they'd be ice-skating.'

Looking around now, Sam can't imagine realistic scenes of this, only stylised pictures: Christmas cards, illustrations on vintage-style calendars.

'You can't fathom it getting that cold now, can you?' Sam says. 'Cold enough for solid ice?'

Sam and Martin walk towards the lake, peering into it. Sam takes some footage of their reflections wobbling on the surface of the water.

'They've pulled all sorts out of here, you know,' Martin says, poking at the water with a long stick he has picked up. 'Dead things, cars, the lot.'

'There were drownings, too, weren't there?' Sam says.

Martin looks puzzled. 'You obviously know more than me.'

Sam films Martin's movements in the reflection of the water. 'I read the stories about a girl falling into the ice and drowning. On a local history website.'

Martin thinks for a moment. 'Heard something about it. I don't remember the details.'

'It was 1898, I think, some time around then anyway. Some say her name was Clara and she was fourteen,' Sam says. 'Others say it was earlier and she was an Emily, and she was just eight. She was skating up here alone and the ice gave way – just in one spot. That's what they reckon.'

Martin's mouth turns down at the edges. 'You have been doing your research, eh? Well, maybe it was Emily that fell in, maybe it was Clara, maybe it was neither. I guess we'll never know, will we?'

'Could have been both.' Sam looks back at the lake into the opaque water, as if it might give them a clue about Emily, or Clara. Or Victoria.

Martin shrugs his shoulders. 'Well, one thing's for sure. Victoria Preston wasn't ice-skating up here, was she? And she wasn't having a picnic either.'

Wordlessly they both step back from the water and begin to walk towards the road, Sam stuffing his camera back into its bag.

'You from here?' Sam says.

'Born and bred for my sins.'

'You followed the case then? Victoria?' Sam asks.

Martin's arms are folded around his torso. 'I wouldn't say I "followed" it, but it was a big thing around here at the time, of course. Everyone in Conley knows about it. In a sense you can't not follow it when you live here. Not that there's been a lot to follow of late. How about you?'

'Me? I'm from Wales. Journo by trade. Made redundant. You know how it is with local papers.'

Martin nods in agreement. 'Ours is a rag. They don't leave the office. They don't get out for stories any more. All rehashed press releases and ads. All written while they're stuffing biscuits into their gobs.'

Sam has to stop himself 'going off on one' about it, as his daughter would say. His job had been swallowed up soon after the owners introduced a content-sharing model across the regional papers, meaning each edition only produced a handful of local stories in-house. The rest were produced by a central team in Liverpool and farmed out to all the regional papers. Sam had been unable to help himself loudly scoffing at the idea whenever he'd got a chance, and he knew it was unlikely to have helped his case when they had to decide exactly where the axe was to fall.

His habit of replying to readers' comments on his stories, and setting them straight on their opinions, might have had something to do with it, too. The new online editor had started finding fault with Sam's articles out of the blue, nit-picking about tiny mistakes – from a misspelled name (it only happened once and, as Sam had pointed out, there were typos in the Bible) to his wording of a headline. Proper journalists strive for accuracy but everyone makes mistakes – a small omission, a slightly off date. You'd be hard pushed to find any articles that are 100% accurate. Writers are humans, not robots – not yet.

'Good to see someone out on a story getting the soles of their feet dirty,' Martin says now, as they approach the dirt track near the road. 'So what brings you here? To Conley?'

Sam hitches the camera bag onto his shoulder. 'Well, I'm unemployed right now... ahem, I mean "freelancing". I've been tinkering about with making films for years – shorts, music videos for mates, and all that. I've always thought about having a go at documentary-making. Got my redundancy and thought it's now or never.' He can feel himself flushing. It sounds pretty pathetic laid out like that. 'This story, Victoria's story, just captured my attention.'

Martin raises an eyebrow, like he's going to say something, then drops it again. He slaps Sam lightly on the back. 'Well, good for you. It's never too late to reinvent yourself.'

'Cheers, hope so.'

Martin isn't ready to let it go, though. He stops, forcing Sam to as well. 'But... I'm curious. Why *this* story in particular? Why Victoria? There are plenty of dead people to choose from.'

Sam swats an insect away that's buzzing in front of his face.

'Sorry, I'm just genuinely curious,' Martin says. 'We don't get a lot of interest like this in Conley. As you might imagine.'

'I covered crime a lot when I worked on the paper. And I've just always been interested, read a lot of true crime too.'

Martin's face is blank.

'Something happened when I was younger,' Sam blurts out, annoyed at himself for feeling such a need to justify himself.

Martin draws shapes in the dirt with the toe of his shoe.

'Well, not to me, to my sister. She's a year older.'

Martin stops dragging his foot and looks at Sam now.

'She was walking home one day when she was about thirteen. There was this area near the house that was just a dirt road. He asked her, this man in a car, if she wanted a lift. She said no, of course. He said he knew our dad. She sensed something was off and she carried on walking.'

Sam feels self-conscious, but Martin's eyes are fixed on him. He finds himself stuttering, his teeth catching on his lips.

'He followed her in the car and it was all just fields around. There was no one else around.'

'So what happened?' Martin says.

The tension breaks a bit then. 'She climbed over a turnstile so he couldn't follow her in the car any more.' Sam can feel his heart thumping.

'Why was she there?' Martin says. 'At the dirt road?'

It takes Sam by surprise. It's not the question he was expecting.

'She was just… she was just walking there, I don't know. We did that then.'

Martin seems happy with the answer. 'So…?'

'The man got out of the car and chased her. He got close, almost within grabbing distance, but she managed to lose him. She knew her way around better than him, I guess. She came tearing into the house, blurting it all out, and Mum called the police. They didn't find anyone, but they said it wasn't the only report they'd had of similar things happening.'

'Blimey,' Martin says. 'You OK? You look a bit peaky.'

'I'm fine. It was in another lifetime. Sorry, it just kind of came out there.'

'Sounds like quite an ordeal. Your sister OK now?'

'Emma? She's fine. But when I read about the Victoria Preston case, it sort of reminded me of that. I'm sure a psychologist would link it all up and have a field day with it. Probably some kind of hero crusade,' Sam says.

'Probably.'

At the side of the lake next to the road there's a small dirt-track area. It looks as if cars have parked there recently, perhaps to sit and look over the water. A road runs past the lake, miles of fields, the odd farm, eventually leading to other towns. It's intersected by another steep, narrow road that takes you back into the town of Conley.

Standing on the dirt track, Martin opens his arms out. 'So, this is where Victoria was said to have been dropped off.'

Sam tries to visualise it. He had on his way into Conley too. He'd come over the tops, driving through the night to avoid traffic and to try to get a sense of what it was like up here in the dark – for Victoria, that night. He was surprised at how rural and remote it felt, as if it didn't belong to the ordinary, seen-better-days town it was officially a part of. He'd hardly seen anyone else on the road, apart from the roadkill every now and then: foxes, badgers, rabbits – unidentified beast-shaped mounds in the headlights. He'd sat there, at the edge of the lake near the road, until it started to get light that first night, and only counted one other car go by.

A ripped paper sign catches on the wind and flaps loudly on a lamp post. 'SAY YES TO THE FOOTPATH' it says.

Martin follows Sam's gaze. 'Oh that. Local walking group wants a footpath to be built between the town and the lake. To make it safer and easier to access, they reckon. There've been people almost run over and killed, a cyclist knocked off his bike coming up that narrow road. Those dry-stone walls make it like a tunnel and there aren't any lights. Drivers can't see people at all.'

'What's the problem, then?' Sam asks. 'With the footpath. Why the campaign against it?'

Martin laughs to himself. 'Oh, it's never that simple round here. You'll see. Some of them say it should remain countryside, they don't want hordes of people trooping up here, "spoiling" it.'

'Isn't there some dodgy stuff goes on up here?' Sam says. 'Maybe some people don't want that disturbed either?' He had seen comments online that the area was used for drug-dealing and dogging, sex workers bringing customers up here in cars.

Martin laughs again. 'Maybe you're right. You really have been doing some digging, eh.'

'That sort of stuff going on when Victoria died?'

Martin shrugs. 'I'm not an expert on the matter, but I'd have thought so, wouldn't you? It's hardly a new phenomenon, is it?'

Sam takes the camera back out of its bag and puts it up to film. The sun is low in the sky now, casting a haze across the lake, a faint rainbow of coloured light refracting in the beam. He kicks at the dirt, as if the tyre tracks from the car Victoria got out of here, twenty years ago, might still be there.

'It just doesn't make sense, does it? Why would she be up here that late at night? Who would she be meeting?'

'Well, that's the question, isn't it?' Martin says, eyes fixed on Sam's shoes. 'That's why it's so frustrating. And so alluring to people like you and your future viewers, I suppose.'

'You going back into town?' Sam asks Martin. 'Want a lift?'

'Yeah, why not. Cheers.'

On the way back into Conley, Sam and Martin sit in silence for a while, watching the fields go by. The road is steep and mostly unpavemented, flanked by dry-stone walls that look like they could tumble down at any moment.

Finally, Martin speaks. Sam had sensed he was working up to something. 'Don't be fooled by Dean,' he says.

It takes Sam a few seconds to process it. 'Sorry?'

'The "ooh I'm so nervous" schtick. He's been dining out on that story since he found her.'

'Really?' Sam asks. He can't picture it. 'How do you mean?'

'He might make out he's reluctant to talk, but he'll tell anyone that'll listen. Doesn't need a lot of prompting. Sometimes none at all. I've heard him in the pub. He was on all the news bulletins back then.'

Sam had seen Dean on some of the TV recordings he'd been able to find online.

Martin doesn't take his eyes off the road. 'And all that stuff about saying he wanted to stay with her, that got embroidered on afterwards. The more times he told the story after, a little bit got added each time.'

'You think he's lying, then?' Sam says.

'Not at all,' Martin says. 'I don't say he's lying as such. That isn't what I said. Reframing, maybe. I'm sure he even remembers it slightly differently now.'

Sam doesn't respond, staring at the road ahead.

'What was at number one that summer, the week when Victoria died?' Martin says.

'Sorry, what?' Sam can hear irritation creeping into his voice at Martin leaping around from topic to topic.

'Just guess.'

'Dunno...' Sam has to think to locate that period of his life. He had recently got married. He was working long hours at the paper. It was a good time to be a local reporter then. The divorce and redundancy, where he was now, wouldn't have seemed possible.

'Um... Blur? Oasis?' he says.

'Try again.'

'Oh, I don't bloody know.'

'Take That!' Martin says, triumphant.

Sam turns briefly to look at him.

'I'd have never got that right if my wages depended on it,' Martin says. 'But it was Take That: "Never Forget".'

'How do you know that?' Sam says. 'And more to the point, what's it got to do with anything?'

'I came across it somewhere quite recently. Pub quiz, maybe. I love a good quiz, don't you? I'm not being flippant, far from it. But it just shows how your memory plays tricks. You think you know something but everything gets... coloured. After twenty years, you're going to have a job on with your true-crime documentary.'

The countryside gives way to a disused farmhouse, then a while later a bus stop, before houses and schools become the usual glut of petrol stations, shops and bars.

'Where'd you want to be?' Sam has to say it twice.

Martin snaps out of a daydream.

'Thinking about Take That, were you?' Sam says.

'Something like that. Just drop me by the library, if that's alright.'

'You sure? I can drop you at home, if you like? It's starting to rain.'

'No, library's fine. Somebody has to use it or they'll get rid of that too.'

'Suit yourself.'

Sam excuses himself and opens the glove compartment in front of Martin and fumbles for a CD to put on, for a break from the small talk. He picks up an Elbow CD.

Martin shakes his head. 'Not that music for bed-wetters, please.' He has started flicking through the CDs, too, and holds up one in a badly cracked case – *The Best of Elvis*. Sam had forgotten he even had it, can't remember where it came from. Maybe one of his dad's that he kept after he died.

'Oh, come on, you've got to love a bit of Elvis. My all-time fave.'

'Is it?' Sam says, genuinely taken aback. 'I wouldn't have had you down as an Elvis fan.'

'No?' Martin looks proud, or perhaps offended. 'Who'd you have said, then?'

'Dunno. John Denver? Mumford & Sons?'

'Doesn't bode well for your investigation. I've been to Graceland twice. Got all the box sets.'

Martin takes the CD from the case and slides it into the player. The jaunty strains of 'Return to Sender' play out and he drums the tune on his knees, trying but failing not to look self-conscious.

After Sam drops Martin off, he drives to Sylvie's house. Judith had called a few days ago to let him know she was back in town.

On his list of interviewees, Sylvie is at the top. Anyone commissioning the documentary would want her.

He arrives in Sylvie's street and checks the house number again against the one he'd noted down.

A small pink bike sits leaning against the wall opposite Sylvie's, but there's no sign of its owner. A slide and Wendy house in one of the front gardens are similarly deserted. Up at the window across the street, a row of teddy bears is lined up, pressed against the glass.

There's something about the day, the silence and the drabness of the air that transports Sam back to his own childhood. To Sundays when there was nothing to do. The house smelled of roast dinner for the whole day, there wasn't anything on TV at night, boring films and sport in the afternoons.

The curtains are drawn at the front of Sylvie's house. Everyone else's are still open. The front patch of garden is overgrown with weeds, the soil dried out, greying. Sam stands on the concrete landing area at the top of the steps, knocks on the front door and waits, but there's no answer. He thinks he can hear someone moving around inside so he knocks louder and the sound stops.

He takes a deep breath and bends down to shout through the letter box. Judith didn't know how long Sylvie would be staying. Sam needs to catch her while she is in town. Letter box open, looking through the open living-room door, he can see baby paraphernalia strewn across the place. The house looks shabby, disorganised, dated décor from the snatches he can make out.

'Hello, Sylvie. My name's Sam. I was hoping I could talk to you.'

He closes the letter box and flaps it loudly one more time. Nothing. He steps back and looks up at the house, half brick, half pebble-dashing. From the corner of his eye, he thinks he sees movement upstairs, in the crack in the lace curtain. But when he looks closer, it's completely still.

CHAPTER SIX

Sylvie

I try to get Victoria ready, but I have to change her nappy and Babygro twice before we're finally ready to leave. My fingers catch on all the poppers and the nappy wrappers. I don't bother to change my own top, just wipe a glob of gluey baby sick off.

The pram is trapped in the door, stuck on the frame, and the more I try to manoeuvre it, the more wedged it becomes. Tension pulses behind my temples. The jolting of the pram has upset Victoria. Eventually, I am able to squeeze past the pram and get outside, catching my coat on the door handle as I do. I pull the pram again, but still it won't budge.

'Here, stand out of the way, will you?'

When I turn, the woman I have seen next door is standing right behind me, her face scowling, all hard lines. We're almost nose to nose.

'Get back and let me. You're breaking my bloody heart with that.' She shoos me out of the way impatiently.

I move automatically, feeling embarrassed and useless, a big lump. She puts the rubbish bag she's carrying to one side. She's wearing leggings, baggy at the knees, with socks and pink slippers. With one swift kick of the wheel to get it into line, she gives the pram a yank and it's out of the house and onto the pavement.

'Thanks. Really appreciate it,' I say, positioning my hands on the pram, ready to push it away.

She gives me a long look. 'Come inside a minute, will you?' She gestures towards her own house, the front door still open. 'I'm freezing out here. Don't be getting yourself in such a fluster. You're going to burst a bloody blood vessel going on like that.'

I go to say I have somewhere that I need to be, but she stops me.

'Oh, just come over.' She drags her slippered feet across the concrete, looking back to check that I'm following her. 'You might want to lock up,' she says, hand on her front door. She shakes her head to herself. I fumble with the keys, lock the door and follow her into her house.

I'm Sylvie,' I say, when we are in her living room.

'I know who you are,' she says. 'And this is?'

'Victoria.'

She's the first person I've met here who hasn't flinched at the name.

'You want a tea or something?'

'Cold drink, if you have one.'

She pulls a cabinet open like a drawbridge, brings out a bottle of own-brand lemonade and tilts it at me, a question. When she screws the lid off, there's no fizzing sound. She pours two glass tumblers and hands me one of them. It's flat, pure sweetness.

'You knew my mum, then?' I say.

'I live next door, don't I?' A deep groove appears between her eyes. 'Are you alright? You seemed to be getting into a right old state there.'

I can hear a pan bubbling in the kitchen, a smell of over-boiled vegetables filling the air. An iron clicks and hisses, a sheet slung over the ironing board, part-way through being pressed. The gas fire is on, too, the air in front of it hazy, shapes and lines blurring through an invisible film. The house feels oppressively hot.

'Joyce.' She puts her hand out and I shake it. Her grip is loose and her hands are cold.

I struggle out of my coat, desperately needing to escape from it in this heat. Joyce sits down.

The house is dark, dingy even, like Mum's. But much tidier and cleaner. The TV plays silently in the background, an episode of *Columbo*.

'Did you know her well, my mum?'

'Well as anyone could, better than most maybe. We used to chat on a bit.'

'Have you lived here long?'

'About ten years or so, I'd say. After your time. My husband lives here too; you'll have seen him coming and going.'

I haven't seen anyone else but her, but I don't say so.

'When I first moved in, she'd given me the total cold shoulder, your mother – bit like you, really,' she says, no humour in her voice. 'But she thawed out after a while, a good few years it took, mind. Started saying hello and that. She took parcels in for me every now and then, when I was still working.'

'Did you go round to the house ever?'

'She came here occasionally. I never went into her house, as I recall. But I saw it – through the window a couple of times, through the door every now and again – if we were chatting.'

I feel a mix of shame about Mum's life and relief that Joyce knew about it and liked her anyway – a queasy lurch in my stomach.

'Did she ever go anywhere? My mum?' Part of me wants Joyce to say that Mum had a busy life, would go to book clubs and into town to meet friends, maybe even had the odd weekend away.

'I can't say I saw her going out much, no. Hardly ever, really. Let's say she was… quite a home body.'

'She didn't work?'

Joyce thinks for a second, looks confused, like it had never occurred to her. 'Not since I've known her, no.'

When I left, Mum was working as a book-keeper at an office in town. She was doing a distance-learning course towards becoming an accountant. Fancied working for herself, she said. I remember the idea of that felt surprising to me, somehow, at the time; her having her own life and plans.

Joyce shakes an orange plastic lighter and lights a cigarette. I tense up. Smoke is already escaping into the air, drifting towards the pram. I want to pick Victoria up, take her outside, but I don't want to appear rude.

The iron clicks and hisses again.

'You feeling better?' Joyce's legs are crossed and she taps her foot in the air.

'Yeah, fine, thanks. I was just having a bit of a moment.' I take a swig of the lemonade, thankful for the momentary relief from the sweltering room.

'You getting much sleep?'

'Not loads, no. Sorry, have we been keeping you awake?'

'Nah, I only need about four hours a night these days. My husband, Tommy, gets a bit grumpy, but he's alright really. Feel free to ignore him. I do.' She waves her glass of lemonade around in front of her as she talks, using it to point and gesture.

'Wish I could sleep more, to be honest,' she says. 'But I'm awake at four if I go to bed at midnight. Typical now I'm retired and I don't need to get up any more, eh? Spent years hardly able to drag myself out of bed in the morning when I worked.'

I take another sip. The heat, the instant sugar hit from the lemonade, are making me feel drugged. The fog of smoke is creeping closer towards us, hovering over the pram like a dark cloud.

We sit in silence for a minute or two and I can feel her looking at me closely while she smokes.

'Is there something special about you?' she says, her eyes narrowed from the smoke.

'Me?'

'Yeah, you.'

'No, why?'

'I was just sorting out the curtains upstairs the other day and I saw that lad out there.' Joyce does a camera gesture. 'He was taking your picture and I wondered if you were famous or something.'

I feel my cheeks flush. 'I don't know what that was all about. I think it was a misunderstanding.' I shrug, shake my head, but she doesn't take her eyes off me.

'And then there was a different fella out there today. And he had a camera, too.' She eyes me through the smoke. 'If someone is bothering you, you just let me know, you hear me?'

'We're fine, honestly.'

'Suit yourself... You've no fella, then?'

I don't answer. She waits a few beats and says, 'Aha, like that, is it? Well, I expect you've your reasons. Can't be easy on your own though, pet.'

'I'm fine. Thank you.' I start to gather my coat to leave.

'She talked about you sometimes, your mother, you know,' Joyce says.

I take a big mouthful of the lemonade at that, as if it's something stronger. The way they drink spirits in the films, draining the glass.

'Oh yeah, what did she say?'

'Just bits. You liked pizza and beaches. You were scared of spiders. You could be quite bossy, she said.' Joyce puts her glass to her mouth and looks at me over the top of it.

I swallow down the hard lump in my throat.

'Did you and her have some sort of falling out or something?'

'I went to live with my aunty in Manchester. After my dad died.'

Dad died three weeks after Victoria. They'd expected him to live at least another three months, Aunty Alice told me later.

'I see,' Joyce says, and I know what it sounds like. Like I abandoned Mum. I know people think that, because often I do too.

'It was very sudden,' I say. 'We both reacted badly. We took it out on each other. We needed time apart.' It's what I tell myself.

'Sounds like you were quite alike to me.' Joyce drains her glass.

It was a Tuesday afternoon, a nothing kind of a day, when Dad died. We were singing hymns during assembly at school. I kept thinking how Victoria should be sitting next to me. I'd look to the side, the shock of her not being there hitting me fresh each time.

A runner brought a slip of paper into the class. She shuffled in, head bowed. There was something about the way the teacher looked up at me, then back at the note, and I just knew. Mrs Richards grabbed me on the way out of the lesson. 'Go straight home, Sylvie. Your mum needs to see you.'

'Is it Dad?' I said instinctively.

'Just go straight home, as I say,' she repeated. That's all she'd say, sticking to the script like a politician.

Since Victoria died, no one walked home alone from school from anywhere really. They weren't allowed. Older brothers would wait for younger siblings they wouldn't normally be seen dead with. Some mums and dads started to come and pick their children up, renegotiating hours at work. My mum didn't come, though. Not with everything that was going on at home.

I remember the burn in my thighs and calves as I powered up the school field to get home that day. The small groups of school kids looked like sheep dotted across the grass. When I got to the spot where Victoria and I had sat drinking so many nights, I broke into a run.

I ran past Victoria's house and the curtains were closed. And when I got home, they were drawn at my house too.

Alice, Mum's sister, emerged out of the kitchen, face tear-stained and blotchy. I pushed past her, didn't even ask why she was there. Didn't need to. There wasn't any sound in the kitchen at all, just a clock ticking loudly. It reminded me of Victoria's house, where it was always quiet.

Mum was at the kitchen table, balled-up tissues everywhere. The skin around her eyes was so puffy it reminded me of raw meat. I sat on her knee like a child, and, by the time I stood up, my limbs had stiffened. It had started to get dark outside.

One thought was so strong I felt as if it was almost audible. Like a strip light about to go, humming and flickering. I couldn't stop wondering if Dad was still in the house, the bedroom where he usually slept throbbing above me. After, I crept up and looked. He wasn't there but the cover was still pulled back on his side of the bed, the sheets crumpled. I climbed in and fell asleep, somehow, in the space where he had been. Later, Mum crawled in too, and clutched me so tightly around the waist I couldn't breathe.

'You clearing the place out? Seen the stuff in the bins,' Joyce says.

I'm relieved to be pulled out of the memory, like I was relieved when Alice drove me to Manchester, away from Conley and from Mum's grief. Seeing it every day was too much to bear, like touching an open wound. I nod.

'You got your work cut out there, eh?' Joyce shakes her head. 'You know what they say about people who collect stuff like that, don't you? I've seen it on these shows they have on telly about it. God knows why I watch them.'

I don't answer, I can't.

'I heard one of them – a doctor in something or other. Degree in junk? I don't know. Anyway, he said it's about remembering someone existed. Not remembering… that's not right… reminding yourself, that was it. Not being able to let go, that's the thing. Makes sense, right? You and your dad and all that.' She leans forwards quickly then. 'Hey, I'm not trying to make you feel guilty, petal. I feel pretty bad myself. Maybe I should have intervened. We were on holiday when she fell. Majorca – we go every year, same place. I think that's why… well, why they didn't find her for a while, you know. We were the main ones who saw her.'

I think of all the possessions building up around Mum, trapping her in, her falling down the stairs, landing. A crack of bones, silence.

'She really never tried to get in touch with you? Bury the hatchet?' Joyce says.

'No.' I coax out the final drops of lemonade, hiding behind the glass. And I think about the calls on my phone not long before she died. I didn't answer. And after that, nothing.

'What a shame, eh,' Joyce says, shaking her head and tutting.

CHAPTER SEVEN

Sylvie

It creeps up on me that Victoria is crying and she has been for some time. Somewhere along the line it had been going on for so long that the noise bled into the silence. Her cries are a solid wall of sound. My ears are starting to ring from it.

Mum's collection of snow globes distracted her for a little while, but not for long.

I shake one and let Victoria watch the golden glitter swirl and fall. It's supposed to be sand. The Prestons brought it back for us from Tenerife one year, when I was about nine, the first in the collection. Everything starts somewhere.

I would spend hours watching it, transfixed. I try it again with a globe with fake snow inside; a New York Christmas scene, although none of us had ever been. Victoria turns her head away. I shake one more; metallic blue sequins to look like water when they settle. Her screaming intensifies. She's putting extra effort into it, digging deep. I worry she will hurt herself crying too hard. I am getting to know her more now, though – usually understanding what she needs better, but not this time. My temper twangs like an elastic band snapping against my skin.

Sometimes, Victoria will only fall asleep when she is moving around. Nathan or I used to take her out in the car in Glasgow, drive around for hours. I didn't bring the car here, though, so I've been walking around the streets. I've found myself needing to clear my head more than ever.

When I was younger I used to dream I could live inside one of the snow globes. It looked like the most perfect place – safe and magical. But now I see it differently. I picture myself trapped under that glass with all these floating things, the air running out.

A knock on the wall from next door again, three hard thuds. I bundle Victoria into her pram and pull on jeans and a jumper over my pyjamas, then put on my coat. Almost as soon as we reach the end of the street, Victoria is asleep, drifting off, fighting it at first but not for long. When Nathan took her out, I would sleep like a stone while they were gone, the bliss of the silence.

Maybe Victoria senses her father's absence. She was sleeping much better before, at home. But since we got here, since Nathan… she must know that something is off; she might taste it when I feed her.

The streets are almost empty, just the odd car creeping past. A jogger runs by and makes me jump. He looks back and offers an apologetic wave from beneath a woolly hat. My teeth have started to chatter.

Nothing's open except the big supermarket – it's twenty-four hours now, apparently. When I lived here, the site was a tinned food factory, bleak and imposing. No one chose to work there; people ended up working there if things went wrong – bombing out of school with no GCSEs or a spell in prison.

Inside, I weave up and down the starkly lit aisles: shiny plastic packages, things floating in jars like eyes, cheap clothes. It seems now that the only time Victoria will sleep is when I don't.

I was always adamant about not wanting children; I made it part of who I was. I liked to wheel it out at parties, as if it made me different, better than other people somehow. Deep down I felt like I'd escaped where others got tangled and snared. But then, it crept up on me, the odd twinge that I tried to push out and ignore. Then it hit me like a wave. I was gripped by this alien, unwanted desperation to have a child of our own, and the thought of not being able to made me feel desolate.

Nathan was surprised at first, didn't quite believe me, but then he just said, 'OK, let's do it! Let's baby,' like I'd asked him if he fancied going to the cinema or if pasta was OK for tea. And that puzzled me.

I thought we'd agreed we both didn't want children, that we were happy as we were. We didn't want to share each other. Was he just going along with that? Resenting me the whole time? It annoyed me to think he could be so non-committal, easy-going even, about something like that.

When we couldn't get pregnant at first, I was afraid I was too old and I hated the blood for coming each month. The doctor said we were both fine, we just had to wait. But it felt like we didn't have time to do that.

Sex was scheduled in around ovulation whether we felt like it or not, and after I'd lie there with my legs up against the wall, counting down fifteen minutes on my phone. We rowed about IVF. He said what was meant to be would be. That sounded ominous to me, quasi-religious. I'd already booked an appointment anyway. But before it came around, it happened of its own accord. Victoria. Something in me felt different, even when it was too soon to do the test.

I tried to resist it; it seemed so obvious, so clichéd. But meeting Nathan, getting our flat and then a child, it was the first time I felt truly contented since before Victoria and Dad died. Before that summer. The first time that I actually allowed myself to be happy too. It felt too good to be true. And you know what people say about that.

The white brightness of the supermarket lighting against my eyes makes me overwhelmed with tiredness. I can almost feel the softness of the pillow against my head, the deep comfort. My skull is starting to thud, pain by my temples. There isn't really anything I need to buy so I just glide up and down the aisles.

I hardly pass anyone else in the shop. Another man with a baby strapped to his chest in one of those contraptions. I'm too scared Victoria would fall out, that I wouldn't have fastened it up properly. Sometimes I get so frightened that something will happen to her, that she'll become ill because of something I do or don't do properly, or I'll drop her. I try to drive it out of my brain, head it off at the pass, because I'm scared, too, that merely thinking about it might conjure it somehow.

Step on a crack... break your mother's back.

'They're a hell of a lot tougher than you think,' a nurse said to me at the hospital.

But everyone's more fragile than you think, too. Something bad can happen at any time, out of nowhere. The floor can drop from underneath you. I've seen that for myself.

The man scours the drug aisle, scratching his head before scrolling through his phone again, cross-referencing against what's on the screen. He gives me a nod and a knowing smile as we go past.

The same woman passes me a couple of times. I try not to look up or catch her eye. I'm not in the mood for someone cooing over the baby at this time of night. But in my peripheral field of vision, I can tell she is slowing down, peering into the pram.

I stare at the shelves for a while, not taking in what I am looking at. As I turn into the nappy aisle, my chin tucked to my chest, the pram hits something, soft but solid. It's the woman again, rubbing at her shin.

'Shit, sorry,' comes out of my mouth before I have chance to register what's happened.

She leans onto the pram, clutching her leg. 'It was me,' she says. 'I wasn't looking where I was going.' She checks around her, then looks up at the big clock in the aisle. The pain is easing out of her face now. 'I was focused on home time,' she says, and smiles at me.

And I see a flash of someone else in her then. I'm transported into another lifetime. *It's Michelle from school.* As it dawns on me, she does a double take, too.

'Is it… is it you, Sylvie? Sylvie Armstrong! Oh my God! I nearly walked right past you.'

'Well, it is the middle of the night. Hi, Michelle. How are you?'

She takes her hand off the pram now and steps back a little. 'Tell me about it.' She rubs her eyes.

I nod at Victoria. 'I've got an excuse for not being asleep at this ungodly hour. What's with you? Do you work nights or something?'

'Yeah, for my sins.' She must be a security guard, judging by the outfit.

We're standing against some cheap, own-brand make-up, the colours of the plasticky nail varnish catching my eye. Hot pink, blue and yellow.

'What are you doing round here? Not seen you since… since forever. It's been far too long,' Michelle says.

'My mum died.' It feels as if it echoes round the empty supermarket. 'I'm clearing out the house.'

'Shit, sorry. We're getting to that age, eh?'

'Guess so… So, what are you up to now?' I ask her.

She throws her arms out to the side: *You're looking at it.*

'Cool.' I haven't used that word since school, but it just sneaks out and makes me squirm. 'Well, it was good to see you, Michelle.'

I wheel Victoria away, pretending to look at tights on the shelves.

'Hey, Sylvie!' she shouts after us, coming back along the aisle towards me. Her voice sounds even louder in the emptiness of the supermarket.

'Don't suppose you… Well, I've not seen any of the old gang for years and… I finish in…' She checks the clock again. 'I get off in twenty minutes. I sometimes go for a coffee or some food when I finish here. I can't get straight to sleep. Don't suppose you fancy it, if you're about anyway? Don't worry if not. If you want to try and get some sleep, I don't blame you.'

'Aw, I'd love to,' I say. 'But I really need to get back. She'll need feeding soon.' Really, I'm hoping she'll sleep for a while longer yet, but I'm too exhausted to sustain more small talk.

'OK.' Michelle tries to put a bright face on it, but I can tell she's disappointed. 'No bother,' she says. 'Maybe another time.' She gives me an awkward wave and sets off back down the aisle, her shoulders hunched, ungainly.

I walk around for a while longer, picking things up and looking at them pointlessly. As soon we stop, Victoria starts to stir. I grab a few random things – none of which would combine to make a meal – and balance them on the pram, before paying and heading for the doors.

When I get through the sliding doors at the exit, Michelle is waiting there, changed out of her uniform into her own clothes. I steal a glance at the time. It's not twenty minutes yet. Sometimes I get so tired I feel like I've missed lumps of the day, spaced out somehow, and occasionally I have. But I look again and it confirms that isn't the case here.

Michelle is wearing a fresh slick of an unflattering brownish lipstick that makes me think of pottery clay, and a white polo shirt, dried out and stiff-looking from many rounds of washing.

A man staggers in through the doors, the smell of fermenting fruit wafting in with him. He looks spaced out and the skin on his face is red and weathered.

Michelle watches him closely as he goes into the supermarket, standing on tiptoes and craning her head as he disappears round one of the aisles. She shakes her head and tuts. 'He's not supposed to be in here.'

I think she's going to go in after him and I'll make my escape, but something makes her change her mind and she turns back to me then peers into the pram.

'Come on. Just one quick coffee? You might as well while the little one is sleeping.'

There doesn't look to be any getting out of it.

We head out across the empty car park. When I look back, the deserted, brightly lit supermarket looks like some kind of weird spacecraft that has landed in Conley. My memory is projecting the old factory.

'Do you always work nights, then?' I ask Michelle.

'Not always, but a lot. I don't mind. It's better money and I get a bit of time to do stuff in the day when everyone else is working. You know what they say, don't you? About night shift. It's for bats, cats and tw---.' She mouths the last word silently and I have to laugh then.

'I can't say I've heard that one, no. But I like it.'

'I don't need that much sleep anyway,' she says.

Just the word sets a fresh wave of tiredness through me.

'Lucky you. I need eight hours or more to feel human. Well, I did. Who knows any more? You got any? Kids?' I am annoyed at myself for asking that; it just comes out. A pre-programmed conversation. But I always hated it when people said it to me; it became salt in the wound.

'No,' Michelle says, but doesn't elaborate. 'Tough going, then?' She gestures at the pram.

'Has its moments, yeah.'

We cross over the road, past the train station and down the dark curved street next to it.

'Erm, where are we going? Isn't it a bit dodgy round here?'

People used to say this was the red light area. I remember being shocked to hear that. Firstly, when I realised what a red light area was. And later that Conley had one; it seemed like something that would happen in big, filthy cities, something far away.

We'd driven past in the car before, and you'd see women standing around in the icy cold, smoking. I'd expected them to be wearing leopard coats, boots, short leather skirts, like on TV. But it wasn't like that. They had jeans on, big warm coats. Even woolly hats some of them.

'It's fine,' Michelle says, looping her arm through mine. 'No one's going to do owt to us. I come down here all the time. Stick with me.'

The buildings on this side of the street are all imposing: old, darkened stone, almost gothic-looking. On the other side everything looks more modern, but dreary all the same: a repair garage; a small, squat gym; a grubby-looking fried chicken takeaway – still open. In one of the doorways, a woman stands checking her phone, her face lit by the glow.

We continue down the street. Every now and then a car slopes past, slower, quieter than usual. Then, out of nowhere, a horn blares out. My heart jolts. The car slows down.

'How much for the pair of you? Do you do BOGOF? Jump in, lasses.'

There look to be four or five people in the car, shoulders pressed up to the windows. The driver beeps the horn again full volume as they go past, but I can't see anyone clearly.

The woman in the doorway looks up from her phone and tuts. 'Wankers,' she says and then her eyes are down again.

'Listen, I'm going to get back, Michelle. I'll get a taxi from the supermarket. Maybe we can have a coffee one afternoon or something.' I start to disentangle my arm from hers, twisting my elbow round.

'Give over. We're there now and she's still asleep.' Michelle nods towards Victoria's pram. 'It's just down here, the place. I'll drop you off at home after. I've got my car parked at the train station. They're just silly little boys; all gob no trousers.'

'Yeah, it's just—'

'We'll have one quick cuppa and I'll take you straight home, right? Anyway, I don't want you walking around by yourself. I've got a car seat from looking after my sister's lot so there's no need to worry about that.'

I'm ashamed to realise that the car seat hadn't even crossed my mind. I look back at the dark, deserted street and give in. 'OK, but just a really quick one.'

'It's so nice to see you. Honest,' Michelle says, her eyes fixed on me. We turn into a large yard with tyres piled up around the edges. The café is actually a large portacabin.

'Give it here.' Michelle grabs the pram and lifts it up the step into the café, like someone who has done it before.

'You always were a massive wimp, Sylvie.' There's something sharper about the way she says it than I had expected.

The image of a speeding car at night flashes into my mind, the sound of the engine getting closer, lights brighter. 'Go on, you wimp. It's your turn,' a girl's voice says to me. A game of Chicken across the road near the park. We used to play it with the boys from school. You had to stand in the road when cars were coming – the first one to move is the chicken. The memory is dreamlike, translucent overlapping images. Michelle's face is there. Victoria's too. She was always the last to move, stepping out of the way at the last split second then screaming up at the sky at the side of the road.

Inside the brightly lit 'café' it's busier than I expected. Three men are playing cards around a small table, with cans of pop beside them and plates smeared with leftover breakfast. They're all wearing dirty orange jackets and heavy work boots. They look out of proportion with the room, too large for it.

I glance at the clock. It's 3 a.m. My head feels so light.

'What do you fancy?' Michelle says, eyes fixed on the menu.

'Um, nothing – I'm alright, thanks.' My stomach is a rumbly mixture of feeling hungry yet nauseous at the same time.

Michelle addresses the woman behind the counter. 'Mel, I'll have a large full English, please. And two teas.' She looks at me for approval and I nod. She points at the buns behind the scratched glass counter, white icing sweating underneath. I shrug my acceptance. 'And two of these. Ta.'

'I'll bring it over, Chelle.'

She hands her some money. I start rooting in my purse for change but Michelle bats me away.

'Least I can do after all this time,' she says.

Victoria's pram is wedged between two tables. I notice a few of the men looking over at us, rare creatures in here. I pray that I won't need to breastfeed any time soon. Michelle bends down to peer in at Victoria, sticking her head into the hood of the pram as if into the mouth of a picture-book lion.

'She's fast asleep. No bother,' she whispers.

'Typical,' I say, rubbing my eyes. The light is making them throb even more. I must look as dreadful as I feel under these harsh lights. There are fine lines around Michelle's eyes too, tiny veins visible under the thin skin. Only Victoria stays exactly the same, cast in everyone's mind by the pictures they used in the paper. If she were to magically come back today, you'd expect her to look just like that.

The waitress brings over the buns and two teas, quickly return-ing with a fried breakfast for Michelle. It's the size of a tray rather than a dinner plate.

I raise my cup to her. 'Thanks. Here's to us: bats, cats and the other lot,' and we clink.

'I shouldn't, I know, but balls to it,' Michelle says, preparing to do battle with the breakfast. 'They say everything kills you now, don't they? In fact, I read the other day that one of the most dangerous things you can do now is shift work. Mucks about with all sorts of internal rhythms and stuff, it said. So I feel like I may as well enjoy it in the meantime, right? Anyway, turns out messing about with your body clock and working nights makes you bloody starving,' she says, knife and fork poised to tuck in.

'You enjoy it, love. You've got to have some pleasures in life, haven't you?' Mel from behind the counter is hovering, watching proudly as Michelle shoves a greasy, bean-soaked sausage into her mouth, orange liquid oozing onto her lips.

'You on nights all week, love?' she asks Michelle, her hand on her hip.

'Yeah, till Thursday.'

'Grand, I'll catch up with you before then.'

'She's a feeder, her,' Michelle calls after Mel. Mel whips her tea towel out to the side and shakes her backside.

I take a bite of the bun; it's rubbery, the icing gritty and sickly.

'I've put two stone on since I started nights over there,' Michelle says, gesturing with her fork.

'Yeah, know the feeling.' I nod at Victoria.

'You used to be dead skinny at school as well,' she says.

I flinch and put the bun down. Michelle was always a little blunt.

'So, how you been anyway? God, not seen you in years.'

I look up and she is shoving a piece of bacon in, looks guilty that I caught her, eyes panicked, the meat hanging out of her mouth like a tongue.

'Sorry,' she says, covering her mouth, her face flushing.

I feel a twinge for her. Michelle was never popular at school. People called her names and mocked her coarse hair. Her clothes were from charity shops – God knows how they knew. I wouldn't have, but some people can sniff out any perceived weakness. And if it wasn't these specific things, it would have been something else. She was just one of those people.

There was an incident at a house party once, and everything got much worse for her after that. It even spread to kids from other schools.

Someone's parents had gone away for the weekend and about thirty of us went to the house. The memory is fragmented, a damaged video tape. There were people jumping out of windows, the sound of a light fitting smashing. An image of someone with blood on their face breaks in. I hadn't thought of that night for such a long time until now, even though we talked about it for weeks. Being back here is dislodging things again.

Victoria and I fell asleep on the sofa – we said we were sleeping at each other's houses. People were laid out everywhere on the floor, under sleeping bags and coats. Then Michelle burst in in the middle of the night, eyes wide and spacey, naked. She'd been taking something – most people had – and she didn't know where she was. I feel guilty looking at her sitting here now with the image of her that night in my mind.

Everyone laughed when she came into the room. Victoria too. But I felt a sensation like a freezing wire running right up my spine. Someone, one of the lads, shouted, 'What's that smell?'

There wasn't any smell but it just went from there. They said she'd soiled herself. By the end of the next week the story was that she'd come in the room covered in her own faeces. Even I started to remember it like that, as if I'd seen it myself. Michelle looked me right in the eye at the time, as if she needed an anchor to focus on and I was it. There was no shit, there was no smell. Just a naked girl, out of it.

Michelle puts her knife and fork down and flicks her eyes up at me. I feel like she knows what I'm thinking about.

'Do you mind if I ask you? What happened?' she says. 'You just didn't come back to school.'

I hadn't been expecting her to just come out and say it.

'I used to go past your house and look for you,' she says. 'I was worried something had happened to you too. Like Victoria. You were just gone. I knocked on your door but no one ever answered. I think your mum was in, though.' Michelle nibbles on a piece of toast, not blinking. 'I thought maybe it was me. That I'd done something.'

'I went to live with my aunty. In Manchester.'

'What about your mum, though?' Michelle says.

I stuff the remainder of the bun into my mouth. 'I thought I'd be coming back,' I tell her. 'But… well, I guess it didn't happen.'

'Until now,' she says, doing jazz hands to the side. 'I used to walk along your street some nights.' One side of her mouth is full of food, and when she speaks, I get the odd flash of it. 'I'd be looking out for you. Sometimes I thought you were back because I'd see that lamp going round in your room. You know the one you used to have with the stars? But then you wouldn't be at school again the next day.'

Michelle had never been in my house; we weren't that close. Her cheeks flush again and I wonder if she has said more than she intended to.

She adds quickly, 'I used to walk past sometimes before you went away as well and I'd see you up there with Victoria. Or just see the lamp going round. Sorry, I sound like a right weirdo, don't I? I was just walking past on the way to mine, though. It's on the way.'

I'm relieved when she changes the subject. 'What's this little one called anyway? Sorry I haven't asked.'

'Er… she's called Victoria.'

Michelle swallows in a hurry, but the lump of food sinks down her throat as if in slow motion. Her eyes look strained and panicked for a moment, as if she's going to choke, and then it's gone.

'Oh right. After…?'

My eyes won't lift to look at her. 'Kind of and it's my…' I was going to tell her it was Nathan's grandmother's name, too, but I drop it again. I don't want to complicate things by mentioning him. I can't face that right now. I know Michelle would seize right on it.

'That's nice. That's really nice.' She emphasises it the second time as if I didn't believe her the first. 'You don't get many baby Victorias now, do you?'

'No?'

'It's all Violets and Emilys and Daisys, isn't it? Our names are well out of fashion now. I expect she'll grow into it, though. You here on your own, then?'

'Yep,' I say, forcing chirpiness into my voice. 'Well, me and Victoria. Where are you living now?' I ask, trying to divert the subject.

'Back with my mum, funnily enough. Or not as the case may be.' She leans forwards and pretends to use a magnifying glass. 'I'm getting tired and over-giddy now. I was seeing someone. But it all went a bit tits up. And, well… I didn't take it too well, let's say. So I'm just getting over that, I suppose. Need to sort myself out financially again. And you?'

'Oh, you know, just getting on with things,' I say, willing her to move on.

She kind of does but not in the way I'd hoped. 'Which reminds me,' she says, wiping her hands with a paper napkin and putting it to one side. 'I couldn't find you on Facebook or Twitter or anything. I always look for you, see if you've joined the modern age.'

'Yeah, I'm not really into all that stuff.'

I try not to stare but the grease on the plate is making me feel sick. I feel hung-over, without having enjoyed the fun part first.

Michelle leans back into her chair, tugging at her waistband.

'All that stuff. Listen to you.' Michelle laughs at me, as if I'm a child and she's the adult. 'I'm ready for that sleep now,' she says.

Eventually, Michelle takes us home. As we pull away from the train station there are three women dotted up the street, walking on the spot, fiddling with phones.

'Did you ever think Victoria might have been coming down here?' Michelle says.

At first I think I have misheard, as she says it so casually, checking both ways for oncoming traffic.

'You know, working down here.'

'What do you mean?'

She doesn't look at me, concentrating on the road, the indicator clicking lightly like a metronome. 'I just always wondered, you know. Because they go up to the lake, don't they, in cars. With men.'

I look out of the window, my transparent reflection staring back at me.

'I'm just saying, you know. I mean, who would she have been meeting?'

Being back here, I feel plunged back into my old life, that summer.

'Can we not talk about this now?' I say. 'I'm shattered.'

'Suit yourself.' Michelle flicks the radio on and we don't talk any more. When she drops me at the house, she insists that we swap phone numbers. Next door's light goes on when I close the car door, a dark silhouette moving behind the glass.

When I look out of the window from the house, being careful not to move the blind so she can't see me, Michelle is sitting there in the car, looking up towards the house.

CHAPTER EIGHT

Summer, 1995

Sylvie and Victoria sat in the grounds of the school at the top of the hill. The view was good from there. Sylvie liked the fact that the school didn't even come into your line of vision when you looked out. It was there below; you could take it or leave it. But the view was beautiful for miles around. Fields like patchwork quilts, lines of traffic wriggling along, a world beyond Conley, people living all kinds of different lives.

Sylvie had never really left the place. She'd been to Skipton and Leeds and Bradford for the day; and to Blackpool and Morecambe on holiday. But never abroad. Even the idea of London felt like a foreign country.

She took a swig and grimaced, the bottle chinking against her front teeth. She was drinking Clan Dew, a gag-inducing mixture of whisky and wine. Victoria had the White Lightning cider, equally disgusting but cheap and did the job. She had to put both hands at the bottom of the big blue plastic bottle to drink some of it. A third of a bottle in each: they were just getting started.

Sitting at the top of the school hill was the extent of their plans for the evening. They'd had Michelle go to the shop for them to buy the alcohol. She was tall, broad-shouldered, so she could get served. She lived near Victoria and they'd seen her walking across the park as they roamed around, on the lookout for something to do.

'Let's ask her,' Victoria had said, nudging Sylvie.

'You ask her,' Sylvie hissed back.

'Chelle!' Victoria shouted across the park. The space was so open and empty that there was a wispy echo.

'Vic,' Sylvie said, jabbing her in the ribs. Sylvie loved it really when Victoria was loud. She felt like just being around Victoria made stuff happen. She was like a magnet for fun.

Victoria asked Michelle to go to the shop for them and she didn't argue. She was nodding even before Victoria had finished explaining what they wanted. She could have been asking her to do anything. Victoria shoved a ball of screwed-up money into Michelle's hand, the exact amount counted out but Michelle didn't check it anyway.

Sylvie and Victoria waited outside the shop, eyes fixed on the door. Sylvie was nervous that someone might come past and see them, or Michelle might get thrown out, but Victoria just sat on the wall of someone's house, kicking her legs out, bouncing her heels off the bricks.

'She's not going to get served,' Sylvie said. 'She probably comes in here for milk and stuff with her mum.'

'Oh, chill out, will you, Sylv? It'll be fine. She practically looks like an old woman anyway. Especially with the…' Victoria made a gesture for big, round breasts and Sylvie laughed along, ignoring a twang of guilt. It was true; Michelle was more developed than anyone else in their year. But rather than it getting her interest from the boys, as you might expect, it somehow made her look matronly and middle-aged. Michelle always got changed in the toilets for PE, not out on the benches like everyone else, but Sylvie imagined her wearing bras like her mum: thick-strapped, full cups, beige or mucky white

They were still laughing when the shop door jingled and Michelle appeared with a carrier bag. Sylvie felt relief at hearing the bottles clinking. Michelle handed Victoria one straining bag.

'Thanks, Chelle. We really appreciate it.'

Michelle smiled. She looked big and awkward. It was too hot for the denim shirt she always had on. She tugged at the sleeves, a film of sweat visible above her lip. She had a bag of her own with one bottle in it. Obviously wanted to be invited along with them, Sylvie could tell.

If Victoria could too, she ignored it. 'See you, then. Thanks again, mate!' she said, and she and Sylvie walked away towards the school. Sylvie looked back and watched Michelle lumbering away towards her house.

'Should we ask her if she wants to come along?' Sylvie asked Victoria. 'She's alright, you know.'

'Not tonight. I can't be arsed,' Victoria said, and Sylvie felt told off. But then Victoria turned to her and added, 'I just want it to be us tonight, don't you?'

'Yeah, course,' Sylvie said, and she linked arms with Victoria.

In the school field, the darkness was properly coming in now. Victoria handed Sylvie back the blue plastic bottle of White Lightning, now considerably lighter. Sylvie already had a buzzy feeling about her. She was loosened and Victoria's face had softened too. Her eyes were glittering, words were getting slack.

'I love you, Sylvie, do you know that? I just really love you.' And she threw her arms out.

Sylvie felt a warm flush. 'I love you too!'

Victoria hooked her arms around Sylvie's neck and Sylvie did the same. And then they were face to face, the tips of their noses almost touching.

'I'm so glad we have each other,' Victoria said. Her face swam in front of Sylvie's. Sylvie felt like her eyes went one way and her brain went another. It was all spinning. She had a rush that she hadn't expected where she considered kissing Victoria. She imagined the softness and warmth of her lips and felt her head lolling forwards.

But Victoria had pulled back. Sylvie was glad to feel the air on her face. It made everything stand still for a second. She was back to herself.

Victoria yanked the Clan Dew bottle from Sylvie's hand and tipped it back. Sylvie took a small sip of the White Lightning, shuddering at the dry taste. She made a contorted face and looked across at Victoria, hoping to get a laugh, but Victoria was still chugging down the Clan Dew, her eyes wide, fixed with determination.

She pulled the bottle away and burped loudly before bursting into laughter.

'You alright? You're on a mission tonight,' Sylvie said.

'I'm fine, couldn't be better!' Victoria said, throwing her arms out like a vaudeville actor. The booze was really kicking in.

They sat and looked out for a while, the bottles on the ground between their legs.

'Anything up?' Sylvie asked. There was something hanging in the air. She knew Victoria well enough to sense it. 'You can tell me, you know.'

Victoria didn't look up. She took a swig from the blue plastic bottle, squashing it inwards to pump the sour fizz out faster. She wiped her hand across her mouth.

'How's things at home?' Victoria said, turning her head to look at Sylvie.

Sylvie looked down and picked at the grass and shook her head. There was an unspoken rule of silence at home. Dad mustn't be disturbed or upset, he needed his rest. Sylvie felt as if she was holding her breath the whole time.

Victoria hesitated then said, 'My dad got beaten up. Came home with a black eye.'

'Really? Why?' Sylvie asked.

'His business is struggling. Think he owes someone money, or he didn't finish off their conservatory or something. Someone keyed his car too.'

'Shit.'

'I hear them every night. He gets back late and says he's been working, but he hasn't, as she checks up on him. So she sits about at home getting herself more and more worked up, then she just flies for him when he gets in. Says he needs to stop drinking the money away, and that he should give in and get a proper job. He doesn't like that.'

'You can understand, I guess.' Sylvie had seen her dad roll his eyes sometimes when Peter talked about how well his building business was doing, the contracts they had coming in, like he was bragging about how much he earned. Sylvie had giggled. It was a little secret between the two of them, her and her dad.

'Flash Harry,' she had heard her dad call Peter to Margaret, when they thought Sylvie wasn't listening.

'Heard her say he's going to get hurt if he's not careful. Over money. He owes people money,' Victoria said. 'And so she's going on at him all the time, so he just goes out more. To "see a man about a dog" or wherever he goes. And she's there winding herself up. Ugh.'

'It'll be alright, Vic.' Sylvie rubbed the top of Victoria's arm.

'You know what he calls her? A bored housewife and frigid. I wasn't in the room but I heard him.' She mimed sticking her fingers down her throat and gagging but something about the words made Sylvie flinch.

'And I can hear her crying through the wall. And other stuff too.' Victoria rubbed at the dirt underneath her legs.

'What other stuff?' Sylvie said, but she knew somehow.

'Doing it.' Victoria said, and they both covered their ears at the same time.

Sylvie had to stop herself from asking more about what Victoria heard. Something was compelling her to demand the gory details.

Victoria's shoulders were slumped. Then she looked up, brightened. 'Tell you what, let's make a pact. Let's never ever get married. No husbands, no kids. Just you and me.'

'Count me in!' Sylvie said, and she meant it. They clinked the plastic bottle against the glass one and guzzled them back.

'Never!' they both said at the same time and started laughing.

They ate mints on the way home and took it in turns to slap each other's faces so their parents wouldn't realise they were drunk. But when Sylvie got in there was no one downstairs. She made a sandwich from spongy white bread and a bright yellow cheese slice, adding in a browning leaf of lettuce that tasted bitter and earthy. She could see light under her parents' door but there was no sound.

She stood outside, listening and waiting, but there was nothing. And after a while the light went out. She waited there for a bit longer on the landing, in the darkness, then finally went to bed.

CHAPTER NINE

Sam

Sam fills the small white kettle in the sink in the bathroom of his room at the Travellers' Rest Hotel. Irritation flares as cold water sprays over the edge of the basin, splashing down his front. He empties two coffee sachets into the tiny cup and adds the now-boiling water, takes a sip and winces at the thin, bitter aftertaste, the synthetic milk. Only the very tip of his finger will fit through the cup handle to hold it, forcing his little finger to stick out.

Why is there a hotel here? he keeps thinking, looking round the room, with its terracotta walls and functional furniture, the duvet flat and thin. Who would come to Conley on holiday? Do that many people really come here on business? He hasn't seen anyone else in the place yet, when he's been outside his room, aside from staff.

Firing up his laptop, Sam loads the SomeoneMustKnow website. He'd heard a radio programme about it – a community of 'armchair sleuths' who sit at home and try to solve crimes. They specialise in long-unsolved murders and finding out who the Jane and John Does are – unidentified bodies that show up with no ID and no one looking for them. The piece was on the radio after the web community had managed to work out the identity of a woman, who'd been found dead on a deserted beach in America a few years ago, by tracing the origin of a small tattoo on her ankle.

After that radio show, Sam had lost hours on SomeoneMust-Know.com, falling down the rabbit hole of board after board, sub-thread upon sub-thread. Reams of facts and theories – not always distinguishable from each other – about dead bodies unclaimed; nobody missing them, or at least owning up to it. Mind-bending murders, impossible scenarios, with no convictions, no endings.

It was here where he had first heard about Victoria too. Hers seemed to be one of the few UK cases currently active on the site, and the name of Conley rang a bell. As Sam read more, he realised he remembered the case from when it had happened, but only faintly – the broad shapes but not the details. They'd probably run something on it at the paper – there'd have been a scramble to tie it to something local, however tenuous – although Sam knows he'd have remembered it if he'd written about it directly.

SomeoneMustKnow drew him because of his interest in true crime, but also because he was looking for something himself – his 'one' as he thought of it. When he'd heard about the website, he'd had an inkling that it would be a good place to find 'his story', the case he could cover. He'd felt guilty about it in some ways, not only about fishing around like that in someone else's misery, but about the cases he hadn't picked, too, like the dogs that get left behind at an animal home.

The threads about Victoria on SomeoneMustKnow had seemingly been dormant for a while, but had recently been revived by Victoria's mother's newspaper appeal and her appearance on the local news. A user called AaronInBetween had posted the video clip and article about the case, asking:

AaronInBetween: 'Does anyone know much about this one? Strange no one has ever been caught?'

It was enough to stir the community's interest.

Most of the posters list their location or a whimsical version of it. Aaron's is listed under his posts as 'Here, there and everywhere'.

Other posters quickly piled in:

PrincessPeaches91: I'd be looking at the family with this one. Mother and father. Grandparents?

Someone else posted an article about another unsolved case of a girl around Victoria's age found in the river in Skipton a few years earlier, the next town along.

'Linked?' PrincessPeaches91 replies says. Sam imagines her wearing oversized glasses. Presumably 'her' anyway.

In another thread, user SeenTheLight has taken it upon themselves to search for Victoria's missing locket, believing this to be a big key to the mystery.

SeenTheLight: My niece was looking for one of these necklaces because she saw a blogger she likes wearing one. They're all over eBay in the UK.

Her profile says she lives in Arkansas. Again, Sam is assuming SeenTheLight is a woman but, looking over the profile again, there's nothing to confirm – or even really suggest – that. The profile picture is a sunset somewhere unidentifiable.

Sam has developed a mental picture of most of the posters now from scrolling through their history on the site. In his mind, SeenTheLight is overweight, late fifties. Curly hair. She has a wooden porch out front of her house. AaronInBetween is a college kid. Skinny, with hair that sticks out from under a baseball cap. Still lives at home.

Sam thinks back to what he's read about Victoria's case, the information Judith has given him – the little that the police would release to her. She said they told her much of it couldn't be made available as it could jeopardise the legal case, should there ever be one. He had to wonder if they just said that to give Judith the impression that a legal case was still a remote possibility.

When Victoria was found in the lake, she had a severe head injury. Although there was no bleeding externally, there was a massive haemorrhage internally. The police concluded that Victoria likely wasn't sexually assaulted, but there were some scratches on her inner thighs and bruising to her wrists, which suggested someone might have tried. She was fully clothed, although some of her clothing was torn – only a gold locket with a heart-shaped pendant was missing. Her parents remember she was wearing it that day and photographs from the party show it around her neck too.

SeenTheLight says they are scanning for lockets like this for sale online and emailing each seller asking them whether there is an engraving on the back. Victoria's said 'VP' in a swirling font, a Christmas present from her parents. Despite a couple of promising leads, so far SeenTheLight hasn't come up with anything.

There's a red envelope flashing in the top right of the page. A private message. Sam had posted on the forum a few weeks ago, saying he was interested in making a documentary about the case and that he planned to travel to Conley, so to let him know of any leads. He clicks into the message.

The message is from someone called TruthBomb. 'Managed to dig this up,' it reads. Sam opens the document and it's a scanned news story from October 1995, a couple of months after Victoria's death. It's an article from the *Conley News* about a spate of flashing incidents in the town. 'Could be worth pursuing.'

The footer to TruthBomb's profile says that his own sister disappeared in 1978, a link out to a thread about the case. She was nine and vanished from their street in Milwaukee, just her bike left behind. TruthBomb remembers seeing the wheel still spinning. She has never been found. Sam has to stop himself reading through all of the hundreds of posts about her disappearance.

He makes a note of the story from the *Conley News*, adding it to the list of things to follow up on – although near the bottom for now, a '??' for who he would interview. He'd need to track down some victims as so far the police have refused to give him much, saying they couldn't comment on individual crimes and didn't encourage speculation.

Judith had told Sam that the police hadn't done enough to find out what happened to Victoria. Even though they'd been tight-lipped with him, what little Sam had garnered through a Freedom of Information request didn't bear out what Judith said. They'd talked to over two hundred and fifty contacts about the case and interviewed almost a hundred of them as witnesses. This scale of work should have yielded answers.

Sam opens up YouTube in another tab to watch a video he's already watched more than ten times before – the original reconstruction of Victoria's last known movements. It aired on *Crimewatch* and the local news shortly after her death. The 'Recommended for You' videos in his sidebar are now other similar programmes that he's morbidly compelled to click through. People getting on buses, going out to work and never being seen again. At least not alive. Bodies in ditches and quarries and even their own homes, no trace of the killer.

Scrolling down the page, there's video after video. He wonders how many of them are solved, who's been found, who's still out there, their bodies rotting away somewhere. Some of them simply don't want to be found. He scrolls back up, presses play on his laptop screen and maximises the video.

It shows the actresses playing Victoria and Sylvie leaving Sylvie's house and walking across the street. Sylvie on the left, Victoria on the right. Strange acting gig, Sam thinks. They're laughing and nudging each other. He always wonders what they were talking about, strains to listen as if he could hear.

There's a patch of grass and Victoria starts running and does a cartwheel, flashing her stomach, springing over. Then she stands tall and straight, pointing her toe and sticking her hands out to the sides for balance, a gymnast finishing a routine. She wipes her hands on her jeans then puts up the hood of her red top. The rain is getting heavier; you can see it against the street lights. Sylvie puts a protective hand across her hair and that makes Sam smile. He's seen his daughter Natalie doing the same thing, on Saturday nights, dashing from the house to the taxi, running in high heels, a little clutch bag held aloft. He wonders if Sylvie remembered that about the hair so they could put it in the reconstruction, the strange details that stick in the mind.

On the screen, the girls get halfway up the hill, stop near the open expanse of the park and say goodbye to each other. Sylvie watches Victoria continue past the park entrance to the top of the street. She turns to wave twice before disappearing from view. The camera follows Victoria alone then. She pushes her fists into the sleeves of the red jacket and pulls the hood around her face.

When Natalie was young she used to believe, like most children do, that people lived inside the television. Sam thinks of that now, following Victoria so closely down the street, like he's right behind her. The rain, the sound of her breathing, the trees swishing. The sound of her breathing isn't on the video at all, though – he realises that's in his head.

The film shows Victoria walking along the road, her head bowed down, looking left and right from time to time. Sam wonders where that detail had come from. Who could know if no one saw her? Was the actress or the police making their own interjection? Something reported to them that hasn't been made public?

Victoria goes into the phone box and jabs at the phone on the corner. She dials a number, lets it ring a few times then puts the phone down. Then she quickly picks it up again and does the same thing. This time someone answers and the coin drops into the phone.

Victoria speaks into the receiver, clamping it to her ear and close to her mouth.

'Taxi please from the phone box on Thistle Street.' A pause for the operator to speak. 'It's for Victoria.'

Another wait.

'The lake. I'm going to Conley Lake… Is it going to be long?' she says.

While she waits, Victoria paces around the phone box, kicking at the ground, stopping and sitting on the kerb for a while, under the street lamp like a theatre spotlight.

After a few minutes, a silver taxi arrives. The clock in the corner of the screen flips by faster to show time has been speeded up for the film. She must have waited longer, of course. Victoria gets in the back of the car. Sam is as close to the laptop as he can get, crouched on the end of the bed, ear tipped in, straining to hear.

Victoria is pressed into the corner of the back seat, forehead against the window. The camera then films the car from the outside, panning further and further back. It becomes a totally unremarkable silver car. No one would notice it, no one would remember, Sam thinks. Someone whizzing right by you, never to be seen alive again.

An involuntary shiver runs over him. Natalie used to say, so casually, that it meant the devil was walking over your grave.

The camera focuses not on the taxi driver or Victoria in the back, but on the car from a distance. It makes sense: it's what someone walking or driving by might have seen. A silver taxi, a girl huddled in the back. The rain would have obscured her, though. The windscreen wipers are going quickly, the downpour heavy.

The camera follows the car up the narrow road to the lake. No other cars pass. At the lake a few street lamps are dotted around the edge, pools of light in the otherwise-darkness. The place is deserted, or it looks to be in the areas that are visible. Victoria gets out of the car, closes the door and walks away. There's a pause and she looks back. She's in the full beam of the headlights and she covers her eyes with her arm. Then she turns and disappears into the darkness. The taxi waits for a few moments then drives off.

A narrator starts reading out the number to call for anyone who has any information, but the clip cuts out halfway through, the screen turning to black-and-white static – taped from the television. Sam thinks of what would happen if anyone called now – it would be a dead line.

The end of the video is frustratingly abrupt. Sam plays it again from the part where Victoria gets out of the taxi. She slams the door and then walks towards the blackness of the lake. Each time, it feels like you're being pulled in, like you're on the cusp of seeing what happened, who she was meeting, and then it's just the static hiss of the end of a videotape.

CHAPTER TEN

Sylvie

I glance at the clock on the mantelpiece: it says 8.30 a.m. Another says 11.48 p.m. The one on the video player says it's midday. The way I feel, any of them could be right, the days are melting into each other, but my phone confirms it's 8.30 a.m. Victoria cried for a lot of the night again, or it feels like it, waking up at 3 a.m. and staying that way, on and off.

I am light-headed, woozy with lack of sleep. If I blink a little longer than usual, bright colours pop and replicate in front of my eyes, kaleidoscopic.

'Shhh-shhh-shhh, baby.' I jog Victoria up and down, but today she seems to have endless reserves for fury. Her nappy is clean, she rejects me when I try to feed her. There's no temperature or anything. When I took her to the drop-in centre they looked her over and said she was fine. 'Sometimes they can just be that way out,' the health visitor said to me with a thoroughly slappable, well-slept smile.

I put my old Walkman on to escape for just the length of a song. I found it up in my room next to my bed and I wonder if Mum was still listening to it too. The batteries look new. I press the cheap spongy headphones onto my ears – I am surprised they have lasted all these years – and click play, turning the volume up as loud as it will go and singing along. 'Common People' by Pulp. The music masks Victoria's crying for a while and finally she starts to calm down.

I spin her round – she's still crying but it's fading. I am careful not to stop for even a moment and her body starts to become more still, heavier. We are spinning round and round.

Something stops me. There's someone outside the window. I push the headphones off backwards and they fall to the floor, dragging the Walkman with them. There's a loud rap on the glass, so sudden it makes me jolt physically and I picture myself dropping Victoria, my heart skipping in my chest. Victoria starts to screech again, even louder, more insistent now because of the shock.

My face is already set hard. I've made up my mind to confront the neighbours about the banging. I assume that's who it is. My stomach drops, though, when I realise it could be the boy with his camera again. But when my eyes focus, it's Michelle at the window, looking in. She holds up a carrier bag, waving. She bangs at the single-glazed window again.

'Alright!' I mouth, Victoria drizzling a stream of warm saliva down the front of my top. I open the door and Michelle pushes her way straight in.

'Thought I'd pop round after work. Picked some stuff up for you.' She lifts up the carrier bag. 'Brekky?' Milk and croissants are poking out of the bag.

'Yeah, alright,' I say. 'Thought you finished in the middle of the night, though?'

Something flickers across her face. 'Oh, yeah, but I worked over today. Had a few things that I needed to clear. And then, you know when you get to that point when you're just not tired any more?'

'Not really, no,' I say, needing to sit down on the kitchen chair, watching her as she makes coffee and warms up the oven for the croissants.

She pauses then says, 'Not being funny, but what's that weird smell?' She looks around then, like she hadn't noticed the surroundings properly before.

I sniff but I can't catch anything. I shake my head.

'Really? You can't smell anything? It's like kind of sweet. Bit rank, to be honest.' She sniffs again, following her nose towards the bottom of the stairs.

'Seems to be round here somewhere.'

'Oh yeah, I smelled it before, you're right – but I can't smell anything now.'

Michelle looks up, screws her face up and heads towards the living room. I follow her in, look back and close the door.

'You must have got used to it, the smell. You OK, Sylv? You look a bit pale.'

'Thanks, I feel a bit pale.' My left eye twitches.

She looks round at the mess, the piles of stuff.

'Tell you what,' Michelle says, her back to me. 'Have this then you go and have a couple of hours' kip. I'll keep an eye on this one, no bother. We'll be OK, won't we?' She shakes Victoria's hand and the baby looks at her, wide-eyed.

'She hasn't stopped crying. She's probably just sick of me,' I say.

'Don't be daft, mate, it's what babies do. They're not that sophisticated, silly.'

Michelle disappears into the kitchen and when I follow her through a few moments later she hands me a plate, putting the coffee on the table next to me. She takes Victoria from me and sits her on her knee.

'My God that's good,' I say, salty butter oozing from the croissant. 'Thanks so much. You sure you're not tired, though?'

'Nah, honest, I feel fine. I'll sleep later, don't worry about me.'

'OK, if you're sure.' I hesitate at first because I've never left Victoria with anyone else except Nathan before. But I feel so tired I could faint and I'll only be upstairs, I reason.

Michelle strokes Victoria's head. 'As my sister says to me, "You wake it, you take it." And I think I woke Victoria up before, didn't I? So… I'll take her for a bit.'

'If you really don't mind, then. I'll leave this in here,' I say, turning on the baby monitor. Michelle looks at the monitor then at me.

I feel the need to explain myself. 'I'm not being funny, but if she's crying I usually know if it's a proper cry, where she wants something, or she's just having a moan, so I'll feel better.'

'If you want,' Michelle says, turning away from me.

I can't tell if she's offended about the baby monitor. She has Victoria balanced on her hip, wiping crumbs off the counter. I put it next to her anyway and pat her lightly on the back to show my appreciation.

I can feel myself relaxing even as I haul myself up the stairs. It's comforting to hear Michelle pottering around in the kitchen, running water, clanging pans. She puts the radio on too. I listen out but I can't hear anything from Victoria. The clatter reminds me of living here as a child, before everything that summer.

I lie on the bed on top of the sheets, fully clothed, placing the baby monitor on the pillow next to me, and the sounds from downstairs soothe me to sleep.

When I wake up I have that woolly-headed, furry-mouthed feeling of oversleeping. The pillow is wet where I have dribbled. I feel disorientated and the light has changed, it doesn't feel like morning any more. The clock in this room says 7.30 a.m. A flash of temper. I need to change them all to the right time.

I get to my feet unsteadily, irritably pulling my top down as it's snarled itself around me. There's a cup of tea next to the bed, which wasn't there before, but when I touch the cup it's cold.

When my mind focuses better, I notice the monitor on the pillow next to me, but there's no sound coming out of it. Suddenly I am wide awake. I have a sudden panic that they will both be gone: Michelle and Victoria. Why did I leave my baby with someone I hardly know any more, that I haven't seen in over twenty years? That's what they'll say in the papers; what people will whisper about me. The whole story is unfurling in front of me.

But when I get downstairs and open the door, Michelle is lying on the floor next to Victoria, who is playing happily on her activity mat, transfixed by the mirrors and bells.

'Shit, what time is it?'

Michelle eases herself up slowly and checks her mobile. 'It's one o'clock.'

'God! Why didn't you wake me up?'

'I tried, Sylv. I came up but you must have fallen back asleep. I brought you a brew up.'

'She must need feeding. Has she not been crying? Did you turn the monitor off?'

I go into the kitchen and check it. Michelle is getting to her feet.

'Sylv, what's the matter with you? I changed her nappy, she's had a little sleep. She's been absolutely fine. I even had a little nap too.'

The kitchen looks transformed. I thought I had made progress on the house but this is something else. I have to look twice to check what I am seeing – the space pops before my eyes. The work surfaces and table are all empty and wiped, the floor mopped. It's the first time I have seen the sink empty and the taps gleaming. There's a pleasing lemony scent in the air.

'Bloody hell, Michelle, did you do this?'

'Yeah.' She looks coy. 'Who do you think did it, the baby?'

'God, you're making me look bad.'

'Sorry I was just…'

My anger at her letting me sleep in is fading now. I am touched that she would do this for me. Baffled at how she's managed it. But still, touched, and relieved.

'God, don't be sorry. I'm sorry for being such an ungrateful, grumpy cow. This is amazing. Thank you so much.'

'It's what mates are for, isn't it?' She punches me lightly on the arm. Then, after a moment, 'I do have some bad news, though, I'm afraid.'

'Oh, what's that, then?'

She opens the cupboard door under the sink, takes out the torch and switches it on, pointing it into the back corner. All I can see is manky old bottles of bleach that look like they're from the 1980s, gunk crusted around the spouts, dirty yellow dusters and a few carrier bags.

'I don't follow?' I pull my head out from the cupboard.

'I think I know where your stink is coming from.' She waggles the torch and I see black drops in the corner. 'You've got mice,' she says, sounding triumphant. 'That's mice droppings for sure. Seen them in the warehouse at work. And that stink in your hallway. You've a dead one in your walls or under the floorboards.'

I put my hand to my mouth, feeling queasy.

She nudges me and I lose my footing. 'Don't worry about it, Sylv. They won't hurt you, you wimp! They're more scared of you than you are of them. You don't want them leaving their mess everywhere, though, with the little one around. Don't worry about it. I'll get it sorted for you next time I'm round.'

'Really, do you think you can get rid of it?'

She laughs. 'It? You never get one mouse, Sylv. There'll be loads of the little buggers. They breed like God knows what.' All the little hairs on the back of my neck prickle up.

'I told you, I'll sort it. Fancy some soup?' she says brightly.

'Ummm, I'm not very—'

'Because I've made us some.'

'Erm, OK, go on then,' I relent.

'Alright.' She claps her hands together and rubs them. 'You sit down and I'll do soup and toasties.'

I don't usually have a chance to eat during the day, not since I have been here. Most of the time, it's a few chocolate biscuits shoved in when I have a moment. The thought of a proper lunch makes my stomach twitch.

I go through to the living room and pick Victoria up from the mat, I don't want her down there now, at mouse level. 'Come on, baby, you need to have your dinner, don't you?'

Michelle pops her head through the doorway. 'Maybe she's just not ready for any food yet, Sylv. Let her play for a bit and feed her when she's hungry, eh?'

My irritation shoots up again and I take a few deep breaths before responding. 'She needs to eat regularly, Michelle. She's a baby.' I push out the thought that she's already been damaged because I slept for too long.

'She'll be fine, Sylvie. Babies are more resilient than you think, you know. If you're all uptight, she'll sense it.'

I purse my lips, avoid snapping. Michelle looks down and fiddles with the can opener in her hand.

'My sister has kids. I looked loads of stuff up when they were born.'

'Ignore me. Sorry, Chelle.' Me calling her Chelle seems to please her and she goes back into the kitchen.

I put Victoria to my breast but she won't feed, struggling to get her face away and crying.

'Come on, please, Victoria. For Mummy,' I say, but she won't.

'You have to keep trying,' the health visitor had said. 'Don't react too much.' So I make an effort to stay calm. I realise that Michelle has sat back down on the sofa and is watching me. I want to cover myself up but it would look obvious.

'You tried formula? Saw you had some in the cupboard,' she says.

I bristle at that, at the thought of her rooting through the cupboards.

'My sister was the same. Switched to formula and she was fine. Started sleeping through the night then, too, putting weight on.

The baby didn't do too badly either.' She laughs at her own joke. 'You don't have to be bullied into breastfeeding, you know.'

Eventually Victoria latches on and feeds hungrily. Afterwards, Michelle and I eat the soup at the kitchen table. I just pick at mine, keep having the sensation of something crawling on me, the way you do when someone mentions insects. The idea of the mice.

Michelle slurps her soup. When she looks up at me, the bowl to her face, she looks young again, like a kid eating breakfast cereal. A twinge of guilt. About how we would leave Michelle out at school. I always saw her as a bit of a drifter. She never really belonged to any particular group. We wouldn't invite her places. Sometimes I think people did that on purpose. Maybe even Victoria. But most of the time, and for me anyway, it wasn't a conscious thing; I just didn't think of her at all.

There was one time when she called for us during the summer holidays. There was only me and Victoria in the house. We hid behind the sofa. We were laughing and I sneaked a glance. Michelle was pressed up to the window looking in, just like she was this morning. It must have jogged the memory loose. There was always just something about her, though. She tried too hard. She wanted to hang around with me and Victoria, I know she did.

We didn't need someone else, though. There wasn't room. You couldn't get a piece of paper between us, Mum used to say.

CHAPTER ELEVEN

Sylvie

After Michelle left, I spent the day playing with Victoria. Her mood was improved. The calm before the storm. I went to bed around ten and I slept fitfully, punishment for a long sleep in the daytime.

Now I am wide awake at 2 a.m. So is Victoria. I bundle her up, put the rain cover on her pram to protect her from the cold air, and we go out. At first I walk, seemingly aimlessly, just to keep warm. But I know where I'm really going.

The past, that summer, the lake itself has a magnetic pull. It's an unhealed scab demanding to be picked at.

I haven't walked this way since the day her body was found. There are no sirens in the distance or police cars this time. No TVs burbling through open windows. All the houses are dark. I use the light on my phone to show me the way ahead, praying that the battery doesn't die. When I get to the narrow path, fields on either side, I run one hand along the dry-stone wall all the way up to the lake. It takes me around forty minutes. It was quicker when I was younger and I didn't have a pram.

Victoria is sleeping now, of course she is, oblivious to where we are, the dark water of the lake, still and stagnant. I have to keep moving to stay warm, and I begin to walk around the footpath. It's an automatic reaction to keep looking behind me every few steps.

The moon is low and Christmassy white over the lake. You can see a shallow perimeter, the fields just beyond the lake with grass almost waist height. Beyond that it's just blackness.

I walk further round, pulled towards the car park. As we get closer, the landscape reveals more of itself. I know I should go back, into the house, into bed, under the covers. But I carry on over the mound. I never could resist following the others.

The hill is steep and bumpy on the other side. I clutch the handle of the pram as tightly as I can, until my fingers ache, the mental vision of it rolling away from me, bouncing over the rough terrain, tipping over.

I walk down slowly, inching bit by bit, feeling my way first with my foot each time for any unseen mounds or holes, grabbing clumps of grass for balance. It still jolts the pram around but Victoria doesn't stir. Strange to think she will wake in the morning and never know that she has been here; the things that happen while you're unaware.

The car park looks empty at first, but then I see two cars parked in the corner, their shapes gradually emerging. I should go back, but I'm incapable: the hooks are in, the need to know more about who could have been up here that night, waiting in the darkness. My steps are speeding up involuntarily now. When we reach the bottom of the hill, the momentum thrusts me further into the car park than I intended; I planned to stay at the edges.

I stop and stand still for a minute, letting the night settle again, and my eyes adjust. One of the cars flashes its lights two distinct times, some kind of Morse code. Then it's black and still once more and I am not sure for a moment whether I imagined it. But there is the flash again. My breath sticks in my chest, my stomach is snakes. A car door opens and closes. I am rooted to the spot just for a second, but then I run and don't stop until I reach the road. As I try to catch my breath, I close my eyes and spring them open, praying that I will wake up at the house.

I walk home as quickly as possible, body tensed the whole way, my feet burning underneath me.

When I get back, I get straight into bed. Victoria sleeps through. I do, too, until shattered glass pierces my sleep and wakes me; a dream of a mirror cracking and breaking of its own accord. The clock says it's 4 a.m. I go downstairs to get water. Victoria will probably need feeding soon. Stepping into the living room, something cracks under my sole. A sharp, stabbing pain on my sole. I check with my fingers; the skin isn't broken. When I flick the light on one of the snow globes is on the floor, broken, bleeding out lilac glitter. The dream must have been caused by the sound of the glass smashing, real life breaking in.

The light in the kitchen is still off and I don't move for a moment, the realisation that someone could be in there. My first thought is Nathan. Maybe he's found out where I am, Mum's address.

'Nathan? Is that you?'

Silence. I grab one of the snow globes with a heavy ceramic base.

A sudden pop of white light across the kitchen floor makes me almost drop it. The security light outside has come on, the motion sensor activated. The silence is broken by the sound of me rushing through, throwing on the light and wrenching the back door open.

'Who's there? Nathan, is it you?'

Surely, he wouldn't creep around like that.

There's just the cool quiet of the night, the panic creeping up around my throat. And it hits me, then. The mice… what Michelle said. One of them could have knocked off the snow globe and set off the light sensor. The tension in my limbs falls away. Relief escapes as a laugh, my breath a fog in the air.

Lighter, I float out into the garden, the cool air refreshing under my nightgown, the grass soaking under my feet. The flowers look otherworldly in silhouette.

Something bright red catches my eye amongst the grass and, when I pick it up, I see it's a red toy car. Next to it are two miniature chocolate bars, one of them squashed and smooshed up. The children who were in the garden must have dropped them.

When I get to the pond, my reprieve is snatched away again. Something is floating in the water. Something flesh-coloured. My mind leaps to the baby, but she's sleeping upstairs.

When she was born, she didn't cry at first. The whole room held its breath for a moment or two, then burst into life and they took Victoria away from me. When they brought her back she was crying and wriggling, purple blotches on her skin. They said it was quite common, not to worry, and left it at that, but sometimes that silent space haunts me.

My hands are already in the water and they're met by something cold and hard. It's a doll, its plastic face moulded into hard lines, dimples more like scars. I reel back, dropping it into the water again. The back of my nightdress is sodden now, sticking to me.

One of the children I saw playing in the garden must have dropped it there the other day.

A light is on in the upstairs window of Joyce's house, but I can't see anyone. Part of me wishes she would appear, insisting on a cup of tea.

I look at the doll again in the water, its marbly eyes staring out, nylon lashes splayed. My reflection is looming over it. When I close my eyes I get a vertiginous feeling and I can just see Victoria dead in the lake.

I yank the doll out quickly, soaking the front of my nightdress, too, and I put it in the outside bin, slamming the lid shut.

After, I lie in bed without getting dry, teeth chattering under the covers.

CHAPTER TWELVE

Sam

Sam sits on the bed in his room at the Travellers' Rest. The smell of smoke clings to everything. It can't have been done out since the ban came in. The tiny TV babbles in the background.

He looks at his phone again, irritated at himself for going round in the endless loop of checking email, Facebook, the news. Almost a compulsive tic. After a few minutes, he shoves his phone and wallet into his pocket and heads down to reception. The foyer is deserted, a radio playing in a back room behind the counter.

'Everything alright with your room?' a girl says, seemingly appearing from nowhere behind the counter, dyed red hair scraped back so tight the surface is almost reflective.

'Yeah, great, thanks,' Sam says, sure the receptionist must know he is just being polite. Even more sure she doesn't really want to know either way. Her gold badge says 'Janine' in black, the name flanked by three engraved stars on either side.

She gestures at the counter. 'Help yourself.' There's a white dish full of doughnuts, drying out.

'I've seen mints before – fruit, even – but doughnuts is a new one on me.'

Janine looks him up and down and shrugs, a non-verbal, '*Suit yourself.*'

*

The car park is dark and gravelly. In one direction, you can see only trees, a dense wooded area. The other way is a main road – a park and leisure centre on the opposite side. Attached to the hotel in the car park is a carvery-type pub. Inside, a young couple sits with a little girl, spooning ice cream into her mouth. It's past her bedtime. Maybe it's a birthday or perhaps they're some of these mysterious people who come on holiday here. An older man and woman sit in what looks like silence, eating bright pink gammon and chips, the peas radioactive-green.

Sam decides to leave the car and walk into town, get a feel for the place. He passes a few closed sari shops, beautiful bright silks and beaded slippers in the window; Indian grocers with vegetables stacked outside. Warm, appetising smells drifting out. The area peters out, and closer to the station there are large supermarkets, all clustered together, two next to each other, one opposite. In the distance, he can see a large turquoise mosque turret. In the local paper, they said there was a petition against building a new mosque in the town, an EDL demonstration planned for the following month. A town that doesn't like change, Sam thinks, remembering the hoo-ha about the footpath too.

Bits of Conley keep revealing themselves to Sam. He'd been surprised in a way by the dispiriting town centre, with its gaudy takeaways, shut-down shops and chain stores, compared to the journey in: the lush surrounding area, pockets of fields and farms. But even in the centre, every now and then between the buildings, or if you hit enough open space, you see a glimpse of the green hills again.

Sam walks around for a while, looking for the place he agreed to meet Martin when he dropped him off after the lake. Most of the pubs look pretty ropy, or empty, mostly both. Eventually, he wanders up a cobbled alley, following the sound of music and voices, somewhere that sounds a bit lively. That's the place: the White Lion pub, the one Martin had mentioned. It looks cosy:

low beams, white fairy lights strung outside. Pretty busy too. Couples having bar meals, a group of loud women crowded round a bottle of rosé wine.

Inside everything is wood and brass, a low ceiling. Sam isn't especially tall, but even he feels like he needs to duck in a few places to avoid hitting his head on copper pots hanging down. The music is playing a bit too loudly, too: an irritating modern version of Tracy Chapman's 'Fast Car', speeded up, bordering on the Chipmunks. Why? Sam thinks. Why mess with a song like that?

He winds his way to the bar and orders a pint of ale, one of the local ones, and some peanuts. The beer tastes hoppy and flowery, just how he likes it.

He takes his drink through to a smaller side room and sits at one of the tables. The room is old-fashioned with an organ in the corner and a space where an open fire would be – if there weren't likely to be so many pissed people around. It's like two pubs in one. A wannabe trendy bar on one side and an old man's pub on the other. He'd stick with the old man's side.

Sam sips his pint in silence. The pub is pretty full for a week-night. A group of lads in football kits and high spirits have just come in. A man brushes past with a tray of drinks, knocking the table.

'Oops, sorry, mate,' he says, as he wipes the spilled beer off his hands.

'No problem.' Sam shoots him a smile and nods. 'Do you live round here?'

The man gives him a confused look. 'No, I just have a summer house here. For my holidays.' He cocks his head towards Sam and says to his football friends at the table next to him, 'Have you heard him?'

One of the friends smirks.

'You parked your yacht up somewhere as well, have you?' the man says.

'I'm not from round here, actually.'

'No shit, Sherlock,' the man says in a poor attempt at a Welsh accent. 'What are you doing here, then?' He takes a slurp from his pint.

'I'm making a film.' Sam can hear the pride tinged in his voice and cringes.

The man's eyebrows shoot up and he swallows his drink hard, his Adam's apple bobbing in his throat.

'You made anything I'll have seen?'

'Not yet. It's a documentary.'

The man's excitement wanes again. 'So, you're making a documentary? Here in Conley?'

Sam nods, looking over the top of his drink.

'Wait wait wait, don't tell me: let me guess.' The man wiggles his fingers, like a hammy psychic. 'Is it some do-gooding piece about the EDL thing and all the nasty racists that live here? Not being funny, but you do look the type.' He touches his chin, gesturing at Sam's beard, then folds his arms and wears a smug look like he's guessed right.

'Nope.' Sam is annoyed at himself for being drawn into the exchange.

'Mmm-hmmm but I'm close, right?' The man is wedged back into the seat at the table next to Sam now, sitting with the group of men. They're emitting a collective musky smell of deodorant.

'Are you doing something on bent politicians? You should be. Robbing bastards,' the man says, beer foam on his top lip.

'No, I'm not here for that either.' Although he makes a mental note to himself. 'I'm here about—'

'Oh, so it's some happy clappy shite about the allotments or something—?'

Sam cuts him off. 'You lived round here long?'

'Twenty-seven years, since I was born.' He gives Sam an exaggerated toothy smile, perfect whitened teeth.

Sam had taken him to be older from the toughened look of his skin, the lines around his eyes.

'I'm here looking into the death of Victoria Preston.'

The man sticks his bottom lip out and shakes his head. 'Not heard of her.'

'Her body was found in the lake twenty years ago. She was fifteen.'

He scowls. 'Oh yeah, I have heard people talking about that. I don't remember it though. Too young.' He picks up his drink and turns back to the group he's sitting with. He says something to them and the table erupts into laughter.

Sam stares down into his drink until he becomes aware of someone standing over him – Martin.

'Sorry I'm late,' Martin says, carrying two pints – one for himself and one for Sam. He sits down at the table.

'Getting acquainted with the locals, I see,' Martin says, looking over at the men on the table behind.

'Something like that.' Sam thanks Martin for the drink with a nod.

'How are you getting along, then?' Martin asks. 'Digging much up?'

'Not bad, yeah. Got some stuff in the pipeline. Think I'll be able to gather enough for the sizzle reel.' Sam feels self-conscious using the terminology he's not entirely familiar with himself.

'The what now?' Martin cocks his head to the side.

'Sorry,' Sam says. 'Jargon. It's like a demo tape to show companies a flavour of what the documentary will be like. You know – the tone of it, who some of the interviews will be. That kind of thing.'

'Ah, I get you. Before they splash the cash.' Martin rubs his fingers and thumb together.

Sam winces a bit at that. 'Just the hoops you have to jump through,' he says.

'You think there might be interest, then? From TV companies?' Martin asks.

Sam shrugs and takes another drink of his beer. 'Hope so.'

'It's all the rage now, isn't it? True crime.'

'Suppose so, yeah.' Sam shifts in his seat.

Sam had been to a documentary-making conference that spring and it came up time and time again: viewers – and therefore TV companies – were hungry for true crime TV. The UK's answer to *Making a Murderer*, the TV version of *Serial*.

Sam feels his neck flush and he pulls himself up straighter on the stool. 'And the good thing about that,' he says, 'is, you know, it could really help find Victoria's killer, if lots of people are watching it.'

It sounds weak, like he's trying to persuade himself, and Sam thinks he can detect the faintest smile across Martin's face, a knowing look. Judging him trying to make money from someone else's misfortune, no doubt.

Martin jerks forwards, beer sloshing down the front of his shirt.

'Watch it. For Christ's sake.' Martin turns to see who has bumped into him. Behind him is a woman clearly the worse for wear, mascara smudged under her glassy eyes.

'Oops, sorry, love, I didn't see you there,' she slurs. She then deliberately tips part of her drink down Martin's back. She covers her mouth and laughs, before the friend she is with drags her away by the sleeve of her jacket. The friend holds a hand out in apology.

Martin leaps from the stool, trying to the hold the fabric of his shirt away from his skin. Sam unrolls some cutlery from a napkin and passes the cloth to him.

'What was all that about?' Sam asks. The woman is nowhere to be seen in the bar now. She must have gone through to the party side.

Martin dabs at his shirt. 'She's a friend of my ex-wife,' he says. 'Not my biggest fan, you could say.'

Martin's smile is tight, his temples flexed. He looks up like he's going to say something else, his expression hard. But his glance wanders and his face softens. Sam turns to see a man weaving his way through the tables towards them. He is grey-haired, slightly built.

'Martin,' he opens his arms out. 'Not often we see you round these parts these days. How the hell are you?'

'Not bad,' Martin says, still dabbing at his shirt.

'Neil.' The man puts his hand out to shake Sam's.

'Sam, nice to meet you.'

'Couldn't help overhearing,' Neil says, helping himself to a seat. 'When you were talking to that lot earlier.' He looks across to the table of football lads. 'You'll get sod all out of the likes of them. Will he, Martin?'

Neil doesn't wait for Martin to respond.

'They probably don't know who's running the bloody country right now, let alone anything else. No sense of history,' he says, shaking his head. He mimics pecking at a mobile phone with his fingers and screws up his face.

'So Martin, what brings you in here? We don't see you much these days.'

Martin shrugs his shoulders. 'You know how it is. Work, eat, sleep... Sam here's a film-maker. Wants to make a film about Victoria Preston.'

Neil swivels on his stool towards Sam. 'Interesting. I thought I heard you asking about that.'

'Neil knows everything and everyone in Conley,' Martin says. 'What he doesn't know isn't worth finding out.'

'So you lived around here then, did you? You know about Victoria Preston?' Sam asks Neil.

'Me? Yes, of course. I've lived around here all my days. I recall it well. They might not tell you as much, but most people do. Everyone who was old enough to remember anyway. It changed the place. Didn't it, Martin? Permanently, I'd say.'

Martin nods and takes a gulp of his drink.

'What do you mean by that?' Sam asks. 'That it changed things permanently?'

'Well, it's never been exactly chocolate-box Cotswolds. I mean look around you.' Neil tosses a look over his shoulder at the group of men at the next table. 'But there was more of a sense of community then. A bit of a spirit of "it's a shit town but it's our shit town" about it, you know?' He gives a flourish of his hand in the air. 'But that, it knocked the wind out of us all. Kids weren't allowed to play out, they weren't even allowed to walk to school without their parents. There was this suspicion everywhere.'

Neil pulls his stool in, leaning further forwards, hitting his stride. 'Do you know, I even think, in fact I know, I caught my wife looking at me sideways once or twice. Can't blame people really. Then especially, but even now, you're looking into people's faces when you're walking round.' He comes close to Martin's face then Sam's for emphasis. '*Was it you? Was it you?* You know?'

'What else do you remember about it, the time around then?' Sam asks. Neil looks at Martin for an answer, perhaps conscious that he has dominated the conversation.

Martin readjusts himself, like he has been woken up in class. 'Well, I agree with Neil. It made things very strange around here. A lot of suspicion.'

Neil is nodding along the whole time and takes the baton back from Martin, impatient. 'And then all these things started to crawl out of the woodwork. Women, girls saying they'd been flashed at. Cars crawling past "offering people lifts".' He makes quote marks in the air when he says that.

Sam thinks of the tip-off he received on SomeoneMustKnow about the flashing, making a mental note to move it up his list.

'And, of course, there was a really nasty rape up in the Brantham estate.' Neil tuts to himself, shaking his head. 'Not that there's any other kind, of course.'

'You thought it might be connected, then?' Sam asks, taking a sip of his pint. It's warm now, he's been nursing it too long.

Neil waves at the air in front of them with his hand, and laughs and breathes at the same time, causing a little snort. He covers his mouth and nose, mock-coy. 'Well, who knows? Oh, of course I don't know anything about that side of it. But the whole thing just left a bad taste in everyone's mouths. We weren't the nice simple Yorkshire folk we wanted to think we were. I could have told anybody that anyway.'

'You've never thought of leaving, then? Moving somewhere else?' Sam says. Neil doesn't strike him as the type of person who fits in around here.

Neil puts his hand on his chest. 'Me? Oh God no! Where on earth would I go?'

Sam can't tell if he's being serious or ribbing him. Probably the latter, he thinks. A twinkle in his eye.

Neil hops up off his seat. 'Right-oh, I am definitely getting myself another drink.' The queue at the bar has cleared. 'Anything for you two?'

'No, you're right, thanks,' Sam says, and Martin shakes his head.

'Suit yourself.'

After Neil walks away, Martin raises his eyebrows over his drink. 'Pub – best place to come round here to find people to talk to.'

'Isn't it everywhere. How do you know Neil?' Sam asks Martin.

Martin shrugs. 'Around and about. Everyone knows everyone in Conley.'

Sam hoped Neil would come back, kicks himself for not accepting his offer of another drink. Over at the bar, Neil has already launched into another in-depth conversation with a few people standing nearby. 'Holding court' Sam's mum would have called it. The group is hanging on his every word, occasionally exploding into fits of laughter.

Sam feels a tap on his shoulder from behind and jumps a little. The man from the next table.

'Old twinkle toes been filling you full of shit, has he?' He tips his head towards the bar.

'Sorry?'

'Honestly, he hardly knows what day it is.' He twists his hand around near his temple.

Martin shakes his head. 'Think I'm going to get off. Work tomorrow. Joys. Keep in touch, won't you? If I can help at all while you're here in town.'

'Thanks, mate. Will do,' Sam says. 'Appreciate it.'

Sam slowly finishes off his pint and grabs his coat to leave. Outside, the woman who spilled the drink over Martin is smoking against the wall. Sam keeps going but she calls after him.

'Where's your mate?' she says.

'Sorry?' Sam turns back to her.

The woman rolls her eyes, exasperated. 'Where's your mate? Where's Martin?'

'Oh, he's gone home,' Sam says.

'Tina,' the woman says, offering her hand. 'You new round here? Not seen you before.'

'Yeah, I'm just kind of visiting. I'm doing some research.'

'Right.' Tina keeps her eyes on him.

'Victoria Preston case. I'm hoping to make a documentary about it.'

'You are, are you? Digging all that up again, eh? What's Martin got to do with it?'

'Got to do with it?' Sam says.

Tina tuts, irritated again. 'How do you know Martin?'

'Oh. Well I don't, really, but we bumped into each other and he offered to show me around. Introduce me to a few people.'

'Oh, he did, did he?' Tina takes a drink from her glass. Looks like gin and tonic. 'Where you stopping?'

'Me? Travellers' Rest,' Sam says.

Tina splutters on her drink, laughing. 'Lucky you!'

'You're not wrong,' Sam says.

Tina starts typing into her phone, signalling that the conversation is over.

As Sam is walking away from the pub towards the hotel, buoyed by two pints of craft beer, an idea occurs to him. Now might be an ideal time to find out more about the taxi driver.

He misses it the first few times, but finds it when he retraces his steps along the high street and checks the map on his phone again. The little side alley, between a bank and a hairdresser's, is completely unannounced. He goes down and it's so narrow – barely wide enough for two people – that it feels as though the walls are closing in.

The bottom of the alley opens into a small yard, boxed in on all sides by the walls of buildings. There's a sign outside one of the doors for Target Taxis. The small window has bars on it, the glass thick and opaque with dirt. Sam goes to open the door but it doesn't move; he needs to press a buzzer.

'Yes, love?' A bored-sounding voice comes through the intercom.

Sam looks up and there's a camera pointing down, right into his face.

'Taxi?' the Dalek-like voice asks.

'I'm looking for Brian Addington.' Sam speaks into the grubby intercom.

There's a long pause. 'All the fares cost the same, love. Doesn't matter which driver you have.'

He goes to press the button to speak again, when the door blares and pops open, and a man comes out. He's tall and broad, a large belly pushing against a straining shirt. He tips his weight back when he stands, jangling his keys in his hands. Wordlessly, he walks up the alley, whistling between his teeth, throwing his arm over to gesture for Sam to follow after him.

'Where you going, mate?'

'Travellers' Rest, please.'

Once they are in the car, Sam catches sight of the driver's badge swinging under the mirror. It is Brian, although he doesn't look a lot like his picture. In the photo he's much younger and slimmer.

Brian tuts under his breath, probably because the hotel is so close to where they are already.

Sam tries to gather his thoughts. He'd planned on finding out more about Brian, trying to get his contact details. He didn't actually think he would be there. He hopes for traffic; should have thought of somewhere further away, but the lake would have been too obvious.

Sitting in the back, on the left side where Victoria sat, Sam stares at the back of Brian's head, his hair threaded with wiry grey streaks. He was thirty-nine then, fifty-nine now.

The air freshener gives the car a talcy, sickly smell. Sam feels like he's inhaling it, like it's gumming up his insides. Brian turns the radio on low. A jingle for a local carpet company. He glances at Sam every few seconds in the mirror.

'Funeral?' he asks.

'Sorry?' Sam says.

'Get a lot of folk stopping there for funerals. Family parties too. But a lot of funerals, it seems.'

Sam decides to own up. 'I'm here making a film actually.'

Brian perks up at that, eyes tilting towards him in the mirror. 'Oh, aye? What's that all about, then?'

'Documentary,' Sam says.

Brian contorts his arm backwards to offer Sam a sweet from a paper bag. They're all clagged together and it brings three others with it, bits of paper welded onto the side of the sweets.

'Listen, it was you I wanted to speak to actually,' Sam says. He can't be sure but it feels like the car does a small swerve at that. 'I'm researching Victoria Preston's case.'

Brian snaps the radio off and spins his head round, taking his eyes off the road for a terrifying amount of time. This time the car jerks unmistakably. The skin on the back of Brian's neck has flared red and the tendons are tightened. He doesn't say anything for a while at first then he pulls into a retail park. It has a DIY store and the back entrance to McDonald's, bins overflowing with burger boxes and cups with straws. They park facing a wall in the far corner of the car park.

Brian spins round in his seat, skin straining like his neck might tear open. 'Are you trying to pull one over on me?'

'No, look. Can I come and sit in the front? This feels ridiculous.'

'You bloody sat there, for God's sake.' Brian turns to face forwards and Sam lets himself out and into the front seat. Brian is staring straight ahead out of the windscreen, chest slowly rising and falling.

'How'd you find me anyway? Not that it's a secret,' Brian says, finally.

'To be honest, I didn't expect you to still be there – at the cab firm. Thought it would be a starting point,' Sam says.

'Why didn't you expect me to still be there? Thought I should have moved away from here, eh? Scuttled off under a rock somewhere?' His voice is raised now.

'No, it's not that. It's a long time. Thought you'd have moved on to a different job,' Sam says.

'Nope. No career progression whatsoever. Thanks for the reminder.'

'I didn't mean anything by it, I was just…'

The silence hangs solid between them and then Brian breaks it, letting out a resigned sigh. 'So, what is it you want, then? What do you want to do me for?'

'You're perhaps the last person who saw Victoria alive that night. So I wanted to interview you.'

'Well, what can I tell you about her? I know as much as you – less probably. She got in my taxi, that's it. I feel bloody bad about it, I do, but that's really all there is to it. There isn't much useful information I can tell you. Every day I wish I had just knocked off earlier that night. People still suspect me.' He shakes his head.

Among the SomeoneMustKnow theories, almost no one thought Brian was guilty of Victoria's death. But in Sam's experience of reporting on crime – inhaling other people's misery through all those books and TV shows – the last person to see someone alive is guilty of their murder a high percentage of the time. He tries to size Brian up.

'I just wanted to hear your side of the story,' Sam says. 'Maybe if people see that, they'll start thinking harder about what really happened to Victoria.'

Brian thinks for a bit, breathing loudly through his nose. He doesn't say anything, but turns to Sam. Something has softened.

'Have you told your side of things before?' Sam pushes on. 'You could maybe provide people that missing clue they haven't had yet. Now is your chance. I'm offering it to you.'

Brian looks like he's on the cusp. Sam stays very still, waiting for his response. Any sudden move could snap him out of it and make him change his mind.

'Alright, I'll do it,' Brian says. 'They'll write and assume whatever they want anyway so I might as well try and have my say for once. I've got nothing to lose.' He twists the mirror towards him and licks his finger to tidy up his eyebrows.

'Can we do it at the hotel?' Sam says. 'It's too cramped in here. I don't have the camera.'

Brian scowls then nods.

They drive the rest of the way in silence. When they go into the hotel, Janine is on reception, reading a copy of a magazine.

She looks up and her eyes follow them as they pass the desk. She's probably dying to laugh about it with one of her colleagues.

Inside the room, Brian is eyeing everything up, like a builder sizing up a job, looking up at the corners and the ceiling, peeping behind the yellowing lace curtain. Sam arranges the chair, trying to find a camera angle which will hide the fact they're in a dingy hotel room. Brian sits down on the cheap wooden chair. He looks too large for it, like it might collapse any second. None of the chair is visible except for the legs.

'OK,' Sam says, positioning the camera and switching it on. He sits on a chair diagonally across from Brian. He wants to move as quickly as they can so Brian doesn't change his mind. 'So, I think the best place to start is, can you tell me about that night, in your own words?' Sam says, setting the camera to record.

Brian gives a big sigh, puffing out his cheeks. 'It was just another night, you know. I've always worked the taxis – it's not brain surgery or city trading or whatever, I know, but I like working when I want, within reason, and I like the wide range of people that you meet. My wife says it suits me because I enjoy gassing on with people and maybe that's true.'

A strip of skin is showing between his jeans and his shirt. It has become partially untucked now and his swollen gut protrudes. Sam adjusts the camera slightly so it's out of the shot.

'So, that night…?' Sam isn't sure if Brian is deliberately obfuscating or just easily sidetracked.

Brian takes another deep breath. 'Yes, so. It was a Saturday night and it had been pretty steady – pubs kicking out and that, but it wasn't as busy as usual because it was towards the end of the month – for paydays and that, you know, and because of the time of year, what with holidays – people were on them, saving for one or skint after getting back. It's always the same. In this line of work you get to know the rhythms of the year.'

He seems to drift off and lose his thread again.

'Would you say you remember the night clearly, Brian?'

He pauses before answering. 'Yes, yes absolutely, as a bell. I have a good memory anyway – you have to remember all the streets and pubs and random little places that people want to go to. We didn't have satnavs and whatnot then and I don't use one now. It's up here.' He taps a finger on the side of his temple.

'So, picking up Victoria?'

'Yes, so Helen, the lass on the switchboard, sent me a job through the system. And she said it was for a Victoria and was at the phone box on Thistle Street. Nothing special in that at all, of course, but it stayed with me because of what happened after. Strange the things that lodge themselves.' He looks childlike fiddling with his hands in his lap.

'And was that unusual in itself?' Sam says. 'To be picked up from somewhere like that?'

'God no, you pick people up all sorts of places, believe me. Places they probably shouldn't be plenty of times. But if it's not illegal – or obviously dodgy anyway – then I try to mind my own. I just drop people where they want to go and that's it. I'd never make any money otherwise. My job is to get people from A to B, not to get involved in why they want to get there or where they've been… So no, I didn't think a lot of it when the call came in, but I did wonder when I turned up and it was a young lassie. Petite little thing she was – you'll know that anyway – and she was sitting out on the kerb in the rain.'

Brian shakes his head, lost in thought. 'I felt a bit sorry for her as soon as I seen her. I'm a big softie, that's what my wife always says too. She looked a bit lost or something. But then I thought to myself it was probably just because of the weather.'

'So…' Sam says, but Brian doesn't notice Sam speaking and drifts into his next sentence.

'You know, I often think the weather worked against her that night. Hadn't rained for weeks either.' He shakes his head.

'So, Victoria simply got in the car?' Sam succeeds this time and it snaps Brian out of something.

He refocuses. 'Yes, she sat where you were sitting today. Not a fact lost on you, I am sure.' Brian gives Sam a snide smile.

'And did she say anything or...?'

'She just said she wanted to go to the lake and I remember saying, "Are you sure?" because of the weather, you know? And the time of night. Anyway, she was upset; she was kind of snivelling a bit. I didn't feel like I could really push it with her so I set off.'

Sam wonders how much of this is true; how much of it is how Brian wishes he had behaved. Did he really just take the money, ask no questions and think nothing more of it? It's what most people might do.

'You didn't think about asking her more?' Sam says. 'Checking she was alright, or telling her you couldn't take her?'

'I have a daughter myself, Layla – it's my favourite name, after the Eric Clapton song, you know the one?'

Sam pictures Brian's thoughts bouncing around, each one triggering a new tangent. Interviewees are like that a lot.

'OK, so I was just asking whether...'

After a pause, Brian ploughs on, though. 'My Layla, she's still my little girl. She was about twelve then. Bit younger than the Preston girl, but close enough. I'd learned a bit about bringing up girls. I knew if I pushed too much, she'd retract. She might try and walk up there to the lake or something, I thought. And that would be worse, wouldn't it? On those roads in that weather. So, better I took her at least, that's what I thought. Sometimes, my daughter, she'll swear black is white just to disagree with me. They're bloody murder at times.' Something passes across his eyes, regret at the choice of term maybe.

Sam has to smile at this, though, as he recognises it from Natalie.

'I suppose I just had to make a decision and go with it and that's what I did. But I do blame myself,' Brian says. 'I should have followed my gut.' He taps his round stomach. 'There was something about it I didn't like, but it was late, I wanted to get home. I was selfish, in a way, although if it hadn't turned out the way it had, I probably wouldn't have thought much of it again.'

Sam nods.

'Thing is,' Brian says. 'She was a young lass; I didn't want to get into a "situation", didn't want to be accused of anything, if I'm honest. You can't be too careful these days. Anyway, that didn't work out too well, did it?' He gives a hollow laugh.

'So, you just drove Victoria to the lake and that was it or…?'

'I asked her once more if she was sure she wanted to go there, to the lake. I asked what she was doing up there on a night like that and she just said she was meeting someone. She was snappy, she didn't want to chat, let's say. You can tell very easily what's what when you been doing this job a while.'

'And what did you think?'

'I just assumed she was meeting some lad. God knows why there, I thought, and perhaps I didn't want to know, having my Layla and that. I thought, she'll be meeting her boyfriend or whatever, probably a no-bloody-hoper who's too old for her anyway, and that was that. I didn't think a huge amount more about it, to be honest. I went home, I had a Chinese and I went to bed. I mean… no that's a lie. I did think about it a bit. I thought again to myself how it was a little odd and how she'd be cold and wet in that weather. I heard the rain when I was in bed and I thought about her. More in a "bloody kids" type way. I assumed she'd be somewhere warm and dry by then. That was it really.'

'Did she say anything? When you dropped her off?'

'Nope she just shoved some money in my hand and she got out.'

'And where did she go? You didn't see anyone else?'

'I can still see her now. She was standing in the headlights and she had her hand up to her face like the lights were hurting her eyes.' He puts his own hand up, palm out. 'So I lowered them, but when I looked up she was walking away, with her back to me. And soon, with the rain, I just couldn't see her any more.'

He exhales quickly, the breath popping between his lips. 'Still gets me, you know?' he says, bumping his fist on his chest.

'And how has it affected you? Do you ever think about it?'

This puts the colour back into his face. 'Are you kidding? I almost lost my wife. My daughter was looking at me funny for months. Even now, people have their doubts about me. They checked my car, you know. At the time – forensics and all that. They didn't find anything they shouldn't.'

Brian bites at his lip at that. There's something he isn't sure about saying, Sam can tell. Waiting usually flushes it out and it works here too.

'I always wash the car on Sunday mornings. Usually anyway, sometimes Mondays,' Brian says eventually.

'What do you mean?' Sam looks up.

'They thought there was something in it that I had washed my car, but you can ask my wife – I often did it Sundays and it was muddy from the weather.'

Sam files that away mentally, keeping his face neutral. He pushes his weight down into the chair. 'But now you have a criminal record, don't you?'

Brian's eyes dart up, but then he regains his composure. He slumps in the chair and a section of the seat is visible between his legs. He points at the camera and shakes his head.

'It's just a few more questions,' Sam says.

'That's not fair – you've got me here under false pretences.'

'Not really,' Sam says. 'It's just about—'

Brian stands to leave and starts to collect his coat.

'OK, OK. Sam gets up and fiddles with the camera before giving Brian a 'tah-dah!' gesture. 'It's off,' Sam says.

Brian sits back down slowly, eyeing the camera cautiously like it's a predator about to pounce.

'Listen, I'm not a violent person, I never have been.' Brian shakes his head, looks up at the ceiling and twists the ring on his little finger. 'I went out into town for my wife's birthday, right. First night I'd had out in ages. I prefer to drink in the house. Full of scum in town. You know the worst of it? I actually had a good night. We had a few drinks, bit of a laugh. It was good to see my wife enjoying herself. For us to have a bit of fun. We should have gone home after the pubs shut but she wanted to go dancing. We went along to Charlie's in town. It's gone now, shut down. Shithole anyway. Some little gobshite starts goading me and that on the dance floor. I said we should just go, but he wouldn't leave it. And it was about Victoria and I just saw red and…'

'And what?' Sam says.

'Boom, there was commotion everywhere and I had a broken bottle in my hand, he had blood pouring out of his face.'

'You glassed him?'

'That's what they tell me. Yeah, I must have done. I just kind of blanked out. I'd had too much to drink. I was so angry. Never happened before, never since. He hit a nerve, I guess.'

'Never?' Sam ventures.

Brian snaps straight back, 'Never. I told you, didn't I?' He looks at Sam. 'So don't be twisting it, right?' All the softness in his voice and expression is gone now.

Seeing Brian get worked up like that, Sam still can't imagine him completely losing it. Enough to kill someone. A customer. Could Victoria have said something, done something, rejected him in some way to make the same happen at the lake? Sam scrutinises Brian, his neck expanding and contracting, blood pumping at the memory of the incident at the club.

'"Missing."'

'Sorry?' Sam says.

'Everything but the Girl. That's the song that was playing when it all happened at the club. Weird that I remember that bit, eh?'

Brian stands up in one swift move, the wood of the chair creaking back into shape. 'Well, good luck with it. With finding out what happened to her,' he says.

Sam fumbles in his pocket, fishing out a crumpled ten-pound note.

'For the cab fare,' he says, but Brian just waves it away.

'Forget about it, mate.' He pauses at the door. 'I hope I don't regret this.'

Sam watches out of the window, waiting for Brian to reappear and get into his car. Brian looks around like he's worried about being seen there. Then he just sits in the car for a while. Sam can't see Brian's face, but his hands are flat on the dashboard.

CHAPTER THIRTEEN

Sylvie

The Roxy pub on the High Street is a confusingly grand building, out of place next to a stationery store and a shop selling unfashionable clothes – skirts with gaudy flowers and elasticated waists, ugly woollen cardigans in dispiriting shades. The Roxy used to be the cinema when I lived here, and the pub retained the name. Now there's just a multiplex on the edge of the town.

Opening the door is an assault on the senses: garish fruit machines, blaring signs for deals on drinks, waiters and waitresses zipping about with plates of chips and stodgy dinners. Some of the tables have the old theatre seats, and the sign outside is a half-arsed attempt at being in the style of an old-fashioned cinema.

I am surprised by how busy it is during the daytime – most of the tables full, a queue forming at the bar. There's no music, just the sound of people chatting and eating, the relative darkness; it's disorientating. It makes me think of secret subterranean worlds.

I scan the room for Michelle, finally spotting her on a raised area in the corner, waving wildly, standing up.

'You blind cow,' she says, punching me lightly on the arm. Irritation flashes in me. I'd been glad of the invite from Michelle at the time, a chance to get out of the house, interact with other people, but now I'm not sure it's a good idea.

She throws a hug around me, clamping my arms to my sides. When she releases me, she leans into the pram and pinches

Victoria's cheeks, making her threaten to cry. I rock the pram to try and soothe her.

There's already a bottle of wine on the table, two poured glasses. Michelle registers me looking. 'Oh, live a little, will you? A glass of wine is not going to kill you. This is my Saturday night this week. I'm working the rest of the time.'

Victoria has settled now and I sit down. Michelle thrusts a laminated menu under my nose. It needs wiping – greasy smears, old food crusted onto it.

'What are you having?' she says. 'I know what I'm having. I always have the surf and turf because it's so cheap. If you order off this list here, we get a discount.' She shoves her finger under my nose so she can point at the menu. Victoria starts to grizzle. The noise of the pub and Michelle's babbling. A cacophony of competing sounds.

'Six quid a bottle,' Michelle says, inspecting the wine label. 'Can't go wrong.'

'God, it's busy in here,' I say, taking a sip of the pink wine, sugary and lurid-looking.

Michelle smiles at me. 'It's a pub, Sylvie. You don't get out much, do you? Me neither. Gotta take a bit of fun where you can get it. See them two over there?' She points with a fork that was sitting on the table.

I turn round to see two elderly women in the window sharing a bottle of wine and a meal. 'In here for a bottle of wine and their lunch twice a week, followed by a whiskey each to finish off. They told me once, it's that cheap that they can afford to do it. That'll be me and you one day.' She beams at me. 'I am so glad you're back.'

'It's just while I sort out my mum's house,' I say.

'We'll see,' Michelle says, pouring more wine into the glasses, filling mine to the brim. 'How's it going? The house? Seen anything of your uninvited little lodgers?' She wrinkles and twitches her nose, mimicking whiskers, and a shiver goes through me.

'No, maybe they've gone now. Now that there isn't any food or anything out.'

'Maybe,' she says, still scanning the menu. 'Droppings looked pretty fresh to me.'

It feels as if she's almost taking pleasure in being right, but I remind myself that my temper is short and I ignore it. 'I've still got loads to sort out before I can sell it. Need to crack on, really.' My own little dig that I'm keen to get away.

Michelle manoeuvres herself out and grabs the menus. She has to squeeze between the table and the wall to get out. It's tight and her face flushes.

'It's on me,' Michelle says, disappearing to the bar even though I haven't told her what I want. I call after her but she doesn't turn.

When she gets back, the mood is lighter. Her work, Victoria's sleeping or lack of. But when the conversation dries up, the awkward silence feels like it hangs heavy between us.

Michelle puts her wine glass down, elbows on the table, and leans forwards. 'So, Sylvie, you're Internet-famous now, you know?'

'What are you on about?'

A waitress butts in and puts two overloaded plates down in front of us.

'I ordered the same for you as me. You were too slow!' Michelle says.

I don't have the heart to tell her that I don't eat meat. Haven't been able to stomach it since the day I saw Victoria's body. I couldn't separate the idea of meat and flesh any more.

The sight of the brown steak, sinewy and glistening on the plate, makes my stomach roll, a faint trickle of watery blood oozing out of it. It's scattered with prawns, peachy little apostrophes.

'You not seen it?' Michelle says, chewing with her mouth open so I can see the mashed-up meat and chips.

'Seen what?'

She tuts and gets out her phone, pecking around on it for what feels like minutes. She hands it over to me and taps on the screen, greasy fingerprints left behind. It's a picture of me outside Mum's house, on the doorstep. It's the picture from the other day, when the boy came to the house. Someone has written 'The best friend: she's back!' underneath. I scroll up and look at the web address. SomeoneMustKnow.com.

'They wanna hear from you, Sylv. There's people all over trying to solve Victoria's case. America, Canada, France. And they all know who you are. Don't you think that's amazing?'

I stare at the phone.

'There's even people doing bus tours, you know, going up to the lake. They want to see where it happened.'

'That's horrible,' I say, as much to myself as Michelle.

'Do you use this website?'

She shrugs. 'I just read it sometimes. Not just about Victoria. Other cases too.'

She tries to take the phone back from me, but I am still gripping it tight. Michelle gives it a hard tug and then wipes off the screen with her sleeve. She gets up and goes back to the bar, jerking the table this time so she can get past. I have to steady the glasses and the wine bottle. I keep checking behind me, and while she's gone I chop up the meat, that livery smell bursting out with each incision, and I gip slightly. I move it around a little to try to make it look like I have eaten some.

Michelle slams two bottles down on the table hard, making me jump. My heart rate takes a moment to return to normal. She has a big grin on her face.

Alcoholic lemonade, a cartoon lemon licking its lips on the side of the bottle, lascivious. 'Like old times. Can you believe this stuff is back in fashion? God, we used to get so drunk on this, didn't we?'

'Yeah,' I say, all those warm, loose-limbed nights flooding back to me.

'What's up with that? Don't you want it?' Michelle jabs her fork at my plate.

'I'm just pretty full. Had a big breakfast,' I say.

She skewers a piece of meat and eats it, smacking her lips loudly.

I look round and everyone is eating, shovelling food in, slurping drinks. It feels like the sounds – the chewing, cutlery, the clanging of the tills – are all turned up too high.

Michelle raises her bottle and reluctantly I clink it and drink, sedimenty and warm, like aspirin dissolved in water. I hold it in my mouth for a while to take some of the sharpness out of it, and I feel like it is eroding and disintegrating my teeth.

'Do you remember…' Michelle says, leaning forwards, her lips still greasy. Something about her expression makes my stomach drop. She pauses to take a long drink, her throat bobbing up and down. 'Do you remember all the stuff we used to get up to at school?'

Michelle and I were never all that close, though. She doesn't feature in many of my strongest memories. Victoria is always there. Sometimes Michelle was out with us, sometimes she wasn't. I don't remember ever calling for her or arranging to meet her. She'd just drift along into the group or happen to be passing when you met up.

'Yeah, we had some times, eh?' The only Michelle memory I can summon is her bursting into the room naked.

She smiles and leans in even further, pushing the table against me. 'Do you remember when we used to go up to the lake?' she says, showing her teeth.

I swallow hard, blood whooshing through my ears, then the sound of someone struggling for air.

'I can't believe we used to swim in that water, can you? Eurgh,' she says. 'They found all sorts in there! Sheep's heads and cars and stuff.'

She's forced it into my mind now, the lake and the image of Victoria's face and hair when they pulled her out.

'I think Victoria needs feeding soon. I'm going to have to go, Michelle.' I start gathering up my bag.

She leans in again. 'I've been thinking about it a lot, since you got back. Do you remember the frogs?' She's looking me square in the eye and holding my gaze, a mischievous glint on her face.

'No,' I say, 'I don't know what you mean.' I pick at the chips on my plate, dipping them into lurid red ketchup. I can't stop myself shoving them in, even though there's nothing I want to do less than eat them.

'Yes, you do, Sylvie!' She's speaking too loudly. The family on the next table over look across. 'We used to put bangers in their mouths and blow them up. God, we were horrible.'

'No,' I say, and my head is shaking. 'That isn't true. Just stop now.'

'And the cat and the firework that time? Oh my God. Where did that cat even come from? All the way up there.'

'No, I wasn't there, Michelle.'

She nibbles at a piece of loose skin on her lip and a small pinprick of bright red blood bubbles up.

'We did, Sylvie,' she says in a sing-song voice. 'You were definitely there. And Victoria too. It was just a kids' prank. You don't need to get so uptight about it. Maybe that's what we need to do with your little mouse visitors.'

I gulp down more of the alcoholic lemonade. 'It was the boys, it wasn't me.' But I have an image of Victoria and me huddled together, her laughing, egging them on, me telling them to stop.

Michelle sticks her bottom lip out, red and glistening. 'You take everything too seriously, Sylvie. Like you said yourself, it was ten million years ago. Lighten up.'

I try to stand up to get to the bathroom, splash some cold water on my face, but the table is jammed in place and Michelle pretends not to notice.

I shove it, and the cutlery flies off onto the floor.

'Alright, alright, what's up with you, grumpy boots! Just chatting about old times,' she says. 'God!'

The 'God'; it's how we used to talk when we were at school.

'Can I ask you something?' I say, taking a glug of my own drink. She shrugs. 'Fire away.'

'You said you had a partner and you split, but you didn't take it well?'

She retreats a bit then, the glee fading from her face. 'Yeah, it's fair to say I was a bit of a mad bitch.'

I nod at her to go on.

'So, I was seeing this guy, Phil. He was married.' Michelle shakes her head. 'We met at work. He worked in the warehouse. So, we got together blah blah blah, we got a flat, we got a cat – the whole shebang. I was mad about him. I was happy, you know.'

'So, what happened?'

'Six months in, he changes his mind, goes back to his wife. They had kids, he was worried they couldn't handle it. Thing is, though, I don't think she even wanted him back, the wife. She just wanted to show that she could. I reckon she'll leave him high and dry in time. Revenge best served cold and all that.' She pushes peas around her plate with her fork.

'That sounds rough.'

'I'm getting there now. But at the time? You would not have wanted to see me then.'

'Why?'

'I was just being a psycho, to be honest, hanging around their house and that. I just wanted to see what she had that I didn't.'

'Sounds intense.'

The colour drops from Michelle's face. 'I slashed his tyres. And some other stuff.'

She scratches awkwardly at her neck, a heat rash gathering. 'You probably think I'm a right nutter.'

I shake my head. I think of the flash of alien temper I saw in Nathan that last time I saw him; it ignited like petrol on a fire. And me and Mum after Dad died. She'd been wearing her dressing gown for days. She didn't look anyone in the eye; she didn't answer when you spoke to her.

She had ignored me again, the zombie-like state was scaring me and I tugged on the back of her dressing gown. When she spun round, I hardly recognised her, her face twisted up. We should have been looking after each other after Dad died, but somehow we couldn't connect. We only had each other to take everything out on.

'What do you want?' she said, gripping my wrist, so much venom in her voice. And I can sympathise with Michelle because the rage in me flared up so fast and so full.

I only realised when my hand connected with Mum's face. The loud slapping sound, the red mark on her cheek. My hand flew round over my shoulder with the momentum of the blow and there was a kind of rush from it, a release. Mum put her hand up to her face for a moment but immediately became impassive again, floating back upstairs.

I couldn't tell if the look on Aunty Alice's face was about Mum or me, but the next day we were in the car on the way to Manchester. This grim empathy makes me feel strangely closer to Michelle, and I think for a moment about confiding in her about the doll, but she speaks and I decide against it.

'Anyway, he went and got a job somewhere else sharpish, thank God. Reckon it was one of the conditions of his re-entry into the marital home. Probs for the best anyway.'

Michelle's eyes shift away and I become aware of someone at the edge of the table.

'Hi, Mr Preston,' Michelle says, a slight slur creeping in.

But Peter doesn't look at her, he's looking directly at me, down onto me. 'Letting your hair down, are we, Sylvie, love? You do right.'

I feel as if I have been caught doing something I shouldn't. Trapped at fifteen again. 'I'm just… just catching up with Michelle. We went to school together.'

Peter gives her a cursory look but then back to me. 'I've been watching you two from down at the bar. Looks like you've been having a right old scream.'

He's been drinking, too. His eyes are shiny, cheeks pink. He picks Victoria up from the pram, even though she shrieks loudly in protest. She looks tiny in his large hands.

'You just out having a few drinks yourself, are you?' I try to change the subject and I hold my arms out for Victoria. She's still crying. But he pulls her in a little closer.

'Yeah, "me time",' he says, and winks.

Michelle goes to say something, but Peter doesn't hear her, or pretends not to. He walks Victoria back and forth along the platform for a minute, jiggling her up and down. Finally, he hands Victoria back to me; her little body contracts in and out, breathing quickly.

Peter pats my shoulder. 'Have a good afternoon anyway, you two.' But he looks only at me. 'Good to see you again, Sylvie.'

Not long after, I make my excuses to get away. Michelle keeps trying to extend the conversation, buy more drinks. I haven't drunk much at all, but on the way home I feel groggy and drowsy. I'm not used to it.

When I get back, I put Victoria in her cot and lie on the bed. The afternoon has left me uneasy… *my picture on the Internet*. I try to ignore it, but the urge is too strong and I bring Someone-MustKnow up on my phone.

The design is poor, blaring banners and ugly fonts. A sea of news stories about death and murder and disappearances. Thread upon thread, hundreds of them, discussing the cases. The screen swims. I scan and see Victoria's name and click in. So much chatter, I can almost hear the competing voices in my head, deafening. The words all rush towards me at once and I close the page. A feeling like vertigo is swooping through me.

The wine and food are sitting heavy and rancid in my stomach, the house creaking.

Then, all I can hear is the sound of the frogs. Hiss, pause, a loud bang. Then a girl laughing.

CHAPTER FOURTEEN

Summer, 1995

'Alright, shit stains,' Jamie said, raising his voice to be heard over the tinny music from the ghetto blaster someone had brought. He lived near Sylvie and Victoria, and was one of the group they hung around with in the park sometimes. They'd bumped into him and some of the other lads earlier and agreed to go up to the lake for something to do.

He flicked his torch up, and in the beam of light, otherworldly, someone was coming towards them. From what he had called her, Sylvie knew it must be Michelle.

'Don't say that to her, don't be tight,' Sylvie said, but no one heard over the music and the chatter. Either that or they ignored her. She wondered whether she'd said it out loud at all.

Another torch pinged on.

'Hi, Michelle, you alright?' Sylvie said.

'Yeah, hi.'

'Just passing, were you?' one of the other boys said. 'Just happened to be walking by all the way up here?'

'Yeah, I just wondered where you lot were, that's all. Thought you might be here.'

Sylvie was sitting on one of the wooden picnic benches around the edge of the lake and she patted the space next to her for Michelle to sit down. Michelle almost fell back the first time she tried to step up, and the boys laughed. Sylvie winced.

Jamie and Harrison started to pretend they were sniffer dogs, Harrison on his hands and knees, crawling along the floor.

'What is that smell?' he said to Jamie, following his nose around.

'Smells suspiciously like... shit to me,' Jamie said.

Michelle shifted in her seat.

'Just leave it now and stop being dickheads,' Sylvie said. She could feel herself shaking, but it seemed to work and Harrison and Jamie stood up and lost interest. Jamie turned the music up and started dancing around, singing up to the moon.

'Where's Vic?' Michelle said.

'She's with Lee somewhere,' Harrison said, and he sent the torch around the lake like a lighthouse beam. 'Why, do you want to go and watch?'

'You don't fancy going for "a walk" with me, Sylv?' Jamie said, winking theatrically at Harrison.

'No, you're alright, thanks.'

Sylvie felt Michelle bristle next to her. Maybe she wanted to be asked.

'So, what's everyone been up to?' Michelle asked, but Jamie and Harrison ignored her, jumping up and down to the dance music.

'Not much,' Sylvie said. 'Just hanging around, you know.'

Out of the darkness a figure emerged, then another. Victoria and Lee.

'Oi oi,' Jamie said. 'Where you two been then?'

Victoria pulled her sleeves over her hands and climbed on the bench next to Sylvie, their arms touching. Sylvie thought she seemed subdued. Lee went over to Jamie and offered his hand. Jamie was about to take it then pulled it away.

'Eurgh, fuck off.' The boys jostled and nudged each other, laughing.

'Who invited shit stains over there?' Sylvie heard Lee say. She tried to cough to cover the words so Michelle didn't hear them, but she knew it was probably already too late.

Jamie ran up the embankment that overlooked the car park and shone his torch.

'Ey up, we've got some action over here, lads.'

'What is it? What's going on?' Michelle sprang off the bench.

'Keep your voice down, will you?' Lee said, a snarl.

Sylvie looked at Victoria to see whether she would say anything, that he shouldn't talk to Michelle like that, but she was engrossed in examining her shoes.

'What's up with you?' Sylvie whispered, nudging her.

'Nothing,' she said, without looking up, twisting her body away. 'Come on, let's go with these.'

Lee and Jamie led the way with the torches and they all clambered up the hill. Harrison ran up behind and pinched Sylvie hard on the bottom as she was bending to grip on to the grass. Her cheeks burned, anger blooming, but by the time she realised what had happened he was already ahead again with the other two boys.

They all ran down the slope on the other side, threatening to crash into one another. When they got to the bottom they each flared out onto the gravel like a Red Arrows display.

'What are we doing here?' Sylvie said. 'I don't like it. Let's just go back.'

'We're gonna crash someone's party,' Jamie said, hopping around with excitement. In the moonlight he looked like some kind of sprite.

They trooped across the car park, all the light from the torch cast in front of them. There was a car parked on the far side.

'Hey, let's just leave it,' Sylvie said.

'Just come on. It will be a laugh,' Victoria said, beckoning her. 'Do you have to be so boring? Man up, will you.'

Sylvie could see that the car was moving from side to side, rocking, and sourness flooded her mouth.

'I'm not doing this. I'm going back,' she said.

'Alright, I'll see you later on then,' Victoria said, lowering her voice, not looking back. 'Maybe tomorrow.'

Sylvie felt herself pulled along with them. Michelle was already up front with the boys. They had turned their torches off now. Sylvie could just hear the crunch of gravel at different angles, signposting where people were. She kept spinning around, looking behind her, thinking she heard it there too.

They reached the car and automatically formed a circle around it. Mentally, Sylvie had felt herself turn and run, back towards home. But she was still standing there rooted to the spot, mouth paper-dry, blood pumping in her ears.

The boys shushed everyone and Michelle stifled giggles.

'One, two, three,' Harrison whispered, and the torches popped on, blinding Sylvie for a second. They pointed them into the car and Sylvie couldn't help but look. At first it was a blur, glare off the glass, but then she could make out a tangle of arms and legs, a naked bottom in the air. She froze and closed her eyes. When she opened them again, she was looking right into the shocked face of a woman through the window, black smudges under her eyes, bare shoulders visible.

A fist against the glass from the inside made Sylvie's heart bounce. The man's fist. The boys exploded into laughter.

'Run!' Harrison shouted as they heard the sound of the car door handle.

Someone yanked at Sylvie and she turned and ran. The noise of the running and scraping on the gravel felt as if it was right up against her ear. Sylvie kept looking back then spinning forwards again, the night around her fracturing into sharp, jagged pieces. Somehow she powered straight up the embankment again and over to the lake. She couldn't tell who was where. She almost stopped to get her breath; it felt like she was swallowing in lumps of solid air. They'd all laugh about it soon.

'Oi! Where are you, you little perverts?' The voice was coming from the other side of the embankment. Distant but closing in.

'Keep going.' Jamie shot past her and stooped, barely dropping pace, to pick up the ghetto blaster.

Someone waved a torch and it gave a strobe-light effect, a disorientating prism. Sylvie didn't know which way to run.

The sound of a heavy splash.

'Wait!' she shouted. But the others ran on ahead. Maybe they hadn't heard her. Sylvie wondered if the man had fallen in. Should she help him out?

'Who is it?' she called and the response was a choked, whooping sound. Someone gasping for air.

'It's me!' It was Michelle.

For a few seconds, Sylvie hopped from foot to foot. There was no sign of the man at the top of the embankment. The impulse to just leave was still strong. She heard another long, pained gasp, and before she knew she was going to jump, she had landed in the water. It was up to her knees. She followed the sounds of Michelle's thrashing. The ground that her feet were on suddenly dropped and the water was up to her waist. It made her fall forwards, grabbing at the lake, foul water going into her mouth. The bottom of the lake was known to be uneven, shelves appearing and disappearing from nowhere. Her foot hit something solid and she tripped, freezing water shocking her face, her hair sticking to her.

Hands grabbed at her, nails digging in.

'Sylvie, is it you?' Michelle was speaking through mouthfuls of water, still splashing her hands everywhere.

Sylvie grabbed Michelle's hands and began to pull her up, the weight almost dragging Sylvie back down.

'Michelle, you're OK. You just fell. You're OK.'

'I didn't know which way to go,' Michelle said, her breathing too fast. 'I walked the wrong way.'

They were both upright now and Sylvie pulled Michelle towards the edge of the lake. Her teeth began to chatter. Sylvie climbed out first, her clothes heavy. She reached down and managed to haul Michelle out, too, her weight almost pulling them both back in.

Michelle's breathing was still laboured and she went to hug Sylvie. Then the voice came again.

'Oi! You dirty little pervs.'

'Run!' Sylvie said to Michelle. Her limbs felt like lead from all the water.

When she reached the lake entrance, Victoria was there, leaning against a lamp post. 'What the hell are you doing?' she said.

'Just run. He's coming.' Sylvie's breathing was loud and whooping, she couldn't drag enough air in.

Victoria grabbed Sylvie's hand and they ran across the road, not stopping to look whether anything was coming. Victoria climbed over the gate into the field. It was a shortcut to their houses.

'Wait, where's Michelle?' Sylvie looked behind her and there was no one.

'Leave her. She must have run down the other way,' Victoria said. 'She'll be fine. Come on!'

Sylvie climbed over the gate too. Water was dripping off the bottom of her trousers now. She checked behind them again. There was no sign of the man or anyone else.

'We shouldn't have left Michelle,' Sylvie said. 'I feel bad.'

'She shouldn't have run head first into the lake, stupid cow,' Victoria said, picking up her pace.

'It wasn't her fault. I was panicking too,' Sylvie said.

'It was just a joke, Sylvie. We were only mucking about. Get a grip.'

They walked the rest of the way in silence until they reached the road.

'Right, I'll see you tomorrow, then,' Sylvie said. She was cold now and she wasn't much in the mood for being around Victoria any more. It would blow over tomorrow.

'Yeah, whatever,' Victoria said and started to cross the road towards her house.

Headlights came on in a parked car over the road. Its engine was humming low and the horn blared out. At first Sylvie thought it was the couple from the lake again, and she started to run. The door opened and Sylvie turned.

There were two people standing on either side of the car. Victoria's dad and Sylvie's mum. Peter and Margaret.

'Sylvie,' Margaret said, schoolmarmish. 'What on earth are you doing?'

Victoria was already walking towards the car. Sylvie drifted over too.

'What's going on?' Sylvie said, confused.

'Never mind you asking, you tell *us* what's going on,' Peter said. 'Look at the state of you both.'

No one said anything.

'I was just dropping your mum off home, Sylvie. I don't expect to see you two traipsing around looking like you've been dragged through a bush backwards. What is going on?' Peter looked between the two girls.

'Well?' Margaret barked. 'Sylvie, you are soaked through. No one is going anywhere until we get some answers. Don't know about you, Peter, but I've got all night.' She looked at him and he nodded.

'I'm in no rush.' He held out his wrist, pretending to look at his watch.

Victoria stepped forwards. 'We went up to the lake,' she said. 'It was dark and Sylvie thought she saw someone and she fell in the lake. She got scared and lost her footing. I helped her out.'

'Is that right, Sylvie?' Margaret scrutinised her face. Her voice was stretched with disbelief.

Sylvie nodded.

'You thought you saw someone or you did see someone?' Peter said.

'We did see someone but we got away,' Victoria said.

'Who did you see?'

'It was just a man,' Victoria said. 'It was dark.'

'Did he say something? Did he try and hurt you?'

'We got away. We're fine.' Victoria had her weight on just one foot.

'I can't understand why you were up there.' Margaret shook her head. 'Who were you with?'

'Just us. We just like it up there. It's quiet and there's a good view of the moon,' Victoria said.

Margaret narrowed her eyes. It was obvious she didn't believe what they'd said.

'Well, you don't go up there ever again, you hear me? Or you're grounded permanently.' Margaret grabbed Sylvie's shoulder and shook her lightly.

Both girls nodded and looked to the ground. Victoria tilted her face a little and winked at Sylvie. Sylvie pushed her head further down to hide the smile creeping across her face.

Peter drove them home, Victoria in the front with her dad, Margaret in the back with Sylvie. No one spoke.

When they got into the house, Sylvie tried to run straight upstairs. Margaret reached up and grabbed her by the ankle.

'Are you going to tell Dad about it?' Sylvie asked.

'No,' Margaret said, 'and neither are you. He's got enough on his mind. Get those wet things off now and go to bed. And you don't ever go up to that lake again at night. You hear me? Ever. Or you will be sorry.'

CHAPTER FIFTEEN

Sam

Sam sits at the kitchen table, marvelling at how spotlessly clean and tidy everything is. There's a chill in the September air today; it's been gradually edging in for a few days. He keeps his coat on – Judith and Peter's house doesn't feel much above the temperature outside.

'So, how is everything going?' Judith says, still not turning round. It strikes Sam how she is very dressed up to clean the house, even if there's nothing for her to get dirty on. He feels a twinge of sadness at the idea of Judith rattling around this house all day in her pristine outfit, bleaching away at stains that aren't there.

'Not too bad, thanks.'

'Do you have children, Sam?' She keeps on rubbing at the same spot on the counter.

Sam considers before responding. What harm can it do? 'I do. I have one daughter, Natalie. She's just started university.'

Judith turns round now, unhooking the apron from around her neck. 'She was so good at art, you know. Victoria. She really had something. All mums say that, but it is actually true. Would you like to see some?'

'Sure, I'd love to.'

Sam waits at the kitchen table, listening to the clock ticking. Judith comes back with a large black folder with handles. She opens it up and spills sheets of coloured paper across the table.

'She never even got to try oil painting, you know. But I bet she would have been good at it. She wanted to. My fault.' Judith purses her lips. 'I didn't want the place getting messy. That stuff doesn't come out.'

She turns over some of the pictures, large sheets with big, loose pastel pictures on. Others are small, postcard-sized watercolour paintings. Sam examines a chalky one of two figures looking out of the window of the house, the artist clearly on the other side of the glass, outside. The picture is smudgy and abstract because of the pastels, and they've blurred over time. But you can also tell straight away that it's Peter and Judith. Somehow, Victoria has managed to capture something of Judith's tense, uptight demeanour, Peter's edge. Must have always had it, even before Victoria's death, Sam thinks.

There's a watercolour of Sylvie on a swing, leaning back, hair almost brushing the floor. Judith pulls out the photo that it was painted from. The sense of movement, the light have been captured in the painting.

'I love this one,' Judith says, sorting through, stopping for a moment to look at each picture. It's another postcard-sized one of Sylvie and Victoria, a sketch in soft red and blue pencil.

'Do you know how she did this one?' Judith says.

Sam shakes his head, knowing Judith wants to tell him herself.

'She drew it in about ten minutes while the two of them were looking in the mirror.' She points out through the kitchen door and into the hall, where a long oblong mirror hangs against the wall. 'She wouldn't let Sylvie move. Thought she was going to burst with trying not to laugh.' Judith takes the picture off the table and puts it to one side.

'Do you mind if I…?' Sam says, getting the video camera out of its bag.

'Fire away,' Judith says. 'I don't think people really saw her as an arty type. It would be good to show that side of her. But don't you think that she definitely had something? I think it could have taken her somewhere.'

'Did she want to be an artist?' Sam asks. 'When she finished school?'

Judith laughs. 'Do you know what she wanted to do? She wanted to go on cruise ships. She'd heard about jobs on board as a photographer and she wanted to do that... I'd have been happy for her to do that, though. I'd have missed her, but whatever she wanted, I wouldn't have minded.'

A key turns in the front door and Judith scrambles to put the pictures back inside the folder, folding the flap over quickly and sliding it behind the door. 'He doesn't like to see me dwelling and moping. It upsets him. So...' She mimes zipping up her lips.

'OK,' Sam mouths.

Peter burps loudly in the hall before coming into the kitchen. 'Oops, sorry, love. Didn't know we had company.' He wafts a stale, beery smell in with him and there's a slight slur to his words.

Judith purses her lips.

'Yes, yes, I had a lunchtime livener. Is there a problem with that, dearest?' His voice has an edge to it. The atmosphere in the room tenses.

'Sam is here to interview us. About our daughter. You might remember?'

'Oh right, yes.' This time he burps more quietly into the O of his fist, releasing another draught of beer into the air. Judith bristles again.

'It's fine,' Sam says, starting to get up. 'I can come back another day. Tomorrow, perhaps.' He doesn't have any intention of actually leaving.

'You'll do no such thing,' Judith says, voice taut. 'We'll do it today.'

She pours coffee into a cup and hands it to Peter, their eyes locked.

'Shall we go into the living room?' It's an order, not a question.

They walk through to the next room. The cream carpet looks brand new, like it's never been walked on.

Peter knocks the black coffee back and grimaces, sitting next to Judith on the sofa. He puts the cup down on the table and Judith slips a coaster underneath it wordlessly. Sam sets the camera recording straight away. He catches Peter rolling his eyes.

'Are you sure you're ready to do this?' Sam asks.

'We'll never be ready, but we'll do it,' Judith says. She grabs Peter's hand and the veins in hers protrude, knuckles white.

'OK, I know this won't be easy,' Sam says, 'but it's important to bring Victoria to life for people, to engage them with her story and who she was as a person. Hopefully jog some memories, rattle some cages.'

Judith smiles tightly and nods, leaning forwards to rearrange a couple of magazines on the coffee table, lining them all up perfectly.

'So, how would you describe Victoria?' Sam says. The small gold carriage clock on the mantelpiece ticks loudly.

'She was just a lovely girl,' Judith says, emotions already rising to the surface. She looks up at the ceiling, the veins in her neck jutting out. 'It sounds so obvious when you say it. Everything sounds like the type of thing people always say when someone dies. It's hard to "bring her to life", as you put it.'

'That's because she's dead.'

Peter's tone is so deadpan, the words he's actually said take a few seconds to catch up with Sam. Judith looks like she's going to react for a moment, but then it's gone again.

'We had our moments.' Peter pushes on anyway. But he and Judith are both squeezing each other's hands tightly now, Judith's irritation with him seemingly dissipated – or glossed over for the camera. 'I mean she was a teenage girl and she'd have her tantrums and all. You know what teenagers are like – it's a live chemistry experiment, isn't it? It was all new to me. I'm one of three brothers.

Michael – Sylvie's dad – and I, we'd have a pint and compare war stories. Sylvie was the same. It was nothing out of the ordinary. I mean, Victoria and me, we'd have some right old ding dongs but we'd always sort things out, wouldn't we, Jude? She was a smart girl, bright – she had a bit of spirit. Crikey, some days it was like an explosion in a fireworks factory round here, but it would blow over and we'd laugh about it. Judith always said she took after me in that way. Didn't you, love?'

Judith smiles and nods at him. 'Both a bit fiery.'

'And what was she like in the run up to her death? Was there anything unusual?'

Peter shifts in his seat, clears his throat. Judith is looking at him, waiting for him to speak.

'I wouldn't say so, no,' Peter says. 'Of course, I've asked myself many times, scrutinised a lot of things that we should have done or that we could have done differently. But, no, she was just a normal teenage girl enjoying the summer holidays.'

Sam changes tack. He has to steel himself to say it. 'So, if we can turn our attention to the night she went missing…'

Judith's expression hardens. Peter's temples flex.

'You'd been to a party at Margaret and Michael's place?'

Judith nods, her lips pursed.

'Was it a summer barbecue or…?'

Judith looks to Peter for reassurance, but he stares straight ahead, his breathing rising and falling slowly in his chest.

'Sylvie hasn't told you…?' Judith says.

'Well, I haven't…. Why?'

Judith looks to Peter again, but he refuses to give in. She starts off uncertain. 'Well, it was a… a kind of… it was a party for Michael.'

'A birthday party?'

'No,' she says, failing to hide the exasperation. 'He was… he was dying. You really should talk to Sylvie. I feel awkward being

the one to tell you. I mean I suppose it's no secret, is it? But still.'
She draws the pendant from side to side across the chain on her
necklace.

'Dying?' Sam says. Nothing he'd read to date had mentioned
that. None of the police reports, nothing on the forum.

'Brain tumour,' Peter says, abrupt. 'Couldn't do anything for
him.'

Judith flinches again, presumably at the brusqueness of his tone.
'Erm... yes, so it was kind of a goodbye in a way, while he was
still sort of himself. He'd asked for it, Margaret said. They used to
have lots of parties and barbecues round at their house. Because of
the garden out the back, you know? He didn't want anything to
change, asked specifically that people didn't talk about his illness
that day. It was a celebration, Margaret said.'

'He wanted it to be a happy occasion. Didn't want people
fixating on the illness,' Peter interjects.

'Was there anything special about the day apart from that?
Anything out of the ordinary happen?'

Judith shakes her head, wrapping her arms around herself.

'Not apart from the bloody obvious,' Peter says.

Judith tries to compensate for him again. 'We went round to
the party in the afternoon. Two or three-ish, I think. Peter and I
came away about ten. Didn't we, love?' She looks at Peter, who
is nodding.

Long time to be drinking, Sam thinks. But not an unusual
amount of time to be somewhere like a barbecue either. He steels
himself again. This is the point where it would be kinder to back
off, but he knows he has to push on.

'And when you got in, after the party, were you waiting up for
Victoria or...? Was it usual for you to come home before her?'

'Her curfew was eleven during the summer,' Judith snaps in
quickly. 'It was still a warm night. There were still a few people
at the party when we left. It was normal for her to be round at

Sylvie's until eleven-ish, yes. Or to stay over. And Sylvie would stay here, too, at least one night a week usually, on the camp bed.'

She carries on of her own accord. 'Usually, most nights, we'd be up until Victoria came home. Always, in fact. I mean, of course we were. That's the thing about it. We weren't these parents that just let their kids run wild. Not at all. We always knew where she was and we'd always stay up until she was in. One of us would anyway. Usually me, because Peter would be working early most days.' She looks at him again for approval but he doesn't engage.

'So, this night you... didn't wait up for her?' Sam asks.

'We'd had quite a bit to drink,' Judith says, pushing her chin down into her chest as if to obscure the words. She pulls it up again. 'Everyone had.'

Peter speaks more forcefully then, still looking straight ahead. 'It isn't a bloody crime having a few drinks, Judith. They wanted us to go round for a party, remember? The man was dying, for Christ's sakes. Least we could do was go along with the whole thing. And, frankly, it was a bit weird, yes. I don't know about anyone else, but I needed a drink to get me through it. I presume most were the same. A few said as much.'

'Of course it's not a crime. And you're right, it isn't every day you go to a party like that.' Sam presses on, glances to check that the camera is recording. 'I am sorry to push you. I just want to be clear. So, you both waited up or...?'

Peter's jaw is tight, mandible twitching almost imperceptibly.

'I went to bed,' Judith says, choking back sobs. 'Sometimes I wonder if someone had been watching the house or something. Because we always stayed up. Did they know we'd gone to bed? Had they been waiting?' She looks at Sam as if he has the answer.

'Judith, please!' Peter's voice. It makes Sam jump and Judith flickers too. 'Talking like that doesn't help.'

The room settles again. The clock clicks round. Sam looks out into the garden; the neatness of the lawn, perfectly manicured flowers.

'Peter stayed downstairs and waited.' Judith rubs his arm and there's a twitch of something across his face. He doesn't look at Sam or Judith or the camera. His eyes are open but his gaze is detached.

'I fell asleep on the sofa,' he says, measured calmness in his voice, sliding his jaw from side to side. He breathes in through his nose and out again slowly. Sam wonders if it's a technique someone has taught him. 'I woke up at about three in the morning. I got a glass of water and I went to bed.'

His voice is unnerving in its calmness. It feels like something he has practised saying. Perhaps as a way to come to terms with it himself, Sam thinks. The obvious question hangs in the air, throbbing and unanswered. Sam pushes himself to let the silence linger but still no one says anything.

'Did you check in on Victoria?' Sam asks, as even-voiced as he can.

'No,' Peter says, blank. 'I went straight to bed.'

Judith fills the space eventually. 'He thought that she was either in bed or staying at Sylvie's, didn't you, love? I'd have been the same, I'm sure. I wouldn't just go into her room in the night, risk waking her.' She pulls lightly at the thick dark hairs on Peter's arm. 'The next morning, I just thought she was having a lie-in. You know what teenagers are like.'

Judith looks at Sam for confirmation and he gives a small nod.

'So, I shouted for her a few times and in the end I knocked and went in. Saw that her bed hadn't been slept in at all. And that's when I called Margaret and Michael's place. We started to ring round. I was worried.'

Sam feels his own heart start to thump at the thought, the exact moment when the panic would set in.

Judith swallows down some tears. 'We never heard it ring. I just can't get past that. I've stood and screamed at the phone as if it's a person.'

'What do you mean?' Sam says.

'They said, from the phone-box records, that she'd tried to call us... before she called for the taxi. But we didn't hear it ring.'

Sam thinks of the reconstruction video. The aborted call.

'She might have wanted picking up.' Judith twists her hands. 'Or maybe she would have told us who she was meeting. It kills me that I missed that conversation.'

He forces his next question out. 'And at any point did you have a sense of where you thought Victoria might be?'

Judith takes a deep breath. 'Honestly? I think I knew deep down as soon as I saw the empty bed.'

Peter shakes his head silently. Disagreeing with what Judith says or just reliving the pain, an awkward tic? Judith registers it but carries on anyway.

'My gut feeling was I knew right away that something terrible had happened. Do you know what I mean?'

'Did Victoria have any problems with anyone that you knew of?' Sam tries to keep his voice light but Judith's expression has already darkened.

'What kind of problems do you mean? Is there something you're getting at, Sam?'

'No, nothing like that. I'm just trying to get a clear picture, that's all. I'm coming to this fresh, remember. And that should be a good thing.' Judith doesn't say anything, so Sam pushes on. 'A fresh pair of eyes can sometimes find a new way into things.'

Judith's face is pinched, staring out at the garden through the rain spattered on the window.

'You talked to Sylvie?' Peter asks. 'She'd be the best one to tell you what they really got up to. Teenage girls don't tell their parents much – you'll know that yourself, Sam.'

'I've not been able to get hold of her yet, but I'll keep trying.'

'Huh,' Peter scoffs. 'Call yourself a reporter.'

'I'll talk to her,' Judith says, robotic.

Peter moves suddenly, raising his voice. 'Ah, just leave her be, will you, if she doesn't want to do it.'

'I think they always blamed us, you know,' Judith says, towards the garden.

'Judith… don't.' Peter's voice has a warning tone and his grip on her arm has tightened but she snatches herself away.

'What do you mean by that, Judith?' Sam asks. He can feel Peter's eyes boring into him, willing him to leave it. He pretends not to notice.

'Michael's death,' Judith says, as if Sam should have somehow known that. 'He died so soon after. Three weeks? They were prepared for months. I always wondered if the shock of Victoria's death had made it worse. Margaret never said directly, of course, but I got that impression.'

Peter shakes his head.

Judith lightens her tone. 'Who can blame her, though? She had such a tough time of it as well.'

'Not exactly the same as losing your teenage daughter. Not the same as a murder really, though, is it?'

'Peter! It's not a competition,' Judith says, pink embarrassment creeping up her face. She shakes her head and turns back to Sam.

'So, let me ask you this,' Sam says. 'Do you have any theories about what happened to Victoria that night?'

Judith's tissue goes up to her mouth, her eyes shining. 'I honestly can't think of anyone who would want to hurt her.' She blots her eyes.

Peter says, 'There are a lot of bad people in this town, Sam. Real wrong 'uns. But the police, the folk round here, they're not interested in unearthing it. They don't want bad PR for the place. It's bad for their stats, whatever. Laughable really, isn't it? If it didn't make you cry.'

This, he and Judith are agreed on, and she nods furiously next to him.

'You know, there was that halfway house right at the bottom of the road,' she says, pointing. 'It's still there – there are druggies, alcoholics, people just out of prison living there. The police went round a few times but nothing came of it. They should have looked harder. Of course, everyone's moved on from there now so the chance is gone.'

'Did you ever have any problems with people from this place?' Sam asks. They're called 'Approved Premises' now, he thinks, but it doesn't seem like a good time to say so.

'We didn't have any problems as such, no, but I was always aware that they were there.'

'I saw a few incidents,' Peter says. 'Couple of pissed blokes scrapping on the grass out front. Someone chucking clothes out of the window. Police car there a few times. They weren't sitting about around the fire singing "Kumbaya" and toasting marshmallows, I can tell you that for nowt. Not like some people would have you think.'

Judith nods her head and she reminds Sam of a cartoon mouse.

'Rehabilitation,' Peter goes on, putting on a whiny voice and contorting his face into a grimace. 'Do you know what galls me? What really gets me? We offered a reward at first. Not a lot, a few grand – much of which people donated. Police didn't want to do it, to be honest. But we had to, didn't we, love?'

Judith nods more vigorously.

'What choice did we have? The police, they said it would bring too many crazies, false leads. They didn't recommend it, they said. Didn't want the admin, more like. That's the impression I got anyways.' His jaw clenches. 'I pushed it. So, what really got me, what made me think I was done with this town is the amount of time wasters we did get. I didn't expect it. And plenty of them were from that place down the road. For money? Don't care how skint you are, you don't do that. I just don't relate to that mentality. At all.'

'I don't say these things shouldn't exist,' Judith says. 'But... it was right across from the park, you know? There's so many kids have always lived round here. It's close to the school.'

Sam takes a deep breath, fills his lungs, then forces the question out. 'Do you think they'll ever find her killer?'

'Isn't that why you're here?' Peter says, a snide tone in his voice.

Judith digs her elbow into him with one small flick of her arm.

Peter looks squarely at Sam, then at the camera. 'No,' he says. 'To be honest with you, I don't. Too much time has passed. No one really cares any more. Everyone is wrapped up in work, going on holiday, buying a load of shit for Christmas. Most people don't even know who she was. And they care even less.'

'I probably shouldn't say this, but sometimes... I wish they hadn't found her,' Judith says. 'I've read about parents whose children are missing for a long time, never found, and they say they think a body might help. Give them closure. I understand where they're coming from, I suppose, but it isn't like that. It doesn't help me. They still have that hope to cling to that their child might be out there somewhere. We don't have that.'

Judith gets up out of the seat, lurching forwards. At first Sam thinks she might fall onto him, that she might be attacking him, but then she's upright and she runs from the room.

'Think that's enough for one day, don't you?' Peter says. He picks up his jumper that's been draped over the arm of the chair and he throws it over the camera as if it's a budgie in a cage. 'As long as you've got what you need for your film, and to get paid, eh?'

Peter gets up and walks out after Judith. Sam packs the camera away and goes out into the hall. There's no one there, but he can hear Judith and Peter upstairs behind a closed door, their voices low.

As he lets himself out, the shock of the cold air is a relief when it hits him.

CHAPTER SIXTEEN

Sam

Sam decides to walk again between Victoria's house and Sylvie's, as if by going in the opposite direction he could rewind the night Victoria died. He finds himself standing at the top of the park across from the 'halfway house' that Peter had mentioned, deciding whether to go over.

At first glance, there's nothing much to set it out from the rest of the large houses that stretch out down the hill like a row of dominoes. Just a small sign, if you're looking closely, marks it out as something different. 'Camden House', the sign reads, a design you associate with hospitals or doctor's surgeries. You might assume that it was a retirement home. A woman in a tabard is sorting recycling into the wheelie bin. She turns once then twice to Sam. 'Can I help you, love?' Her tone is open, not confrontational. Sam crosses over the road.

'My name's Sam,' he says.

'You looking for some help?' The woman looks confused; she's eyeing Sam up, trying to work him out.

'Not exactly. I—'

'I'm sorry, love. It's referral only here. I can give you some information, though, if you like.'

'I'm looking for someone.'

'I see. Listen, I can't give you any details on people staying here. Not even for family. Sorry, love. That's up to them.'

Sam goes closer to the gate. 'It's not that.'

The woman shifts further round now, more defensive, the light from inside the building behind her.

'I'm a film-maker. I'm making a documentary about the death of Victoria Preston.'

He waits for the woman to go into the house, slam the door, but she doesn't. 'Oh, right, I'd heard you were in town. I was wondering when you'd come over. I expected it to be sooner.'

The woman looks up at the windows above, then at her watch. Some lights are on upstairs. 'I've got fifteen minutes now, if you want to come in?'

They go inside. 'Tracey,' the woman says. 'Come through here.'

They go into a small narrow room with no windows. Against one wall is a table with a computer on it. One chair in front of it, one at the end of the table. It reminds Sam of a doctor's consulting room. Tracey gestures for him to take a seat.

'So, how's it going? Your "film",' Tracey asks. She makes quote marks in the air with her fingers.

'Not bad, you know.'

'Like trying to get blood out of a stone?'

'In some ways, you could say.'

'I'll bet.'

There's a knock on the door.

'What?' Tracey says and a man pops his head in, an arm in a stripy jumper coming round to hug the door. 'Is it urgent, Terry?'

'I'll come back,' he says.

'Thanks, love.' She winks at the man at the door, then turns back to Sam.

'How long have you worked here?' he asks.

'I've worked here about seventeen years or so, since I was in my mid-thirties.'

'So you weren't working here when Victoria died.'

Tracey hesitates, her tongue on her upper lip. 'I said I've worked here seventeen years. I was here the summer Victoria died, as a resident.'

'Right.' Sam doesn't know how to react.

'I had some issues myself when I was younger,' Tracey says. 'I like to think it gives me an insight into where people are coming from. Or something. Except everybody's weird; everyone has their own idiosyncrasies, don't they? Tell you what, you could make a documentary about this place. We've got some great stories of people who've turned their lives around.'

'You don't find that people round here mind?' Sam says. 'They don't bother that somewhere like this is on their doorstep?'

'Somewhere "like this"?' Tracey does the air quotations thing again.

'You know what I mean.'

'And I'm sure they've told you they mind?'

Sam holds his hands up, caught out, and Tracey raises her eyebrows, good-humoured.

'We've a few Nimbys, of course. It's to be expected. And we've had our moments. But I'd say we've a good relationship with the community now. The police, local residents. We rub along OK.'

'So did you know Victoria?'

'Not as such, no, but I know she lived round here. I saw her in the paper and on the telly and I'd seen her coming and going.'

'Did you hear any rumours about what might have happened to her?' Sam says.

'What, because of the kind of people who stay here? They're covering up what happened to her?' Tracey shakes her head to herself.

'I didn't say that,' Sam says. 'Would you be up for being interviewed for the film?' He starts to get his camera and tripod out. 'It's not actually commissioned yet, but I'm making a reel to start pitching it out.'

'Not on camera.' Tracey looks across at the door, playing with loose skin on her lip between her teeth. 'I don't want this place dragged through the mud.'

'OK...' Sam says, a flutter in his stomach. That feeling that he might be on to something. 'Did you see something?' he prompts her.

'Well, it maybe isn't much, but it's always stuck with me.' She picks up a biro and lets the tip bounce off the desk over and over.

Sam shifts forwards in his seat.

'This has already been reported to the police, you know, and they weren't interested. That's the only reason I'm telling you. At least you've had the good grace to ask.' Tracey shakes her head.

'What did you see?'

'I think the police thought I just wanted the reward money. That I was a drunk. I guess I wasn't the right kind of witness.'

'What did you tell them?'

Tracey lowers her voice. 'Sometimes I wonder if I imagined it now. But I'm sure I didn't. I know I didn't.' There's a long pause then Tracey says, 'Follow me.'

They leave the office and go up a staircase with a wooden bannister and a shabby carpet. At one time, this place would have been a grand old house. Tracey checks around then opens the first door at the top of the stairs with a key from a bunch hanging off her waist.

'We've no one staying in this one at the minute,' Tracey says. 'But it used to be mine.'

In the room there is just a single bed, a small chest of drawers and a cheap, mismatched wardrobe. A paper shade covers the bright, white bulb. There's a big window with no curtain or blind, just a deep ledge like a shelf with two flattened cushions on it.

Tracey pats it. 'I used to sit in the window. Best seat in the house.'

Sam goes closer and looks out. From the outside, the window doesn't stand out, obscured by the trees. But from in here you can see clearly right across the park and along the street.

Tracey comes and stands next to Sam. 'It made me feel calmer just watching people walking around, and the traffic and the night,' she says. 'I'd seen the two girls before, coming and going. Hanging about in the park. I'd seen them say goodbye halfway a few times before, like they said they did that night.'

'OK and you saw something the night she died?' Sam asks.

Tracey steps back from the window. 'Well, it wasn't exactly something. It was someone. Well, not "someone", really.'

'Victoria?' Sam says.

'Yes, I saw Victoria. And she went past the park, towards the phone box. Like they said on the news and all that.'

'OK, so...' Sam can feel himself deflating. She hasn't given him anything new.

'That's the thing, you see? I only saw one of them. The other one... Sylvie, wasn't it...? She wasn't there. I'm sure of it. There was just one girl.'

'And how can you be sure it was *that* night?'

'It was the first thing I thought of when I heard the story on the news. And then when I saw the reconstruction film, I was sure,' Tracey says straight away.

'Only Victoria was there?' Sam says it as much to himself as a genuine question.

'Don't believe me if you don't want to. I'm just telling you because I've tried everything else. The police, the family.'

Sam looks out across the park. 'Hang on. You say you've told the family?'

Tracey nods. 'At the time, just after she was found, I phoned the helpline like they said. But the police just dismissed it. When I saw the mum on the news a few weeks ago, I sent an email into that website they have asking for information.'

'So it was recent then?' Sam says.

'A few weeks ago, a bit after I saw her on the news. I dithered for a while because I've tried before, like I said, but I did email. ' Tracey narrows her eyes at Sam. 'Do you not believe me?'

'I didn't say I don't believe you,' Sam says. 'I'm just thinking.'

'I'll show you.' Tracey sets off out of the room and waits for Sam to follow her so she can lock it. Back in the office she wakes up her computer and stands leaning over the desk, scowling at the screen.

After a few clicks the printer starts whirring. She snatches the paper off when it's done and hands it to Sam, putting her hands on her hips. There's an auto-response confirming the email has been received and Tracey's email detailing what she told Sam she saw.

'Can I keep this?'

'Well, I don't need it, do I?' Tracey shuts the email down again. 'Sorry, Sam, but I'm going to need to get on now.'

'OK, well, thanks for the info.'

She sees him to the door. 'And think on, you know where we are if you wanted to give people a real look at what it's like here, who the residents are,' Tracey says, the door already coming towards Sam.

'Will do,' he says, hitching his camera bag onto his shoulder.

'Trouble is it just wouldn't pull the viewers in like a pretty dead girl, would it?' Tracey closes the door and becomes a dark shape behind the small pane of glass.

Sam gets back to the hotel as quickly as he can, not even taking his coat off before delving into the bottom of the wardrobe and retrieving the thick ring binder Judith had given him when he first contacted her. He's already been through it once to pull out any anomalies or urgent things to follow up. Tracey's comments didn't ring any bells.

Judith has neatly placed all the emails and statements released to her by the police into the binder in date order. Not even the edges of the paper are curled or crumpled. There are around fifteen emails since Judith's recent appeal on TV. One says they've seen someone who looks like Victoria in another town, another that they'd heard someone scream in the street that night but nowhere near the lake or Victoria's house. The police had already ruled out a connection, but Sam planned to follow it up later anyway. Mostly they reiterate what's already known: there was a party at the house, the girls often hung around in the park. But there's nothing from Tracey, nothing saying that Victoria walked home, or to the phone box, alone that night.

Sam checks the date of the email and cross-checks in the file. There are emails either side, but Tracey's... it isn't there.

CHAPTER SEVENTEEN

Sylvie

I have drifted in and out of sleep and I awake to a gentle hissing of rain. It's soothing and Victoria is still sleeping.

A sharp knock on the door breaks me out of the delicious wooziness. I look out of the window. It's not Michelle or Sam. It's Judith, shuffling from foot to foot, pulling the belt of her coat so hard I can imagine the sensation across my own stomach, the squashing of her insides. Peter is there too. I can just see the top of his head, the collar of his jacket.

I run my hands through my hair. On the way past the bathroom, I swill some mouthwash around my mouth, holding it for a few seconds longer so it starts to tingle and burn.

Judith looks surprised when I open the door. 'Hi,' she says, her expression too enthusiastic. 'I just thought I'd come round and see you, since you're here.'

I sense a dig that I haven't been round to see her again. She looks even more tightly wound than usual.

Judith looks up and down the exterior of the house, the grey stains, the missing bits of plaster and the chewed-up garden. Peter's eyes are down, he's kicking at the edge of the doorstep, reminding me of a schoolboy.

'OK, yeah, 'course, come in,' I say.

Judith thrusts a tin and a plastic tub into my hands. 'Just a few bits; thought you might not have a lot of time to cook. Some beef casserole, and coffee and walnut cake. I was making it for us anyway, so no trouble.'

She leaves it in my hands and glides past. Peter brushes past me too. I follow them in. Judith's eyes are darting everywhere, gaze bouncing off every surface.

She undoes the knot in her belt. 'Wow,' she says. 'Can you believe it?' She's still fiddling with her coat, fingers failing to grasp the buttons. 'It's like stepping back in time.'

Peter nudges her with his elbow, fists shoved deep into his trouser pockets, but she ignores him.

My phone rings in my bag on the sofa. Everyone's eyes go to it.

'Everything alright?' Judith edges forwards to try and get a look at the phone.

'They'll ring back,' I say.

The phone stops and starts again. When I get closer I can see the name illuminated. Nathan.

Judith's and Peter's eyes are still on me.

I reach in the bag, as if I'm going to answer it, and I reject the call, turning the ringer down to silent on the side of the phone. I pretend to try to answer it. 'Always happens, doesn't it? The minute you get to it, they ring off.' I place the phone face down on the table.

Judith puts her hand up to her throat. 'The décor hasn't changed at all.' There's a pained expression on her face.

'Aye, it's been a bloody long time,' Peter says, brusque.

I turn the baby monitor on, Victoria is still upstairs. 'Can I get you a tea or coffee?' I say.

Judith doesn't hear me, or if she does, she doesn't let on. She is still peering round into each corner of the room, staring down into the carpet, focusing in on the worn, threadbare patches. I can almost feel her shrinking away, recoiling from twenty years of dirt. Once again I get an unexpected rush of feeling protective of Mum, of people judging her.

Judith nods. 'I'll have one,' Peter says. 'Tea – milk, two sugars.'

As I'm making the drinks, Judith drifts in. I am conscious of her hovering behind me, sizing up the kitchen too.

I can feel her eyes in my back. She isn't moving around any more. I wait for what I know she is thinking, what she is going to say.

'Do you need any help?' she says.

'No, I'm right, thanks. Do you take sugar?'

'Ooh, God no, not for me, thanks.'

I should have known that. I put two spoons of sugar in mine. I need it. Judith sneaks up behind me and hands me a box of sweeteners, and I click one into her cup. We take the drinks and she follows me back into the living room as if we are attached by string.

'So, where is she?' Judith says, blowing on her tea then putting it down, not drinking any. It's what people always want to know since I had a baby. Sylvie and Victoria, Victoria and Sylvie again.

'Sorry, she's asleep. We had a bit of a bad night last night. So I'm going to leave her, let her catch up a bit.'

'Really…?'

'Mmm-hmmm,' I say, hiding behind blowing on my cup.

'I always felt it was better to have some kind of routine, person-ally,' Judith says, as casual as she can. 'You know, naptime, dinner time, bedtime, stays the same no matter what. It isn't always easy, but it can help. You don't want to make a rod for your own back.'

'Jude,' Peter cuts in. 'Leave the lass to do things her own way, will you?'

He's making me nervous standing on the edge of the fireplace, leaning backwards and forwards, his foot scraping against it.

She tuts. 'Oh, give over, Peter. I'm just telling her, one mother to another, what I learned. I'm just trying to…' She trails off.

'It's fine, thanks, Judith. I appreciate your support and you coming round.' I rub the top of her arm. I know she means well.

She sits down. 'Do you think Victoria would have had a baby, Sylvie?'

I freeze. The room sways. Peter tuts and sighs.

'I'm going to answer a call of nature,' he says, going upstairs.

'I don't know; we didn't really think about it then. We were too young.' I remember the pact we made, in the school field that night. *Let's never ever.*

'I think she would,' Judith goes on. 'She always fawned over her little cousins. I would have so loved a little grandchild. Peter too.'

She stares into the cup, but doesn't drink anything, the distaste showing faintly across her face again. Then she shakes her head quickly, rolling her shoulders back. 'Listen to me, coming round here all doom and gloom. It isn't good for any of us, is it?' She slaps her hands onto her knees. 'I actually came round to ask you something. A favour, I suppose.'

'OK… what's that, then?' I say, playing for time.

Peter bangs around upstairs, flushing the toilet, running the tap. Victoria will be awake very soon now.

'Sam. His documentary,' she says, still focusing on her drink. 'I do understand how difficult this has been for you, you know, how much it must have affected you, with your mother and everything else too. But Peter and I would just really appreciate it if you would participate. Well, me really. Peter's a bit upset about it all. What they've been saying. He says it's all dirty-linen-airing, but I don't care what they say if we get to the truth. Why should I care? I've nothing to hide.'

Before I can argue, Judith says, 'It might be our last chance, Sylvie. Sam might not be here that long. If he had you on board… he says he'd have more chance of them picking it up if you're on board.'

'I'll do what I can,' I say.

'You'll talk to him?'

I give her a half nod.

Judith's face floods with happiness. 'Thanks so much, Sylvie. It really does mean a lot to me.' She jumps up from the chair, her face bright again. 'Now, I'll get these washed up.' She starts gathering up the cups. Peter's and Judith's drinks are untouched.

'You don't have to do that.'

'No problem. I know how it is, don't worry. You don't get a minute to yourself, eh? You sit down for a bit.'

She goes into the kitchen, running the tap loudly, humming to herself.

Victoria's murmuring breaks through on the baby monitor. I set off to go to her, then stop. *Peter's voice.* I knew he would wake her.

'Hello, hello, gorgeous,' he says. 'Have you had a lovely sleep? Have you? Haven't you got a pretty name? Yes, you have.'

She gurgles at him.

I hear him strain, like he's reaching or stretching. The monitor crackles.

'Look at this, Victoria. Just look at this.' The straining sound again. 'Your mummy is a dirty bitch, isn't she, just like her mummy was as well.'

My breath catches in my throat. I think of my underwear, dumped on the bedroom floor.

Then I hear him again. 'Are you going to grow up just like your mummy? No, you're not, are you?' His voice is soft and playful, detached from what he's saying.

Judith comes back in and looks at the baby monitor, and I realise I had been staring at it too.

'Everything alright, love?' Judith says.

Victoria lets out a wail and Judith gives me one of her fixed smiles. I think of my Care Bear upstairs, its plastic eyes.

Peter is coming down the stairs slowly. The cry has gone from the baby monitor and is getting closer. He appears with Victoria in the doorway and lifts her up in the air, jiggling her. Over-fussing with her when she's just woken up.

'She's such a grand little thing, isn't she?' He rubs Victoria's cheek gently and she smiles at him. Peter gives me a big, warm grin and ruffles my hair like he used to when I was waiting for Victoria to come downstairs.

It was less than two minutes ago that I heard him on the monitor, but that doesn't seem real now. The feeling of disconnection makes it hard to focus, and I fix my eyes on a spot on the ceiling.

Peter strokes Victoria's cheek and hands her to Judith. 'I was just saying,' he says, 'how much she looks like you and how much you look like your mum.'

Finally, after a while fussing over Victoria, Judith says, 'OK, darling. Time to say bye-bye to Nanny Judith.'

My body tightens. She steals a look across at me and I try to quickly rearrange my face so I don't hurt her feelings. I force on my own smile and she says it again, pushes it a bit further, less hesitant this time. 'Nanny Judith loves you, doesn't she? Yes, she does.'

Judith leans in closer and kisses Victoria's mouth, leaving a light trace of brownish-red lipstick. I stand up and hold my arms out to take her back. Judith hugs me then. She smells sweet, highly scented. Peter kisses me on the top of my head then ruffles my hair again. Finally, they leave, and I watch them walk towards the car.

I wipe Victoria's mouth with a wet wipe and it makes her cry. She won't stop for a long time. Eventually we go into the garden and I walk her round and round, even though it's drizzling. We walk down to the end of the garden, the rockery that Mum and Dad once loved all overgrown and decaying.

The swing seat is filthy and rusting; I sit on it anyway, pushing off leaves and tipping off a slug. At first it feels rigid, but after a few pushes with my feet off the floor, it starts to ease up and we can gently swing backwards and forwards, a grating, squeaking noise cranking out each time. This calms Victoria and she starts to rest easier on my chest, giving in to the movement.

Up at the window next door, someone is looking down at me. But it's not Joyce; it's a man, must be her husband. I don't look away; I hold his gaze. Uncertainly, he waves his hand and I wave back, then he pulls the curtain across and is gone.

We stay out on the swing seat until the sky becomes darker and more overcast and the drizzle turns to rain. But, for the rest of the day, Victoria is calmer. She plays on the mat, grabbing for the Velcro windows, pressing a duck's beak and turning to look at me, equally surprised each time when it emits a noise.

I flip my phone over quickly and force myself to check it. Eight missed calls from Nathan. As I'm staring at it, it starts to light up again and I answer.

'You're alive, then?' It's Beth, from work.

The memory slams in now that we'd had a plan to meet one day for coffee on her day off.

'Shit, sorry,' I say. 'Was it today we were supposed to meet?'

'Noooo,' she says. 'It was last week, actually, but I figured you had your hands full. But you hadn't replied to my email either so I thought I'd have to bring the big guns out and phone you. Terrifying, eh? The lengths you've pushed me to.'

'Sorry,' I say again. 'I'm away at the minute.'

'Oh right, great. With Nathan?'

'No, it's er… a family thing.'

'Right.' That seems to suitably dampen her interest.

'How's work?'

'Ah, you know. Dead as. The usual.'

We chat for a while about the shop and Victoria and lack of sleep.

'Listen,' Beth says. 'There was something I wanted to ask you about. There's been someone in the shop asking me about you.'

'About me?'

'Well… he was asking about a Ruby,' she says. 'But he meant you.' Her voice sounds reinforced, like she's delivering information that she'd prefer not to.

A sinkhole opens up inside me.

'Sounds like a misunderstanding,' I say, embroidering confusion onto my tone.

'Didn't seem like it,' Beth says, firm. 'He seemed pretty sure of himself. He recognised me from that night out we had this time last year – the one that got a bit lairy. He said he saw us together earlier in the night. He clearly wasn't as shit-faced as us. But he did ring a bell once he mentioned it. I saw you talking to him before I left the club. Remember? You didn't want to leave. I thought it was a little bit odd, that's all. He described what you were wearing, your hair, the lot. Definitely you.'

'I honestly don't know what you're talking about.'

'Suit yourself. Is everything alright, Sylv?'

'It's fine.' My voice is thin and tight. 'I'll have to go soon. Got some family stuff to deal with.'

'OK,' Beth says. 'If that's what you want. You know where I am if you need me, though, for anything. Hiding in the stockroom that's where.'

'Thanks, I appreciate it. I'll let you know when I'm back in Glasgow. Beth?'

'Yes?'

'What did you tell him? The man asking for this Ruby?'

'It's like you said, isn't it? I told him I thought he must have the wrong person, a misunderstanding.'

CHAPTER EIGHTEEN

Sylvie

'Did you not get my text?' I say, opening the door after Michelle has knocked hard a second time, clattering the letter box. I have to raise my voice to be heard over Victoria. She's been interrupted during a feed.

'No, sorry. What's up? You alright? You look at bit…' Michelle says, breathing heavily, face glowing as if she's been running. She roots around and pulls her phone out of her bag. 'Oh, sorry, mate. I didn't see it.'

I try to hide my irritation. After Beth called, sleep wouldn't come last night.

'It's just that I was going to say not to come round this morning, that's all. We've had a bit of a bad night. Doubt I am the best company. Sorry. And you've probably got loads of stuff you need to be doing.'

Michelle has been coming round after work for a few days now, bringing carrier bags of reduced items from the supermarket, cleaning up the house for me. I should be grateful; I am. But I couldn't face seeing her today. I don't have the energy to make conversation.

I think she's lonely, too. That's why she comes. Occasionally over the years, right out of nowhere, I've thought of Michelle. Often when I haven't been able to sleep. Lying awake in the darkness, suddenly feeling a creeping guilt for the way she was

treated at school, for whatever part I might have played in it. I've
wondered how things turned out for her, whether we affected the
way her life went.

Seeing her standing there, I think now of the time we went to
the pictures on the bus with her, Victoria and me. We wanted to
go to the big cinema in the next town. The film was called *Alive*,
about someone who had to eat their dead friend to survive after
a plane crash. It was based on a true story. When it was our stop,
we rang the bell and Michelle went down the stairs first and got
off. Victoria pulled me back by the collar on my coat. I didn't get
it at first; didn't know what was happening. We didn't get off the
bus. We stayed on and went all the way to the city. Victoria went
to the window and waved at Michelle, laughing as the bus pulled
away. Michelle just stood there until she became as small as a toy
soldier. Victoria punched me lightly on the arm and I laughed
too. Michelle never even mentioned it, not the next time we saw
her and not after that either.

Michelle's expression darkens for a moment. Then just as quickly
it brightens again. 'Well, I'm here now, aren't I? And I don't really
have much on today anyway.'

She steps forwards to come into the house, pushing me gently
out of the way, then giving me a short, shallow hug. Flopping down
on the sofa, Michelle opens some crisps from a huge pack with a
yellow 10p sticker on the side. She tips it towards me.

'It's a bit early for me,' I say, wincing at the volume of Victoria's
wails.

Michelle covers her full mouth and blushes. She rustles the
carrier bag. 'And, my dear, I've brought something to get rid of
our little furry friends.' She makes a noose and hanging motion.
'Leave it to me and they'll be gone in no time. You'll never know
they were here.'

Her voice feels more distant, lower, a murmur.

'You OK, mate? You don't look too good.' Michelle's hand is on my arm, yellow crisp dust on her fingers, the smell on her breath. She manoeuvres me to sit down.

'Victoria. She just won't stop crying,' I say. 'Sometimes I just think I can't take it any more; I feel like I'm going to lose it.' The image of the doll in the pond breaks in.

She looks down at me, concern on her face. 'Right,' she says, dusting her hands off on her jeans, and I am relieved when she scoops Victoria out of my arms. 'I'll tell you what it is. You need to get out of here, pal. You need a break.'

She carries Victoria over to the window and opens the curtains. The light shocks my eyes and makes everything blur for a moment.

'Oh, I don't know. It's nice of you, but I've not really left her at all before, only with…'

She turns to wait for me to finish the sentence, but I don't. I don't want her asking about Nathan now. Victoria lets out a fresh blast of rage. I consider doing the same myself. My ears ring, teeth grinding together.

'Oh, come on. It'll do you good. Two hours, one even. We'll be alright, won't we, baby?'

'I'll have a shower and I'll think about it, OK?'

'Suit yourself.' Michelle turns back to Victoria, trying to engage her in looking out of the window, and they babble on together as if I'm not there.

The hot water running over me, the zingy smell of the shampoo; I start to feel more wide awake than I have in a while. Just to have a moment to myself… some of the tension is already draining away with the water. I stay in the shower for a long time, letting the tightness go out of my shoulders and neck. Afterwards, I lie like a starfish on the bed, naked, and let myself air dry. Looking in the dressing-table mirror, framed with the pink feather boa and tiara, I rub a little make-up on my face.

'Go on, then,' I say, putting my coat on as I go into the front room. 'I'll just nip out and I'll be back again by the time she needs feeding.'

'Good lass.' Michelle is sitting in the chair, legs hooked over the side. Victoria has stopped crying and is lying down on her back on the play mat, murmuring gently, reaching out into thin air. Michele looks up from the magazine she is reading, Lorraine Kelly chattering on the television.

'I don't know how you do it,' I say, trying to stop the defensiveness showing in my voice.

'Call me the baby whisperer,' Michelle says, a huge grin on her face.

'Right…' I say, hovering in the doorway, looking at Victoria again, unable to believe she's stopped crying, finally, after her marathon screaming session. *Maybe it's me.*

'Just go!' Michelle says, tone light-hearted. 'We will be fine. You'll be fine.'

The day is surprisingly crisp and bright. Autumn is moving in fast now. I stand outside the house for a few moments, my ears still recovering from the onslaught. Feels like I can still hear faint, echoey cries but when I look through the window, Victoria is still on her mat, Michelle engrossed in some celebrity article.

I start to walk, feeling looser, lighter already. The sun is bouncing off cars and windows, making everything look softer, dreamy. It gives me that peculiar sensation of déjà vu.

I walk on towards town. Not having Victoria with me keeps making me panic momentarily, then I remember she's with Michelle. I carry on, the fresh air making me feel cheerier. It will be good for me, Michelle is right. I stop and look in a few estate agents' windows. The prices around here are higher than I imagined. I might get more than I expected for the house. It spurs me on to get it sorted out. A new start, another one.

When I get into town, I wander round some of the shops. I buy a couple of cheap lampshades and vases, thinking they'll be handy for when I come to have people looking at the house. The agent needs to pitch it to someone who wants a 'fixer-upper', who sees the potential in the place, beyond the cosmetic, he says.

I sit by the fountain in the centre of the square for a while. A toddler in a bulky red coat runs unsteadily, making everything in me tense up. His grandmother bends down and gives him a bag of bread, and he throws chunks out onto the ground like firecrackers, shrieking with delight. What feels like hundreds of pigeons flock over, swooping in from every direction, pecking and bobbing their heads at the bread, their wings flapping so close to my face, the beating sound loud in my ears. The boy screams, excited or frightened, and runs into the crowd of birds, sending them exploding out in all directions.

When the commotion dies down, I move along and walk by the library where Mum used to take me. It's glass-fronted now, where before it was stone, and islands of computers have replaced many of the shelves of books. Sometimes she'd drop me off at the library for a few hours while she went and did her shopping. She knew I wouldn't go anywhere. I'd wander the aisles, running my hand along the spines of the books, picking one up at random, letting the pages fall open anywhere and starting there. I didn't worry about what had gone before in them, what was going to happen next.

In the reflection in the glass I see it then, across the street. The building is there but it's burned-out now and it stops me in my tracks. It is one of the last times Victoria and I went out together, as us: Victoria and Sylvie, Sylvie and Victoria. With distance I can see that night changed something between me and Victoria.

I turn and cross the street. As I get closer, I have to strain my neck to see the full size of it. It had been an old dance hall once, Mum told me when I was little.

A voice in my ear makes me jump.

'Massive fire, year or so ago,' an old woman standing at the bus stop close by says.

'I used to go there,' I tell her. 'What happened?'

'Well, it weren't an accident, that's for sure. Arson,' she says, nodding her head enthusiastically. She looks around before she says the next bit, seemingly to check that no one is listening. 'But most people reckon it's an inside job. For the insurance,' she says, rubbing her thumb against her fingers. 'A money job.'

'Aren't they going to do anything with it?' I say, looking up again at the dirty, white, art deco façade, the blackened inside visible through rusted window frames: twisted metal, tangled wires poking out.

She shakes her head, checking whether her bus is coming. 'Listed building so they've got to be careful how they use it. We've been going to have a posh furniture shop, a restaurant, another bloody nightclub, but here it still is.' Her voice is getting more distant, and I turn to realise she has drifted towards her bus as it approaches, her arm shoved out into the road.

I go right up to the building and look through the old doors into the foyer of the ice rink. The coloured, swooshing stars on the purple carpet remain visible in some places under the dust. There are still vending machines in there too, the chocolate rotting inside. Here and the shopping centre would be my and Victoria's favourite places to come on the weekend or in the holidays. The memory of the excitement that would build is still vivid, the military planning of what to wear.

The nights lived up to the build-up, too. Not many things do. The chill coming off the ice, the swooping coloured lights like a gymnast's ribbon, the feeling of gliding, like flying. I push my fists into my pockets instinctively. Mum said that's what you had to do, and wear gloves. She didn't like me and Victoria going there. If you fell and put your hands out, your fingers might get skated over, sliced off by the blades.

I pull myself out of the world of the ice rink and that summer, and back into my own. I have time for a quick coffee before I need to get back. It's something I miss, sitting on my own, watching the world go by.

I sit outside the Coffee Pot café this time, a half-hearted attempt at café culture that doesn't quite come off here in Conley. Pigeons strut close by.

I reach for my phone to give Michelle a quick ring to check in on Victoria and I realise I don't have it: I must have left it back at the house. I neck the coffee back quickly, relaxation bubble burst immediately. A black, solid-looking cloud is looming now, the same colour as the concrete. It makes the shopping centre look like a collage picture.

My stomach drops when I realise that I don't have my purse with me either. I rush back into the café, trying to remember where I put it down. The girl behind the counter spots me and looks confused.

'I left my purse in here and maybe my phone too, I think.' I can't get the words out quickly enough and she doesn't look as if she is trying to keep up.

She scans vaguely around the room, without actually looking. 'Sorry, nobody's handed anything in.'

'They must have done; I was only in here a minute ago.' My hands are in my hair and she eyes me from a distance. Her expression makes me wonder if she thinks I'm lying. I duck down and underneath the tables, some people tutting and looking annoyed at me, others making a show of having a look around themselves.

'Are you sure?' I go back to the girl at the counter.

She's frothing milk. 'Sorry, love,' she shouts over the sound of the hissing steam, gives me a not-my-problem shrug.

A little girl looks up at me, her eyes quickly looking away again when they meet mine.

'You couldn't lend me some money, could you?' I say to the waitress behind the counter.

She doesn't come any closer and looks at me with suspicion, like I might attack her.

'Sorry, it's just I need to get back to my baby. I was just here the other day? I'll drop in and pay you back tomorrow.' I think this will soften her but she takes another step back.

'Sorry, love, I can't. I would but I just can't.' She gives a little shake of her head then refuses to look at me again. I can feel other people prickling around me, on edge.

I relent and leave the café. When I glance back, the waitress is whispering to her colleague, looking out after me. Outside the sky has lightened, but it has started to rain too. I root in my pockets, praying for some loose change for the bus or to use the payphone. I don't know Michelle's number anyway, but I remember Mum's house phone number still. I need to get that cut off. Disconnecting it; it feels very final. I remember Judith and Peter's – Victoria's – number off by heart too.

I open my mouth a few times to ask people for some change for the bus, but they flinch as I come towards them or turn away, pretending to be busy. May as well walk, even though the rain is getting heavier, making my clothes stick to me. It will take me over an hour. I'm already late. Victoria will be hungry. I hit every traffic light, every slow walker, old person and pushchair, impatience bubbling in me. The rain slows down and a rainbow breaks through, picture-book colours against the dark grey.

When I get to Mum's street, there's a car outside the house and I recognise it from the other day when he knocked. It's Sam's, and my pace quickens. I'm out of breath, a stitch gathering in my side.

Through the window I can see Sam sitting talking to Michelle, his ankle rested on his knee, leg bent at a right angle. They're drinking tea and there's a plate of biscuits on the table, as if Michelle owns the place. They don't see me.

The window is open slightly and their voices are drifting out, distorted and vague at first, but eventually my ears adjust and I can tune in.

'Victoria… School… That night?' It's Sam. I want to barge straight in but I force myself to wait and listen.

'You know there were all those reports of some weird guy around that time, don't you? Someone was going round flashing at people,' I hear Michelle say.

'I heard something about that, yes.' Sam sounds casual, but something about his voice tells me that's manufactured. He's squirrelling every word away.

'Did you also know that Sylvie and Victoria saw him?' Michelle sounds proud of herself, as if she's telling someone about a personal achievement.

'When?' The question flies out of Sam's mouth like he's caught wind of some especially juicy gossip.

'Dunno. One night in town. You'd have to ask Sylvie. She's a bit moody at the minute.' Michelle gives a strange laugh. Is she flirting?

'Assume this flasher was mentioned at the time?' There's a definite hardness under Sam's chatter.

'People knew, yeah. Not that Sylvie and Victoria saw him – maybe the police and papers didn't want to scare people or maybe they caught him already. I dunno. Probably long gone by now. Or dead. Or watching telly with his wife!'

Michelle's laugh sets my teeth on edge.

'Did Sylvie and Victoria report seeing him?' Sam again. I dare not look, but I picture him pulled forwards to the edge of his seat.

'Dunno. Like I said you'd be best off asking Sylvie. It wasn't like they were bothered by it. If you weren't here asking me stuff, I wouldn't have mentioned it. I didn't even connect it at the time, to be honest. Just thinking now. They just laughed about it.'

The sound is muffled then for a moment, clattering of crockery.

Then I hear Michelle say, 'I mean, Sylvie seems to have reinvented herself as this mousey little bookish thing.' My jaw clenches. 'But at school, Sylvie and Victoria were the popular ones.'

'What do you mean by "popular"?' Sam asks, emphasising the word.

'Well,' Michelle says, conspiratorial, 'I mean they were popular – people liked them. Teachers, they had friends, all that. But they were *popular* popular too, if you know what I mean? Victoria especially.' She makes a horrible clicking noise with her tongue and teeth and I imagine a wink going with it.

I hear the inflection of a question, Sam's voice, but I can't hear what he says. Then, 'Mmm-hmmm,' like he's scribbling furiously in a notebook, or maybe the camera is rolling, recording everything, immutable.

Michelle's fake girly giggle again. 'Victoria was the first to do a lot of things at school – if you catch my drift. I mean it's fine, I have no problem with it, of course I don't. I'm not going to get quoted on this, am I? In the film?'

Sam's response is inaudible.

'Where'd they hang out then?' he says, clearer.

'Usual places, you know. I doubt it's changed much today. Parks, people's houses, the lake… Anyway,' Michelle says. 'Victoria got a boyfriend then, Ryan, so she was suddenly always with him.'

'Boyfriend?'

I barge in then, I can't stand it any more. Sam glances up then puts his cup down on the table, but Michelle jumps up from her seat.

'You OK, Sylvie?' Michelle says, her face tight. 'Did you have a nice time in town?'

I fake being a little out of breath. 'Yes, just got a few bits for the house. A lampshade and a couple of—'

Michelle and Sam look at my empty hands. I have left the things I bought at the café. I can picture them pushed under the silver table where I drank my coffee.

'I lost my bloody purse and phone, didn't I? Such an idiot.' My voice cracking.

Michelle guides me to sit on the arm of the sofa.

'I had to walk home and I was so worried about Victoria. And…'

Sam stands up. 'I'll let myself out. Maybe it's not a good time.'

Michelle is rubbing my back, like my mum used to when I was little and being sick in the night.

'There is something though, Sylvie, that I need to talk to you about pretty urgently.' Sam's eyes lock on mine.

'What's it about?'

'It's just some basic details I need to check about the night,' he says. 'I think it's best if I hear them from you.' He says the last bit with his back to Michelle, blocking her out. His voice is unmistakably lowered so she doesn't hear.

'Maybe not now, eh,' Michelle says to Sam, guiding him to the door.

'I'm staying at the Travellers' Rest anyway,' Sam says to no one in particular.

They talk on the doorstep for a minute, and I take a deep breath before I go to pick up Victoria. I don't like her to see me upset, worried about what she's absorbing, what she'll remember. But when I go over to her, she's fast asleep.

Michelle comes back in, slamming the door shut, whole room rattling. Even then, Victoria doesn't wake.

I touch her cheek, afraid she'll be hot. Or worse, cold.

'We need to wake her, Michelle. She hasn't eaten in hours.' I'm trying to wrangle out of my clothes and pick Victoria up at the same time.

'It's fine,' Michelle says, lowering her voice, beckoning me into the kitchen. She looks sheepish. I sense that something is up. I look back once more and follow her in.

'What's wrong? Is Victoria OK? Tell me what happened. I knew I should never have gone out, Michelle!' I'm shouting and she hushes me to lower my voice.

'She's fine. It's just...'

Then I see it over her shoulder. A bottle and the tin of formula milk on the worktop. The steriliser out of its box.

'Michelle. You didn't... That isn't for you to do!'

She holds her hands out, palms towards me. 'I'm sorry, Sylvie, but what could I do? I couldn't contact you. It was there. I knew you were trying with it anyway so I assumed you'd be OK.' She looks down at her own chest and then at me. 'She's fine, Sylvie. She needed to eat. You weren't here. I couldn't reach you. I mean, what would you have had me do?'

'And what was that stuff you were telling Sam?'

'What stuff?' She talks down to the floor.

'About me and Victoria basically being the school slags?' I can feel my temple pulsing, a sharp headache gathering behind my eyes.

'Don't be ridiculous, Sylvie. I didn't say that. At all. I wouldn't say that.' Her face is flushed.

'And about me and Victoria seeing that creepy guy?'

'Well, you did, didn't you? I remember Victoria telling me.'

'They aren't your stories to tell, Michelle. You weren't even there.' That makes her flinch and I half regret my spite. I notice bright blotches on her neck now like pink dandelions.

'You don't own all the stories about her,' Michelle says, casting her eyes down, and guilt starts creeping in more, but it gives way to anger again.

'I think you should just go.'

Michelle recoils slightly, flinching.

Does she really think I would hit her?

'Your phone,' Michelle says, gesturing towards the dresser in the living room, where it's lying face down. 'You left it here. You had loads of missed calls. Nathan?'

I must have left my phone here and put my purse down somewhere in town.

'Have you been riffling through my phone as well?'

'It just rang, Sylvie.'

Michelle reaches into her bag and takes out some notes and holds them up at me, before placing them on the dresser next to the phone.

'What the hell is that for?' I take a step back like the money is a firework that hasn't gone off yet.

Michelle looks down, deflated. 'Your purse?' she says. 'I thought you'll probably need some money to tide you over?'

She looks at me again, hesitates, and then grabs her coat and leaves. She turns back once more and the expression on her face triggers shame in me. I think of the bus pulling away that night. I go to call after her, but no sound comes out. She's already slammed the door and she's away down the street.

That night sleep refuses to come. In the space in between, I hear a banging noise downstairs. This time I don't creep down the stairs or grab a weapon; I walk straight into the kitchen and put the light on. The noise stops for a second or two then starts up again. Rustling and clattering. It's coming from the cupboard. I think about opening it, but instead I grab some parcel tape from one of the overstuffed drawers. There are eight rolls to choose from, more of Mum's clutter. I tape up the cupboard so the mouse can't get out. If I cut off the food supply, it can go back to where it came from. Outside. Then I add on extra tape for good measure.

I grip the side of the sink, my head pulsing. Through the window, I notice Michelle has hung washing on the line, and arms and legs jerk themselves out at impossible angles in the wind. Victoria's Babygros like small, headless ghosts.

CHAPTER NINETEEN

Summer, 1995

'Do you reckon Ryan is going to be there?' Victoria asked.

Ryan was older, but they'd seen him around in the town centre, sometimes in the park. They would report back to each other immediately if he had been spotted in the wild. When Sylvie thought about him, or if he was close by, a feeling like warm water rushed through her stomach. She'd never spoken to him, but she'd caught his eye a few times. And she and Victoria had done their research. They knew a lot about him. Where he lived, who he had been seeing – and, importantly, when they broke up – and where they were likely to see him next.

Sylvie shrugged her shoulders and they both grinned at each other. They were sitting on the patch of grass outside Sylvie's house; Victoria stretched her arms out, as if she were lying in the snow. It had been on the radio earlier in the day that it was the hottest day of the year so far. On TV, there were women in bikinis on the beaches in Brighton and Bournemouth. They said the weather was going to break soon, though. The sun was fading to a haze, making all the colours in the street pop brighter.

Sylvie was counting money, dividing it into two piles, mentally doing the maths. She would never say it out loud to anyone. She couldn't. But she'd thought it. One of the upsides to her dad being ill was that she had been allowed more freedom than ever. She had missed her 11 p.m. curfew a few times and her mum hadn't said anything. She didn't even seem to have noticed. Before, she'd have been waiting at the door, looking up and down the street. Her mum rarely asked where she had been or what her plans were any more. Sylvie sometimes felt she was moving through the house like a ghost.

Sylvie was wearing her green jeans and a black body top; the corners on the gusset were square and badly designed, cutting into the creases of her thighs. Victoria wore red jeans from the same shop and a striped body suit. Sylvie's dad used to say they looked like they were in a 'pop duo'. They both laughed at his old-fashioned phrasing, but Sylvie liked the idea of learning to play the guitar or even the drums. When things blew over at home, after her dad was better, she would ask her mum about lessons.

Sylvie's foot was going dead. She adjusted the way she was sitting, twisting her legs one way then the other. It felt like her flab was bulging over the top of her jeans, uncontainable. She hated the way her thighs spread out when she kneeled down. Victoria's still looked so narrow.

Sylvie's mum was always on a diet. Sometimes she'd only eat grapefruit and cottage cheese for weeks on end, before giving in and eating half a packet of chocolate biscuits. Once she bought some weird concoction from a woman in a caravan over the tops. Sylvie waited in the car while she went inside. You had to add water to it and her mum gipped over the sink as she forced it down.

This special diet food was cordoned off in the fridge; Sylvie couldn't have it.

Some days now Sylvie had to fend for herself. Others, her mum would spend hours baking and cooking – apple crumble and steak and kidney pie, although she didn't eat any herself. Sylvie found herself eating to bursting point, like today. She felt too guilty to turn it down. She didn't want to hurt her mum's feelings, couldn't risk disrupting the careful calibration of the house. Sylvie readjusted her trousers again, trying to tuck the small bulge of fat under the waistband of her jeans.

They went into town first, into the disabled cubicle in the public toilets in the centre. It was filthy but it was somewhere to sit and have a laugh, to have some privacy. You could have fun with Victoria anywhere, though, that was the thing. They locked themselves in, double-checking the door. Victoria had got hold of some alcohol from home. She stole a bit from each bottle, all mixed up in an old water bottle. They'd even drunk aftershave once before, retching up everywhere but carrying on anyway. That night's concoction tasted disgusting. Sylvie took a big swig, then hung over the toilet gagging, strings of saliva bungeeing up and down. She wiped her mouth and laughed, before taking another large gulp, shuddering and contorting her face, waiting for it to be over.

They both laughed before Victoria broke the spell. 'You nearly got me into trouble the other day,' she said, taking the bottle from Sylvie. Her face was harder now.

Victoria took a sharp sip. They were both crouched down in the cubicle with their backs to opposite walls.

'What do you mean?' But Sylvie had an inkling. She'd called Victoria's house and discovered that she wasn't there. Victoria had told Peter and Judith she was staying the night at Sylvie's.

'Ringing the house. I got a right rinsing off my mum.'

'You nearly got us both into trouble more like,' Sylvie said. 'Where were you anyway?'

'Just out with some mates.'

'Why did you lie to your mum?'

'If I say I'm coming to yours, she doesn't ask questions. If it's someone new, she's on and on at me about their life history.'

'Who is the someone new?' Sylvie's voice went high-pitched.

'Some mates.' Victoria had a snappiness to her now. 'You don't know them. We don't have to do everything together, you know.'

Sylvie swallowed down the hard stone in her throat.

Victoria burped. 'What did you want anyway?'

'What?'

'When you rang?' Victoria said, impatience thrown in now too.

'Oh, I just wanted to see if you wanted to come over. It gets a bit oppressive round there, you know, with my dad and everything.'

'Oppressive,' Victoria said, rolling the rrrrs and giving a flourish with her hand. 'That's a big word for you.'

It was supposed to break the tension, but to Sylvie it seemed flippant and untactful. She snatched the bottle and swigged back a big gulp of the concoction.

She sneaked a glance across at Victoria and something caught her eye – a dirty-looking mark on Victoria's neck.

'What's that?' Sylvie said, pointing at the same place on her own neck. Victoria slapped her hand across the mark. Panic rippled across her features.

'Oh, I just… I banged it. It's a bruise.'

Sylvie knew what it was, though.

There was a knock at the toilet-cubicle door. Sylvie and Victoria looked at each other automatically and stifled laughs. They flapped their arms around and covered their mouths. It could be the police.

'Who is it?' Victoria shoved the bottle down the back of her jeans and pulled on her hooded top.

'Can you see it?' she mouthed to Victoria, turning to show her.

Sylvie gave her the thumbs up, confirming that it was hidden. Victoria gestured with her head that Sylvie should be the one to open the door.

The knock came again, louder.

Victoria gave Sylvie a gentle push from behind and she opened the door.

A man was standing there. Not the police and not looking as if he was there to use the facilities. Sylvie froze. Something about him was skittish, her alarm bells were going off. His face was pale, eyes flickering and rolling back. He looked like he was off his head on something, and he was blocking the doorway, so it wouldn't be easy for Sylvie and Victoria to leave.

'Alright, mate. You need a slash or you just knocking for a laugh?' Victoria's voice was upbeat, an edge of cockiness. She just came right out and said it. But Sylvie was on edge. Something about the strain in his jaw, the way his eyes were darting around, she didn't like it.

He made a sudden movement and Sylvie felt herself flinch. Then she realised. Her eye was drawn. He was flashing them. A hot spurt of vomit leapt into her throat, pungent with the alcohol.

His fingernails were dirty and he had this look on his face, lurid and sleazy. Sylvie was frozen solid to the spot.

Victoria had pushed herself forwards so she was level with Sylvie. She put her hand on Sylvie's shoulder to stop her from shaking. Sylvie couldn't take her eyes off the purple puncture wounds up his arm. She felt something swelling in her, sweating, shaking, she couldn't catch her breath. She sneaked a look across at Victoria. At first her face was blank with horror, too, but then something else was creeping in. It was turning into a smile and, before she knew it, a fit of the giggles.

The man looked confused. Victoria was doubled over, covering her face, hysterical. Sylvie couldn't help but join in too. It must have been all the alcohol.

The man moved again and they both adjusted their stance, to be ready. But he was fumbling with his pants and putting himself away. 'Fuck yous, you little slags,' he said, his voice whiny. 'I'll be seeing yous two around.' He looked right into their faces, first Victoria then Sylvie, then back again.

He picked up his carrier bag and shuffled out of the toilets again. Sylvie shut the door and quickly put the lock across, trying to steady her breath.

Victoria was still trying to recover from the giggles.

'D'you recognise him?' Sylvie said.

Victoria thought for a minute, looking up. 'Yeah, you shagged him, didn't you?'

'Piss off! Eurgh. Don't you think we should be worried? You heard what he said.'

'Dunno. Probably one of the smackheads from Camden House – who cares? Don't worry about it, Sylv. He's just some old druggy. He'll be passed out and won't even know what day it is soon.'

Sylvie tried to believe her, to forget about it. But the incident had set her on edge.

When they left, the man was crouching outside the toilets next to the railings. He was muttering something Sylvie couldn't make out under his breath, and when she looked back, his eyes were following them down the street. She linked up with Victoria and soon he was out of sight. She felt warm-faced and bellied from the booze and decided to put the love bite and the snappiness behind them for now, and enjoy the night, the music and lights at the rink stretched out ahead of them.

Throughout the rest of the evening, Victoria kept doing the tiniest of gestures. Most people probably wouldn't even notice it. Pretending to flash Sylvie, pulling a silly face or crossing her eyes, and they'd both burst into fits of giggles again.

This shared joke, a little secret between them, it made Sylvie feel close to Victoria.

At the rink, Sylvie and Victoria glided around the ice. They could stay upright most of the time but there were speed skaters there, too. When they zipped past, Sylvie could feel the air between them and each time it made her wobble and falter. They'd skate backwards and spin in the air.

Sylvie tried to follow the swirling lights with her feet. She got her skates into a tangle and fell over onto the ice. Victoria creased up laughing. The icy water seeped into Sylvie's jeans. Victoria put her hand out to help her up, then kept pulling it away at the last second, laughing even harder. Sylvie eventually managed to get herself up again, feeling big and clumsy.

To get off the ice, Sylvie and Victoria had to hold on to the barriers at the edges, where groups would gather, posing and showing off, dancing to the music. Serious faces, small nonchalant moves. Groups of lads they'd seen in the town on Saturdays. Striped jumpers, gelled hair.

Victoria grabbed Sylvie's arm, hard, using her to stop herself from falling over. 'Let's go over there.' She gestured towards one of the groups. The shifting, twirling lights made it hard to make faces out, but Sylvie had studied him long enough – the height, build and stance. Sylvie could see that at the centre of the group was Ryan.

Before she had a chance to say anything, Victoria set off out in front and his eyes narrowed as she got closer. When the lights flashed on his face, Sylvie thought she saw him run his tongue across his teeth and top lip and nudge the lad next to him. The strobe light effect was disorientating, making people's movements stutter and judder. Ryan was beckoning them over. Sylvie's stomach skipped and her legs skidded around – for a moment she thought she would fall over again.

Sylvie reached out to tap Victoria's shoulder, but she was too far ahead, already going towards him, speeding up. When she got there, Ryan put his hands on Victoria's shoulders and whispered in her ear. He pushed Victoria's hair back off her face. His hand was on her neck, right at the spot where the mark was. Sylvie was still on the ice and skidded again for a moment. The way Ryan had greeted Victoria had a tenderness about it – it wasn't a first-time introduction; it was like they were close.

Finally, Sylvie managed to stagger off the rink. The fact she was focused on Victoria and Ryan, and the sudden change from ice to solid ground, made Sylvie lose her footing again. She flailed around behind them uselessly, a spare part, Victoria's back to her. Ryan caught Sylvie's eye over Victoria's shoulder and the strobe gave him a wild look.

She felt a hand on her shoulder, a head close to hers, lips pushing through her hair and touching the skin of her ear, sending small shocks down her neck.

'What's your name, love?'

It was one of the other boys from the group. His face was pocked. He was definitely older. And quite short, Sylvie noticed. He was leaning into her with his hands behind his back. Lots of the boys stood and walked like that.

'Sylvie!' she called out, looking past him at Victoria and Ryan. She was shouting but it seemed like no sound came out; it was swallowed up by the music.

'It's a pretty name,' he said. 'For a pretty girl.'

'Thanks.' Sylvie wished she could say more, but she couldn't think of what.

'Maybe see you around later, yeah?' he said, looking her up and down slowly.

He had turned back to the group. He said something to them and they all looked at her, grinning and nodding. One of them punched him on the arm.

Victoria turned round. 'Come on,' she said, dragging Sylvie to the seats, where they took their ice skates off.

'What's going on?' Sylvie shouted, but Victoria didn't look up – she was focused on her boots.

Sylvie wasn't feeling so drunk any more. As they dawdled towards the exit, the decision to leave unspoken, the group of lads was at the bottom of the stairs in the foyer in front of them. Sylvie looked back and the rink was almost empty now, closing down, just a few speed skaters left on the ice. She nudged Victoria. 'Here, look who's with them. It's Charmaine Simmonds.'

Charmaine was notorious locally. Her whole family was. People said she was hard. She was rumoured to have beaten up two girls in a pub by grabbing their hair from the back and smashing their faces into each other. Sylvie didn't know if it was true, but she winced to think about it. She was the only girl amongst the group of boys.

When Sylvie and Victoria reached the stairs, Ryan's group was standing around. Sylvie got the impression they were waiting.

Ryan said something to the others, then to Victoria, 'You coming round to mine again?'

Again? Sylvie looked at Victoria and her face was glowing pink. She refused to look at Sylvie though.

'Yeah, can do,' she said to Ryan. The casualness in her voice was a total act, Sylvie could tell.

The boy that had been talking to Sylvie walked towards her, and Charmaine too. She had black permed hair, half up with a spotted ruffle on top of her head.

The boy who spoke to Sylvie earlier put his hand out. 'I'm Jimmy,' he said. 'And you're Sylvie.'

Sylvie blushed.

'This is Ryan. And Charmaine.'

'Alright.' They both nodded. Charmaine eyed Sylvie suspiciously.

'We're off to a house party up Brantham, if you fancy it,' Jimmy said to Sylvie. She thought she detected a bit of a smirk across his face.

Before Sylvie could say anything, or catch Victoria's eye, Victoria had answered, 'Yeah, she'll come. Sounds like a laugh, doesn't it, Sylv?'

'Sound,' Ryan said.

'What about you? Cat got your tongue?' Charmaine glowered. Sylvie could feel her heart fluttering. 'I'm talking to you, you ignorant cow.'

'Sorry, I…' Sylvie could hear how weedy she sounded.

'Don't be a bitch, Char,' Jimmy said. 'She's alright, leave her.'

Sylvie looked across at Victoria, but her face was impassive, flitting between them, waiting to see what happened.

Charmaine made a sudden lurch towards Sylvie, making her chest explode, then she just laughed. 'Chill out, will you, I'm kidding.'

Sylvie looked over and Victoria was deep in conversation with Ryan. She hadn't even bothered whether Sylvie was OK.

Jimmy put his arm around Sylvie, his hand dangling close to but not quite touching her breast. 'Don't worry about Char. She's only jealous,' he said. But Sylvie was spooked and she was tired and sober now. She wanted to go home.

'Just a sec,' she said, shrugging him off. She went over to Victoria.

'V, can I talk to you for a minute?'

'What?' Victoria said blankly.

'I just need to have a quick word with you, on your own.'

Victoria let out a sigh. She looked at Ryan, and he nodded. Did she need his permission now? She walked towards Sylvie.

'Listen, I'm gonna go home. I don't fancy it, to be honest.'

'Suit yourself.' Victoria was already turning away.

'Is your mum not going to be worried about you?'

'No, because I'm going to go to the phone box and tell her I'm staying at yours. I was going to suggest you do the same, but it's up to you. I'm going to the party.'

A lump bobbed into Sylvie's throat. Suddenly all she wanted was her room, her own bed.

Victoria relented a bit, her voice softer. 'Look, why don't you just come, Sylv? It'll be a laugh. This is our chance. Jimmy likes you.'

Sylvie thought for a moment. She was sure Victoria would give in and walk back with her.

'Nah, I'm going to go back, V. Next time I'll come, I promise.'

Victoria shrugged but she was already on the move. 'Suit yourself. Who says you're going to get another chance, though?' she said over her shoulder, throwing her hands up before turning away.

When Sylvie got in, the living-room door was open, a mound shape on the sofa. When her eyes adjusted and the silence settled, Sylvie could make out her mum in the darkness, head on the cushions, asleep. She had taken to sleeping downstairs so as not to disturb Sylvie's dad. He needed his sleep, she said, and the nightmares didn't help. She didn't say who the bad dreams belonged to.

Sylvie crept in and draped the thin blanket from the back of the settee over her mum, before quietly going upstairs. In bed, she lay awake, wondering what Victoria was up to, thinking about that mark on her neck and what she was doing with Ryan.

Before she fell asleep, Sylvie heard the door creak downstairs. She leaned over and pulled the curtain back and saw her mum jogging off down the street, leaving a trail of fog with her breath.

When she went jogging, it usually meant there'd been bad news at the hospital or a new mysterious symptom had appeared with her dad. Sylvie could time it around the appointments or the whispered fussing. Her mum would become tighter, more manic —sometimes she'd run twice a day, early in the morning and last thing at night. She'd hardly eat anything. Tomorrow morning, she would probably cook Sylvie a breakfast; more than she could face – bacon or waffles with butter. Sylvie's stomach twisted.

CHAPTER TWENTY

Sylvie

I am heading out for a walk with Victoria when Joyce appears out of her front door, making me think of a cuckoo clock.

'Sylvie! Do you fancy coming round for a cuppa?'

'OK, why not?'

She always seems to know when I'm passing, but it's nice to have someone to talk to, too.

The heat of her house hits me again as soon as I get inside. There's a partially completed jigsaw on the table, coloured pieces strewn across.

Joyce sees me looking. 'Grandchildren sent me it for my birthday. Want to get it finished and framed so I can show it to them,' she says proudly.

'Oh,' I say.

She nudges me. 'Don't suppose you want to finish it for me? I'm not really into jigsaws – who is? – but it was very sweet of them, so I want them to see it all put together. They obviously think of me like a proper old granny to buy me that, eh?'

I push away the twinge of sadness that Mum never met her granddaughter.

'It's the festival in Bristol,' Joyce says, turning the box over – hundreds of brightly coloured hot-air balloons floating in a cloudless blue sky. 'It's where Tommy's from, Bristol,' she says. She points upwards and I can hear him banging about upstairs.

'This would be more your mother's thing than mine, I think,' Joyce says, forcing a jigsaw piece into place. 'She used to pop round sometimes asking if Tommy or I could help her with the crossword clues. Don't think she really needed the help, though, if I'm honest. She knew a lot more than us.'

It's comforting to think of Mum having neighbours she could call on.

'And I saw your mum's friend was round to visit you? Now isn't that nice?'

She rubs me on the top of the arm.

'I hope it makes you feel a bit better. About your mum and everything? She did have people that cared about her, you know. You see?'

I process what she just said properly. 'Sorry, but who are you talking about?'

'Well, I don't know his name, do I?' She scowls and thinks. 'He was with a woman. His wife, I suppose. The older couple that came around.'

'Peter and Judith? Not sure it would have been Peter. He hasn't seen her in years.'

Judith straightens up as if I've slighted her. 'Well, I'm just telling you what I saw. I just see the odd thing when I'm passing, or at the window, you know. It isn't like I'm checking up.'

'I just don't think—'

'Suit yourself,' she snaps at me. 'I'm only telling you what I've seen.'

'How long ago did you see him?'

'Oh, it was summer, late summer. Thought maybe he was doing some work around the house or something, but I saw them out the back a few times, drinking tea in the garden. And I thought that was quite nice. I asked her if she'd got herself a fancy man. She didn't like that!' Joyce gives a mischievous laugh. 'Do you know him as well then?' she asks.

'Yes,' I say, and she looks at me, now clearly on the scent of more information.

'Old family friend, that's all.' I think of the day at the theme park, Peter and Mum on the ground while we were on the ride, all the teeth and hair and screams.

'These your grandchildren?' I pick up a photo on the mantelpiece, changing the subject. A boy and a girl – around seven and eight – with pale blonde hair and blue eyes.

'That's them. Katy and Ethan. Twins.'

'Do you see them a lot?'

She takes the picture off me and puts it down, wiping her hands down her jeans.

'Oh, not so much now,' she says. 'They moved to Australia last year, so…' She twists her hands together. 'My daughter, Caroline. Her husband got offered a job over there. They had to go. Be daft not to, wouldn't it? Oh, they'd be mad not to take it. They've a great life over there. Lovely house, beach, sunshine. They're always outside, not like here.'

'You going to go over there and see them, then?'

'Saving up, but we'll see. Getting a bit long in the tooth to be sitting on a plane for that length of time, aren't we?'

'You should get yourselves over there.'

'We'll see. Never been on a computer in my life before this, neither of us had. You can get them up on the screen and everything, you know. It's quite amazing.' She gestures to the laptop sitting on the table, a green light blinking on the front. 'I'm always on the damn thing now.' She shakes her head.

I scan her face, wondering if she's been on SomeoneMustKnow, too, reading about Victoria, the picture of me.

'Bloody bingo on it every night.' A man's voice.

We turn and her husband has appeared in the doorway. He is tall and broad-shouldered; takes up most of the door frame. He's wearing a checked shirt and a green gilet.

Joyce laughs. 'Eeh, give over. I'm allowed some vices, aren't I, at my age? What am I going to do? Bloody jigsaws all day every day? Sylvie, this is Tommy, my husband. Tommy, Sylvie and little Victoria. This is Margaret's lass, Tommy.'

'I know that, thanks, Joyce.' He tuts.

'And anyway,' Joyce says, 'I'm on it for all sorts, thanks very much. News, recipes, everything. You're just jealous because you can't work out how to use it.' The exchange between them remains light-hearted, but it's gaining an edge.

'Ha! News?' Tommy nudges me. 'She's always looking up bloody conspiracy theories. Ask Joyce and she'll tell you Elvis is still alive and kicking and living in Milton Keynes, and the prime minister's a bloody lizard in disguise. Ghosts, UFOs; it's a load of old mumbo jumbo.'

Joyce rolls her eyes. 'I don't think that. I'm just interested, that's all. Maybe I don't want to become so set in my ways as you. I remain open-minded.' She looks at him over her glasses.

Tommy laughs and shakes his head, defusing some of the tension. 'Have you given her the veg, Joyce?'

'Not yet. Sylvie, Tommy has gifted you some of his prized carrots and asparagus from his allotment. He spends enough time there.' She gestures through to the kitchen, a bulging, striped carrier bag sitting on the side.

'Put hairs on your chest that lot, and the bairn.' His voice is deep and booming. 'Speaking of... you sorted out the vermin problem round there yet?'

'Tommy!' Joyce cuts in.

'What?' His voice is booming, self-important. 'I don't mind telling you, Sylvie love. I called the council out a number of times about the bloody things. I know she wasn't happy about that, your mother. But it wasn't about getting your mother into trouble or anything like that. They were getting everywhere in the street. You can't let things like that run and run. Those little critters multiply like no tomorrow. They gnaw through electricals, spread disease and all sorts. Won't help with selling the place.'

Joyce fixes him with a hard stare but he ignores her.

'She's getting the place sorted the best she can, aren't you, petal? It's not her fault it's like that, Tommy. It's the way she found it.'

'I am. I'm getting it sorted out. Sorry you've had trouble with it,' I tell him.

'Traps?' he asks.

I nod.

'And?'

'Well, I don't know. My friend put them down. I haven't been able to...'

He tuts and looks up at the ceiling.

'I'll have a look for you, will I?' Joyce smiles at this, proud.

'OK,' I say, and we all troop round, Joyce running back for the bag of vegetables.

Tommy claps his hands together and then rubs them. 'Right, then. Where are we looking?'

I point him through into the kitchen and under the sink.

Tommy is crashing around under the sink, mangy bleach bottles and carrier bags clustered around his feet where he's kneeling down.

'What are you doing with all this flaming tape?' he says, tearing it off the cupboard door, all the strips sticking together and onto his fingers in a large knot. But before I have time to answer he says, 'Oh, blimey,' his head buried in the cupboard, bottom in the air, and he starts retreating.

'What's wrong?' I say, but he doesn't answer. Joyce and I go through.

'Tommy, what is it, love?'

'Who the bloody hell put these traps down?'

'A friend,' I say.

'You don't want to be using glue traps.'

'I didn't know. I... She just...'

He holds up a board with a shiny surface, a lump of dark fur matted to it. The stench hits me in the back of the throat. Joyce lets out a squeal. Tommy steps towards us, his arm holding the trap out in front of him, and I instinctively reel backwards, almost knocking Joyce over.

The bulk of the mouse's body flops down, revealing a raw bloody patch of flesh. And something else, something pink is detached, remaining stuck on the board.

'It's torn or bitten its own foot off and ripped off a big lump of fur, trying to escape,' Tommy says, holding it aloft as if it's a fish he's proud to have caught.

My mouth is filled with hot, sour vomit that I am forced to swallow down again.

'Is it dead, love?' Joyce says from behind me, her hand on my shoulder.

'I bloody hope so for the damn thing's own sake. What a terrible way to go.' Tommy is shaking his head. 'Right, shoo, you two. Get yourselves through there while I clear this mess up.'

He chivvies us along with his hand without making contact and we both obey, not wanting to be anywhere near the little rotting corpse.

Tommy bangs about for a while, cupboards opening and closing, the tap running. Then the sound of the back door unlocking. A few minutes later he comes back through, holding two devices with plug prongs in them.

'We used these and they helped, didn't they, pet? Because once mice're in one house, they get into the others too. And didn't we know it! You plug these devices in and they send out ultrasonic wotsits, or something that the little critters don't like, so they keep away.' He makes a wave motion with his hands. 'Less barbaric than those glue traps. Bloody hell, it's torture. You want to have a word with whoever put them in for you.'

I feel a hot flush of shame that I let Michelle use them, about the problem Mum created. Joyce rubs my back soothingly.

Tommy pushes his hands into his coat pockets. 'Anyway, ladies, on that delightful note I'm away. Give us a knock if you need some more help with this, you hear me?'

'Bye, love.' Joyce tiptoes on one foot to reach up and kiss him.

After he closes the door behind him, I apologise, my hand on my forehead to try to suppress the cringe washing over me.

'Oh, don't bother,' she says. 'I honestly think he'll be glad of being useful. He retired a couple of months back, you know, and he's never in. Out every day at the allotment or I don't know where. If he stays in the house, he gets cabin fever by lunchtime. Not me, but he's terrible.'

I look out of the window, at Tommy disappearing at the end of the street, striding purposefully.

'You don't have to go out at night, you know? Because of the baby crying,' Judith says, out of the blue.

'It clears my head. I get that from Mum. She used to do it, too.'

'Where do you go?' Joyce says, genuinely interested.

I shrug. 'Around. Sometimes to the supermarket. Or the lake.'

I expect her to tell me it isn't safe, that I shouldn't go there on my own at night, but she just smiles and nods like she isn't surprised, like she gets it. 'Well, mind how you go, eh?'

It's obvious Joyce is considering whether to say something else or not.

'Everything alright, Joyce?'

'Yes, it's nothing… I just. Never mind. It isn't helpful.'

'Oh, come on, please just say it.'

She unfolds her arms. 'I think it was the mouse that did it. One of them anyway.'

'Sorry?'

'Your mum.'

I shake my head, exasperation rising.

'She was up in the night a lot anyway, but especially so with this flaming mouse. We'd hear her crashing about. I mean he wouldn't say so, but that's partly why Tommy wanted her to get it sorted. For her own safety and so she could get some sleep. I mean, yes, and us. But he's a right old softy really. They were driving her crackers, but she'd not get anyone round. She didn't want to set proper traps because she said they were cruel.' Joyce bites at her nails. 'She wouldn't have liked them things your mate used. She was trying to catch them in jam jars with jelly beans. I think it was making the situation worse, to be honest. They were scoffing all the bloody jelly beans and inviting all their mates round, no doubt, for a flaming party. I think she must have heard one and got up to get it in the night, and then fallen.'

I wince again to think of Mum stepping out into the dark during the night, landing at the bottom of the stairs.

That evening, when I'm going up to bed, I notice a thick brown envelope on the mat. It stops me in my tracks and I pick it up and turn it over. I wonder if it's from Sam – an offer of money to talk to him. Or something from Michelle – one of her thoughtful little gifts. She might be trying to make things up to me after the other day. I didn't hear the letter box.

A sense of déjà vu. The days in Manchester with Aunty Alice stretched to weeks and then months. Around birthdays and Christmas, I would find a gift left on the doorstep. They always looked so strange there in the bright morning sunshine. Make-up brushes or nail varnish, a diary. I knew they were from Mum, although there was never a card.

Occasionally there'd be a phone call, too, but then no one on the other end, just silence. I promised myself I wouldn't, but once or twice I'd cracked and phoned the house. Mum answered, but she'd never speak. She'd just sit on the line in silence, sometimes for up to ten minutes or more. Occasionally, I would talk anyway, about what Alice and I had been up to – walking the dog, a short holiday to the seaside. Other times I wouldn't say anything either; just sit there in silence too, breathing, trying to send some kind of feeling down the phone, to let Mum know that I missed her. Hated her too. Alice would just shake her head or shrug her shoulders apologetically at me.

After a while, though, I hardened. I could feel it inside myself. I started refusing to go to the phone on the odd time when Mum did ring. Why should I? She'd abandoned me when I needed her the most. I started to busy myself with other things. Eventually, the pain wasn't quite so raw.

The front of the envelope is completely blank. It feels light, empty even, but I shake it and something shifts around. I tear off the top, grey powdered paper poofing into the air, and hold it open. Inside is a solitary photograph, a Polaroid. I go and look out into the dark street, but it's still completely deserted, a faded impression of the living room reflected onto the window. I take a deep breath and slide the photo out, not yet daring to turn it over.

When I thought I was pregnant with Victoria, Nathan and I sat in the bathroom, me on the edge of the bath, him on the loo seat. 'You've got to do it now,' he'd said, 'or it might be invalidated'. He was shaking the instructions at me. He took a deep breath. 'One, two, three!' he said, but I kept my eyes closed, and then he was grabbing my shoulders gently and laughing. 'It's happening, Sylv. You're pregnant. We're pregnant. It's happening. We are going to have a baby!' He threw his arms around me and we fell backwards across the bath. A wave of something rushed through me. I couldn't be completely sure if it was excitement or dread, or where one began and the other ended.

This time, there is no one here to take a look for me, though. I have to do it myself.

'One, two, three,' I find myself saying out loud. I flip the Polaroid over and force my eyes open. It takes a few seconds for them to focus. The photo is dark, it's hard to make it out, at first. But it becomes clear, then. It's a picture of the lake, taken at night.

Michelle's words float up, about the bus tours to the lake, SomeoneMustKnow and Sam digging around. I keep having this sensation of being in front of a two-way mirror. Everyone sees me, but I can't tell who's there.

Saliva collects in my mouth and I try to swallow but it won't go down. It makes me think of what it feels like to drown.

CHAPTER TWENTY-ONE

Sylvie

'I'm here to see Sam,' I say to the receptionist at the Travellers' Rest.

She raises one eyebrow at me. 'Last name?'

My brain is blank. 'Erm…'

'You a relative?' she says, peering over the counter at the pram.

'Just a friend,' I say, and I can see her jumping to conclusions, a small smirk appearing on her lips. She twists her mouth, thinks, then taps at the computer keys with the ends of her talon-like nails.

'Room eight. You'll have to go and knock,' she says, before turning her attention back to the screen.

I'm surprised she's let me through so easily. I'd expected her to ring him in the room rather than let me go straight down there. People are never threatened when you have a pram. I don't wait around for her to change her mind, though, and I head through the fire doors and along the dingy corridor, door after identical door. I notice that they open with old-fashioned keys rather than the cards you get in almost all hotels now.

Scared I'll lose my nerve, I knock on the door without pausing.

I hear some music or the TV go off, so I knock again. Someone comes close to the door then there's a lull. Some scrabbling around with the lock and the door opens.

Sam looks surprised to see me. It's hard to tell if he's putting that on, since I'm almost certain he looked through the spyhole before opening the door. He certainly isn't dressed to see anyone.

He's wearing grey jogging bottoms, a scruffy-looking T-shirt and stubble. He looks as if he may have just woken up.

'I wanted to come and see you after you turned up at the house the other day and… to see whether I can be any help with Victoria's documentary.'

It takes him a moment of recognition to twig what I'm referring to, but part of me suspects that's an act too.

'Can I come in then?' I say, already pushing the pram forwards so that he has to move out of the way. The inside of the room is no improvement on the corridor.

Sam overtakes me, grabbing underwear off the floor and sweeping a crisp packet and Coke can into the bin. He slams the lid of his laptop shut and pulls a jumper on over his T-shirt.

'Thanks for coming over,' he says. 'I'd have come to the house again. You should have given me a ring.'

'No problem,' I say. 'It does us good to get out and about.' The truth is I wanted to catch him on my terms, not wait for him to come back to the house. And, if he hadn't already, I didn't want him filming Mum's place either. I don't want her life displayed like goldfish in a bowl.

On the inside of the wardrobe door, I catch a glimpse of Post-it notes dotted around – I see Peter's name and mine, before Sam sees me looking and swings it shut. Neither of us mentions it.

'I'm surprised you came,' Sam says. He scrapes the curtains open, lifting the room from its gloom.

'Oh, no. I've just been busy with the baby and Mum's place, that's all. Of course I want to do everything I can to help.'

'Great.'

I knew I couldn't keep Judith at bay much longer either.

I sit on the bed and feel like I'm sinking into it, being swallowed up. 'So… the other day you said there was something you wanted to talk to me about?'

Recognition falls across Sam's face. 'Ah right, yeah.' He springs into action and starts preparing his camera. 'So, it was just really to check some basic details with you.'

'Oh, OK. It was just that it seemed like it was urgent?'

'Well not *urgent* urgent, but you know,' he says, turning the camera on me. 'You don't mind, do you?'

I'd expected that and have put some make-up on. I tidy my hair with my hands. 'Shoot. I mean, I don't think there's much I can add. I've told the police everything I know. But if it helps to go over the facts.'

Sam clips a small microphone onto my collar. Then he turns one of the hotel's cheap chairs backwards, straddling it.

'So, what I want to do is bring Victoria to life, and find out a little bit more about the last few weeks and days of her life, to see if it offers any clues about what might have happened to her, or perhaps jog people's memories. It seems like you're one of the key people to ask.'

'Fine,' I say. 'We were best friends. But like I said, I don't think there's anything new I can tell you.'

Sam is looking at the camera viewfinder, not me, and that makes me feel a little less uncomfortable, but then he stands up and comes and sits next to me on the bed. I'm surprised to see that he's wearing a microphone, too.

He looks once at the camera, clears his throat then turns to me.

'Well, everyone thinks that, but I believe there may be things. You'd be surprised. How people remember things differently. Or how what they say can set off a chain reaction in someone else's memory.'

'OK, fine.'

Sam gestures for me to look at him not the camera but my attention keeps drifting over. It feels like an extra person in the room.

'Can you tell me about the friendship you two had? Can you tell me about Victoria? How you met, what she was like, that kind of thing.'

'Well, let's see where to start. It's been a while, you know. You kind of block things out after a bit.' I feel like I am trying to get an old oil can going, pressing at the handle but nothing coming out.

Sam waits, looks at me impassive, patient. He isn't in a hurry. He's got me for his film now. He isn't about to let me get away.

So I start. 'Victoria… she was always just fun, you know. Like not in a generic way that you'd say about anybody. She was different, she had something special about her. Really special.' The words start to come easier. *They're the truth, after all.*

'You couldn't have a boring time with her – something would always happen, or she would just make you laugh. Or you'd be hanging around doing nothing much at all, but you'd go home feeling like you'd had a brilliant time.'

'So how long had you two been friends? Best friends?'

'You know, it's funny,' I say, 'because I've been thinking about that a lot lately, being back here and everything, because of my mum. Victoria and I, we would go round kind of boasting about how we were the best friends ever. And it's true, we were. I mean, we were like sisters in a way. We were both only children, so we sort of played that role for each other. But we had this thing where we would tell everyone that we met one another on the very first day of primary school. We would tell people that Victoria had marched up to me at primary school and asked me if I liked Madonna, and that I did a little dance to "Lucky Star", and after that we never left each other's sides.'

'That's pretty cute,' Sam says, nodding along. 'You said you would tell people that? It wasn't true?'

'We definitely did do a lot of dancing around to Madonna around that time, but I am not sure that's quite the way it went.

Even our parents will tell you that's how we met. I like the sound of it anyway, though, don't you?'

The story comes out sounding much more sinister than the playful rendition I had intended.

I carry straight on as Sam digests it. 'So, we met because our parents were friends and we went to the same school.'

'That's nice,' Sam says. 'And what was your friendship like?'

'Like I say, we really were like family. We used to go on holidays together and we even spent some Christmases with the Prestons. We'd always be staying over and in and out of each other's houses.'

'That must have been nice to have had a sister-like figure,' Sam says. 'I'm an only child too. I wish I'd had that.'

'Yeah, it was.'

Outside the wind is blowing the trees from side to side. They look as if they're trying to get my attention through the window, friends trying to distract me from a detention at school.

Sam clears his throat. 'So, Michelle said you were flashed at, you and Victoria. Not long before she died?'

'I don't really know why she mentioned that. It wasn't all that big a deal and she wasn't there.'

'Did you know that around the time before and after Victoria's death there were reports of a number of women being flashed at? Indecent exposure?'

My head snaps round. 'There were other reports too?'

Sam nods. 'A number of them, yes. I understand that you saw something that summer, too. You and Victoria?'

'Yes, but like I said, it was nothing really.' The image of it comes back into my head, grubby skin.

'So, did you tell the police about it?'

'Erm, no, we didn't... I didn't... I don't think Victoria did. We were daft teenagers. I think we just thought it was kind of funny at the time.'

'You didn't tell them after Victoria died?'

I think back and feel stupid and exposed then, feel my face reddening. 'I don't think I did. But there wasn't any reason. I honestly didn't think of it. Do you think it's connected?'

Sam shrugs. 'It's worth looking at everything again now, isn't it?'

Victoria starts to stir. 'Do you mind if I quickly...?' I start to get up and go to her.

'No worries. I need to answer a call of nature anyway.' Sam goes into the bathroom. The walls are so thin, I can hear the water splashing loudly in the bowl.

I rub Victoria's tummy and she seems to settle again.

On the side, near the kettle, there's a pack of photos, still in the envelope from where they've been developed. I check the bathroom door; I haven't heard the toilet flush yet, so I slide the pictures out. They're of our house, the day of the party at our house. One is taken from outside – must have been before the party started. The living room is empty, except for the decorations. There are pictures of the food, too – fleshy-looking hotdogs, anaemic crisps. Quickly, I flip deeper into the pack. Maybe Sam planned to show me them anyway, but no harm being prepared.

There's one of Mum, dancing with Peter, a huge glass of wine in one hand. She looks happy in the pictures, happier than I remember her looking the whole summer before. A glimpse of the old Mum. There's a few of Dad, too, posing with people I don't recognise, slightly stiff and stilted. How pale he looks is startling now. In one photo, he is sitting on a chair in the middle of the grass. He looks completely still, while everyone else around him is moving.

I quickly skim through the rest of the photos, but one of them snags in my mind and makes me go back again.

Right on the edge of the picture; it's those coloured jeans we all used to wear, that same striped T-shirt we all had. But it isn't me or Victoria... I pull the picture up closer to my eyes. It's Michelle.

She's half cut off, standing off the lawn away from everyone else, and she's looking up at the house.

I think back to the day again, the party. And I'm certain Michelle wasn't there. There's no way she would have been invited. The toilet flushes and the tap runs, then stops. I shove the pictures back in as best I can and flip the envelope lid shut.

Sam is wiping his hands on his jogging bottoms, sitting back down on the bed.

'There was just one more quick thing I wanted to ask you about.' It's clear he's waiting for me to sit back down too.

'OK, but I'll have to be getting away soon.'

'No worries,' Sam says. 'Little one will want feeding, eh? So, I just wanted to get a bit more background on what happened after the party.'

It's getting windier outside and the trees remind me of those inflatable things you get outside car showrooms, blowing in all directions.

'OK,' I say. 'What do you mean, after the party?' I have to manage my breath, thinking about what happened to her after, where she ended up.

'So, people started to leave, go home. What did you and Victoria do?'

'Well… we cleared up a little bit. Mum was picking all the stuff up from the garden. Then I think Mum went up to bed. Dad was already asleep. Victoria said she was tired and she wanted to go home.'

'She didn't want to stay over.'

I shrug. 'Not that night, no. Sometimes you just want your own bed, don't you?'

'Absolutely,' Sam says, gesturing around the hotel room. 'And had you been drinking, you and Victoria?'

'A bit, not a lot.'

'Did your parents often let you drink? When you were under-age?'

I feel my face twist, but I remember the camera and I recompose myself.

'Sometimes they let us have half a glass of wine topped up with lemonade. We might have had a bit extra at the party – when they weren't looking. They wouldn't have let us get drunk, though.'

'The post-mortem suggested Victoria had been drinking, didn't it?' Sam doesn't take his eyes off me. The mental flash of the procedure, scalpel into flesh, makes me squeeze my eyes shut for a second.

'I don't really know about that. I didn't dig into it, funnily enough. Maybe she had been drinking after… after the party. At the lake.'

'I guess so,' Sam says. 'So, you're saying she wanted to go home, sleep in her own bed. What happened then?'

A sigh escapes from me. 'You know all this. I walked her halfway home, like always.'

'Can you tell me more about that?'

'Well, there isn't anything to tell really. I would walk her halfway home or she would for me if I was at her house. Then when we got in we'd do three rings so we knew the other was home safe.'

'That's what I thought,' Sam says. 'And that's what you always did? And what you did that night?'

'I've said so, haven't I?'

'Are you telling me the truth, Sylvie?' Sam asks. 'I think there might be things you're not telling me about that night.'

My breath catches in my throat. The camera is at point-blank range. I try to get myself together.

'Someone saw Victoria that night.' Sam is looking right at me and I feel my eyes expand and contract. 'And you weren't there.'

'Sorry, Sam. You've really lost me now.'

'I spoke to someone…'

'What *someone*?'

'Well, that doesn't matter for now. But, I spoke to someone who said they'd seen you and Victoria before. Walking up near the park. Parting halfway, like you said.'

'Yeah, like I said.'

'But they said that night, they didn't see you.'

'You're talking in riddles. Can you please just get to the point?'

'OK. You didn't both walk halfway that night, did you? You didn't go with Victoria, did you? Did you have a row? Did something happen?'

'No, that isn't it. Victoria didn't walk on her own; I wouldn't have let her.' I look Sam straight in the eye, then I get up and start gathering my things. 'So whoever you've been speaking to is wrong; they've made a mistake.'

On the way out of the hotel, the receptionist eyes me with that smirk again. I think she thinks something entirely different has been going on in the room. When we get home, I dive into bed for comfort like I used to do when I was a teenager. I pull the covers over my head. It brings back a memory. Victoria is everywhere again now.

CHAPTER TWENTY-TWO

Summer, 1995

Sylvie's eyes opened and she sensed she had been woken by a noise. It wasn't unusual. When he was well, Sylvie's dad often left for work in the middle of the night. Two or three in the morning, if he had to drive the lorry to Aberdeen or further. For a moment, she imagined everything was back to normal before reality crashed in. *Her dad wouldn't be working.*

Sylvie looked at the clock on the bedside table. It was 5.16 a.m. If her mum was out running, that meant she might be in the kitchen again soon, crashing around and cooking food for breakfast, which she wouldn't touch herself. What was the bad news now? Sylvie's stomach belched up some acid in protest. She plumped the pillow and tried to get back to sleep.

Then there was a click at the window. Tired and disorientated, Sylvie thought maybe it was hail-stoning. Because of the snow globe on her bedside table perhaps. But it was the middle of summer.

The next click was louder and it was followed by a cough. It woke Sylvie up like cold water to the face, and she padded to the window, pulled back the curtain and wiped away the condensation. Long strands of light streamed in. The sky was powder blue and hot orange. Sylvie hadn't seen the sunrise before.

Movement drew her attention down. There, in the front garden, straining to look up at the house, was Victoria. She was hopping from one foot to the other and Sylvie wondered if she was hurt. Victoria started to flail her arms and beckon Sylvie.

'Wait there,' Sylvie mouthed, and she ran downstairs in her pyjamas as quietly as she could. Her mum was asleep on the sofa, snoring gently. It looked squalid somehow in this light. Sylvie cringed at the sound as she unbolted and opened the front door. She closed it behind Victoria as gently as she could.

'What are you doing?' she hissed, but Victoria put her fingers on her lips and gestured for Sylvie to follow her up. Every single step seemed to creak and Victoria held her hand out to the side like an orchestra conductor to set the timing so that they both moved at exactly the same moment, creating one pair of feet on the stairs, not two.

They heard Margaret snort loudly and move, so they stood still like statues for a few seconds until her breath became regular again.

Victoria pointed to the spot outside the bathroom and Sylvie understood she was to wait there until Victoria came out. Even the wee seemed thunderously loud, and Sylvie kept glancing anxiously downstairs and at the bedroom door.

Finally, they went into Sylvie's room and closed the door.

Victoria bent over, holding her abdomen. 'Fuck!' she whispered. 'I've needed a wee for about an hour. My bladder was rock hard. I think I might have poisoned myself.' She bit her bottom lip and screwed up her eyes, rocking gently, relief slowly washing over her.

Sylvie was wide awake by then.

'Have you got a nighty I can wear?' Victoria asked. Sylvie opened the drawer and Victoria grabbed a nightshirt, a faded, oversized T-shirt with teddy bears on the front. Victoria turned away and took her clothes off, slipping the nighty on. Her backbone and ribs were protruding out, and there was a gap between her thighs that Sylvie didn't have. The nightshirt swamped her, making her look childlike.

Sylvie got into her bed at the top end and Victoria jumped in at the other end. Sylvie threw her a pillow.

Getting a better look at her, Sylvie was startled by Victoria's appearance. Her face was pale, her eyes big and glassy. Her hair was stringy at the front, lacking its usual bounce and sheen. 'What's going on?' Sylvie whispered. 'Are you alright?' she added to soften it.

Victoria pointed and they both put their heads underneath the pink covers. It felt womblike, reminiscent of the cringeworthy educational videos they'd had to endure at school. The heartbeat thudding in Sylvie's ears intensified the sensation.

'Yeah! It was an amazing night! You should have come, Sylv. I missed you!'

Sylvie felt a pang of regret that she hadn't gone with her to Ryan's after the ice skating. Victoria's feet were cold against her. She wrapped them in the duvet and rubbed at them.

'Right, so… tell me, then!' Sylvie said.

'We went up Brantham to Ryan's house.'

'Were his parents away?'

'Nah, he's got his own house. It was such a laugh.'

'Who was there?'

'Everyone, like Jimmy, Charmaine. Loads of people. Like twenty people or something.'

'Ugh, that Charmaine is a bitch.'

'She's alright really.'

Sylvie bristled at that, especially after the way Charmaine'd spoken to her at the ice rink, when Victoria was there.

'Vic, have you been home…?' Sylvie almost didn't want to know the rest, but morbid compulsion drove her on.

'Not yet, no. Told you, I said to my mum I was stopping at yours. So, if anyone asks, I was here, right? I am here anyway.' Victoria's lips looked dry and powdery, like the skin might split.

'OK.' Sylvie shrugged.

'Thanks, mate.'

Something was off. There was a strange speed and intensity to the way Victoria was talking.

'Are you alright, Vic? What have you taken?'

'A trip.' Victoria couldn't hide the proud smile that had cracked across her face. 'It was so weird; it was like a little bit of paper with a cute little face printed on it. Like that edible paper you used to get from the sweet shop. I swallowed it, but this other lad, he put it in his eye. Said it hits you faster that way.'

'Eurgh.' Sylvie instinctively put her hand up to her own eye at the thought. It bought her some time, too, to play it cooler than she felt about Victoria and the drugs. And the rest.

Victoria was opening up now, getting into full swing. 'I just had one, but this other lad, apparently he'd had about five, and he was just sitting in the corner and he couldn't like speak or anything. He was chewing at his lips and they were all bleeding and stuff.'

'What was it like for you?'

'It was like… I just felt all floaty and like everything was more intense. Sounds stupid – I felt like I was in a computer game or something.'

Sylvie tried to hide her wide-eyed astonishment, the fact she was hanging on Victoria's every word. 'Was it scary?'

'Nah.' Victoria laughed. 'Although I dunno about that lad who'd had a face full.'

There'd been a rumour at school about someone's friend of a friend who'd taken drugs and thought a Mars bar was chasing him down the street. They said that his cousin had found him opening the window of the bedroom and climbing out onto the sill. He thought he was going to fly. They'd all laughed at the time at school… about the Mars bar bit anyway.

'So how much that cost you?'

'Nowt, Ryan gave us it. I didn't have much cash with me. Don't have any anyway at the minute. And Charmaine…' Victoria went on. She had to pause to take a chance to swallow. 'We did a Ouija board and her eyes were like rolling back in her head and everything. She was just pushing the thing with her hand, though, you could tell.'

Victoria chewed on her lip, like she didn't know whether to say something else. Sylvie noticed another bruise-like mark on her neck. She pointed at it. 'You walked into something again, have you?'

Victoria didn't answer and they lay there in silence for a while. Sylvie started to drift off again, until Victoria tapped her on the foot.

'I did it, Sylv. At least… I think I did. Do you hate me?'

Sylvie froze. She considered pretending she was asleep, but she couldn't leave it like that. It wasn't like she would be able to get back to sleep anyway.

'What do you mean?'

'Ryan.'

Sylvie tried not to let her face distort. She focused all her energy on not allowing a single tear to escape.

'Sorry, I know you liked him, Sylv. But I liked him too. We both liked him, didn't we? And Jimmy, he's after you.'

'Is he?' Sylvie's words sounded high and strained. 'So, what happened? What was it like?' She squeezed Victoria's foot and tried to sound chirpy.

'Let's just go to sleep, yeah. I'll tell you later,' Victoria said.

They both lay down and Victoria pulled Sylvie's feet in close, hugging them to her chest.

Victoria fell asleep almost instantly, a serene look on her face. Sylvie took the opportunity to study it closely, undisturbed, the curve of her lips and the light down around her hairline. Victoria's skin was completely unblemished, almost translucent. Its paleness and the mark on her neck gave her a vampiric quality.

A strand of blonde hair fell over Victoria's face and Sylvie brushed it away. She looked so vulnerable lying there like that. Sylvie thought of her and Ryan together and how Victoria would always just be one of those people who could have whatever she wanted.

CHAPTER TWENTY-THREE

Sam

Sam decides to go into the carvery restaurant next door to the hotel, a sudden rabid craving for broccoli. His Conley diet of crisps and garage sandwiches is taking its toll.

'Table just for one?' a teenage girl in a maroon waistcoat asks.

Less of the 'just', Sam thinks.

Only a couple of the other tables are occupied. Two men having what looks like a business lunch and a group of older ladies around a large circular table. The food doesn't smell great. Generic, intense savoury, but it still makes Sam's stomach contract.

The layout of the place is disorientating; a slight hall-of-mirrors effect from all the identical dark tables and the shelves that break up the space. There's a couple with a baby in a high chair that is splattered with food. At a noisy machine a toddler is reaching up, loading the whipped ice cream with brightly coloured smarties and jelly sweets.

The waitress shows Sam to a seat and returns a moment later with a large, warm plate. 'Just go over and help yourself,' she says. Sam tries to avoid thinking about how dubious the meat looks, how long it's all been sitting there. He fills his plate up with as much veg as he can, even skipping the gloopy gravy. For the first round, at least.

As he's sitting down, Sam spots Sylvie's friend from the house. Michelle, head down over her meal. He goes over, his hand starting to wobble under the weight of his plate.

'Hey, Michelle, isn't it?'

He regrets approaching so quietly, as he catches Michelle mid-chew and the seconds tick on for an awkwardly long time while she clears it. Sam slides into the seat opposite her. Michelle looks flustered and swallows hard.

'Sorry, I didn't see you come in.'

'Sorry for interrupting your dinner,' Sam says.

'No problem.' Michelle wipes at the corners of her mouth for stray food. 'I forgot you said you were staying here.'

Sam wonders if that's really true. Something of a coincidence to bump into her so soon.

Michelle takes a big glug from her pint of Coke and suppresses a silent burp.

'Day off?' Sam remembers Michelle saying she worked at the supermarket.

'Yeah, for once. You?'

'Never,' Sam says. *Or every day, if you think about it.* 'Just trying to top up my vitamins.' He takes a quick bite of the pale green broccoli on his plate. It almost disintegrates on contact with his mouth. He pushes the plate to one side.

'So, we got interrupted the other day. I was going to ask you a few more questions, actually.'

This seems to please Michelle and she sits up a bit straighter.

'How good friends were you, you and Victoria? You seemed to know a lot about her when we were chatting at Sylvie's?'

Michelle pushes a potato around her plate, an internal struggle about whether to eat it. 'Pretty good, actually. Sylvie makes out they were like some power couple or something. But me and Victoria were close, too, especially that summer.'

'Yeah, how's that, then?'

'Knew her boyfriend.'

'Oh right, that Ryan, is it?' Another one on Sam's list of people to talk to, and soon.

'Sylvie not told you, then?'

'I've not had a chance to chat with her in that much detail yet. There's a lot to cover, you know. Maybe you can fill me in, though, since we're here. Guess Sylvie has a lot on at the minute, with the baby and everything.'

Michelle turns her mouth down at the sides into an unflattering expression. 'Yeah, Sylvie's had a tough time.' She shrugs. 'Who hasn't?'

'You two had some sort of falling out or something?' Sam asks.

'No, don't be daft. She's just tired and a bit baby-brained. She'll get used to it. She needs help, that's all.' Michelle eyes the potato, continuing their stand-off.

'Help?' Sam says.

'Round the house, sorting that place out. She can't do it on her own. She's just getting herself worked up and I've been trying to look after her. She's an old friend.'

'Worked up how?'

'She isn't getting any sleep. And Victoria, she's an agitated baby. She senses Sylvie being worked up and it goes round and round… but Sylvie won't listen to me. Doesn't want to hear it. You can understand. My sister was the same when she had her first one. That's how I know.'

'You don't have any, then? Children?'

'Me? God no.' Michelle starts to play with a beer mat, tearing at the paper on it.

'So, you mentioned Victoria's boyfriend the other day?'

'Yeah, Ryan Thompson.'

Sam tries again, with the meat this time, but it's tough and dry, a nasty aftertaste.

'Had she been with him long?'

'Not long. Met him at the start of the summer.'

'Was it serious?'

Michelle see-saws her hand from side to side. 'Much as it can be when you're fifteen, I suppose. But they saw each other nearly every day in the summer. Think so anyway.'

'Right – he from school, was he?'

'Nah! Older. Eighteen. She was going to meet him that night, but she didn't turn up…' Michelle trails off. 'I always wonder how that's made him feel. Maybe she was on her way there, you know. And whatever happened, happened.'

This catches Sam's attention, a comb snagging in knotted hair. 'Sorry? Did you say she was meeting him *that* night?'

'Yes?' Michelle sounds hesitant now. 'But like I said, she didn't turn up.'

'Did you tell the police that?' Sam says.

'Me?' A guard is going up. 'Well, *I* didn't, personally. Nobody interviewed me. I'm obviously not important enough. But I'm sure someone did. Sylvie. Or Ryan.'

'How do you know she was meeting him, Michelle?'

'Erm, I don't remember now. Victoria must have told me. And… and I was at Ryan's later that night.'

'The night Victoria died?'

'Yes.' Michelle tries to take another drink, but her glass is empty.

'Were you there all night?'

'No, not until later. I got there about ten.' Michelle's voice has an unmistakable undercurrent of panic.

Sam doesn't let up. 'Where were you before that?'

'Nowhere. Just at home.' Michelle stands up quickly, reaching for her bag. She accidentally pulls a serviette off the table, cutlery clattering loudly to the floor.

'You know where he lives, this Ryan?'

Michelle picks up the cutlery and sits back down, as if trying not to put any weight on the chair.

'Well, I know where he used to live, obviously. Last I heard he was still there.'

Sam gets notebook and pen out of his pocket and puts them on the table in front of Michelle.

She blinks and looks at him as if he's done a magic trick. 'Well, I don't feel right about giving people's addresses out.'

'It's not like I'm flogging something, is it? It's for Victoria.'

Michelle thinks for a second, then picks up the pen. At first it won't write and she scribbles hard on the pad. She writes the street name down, and then puts the pen in her mouth and closes her eyes. She puts one hand out, hovering it over the table, looking like a bad psychic.

'I'm just trying to visualise the number.'

Sam doesn't interrupt her and, after a few seconds, she snaps out of it and quickly scribbles a number down. She looks pleased with herself.

Sam switches tack.

'So, what did Victoria's parents make of her seeing an older lad like that? Not sure I'd have liked it.'

'You would when you were fifteen!' She's hooked back in. 'Her dad didn't like it. At all. Tried to ground her and everything. But she kept seeing him.'

'What about Sylvie? How did she feel about Victoria's new boyfriend?'

Sam thinks he can detect a small glint in Michelle's eye at that.

'Think she'd have liked to have Victoria all to herself. But that's what fifteen-year-old girls are like, isn't it?' Then she adds, 'This is all just teenage stuff, you know.'

They sit in silence for a while. Michelle runs her finger along her empty plate, scraping up a fine film of the remaining gravy and putting it in her mouth. She catches herself and shoves her hands underneath the table. A few moments later, she gets up to leave.

'Anyway, it's been nice chatting to you,' she says. 'Good luck with it all.'

On the way out, the waitress shouts across to Michelle just as she's about to get into the revolving door. She's forgotten to pay.

Sam feels the areas of the town change from street to street, an invisible line between them. One minute you're in a well-to-do area – tended lawns, hanging baskets. The next street along, something has changed to boarded-up houses and broken glass. He has reached Brantham now and quickly checks the address in his notebook again. One house has newspapers covering the windows. A large Alsatian roams the garden like it's searching for something in the overgrown grass. A child on a scooter goes past and the dog leaps up at the wooden fence. It looks like one decent run up and it would be over and on the loose.

He drives round the small roundabout twice more and is grateful that the satnav finally kicks in and tells him where to go. As he passes a group of boys sitting on a wall outside the shop, one of them makes an obscene gesture with his hand and they all laugh. He's driving along Wagon Way. Rows of small, red-brick houses, steps up to them a bit like Sylvie's. He sees number twelve and pulls over to park. A large St George's flag hangs out of one of the windows, flapping loudly in the breeze. He takes his camera out and films it. The boys across the street eye him with suspicion, all facing towards him. He unlocks and locks his car again before going up to the house.

Quickly after Sam knocks on the door, a small woman opens it, wearing leggings and Ugg boots. Sam only knows the name of them as he bought Natalie some for Christmas a few years ago. He couldn't believe how much they cost, had got annoyed to see the way Natalie slouched in them, seeming to roll onto the sides of her feet, the soles wearing away unevenly.

Despite the casual outfit, the woman's face is perfectly made up, icy-pink lip gloss freshly applied, smooth foundation, a biscuit shade. She squints at the light.

'Yeah?' she says accusingly, her perfectly smooth forehead crumpling up as if an invisible thread has been pulled. 'Can I help you?' She looks behind Sam to see if there's anyone with him.

'I'm here to see Ryan; I'd like to talk to him, please.'

The woman brings her hand up to her face to shield her eyes. She closes an internal door behind her.

'Is he in?' Sam says.

'Who's asking?' She has mostly closed the front door now, too, and just her head peeps out.

'My name's Sam. I'm a film-maker. I'm researching a documentary about Victoria Preston.'

That thread across her forehead is pulled tighter still.

'What?' Her tone is impatient, defensive.

'Victoria Preston. She was murdered twenty years ago. Her body was found in the lake. I believe Ryan knew her.'

She starts to close the door, but Sam pushes his hand forwards and stops it.

'Listen, I'm not trying to cause trouble or anything; I'm talking to lots of different people who knew her.'

The woman scowls again, deep grooves etching themselves between her eyes.

She looks at him once more and slams the door.

Sam starts to back away from the house, thinks of heading back to his car to write a note for Ryan, push it through the letter box. But there's a scraping sound of the chain being adjusted and the door springs open again, wider this time. It's a man.

'I'm Ryan.' He opens the door wide. He looks much older than thirty-eight, his face weathered, skin puckering around his mouth and eyes, a greyish tone to it around the crevices. He's wearing an NYPD T-shirt and jersey bottoms.

'My name's Sam Price. I'm a film-maker. I'm researching Victoria Preston's case. I believe that you knew her.'

'Yeah, I knew her,' Ryan says. His voice is gentle, even. 'You better come in. You'll have to 'scuse the mess, though.'

Sam notices that Ryan walks unevenly with a distinct limp. As they go into the living room, Ryan picks up a games console balanced precariously on the edge of a squashy sofa and kicks a doll out of the way on the floor at the same time. A girl with pale-pink plastic glasses and a school uniform is sprawled across the carpet, taking up most of the available floor space, colouring in, swapping coloured felt tips every few seconds. She looks up at Sam and gives him a grin, tiny teeth missing at the front.

'I told you to take your uniform off,' Ryan says to the little girl. Then he points to her picture. 'You've missed a bit.'

A slightly younger boy appears, tearing out of the kitchen, wearing a cape and making a roaring noise like he's pretending to be a plane. The boy wends between Sam and Ryan, making Sam feel off-balance. Ryan opens his mouth to tell him off, but the boy's already flown back into the kitchen. He shakes his head good-naturedly, gesturing for Sam to sit on the sofa, moving a pile of folded washing out of the way so that he can. Sam had expected more hostility.

'So, what is this?' Ryan's legs are spread wide open, body language relaxed.

The woman who had answered the door is busy in the kitchen, opening the oven door, shaking a tray of food, but Sam can tell she is paying attention, listening in. When he glances in, the woman moves quickly, pretending to be concentrating on the cooking.

'People tell me you and Victoria were seeing each other?' Sam says. 'I'm looking to interview people that knew her. About what happened. And what she was like.'

Ryan takes a deep breath, puffs the air back out. 'If you like, yeah. I was seeing her. We were knocking about together, yeah. I wouldn't say it was serious.'

'Are you going to be on the telly, Daddy?' the little girl says, her glasses at an awkward angle.

'No, Kirsty, I'm not. Get back to your colouring in.' Ryan gestures for her to turn back around. 'They don't miss a trick, do they?' he says to Sam.

Sam looks at the little girl and back to Ryan. 'Might be better if we do this somewhere quieter,' he says. 'Away from little ears.'

'She's alright,' Ryan says. But the girl turns around again, trying to straighten her glasses, and says, 'Who is Victoria, Daddy? Do we know her?'

'No, darling. Never you mind, nosey. Close your ears.'

She giggles at him, her tongue poking through her teeth, and puts her hands on the side of her head.

'You don't seem surprised to see me, Ryan.' Sam decides to carry on.

'I heard there was someone sniffing about so I wondered if you'd want to talk to me. It's a small place round here.'

'Do you mind if I ask what happened to your leg?'

'Accident at work,' Ryan says, automatically reaching out to touch it.

'Yeah? What is it you do, then?'

'I work in a bookies now. Was training to be a painter and decorator at the time. Fell off a ladder, knacked me leg in.'

'Sorry to hear that.'

'Don't be.' He grins at Sam. 'I weren't very good at it. Put it this way, you wouldn't want me doing your place up.'

The little girl cranes her head around again. 'Stop telling fibs, Daddy. If you tell fibs you won't get any presents from Santa at Christmas.'

'Oi! I told you to stop earwigging and colour that picture in for me, didn't I? We need a new one for the fridge.' He tickles the bottom of her feet, shaking his head at Sam.

The girl's expression darkens and her face sets harder. 'I heard Mummy telling her friend that some bad men took you up on the moors and hit you on the knee. A long time ago. Before I was even here. If I lie, too, I won't get any presents either. That's what you said.' She scowls, confused.

Ryan's face flushes red. He leans back in his chair and knocks on the kitchen door. The woman appears, face glowing, pushing her hair off it with the back of her hand.

'Can you take her in there, please, Charmaine?'

The woman tuts, beckoning the girl through. 'Come on, your tea is nearly ready. Can you set the table for me?' She says to Ryan, 'Everything alright, babe?'

'Yeah yeah, sound. I'll be through in a minute, OK?' Ryan shoos the woman away.

The girl hops up to her feet in one swift movement. Ryan reaches out for her but she swerves out of the way. When she walks past Sam, she slows down and looks him closely in the face, then giggles. The kitchen door closes.

'Is that true?' Sam asks. Ryan has had time to shut down, though.

'I told you. Work accident. I thought you were here about Victoria not my career.' His hand is clutching at the back of his knee again, as if for support.

'You and Victoria were dating, then?'

'I wouldn't call it that, but yeah, if you say so.'

'What would you call it, then?'

'Well, it's just a bit old-fashioned, isn't it? Like courting or something.'

'Alright. Seeing, then? Whatever you want to call it.'

'Yeah… I guess. Sorry, I ain't being funny or nothing. It's just a bit weird, you know, being asked about a girl from that long ago. It's ancient history all that stuff.' Ryan's eyes dart around the room.

'Not to Victoria's parents it's not.' It escapes from Sam without him expecting it.

'Yeah, and I get that. That's why I've let you in, isn't it? I got my own kids – my oldest is fifteen now; I get it.'

'So where did you meet, you and Victoria?'

'Just around and about; you know how it is. I used to see her and her little mates down the shopping centre. It's what everyone did on a Saturday afternoon, or when they finished school.'

'So you knew her already?'

'Not as such, no. I knew Michelle. Was mates with her brother. I'd just seen Victoria. Then we got together.'

'Right, so you asked her out, or what?'

Something changes in Ryan's demeanour. His posture becomes more aggressive. 'Sorry, mate; I'm talking to you out of my own free will. Are my teenage dating moves really relevant here? Do you wanna start telling me about yours?'

'This is about building up an idea of Victoria's movements, what she was like, who she hung around with. What that summer was like.'

Ryan blows air out through his mouth, rubbing his hand across what's left of his hair.

'I didn't ask her out really, no. It weren't like that. It's not an Enid Blyton book, you know? I saw her in the park one night and got chatting with her and you know how it is… Saw her a couple of times then we met up again at the ice-skating rink and I guess we were kind of a couple after that. I invited them back to my house.'

'Them?'

'Vic and her other little mate, Sylvie. She didn't come anyway.'

'How come?'

'Dunno.' He shrugs, unfazed. 'It's twenty years back. Fuck's sake. She needed to get back or something. I don't know, do I? I think Vic said that there was something going on at home with her dad. She was a bit snooty, to be honest, but so what? Can't please everyone, can you?'

'So, this party... these parties you had at your house...'

'It weren't really a party; it was a "gathering".' He gives Sam a grin, displaying yellowing teeth. Then he puts his hands up in surrender. 'It were just a few people sitting around, having a few cans, chatting, watching shit on telly.'

'Drugs?'

Ryan looks down at the floor.

'I'm not looking to name any names on this,' Sam says. 'My focus is Victoria and building up a picture. If it's not connected, I'm not interested.'

Ryan allows himself to look up. He checks the door before answering. 'Sometimes, yeah. Es, trips. Bit of weed. Nothing major. Everyone was doing it.'

'Any harder stuff? Heroin?'

'Nah! Calm down, mate. I was an idiot but not that much of a fucking idiot.' Ryan checks the door again. 'I ain't into any of that no more. I was a kid. I've got a family now.'

'You gave them to Victoria? Es, trips...?'

He twists his mouth. 'Yeah, but I didn't force her or nothing. We were all doing it.'

Sam can see him clamming up again so he changes tack.

'Was this your parents' house?'

'No, it was mine. Council place. Me and a couple of lads.'

'You didn't live with your parents?'

He lifts his head up fully to look at Sam square on now, enunciating his words. 'No, I didn't. We had our differences – me being a little shit, mainly.'

'So, what did you and Victoria do? It was the school holidays. Where did you hang out?'

He shrugs. 'The usual: my place, town, park, whatever. Weather was nice that summer so—'

'The lake?'

Ryan makes a sharp, sudden gesture like he's about to say something or jump up, but then he gathers himself again. 'Look, we did go to the lake, yeah. So what? I'm not going to lie about that because I have nothing to hide.' He throws his arms out to the side. 'But I had nothing – you hear me – *nothing* to do with what happened to Vic. It isn't me, it isn't who I am. And even then, I wouldn't have got mixed up in anything like that. I did some stupid shit but not that.'

'So, you told the police everything?'

He raises his eyebrows. 'What do you mean?'

'That you were supposed to meet Victoria later that night.'

Ryan's face darkens. 'No, I never. We weren't meeting that night. What's this?'

'I heard,' Sam says, 'Victoria was planning to come to your house after the party at Sylvie's.'

Ryan is shaking his head now. 'Is this her mate saying that? Sylvie? I heard she was back here too. I never... I didn't plan to meet her that night. It was cooling off, to be honest, for me anyway. I was avoiding seeing her a bit more. Look, I'm not sure I'm happy about this. I had everyone, the police, asking me at the time, and I told them the truth.'

Sam lets the tension dissipate out of the air. 'So how did you feel then? When you found out what happened to Victoria?' he says.

'Honestly? I was upset, I was shocked. I couldn't take it in. But I was scared too. Course I was. I was scared they'd blame me. I was on their radar. They had me down as a wrong 'un. They knew my name. I was scared that they'd pin it on me. But I was at my house the whole night. You can ask my mates. I'll give you their names.'

'So, if things were cooling off, you didn't love her then?' Sam asks.

The kitchen door opens. 'Now that isn't fair,' Ryan says. The door closes again quickly, the smell of something savoury wafting in, a blast of warm air.

'We'd only been seeing each other a few weeks. It weren't like she was the love of my life or something. I think people would have preferred it if it was some big Romeo and Juliet thing but... it just wasn't. And it still isn't. I'm being totally honest with you.'

Sam can hear Ryan breathing steadily through his nose. In fairness, it would be easier for him to say he did love her, it would paint him in a better light for some people.

'I had to distance myself. I have to,' Ryan says. 'Sorry, but time passes, you move on. It's been twenty years.'

'How did she take it, Victoria? About you backing off?'

Ryan raises his eyebrows slowly and takes a half-breath. 'I don't think it's what she wanted. She started trying a bit too hard, coming on strong, you know?' Ryan wriggles in his seat a little. 'She wanted us to carry on. Maybe we would've, I don't know. I really don't know.'

'You ever see Sylvie again? After that night at the ice skating?' Sam says.

Ryan looks confused for a second. 'Her mate? Couple of times, yeah. She hung about with us in town a few afternoons, but not loads, nah. Told you, she thought she was better than us.'

'What about Victoria's parents?'

'Huh. Here we go.' He gives a little laugh to himself. 'Met him once or twice, yeah. Fucking nut job.'

'Peter?'

'Yeah. He came round one afternoon and practically dragged Victoria out of here by her hair.'

'For what?'

'Dunno. He must have followed her, she said. I didn't ask her to, but she just snuck out of her house anyway. She knew her own mind, that's for sure.'

'You think she was scared of him? Her dad?' Sam asks.

'I don't think he put her in the lake, if that's what you're saying,' Ryan says. 'Like I said, he was a fucking nut job but I'm older now. I get it. I got kids of my own, a teenager of my own, and yeah, I'd go round and I'd drag her out if she was hanging around with people like me and my mates were then. It's what dads do.'

The door pops open again and there's a commotion in the kitchen, chairs scraping, cutlery clattering, children running underneath hot baking trays held high in the air. The woman gives Ryan a look.

'Any chance of a hand in here?'

'I'll be in in a sec, Char. Just give me a minute, yeah.'

Ryan stands up.

'I'll see myself out,' Sam says.

'Look. I want her parents to find out what happened to her, I do. I get it. But I promise you it ain't nothing to do with me.' Ryan puts his hand on his chest.

He goes into the kitchen and sits down at the table, looking up at Sam once more before turning his attention back to the little girl, pulling her seat in as she bounces her knife and fork off the table, legs dangling in mid-air.

As Sam is leaving, the woman follows him out, pulling the gilet tightly around her, phone clamped in her perfect, French-manicured nails.

'Listen,' she says. 'You're not planning on bringing trouble round here, are you?'

'No,' Sam says. 'I'm looking for information, that's all.'

The woman eyes him suspiciously. 'Looking for people to be in your little movie, more like.'

Sam turns to go.

'You know who did that to his fucking leg, don't you?' The woman's voice again from behind.

'What do you mean?'

'Oh, work it out. You're making the bloody documentary. They thought Ryan knew something about it but he never... I was there that night. He was at that house all night. He's turned himself around, right? We're making a life for ourselves here. You think before you go causing trouble for people, you hear me?' She closes the door.

As Sam walks down the path, he looks through the window and sees them all crowded round the small dinner table, Ryan's leg stuck awkwardly straight out to the side.

CHAPTER TWENTY-FOUR

Sylvie

I put Victoria into her cot and set the lamp going round. I find a tinkling version of 'Twinkle, Twinkle, Little Star' on my phone and let it play out, and I sit with her for a while and watch her eyes try to follow the shapes, make sense of the patterns.

There's a light tapping at the door downstairs, more of a scratching against the glass. As I approach, there's a dark blue shape through the small pane. Then the letter box rattles and moves, fingertips poking through. The letter box rattles again.

'Sylvie, are you in there?'

It's Michelle.

I think of the Polaroid and the photo of Michelle at the party, and I suddenly feel wary of her now. 'What do you want, Michelle?'

'Sylv? Let me in, will you?' She rattles at the door handle, shaking the glass. 'I'm sorry about the other day. Really I am. Is Victoria OK?' She slaps her hand against the glass like someone locked in a cell.

'Did you put something through the door, Michelle?'

'Like what? Sylvie, just open the door.' Michelle's voice is louder through the open letter box.

'I'm sorry, you know, about everything.'

'What do you mean, Sylvie? What's going on?' She withdraws her hand.

'I'm sorry about the night at the pictures when we stayed on the bus. And the night at the lake when you fell in.'

Michelle didn't turn up at school the next day. The teacher had asked if anyone had seen Michelle that night. Victoria said we shouldn't say anything 'just in case' and I let myself be swept along with it. A few days later, I heard Michelle had twisted her ankle badly when she fell. It had taken her almost all night to hobble home alone.

'Don't be silly. It's all kids' stuff now.'

'Don't you think about it any more?'

Michelle doesn't answer.

I slide down the door and sit on the mat, the bristles poking into my backside. Michelle has the letter box pushed open, cold air hitting the back of my neck.

A few years ago, I was on the other side of this door. I took the train from Glasgow and came here. We should talk, me and Mum, I thought. I felt ready, tricked by contentment. I called ahead but Mum never answered, of course. Left my number but she didn't ring back. I think of all the calls I have ignored from Nathan.

Me and Mum; we're not that different.

I'd travelled all that way; I'd assumed she'd open the door.

I knocked and heard her shuffling around. She got to the door and I made the mistake of speaking. 'It's me, Mum.' Then nothing; silence.

But I knew she was there, just on the other side, within arm's reach – standing still, like I'd think she wasn't there. I had bent down and opened the letter box, just like Michelle. All I could see was the swathe of her floral skirt. At first she still didn't move, then she suddenly just scuttled away and into the living room, door slammed behind her.

I sat there until it got dark, but she never came out, never put the light on. In a snap decision, a weak moment, I scribbled my phone number and address down and shoved it through the door, scraping my hand, drawing blood on the letter box. I regretted it the second the paper left my fingers. I already knew, deep down, but I decided then once and for all, we were done.

You never are, of course.

As far as I was concerned, she didn't exist to me any more; I said that to Nathan and he knew not to argue, but I saw that flicker in his face too – what kind of person cuts out their mother? What kind of person do they have to be for their mother to reject them like that? Occasionally he'd pick at the edges of me and Mum, but he learned to know better than to sour the day or negate the evening ahead.

'Did you come to the party that day, Michelle?'

There's a long pause. I wonder if she has gone, but I can still feel that cold air turning into a headache at the back of my skull.

'My dad's party. The day Victoria died.'

There's another long pause.

'Yes,' Michelle says, barely audible.

'Why?'

'You asked me,' she says, her voice strained.

'That's not true. I didn't invite you. You didn't even know my dad.'

There's another pause and she says, 'I was walking past the house and I heard voices and the music. I just wondered what was going on.'

'So you just let yourself in?'

A police siren whistles past in the distance.

'Yeah,' she says.

'But I didn't see you. At the party.'

'I came later. No one noticed me really. Everyone was well smashed. You were upstairs,' she says.

'You came into the house?'

The wind is whipping up outside, the trees swishing.

'I was looking for you, that's all.'

'How long did you stay?'

'A while.'

'Please just leave us alone, Michelle. I don't want you to come round.'

'I don't understand why you're being like this, Sylvie.'

After a while, the letter box clatters shut.

I stay sitting on the mat for I don't know how long. My back is icy cold. I open the door to check and Michelle is gone.

CHAPTER TWENTY-FIVE

Summer, 1995

Sylvie woke early on the day of the party. She was anxious about the weather. If it rained, they'd have to have it indoors; it wouldn't be as much fun. She went downstairs, barefoot in her lemon silky pyjamas – shorts and a shirt, a birthday present. Her mum was already busy, loading drinks onto the trestle table and slathering bright yellow margarine onto stodgy white teacakes.

'What shall I do, Mum?' Sylvie asked her. Normally her mum would have asked her to mop the floor or dust the living room, but she just gave her a kiss on the cheek and handed her a cup of tea and some white toast.

'I've got this under control, I think. You take that up to your dad, then get yourself ready.' Margaret looked at her delicate gold watch. There was still ages before anyone would arrive.

Sylvie sat with her dad for a while. He propped himself up in bed. It felt a bit weird seeing him with his top off. He lolled his head to the side and reached out for Sylvie's hand, smiling at her. The intensity of it spooked her, the way he was looking at her. It was almost more than she could bear. She squeezed his hand back but didn't move any closer.

'We're going to have a good time today, you'll see,' he said. The purple shadows under his eyes reminded Sylvie of the coloured segments from Trivial Pursuit. Her parents played it sometimes with Victoria's mum and dad. The room would be scattered with empty wine bottles the next morning.

Michael squeezed Sylvie's hand. 'You be good for your mum, won't you? Do as she says?' The future he was referring to went unspoken.

'Are you going to be alright?' she asked him. She meant, 'Are you going to get better?' and that was the question he answered.

'Stranger things have happened at sea,' he said, one of his phrases.

After a while, he fell asleep and Sylvie disentangled her hand.

Sylvie busied herself getting ready. In the bath, she shaved her legs, using one of the pink razors her mum left on the side. It was blunt and drew tiny droplets of blood up her shin. Saturday programmes played in the background on her little portable TV. It was never fully tuned in, lines across the screen warping the picture.

She decided on wearing red jeans and a navy crop top that buttoned up the front, the thinnest strip of flesh visible. She wouldn't get away with any more. The hem of the top was squiggly like a phone cord and she liked that detail. Victoria had the black version of the top because they got them one Saturday afternoon – two for five pounds, or they would have been if Victoria hadn't sneaked them into her rucksack and sauntered out, not telling Sylvie until they were on the bus home. Sylvie looped coloured beads around her neck once, tightly like a choker, and then let the rest of the slack hang down.

She admired herself in the mirror. The fresh foundation gave the illusion of clear skin. Later, especially in this heat, she knew the cheap make-up would wear off. Stubborn clumps would cling on and remain, the colour somehow turning orange. Her spots would start to creep through. New ones would appear out of nowhere.

She sprayed herself with a cloud of fruity-smelling body spray and went downstairs. Her mum was in the hallway and Sylvie braced herself for a comment, steeled herself for a row, but Margaret just kissed her on the cheek and said, 'You look lovely, sweetheart.'

Sylvie pretended to be embarrassed, or not to really notice, but she loved what her mum had done with the house. She had transformed it into something magical. Across the hallway, Margaret had hung coloured paper streamers. Loads of them criss-crossing all the way down the hall. At the corners of the doors and along the spindles in the bannister she had tied clusters of bright balloons.

'Looks good, Mum. I still don't know why we're having this party, though.'

'I thought it would be nice, while the weather's good.' Margaret's smile was tight.

Something was going on behind the curtain of her expression. Unease churned in Sylvie's stomach. She hugged her mum stiffly and Margaret squeezed her back harder than usual, kissing her on the top of her head and smelling her hair. Then she gently pinched Sylvie's stomach where the crop top was showing it, but for once Sylvie didn't recoil or pull away.

'Come and look at this food, Sylv, will you? See if we are missing anything.'

Margaret lifted the paper tablecloth off the buffet. It was only lightly touching everything, almost floating. She'd even bought the tablecloth especially – usually she would have used one of the ones left over from Christmas, but this one was bright pink with yellow stars and she'd got matching napkins, cups and plates, too.

On the table there were egg sandwiches, ham sandwiches, cold pizza, sausage rolls, chicken legs, crisps, chocolate cornflake cakes and a Swiss roll. So much food. Sylvie had managed to dodge breakfast and her mum had been too busy to notice. The sight and smell of all this food unleashed a surge in her, hunger, stronger than her willpower. She stole a sandwich when her mum wasn't looking.

The first people to arrive were Mum's friend Aileen from work and her husband. Sylvie didn't catch his name. Everything about Aileen was loud. She had a bright pink skirt on and a tight T-shirt with a palm tree. Her fake tan made it hard to make out what she actually looked like. All you saw was the tan and the pattern on the clothes; her features were hardly there.

After Sylvie had taken the coats upstairs, she came back down and they were still standing in the doorway, carrier bags swinging off their wrists, a bottle of wine in a blue bottle half-heartedly held aloft. Her mum took the wine and gave Sylvie the carrier bag.

'Put these out, will you, petal?' Margaret said to Sylvie, without looking at her. In the bag were some chocolate fingers and a big family bag of crisps. They never usually had this kind of stuff in the house, especially during a cottage cheese and grapefruit period. Sylvie emptied the fingers onto a plate and the crisps into a bowl, stuffing a handful of each into her mouth. She had to pretend she was looking for something in the cupboard under the sink, when Margaret, Aileen and her husband came past, because her mouth was still full.

Next to arrive were some of the neighbours from along the street, with an armload of cans of lager and a box of wine. More crisps, and cheese and onions on sticks stuck into a foil-wrapped orange. Greasy, wizened little sausages. One of each went into Sylvie's mouth, the cocktail stick scratching and drawing blood from the roof of it.

After that, the house suddenly seemed to become very crowded. People were wedged into every nook and cranny downstairs, and each time Sylvie took coats to her parents' room, she had to wiggle past people coming up and downstairs.

From the kitchen, Sylvie watched her dad out of the kitchen window, while she filled a vase with water for flowers that someone had brought. He was laughing and talking away.

Eventually, Victoria emerged through the living room, pushing through crowds of people, a red top tied around her waist. At the front of her long hair were two very thin plaits. Sylvie was struck by how pretty she looked, followed by an aftershock of resentment, papered over with a smile. Victoria soon broke off from her parents, and she and Sylvie were in their own little world.

The party went on around them, but it didn't look like much fun to Sylvie. Just people sitting around sipping drinks, chatting about DIY and work and mortgages. Sylvie saw one of her mum's friends pat her husband on the bottom, pinching it lightly. He turned and looked at her as she drank her wine. The way their eyes were locked made Sylvie shudder.

Margaret rushed past with some empty paper plates and a bin bag. 'You OK, love?' She ruffled Sylvie's hair, which she never did these days, and Sylvie patted it down again to smooth it.

Sylvie went to answer her but her mum was already gone.

It started to get late and dusky, a Tizer-coloured sky and candyfloss-pink clouds. People's chatter and laughter got louder; some people were visibly drunk, staggering backwards and trampling on the flowers. Sylvie ventured uncertainly out into the garden, threading her way through people dancing unsteadily, small groups standing chattering. Shoes were off now, women standing in their tights, dirtying their soles on the grass.

Her dad was sitting on a chair at the bottom of the garden, chatting to a couple of people, and she went over. He waved to her and winked. He'd caught some colour from the day's sun, evenly across his face. It made him look well again.

Back inside, Victoria was sitting on the sofa in the dim living room, flicking through the TV magazine.

'You OK, V?' Sylvie said, and when Victoria turned to her, in this light, something about her looked sly, the gloom casting deep shadows underneath her eyes.

Victoria jumped up. 'Let's get some booze.'

She went into the kitchen and Sylvie followed her. Victoria reached behind a group of people. A woman was hanging off a man's every word. They eyed Victoria suspiciously, but soon went back to their conversation. Victoria handed Sylvie a bottle of wine from the fridge and she handled it like Kryptonite, standing there 'catching flies' until Victoria gave her a push towards the stairs.

They both ran up towards Sylvie's room. Margaret was coming down the stairs. Sylvie felt herself tense up, her heart quicken, but

Victoria just gave a little wave and pushed past. Margaret turned and watched her go. As she passed, Sylvie noticed her mum looked flushed and glassy-eyed, as if she had been sick.

Sylvie closed the door behind them and they laughed until they were breathless. But something didn't feel quite right too. Victoria had one of her edges to her.

Victoria tossed the wine on the bed and it bounced. She started to unpack the small bag she was wearing across herself. She pulled out four miniature bottles of vodka, three chocolate bars and a serviette that was stuffed with sausage rolls from downstairs.

'Fuck that boring lot. No offence to your parents, but let's have our own little party! Stick some music on.'

Sylvie's stomach already ached from all the food she had eaten, but she popped one of the sausage rolls in her mouth to soothe her nerves, grease oozing from the salty meat.

They sat on the floor, backs to the bed. Victoria put plaits in Sylvie's hair just like the ones she had. The pulling against Sylvie's scalp made her eyes water.

'Ow,' she said, and the tension increased. 'So, where you been all week?' Sylvie asked. 'Not seen you at all.'

'Around,' Victoria said moonily, a strange smile on her lips like sunlight catching on water.

Sylvie got a flash of déjà vu and then it zipped away again. She had seen that type of look on someone else. They're with you, but they're thinking about someone else. The curtains are closed.

'You been seeing Ryan?' Sylvie forced it out like when she played Pontoon with her dad. No matter what her hand of cards, she would always twist, twist, twist. Say it fast enough and it's too late to change your mind.

'Might have been.' Victoria swayed her legs from side to side and screwed the cap off the wine. Sylvie felt too full and sick to drink.

'Be careful, V. My mum's gone to a lot of trouble for this party. Let's not spoil it, eh?'

'Oh, boohoo. Your poor mum,' she said, waving her arms around. 'Live a little, will you? Everyone else here is pissed.'

Sylvie took a swig of the wine to try to smooth things over.

'The other day Ryan and me went to Morecambe. He's got a car, you know. We stopped off on the way. On the moors.' Victoria's tongue was in her cheek. Any guilt she'd had about Ryan, and Sylvie's feelings, seemed to be gone. It felt as if now she was twisting the knife.

'So, are you going out now?'

'Dunno – I'm going to see him tonight, though. Surprise him at the house.'

There was a scuffle against the door, and Sylvie's and Victoria's eyes met. Sylvie turned the music down and they both listened, staring at the door handle. Sylvie was worried her mum or another adult was about to find them. But it fell silent, just the distant sounds of the party downstairs.

'Tonight? When?' Sylvie looked at the clock. It was already after nine.

'*Later* later. There's a party round Ryan's so I'm going to go. You better not say anything, though. If anyone – and, I mean, anyone – asks, I'm staying here, right. I'm going to sneak out after.'

Her tone had a shade of threat in it. 'My dad thinks we've finished so I don't want him knowing,' she said.

The shuffling sound outside the door was back, two long shadows in the crack of light; legs. Victoria put her fingers on her lips and Sylvie held her breath. After a few minutes, the dark shapes went away again. Sylvie turned the music up loud.

CHAPTER TWENTY-SIX

Sam

Jiggling on the step to keep warm, Sam waits outside Peter and Judith's. Eventually, Peter answers the door.

'Oh, it's you. Thought it was bloody Jehovah's Witnesses again,' Peter says. He says it like that would have been preferable. Judith appears behind him, a smell of cooking following her.

'Come on in, then,' Judith says over Peter's shoulder. Inside only the light in the kitchen is on. The rest of the house is in darkness, except for the TV flickering in the front room. A quiz show, on silent.

'Sorry for interrupting your dinner,' Sam says.

'No worries, it's not ready for a while yet,' Judith says. 'You're welcome any time.' She gestures into the living room and puts on the light. She and Peter take up their customary positions. Judith is poised on the edge of the seat.

'We haven't talked about Victoria's boyfriend? You didn't really mention him,' Sam says.

Judith sits back. She'd been expecting news. She presses her lips together.

A hot pink tide rises up Peter's neck. 'Boyfriend?'

'Ryan?'

'I wouldn't say he was her boyfriend,' Peter says.

'The police knew all about him,' Judith says. 'She hadn't been seeing him long.'

'He wasn't her boyfriend,' Peter says through his teeth.

Sam pushes on. 'Mr Preston, I spoke to some of Victoria's friends and even to Ryan himself. They were seeing each other.'

'Well, why are you asking, then?' Peter says, voice even.

Judith's eyes glitter as they look between him and Sam.

'I went to see him… Ryan,' Sam says.

'Still lives round here, does he?'

'Yes, he has a family now. Three kids.'

Peter's lip curls. 'Has he got a proper job, though?'

'He works in a bookies. He had an accident.' Sam floats the idea. 'Couldn't work any more as a painter and decorator.'

'What kind of accident?' Judith says, her voice strained. But Peter's face hardens.

'Someone beat him up, by the sounds of it,' Sam says. 'Up on the moors. Damaged his knee permanently.'

Judith's face twists and she looks at Peter.

'He was obviously a wrong 'un, love,' Peter says. 'I am sure he got what he deserved from somebody.' Peter's voice is lower again now. He gives a small, sneery laugh. 'I think I heard something about that at the time, actually.'

'What do you mean by that?' Sam asks.

'What do you mean?' Judith repeats, addressing Sam.

Sam doesn't answer, keeping his eyes on Peter.

Peter stretches his hands above his head, casual. 'I heard some lads took him up on the moors and cracked his kneecap. Left him up there. So what?'

Judith lets out a strange, whimpering sound. The colour has drained from her face.

Peter grips her hand. 'Don't worry about him, love. People like him, they get what they deserve around here.'

'You know who did it, Mr Preston?'

'Me? Honestly? No. Could have been any one of a number of people who don't like his sort. Would I tell you if I did know? No, I wouldn't.'

'He says he was at home all night, the night Victoria went missing.'

Judith blinks, waiting for more.

'Seems like maybe Victoria was planning to go round and see him later, but she never got there.'

Judith shakes her head. 'Don't think so. She wouldn't have told us anyway, would she? But she'd have told Sylvie.' She rests her hand on Peter's knee.

'We wouldn't have bloody let her go and she'd have known it,' Peter cuts in. 'I told her she wasn't seeing him any more.'

Judith's eyes look like those of a frightened animal. She looks as if she's thinking about saying something, forming silent shapes with her lips, then stopping again.

'There's one other quick thing,' Sam says.

Judith seems to cower, waiting for the next blow.

'The emails you've had through the campaign website. Could I have another quick look through the folder?'

Judith thaws out at this. She is already getting to her feet. 'I printed them all out for you.'

She retrieves the folder from a drawer and hands it to Sam. 'What are you looking for?'

'It's nothing really. Just a quick detail I want to check.'

Judith hovers while Sam flicks through. The clock ticks round, punctuated by the sound of Peter's disgruntled breathing. The email from Tracey isn't there.

'How often do you check the inbox?' Sam says.

'Every day, of course. Morning and evening. Either Peter or I check in every day. We check junk and everything. Why do you want to know?'

'It's really nothing. Honestly.'

When Sam catches Peter's eye, he looks away.

'Is there *any* news?' Judith's eyes are turned up, willing him to give her something.

'Nothing at the minute, but I am making progress, Judith. I promise.'

Peter stands up and throws his newspaper onto the sofa. 'Seems to me you're achieving nothing more than upsetting my wife. Well, you invited this vulture in, Judith.'

'You will let me know anything, won't you, as soon as you know?' Judith says.

Peter walks out slamming the door behind him.

'Course. As soon as I can.' Sam avoids her eye. He chooses his words carefully. He'd initially planned to tell Judith and Peter about what Tracey said, but the missing email is stopping him. One of them has seemingly deleted it. Why? Deep down he knows that isn't his only reason, though. He doesn't want to spoil his chances of getting a scoop.

Sam leaves Judith leafing through the folder and lets himself out, closing the door quietly behind him. The smell of the cooking is stronger now. He pictures Judith and Peter eating in silence: determined, joyless chewing. After his visit, maybe they'll bin it altogether.

As he walks to his car, Sam thinks about Peter's reaction to Ryan. It's clear that Peter was either there on the moors when Ryan got attacked, or that he knows who did it, and likely encouraged them to do so. Who else would be that mad at Ryan?

More than that, though, Sam is surprised by the feeling that Judith knows something too. The tiniest shift in her expression gave it away. Maybe she'd known before tonight, maybe she hadn't. Maybe she'd never admit it anyway, not even to herself. But she knew about what had happened with Ryan. And yet, when they were talking about it, she'd put her hand on Peter's knee anyway.

Sam is fiddling with his phone when he gets into the hotel. Someone clears their throat from behind the desk. Janine. She scratches the end of her nose with the very tip of her nail.

'Someone waiting to see you,' she says. 'Woman.'

Sam thinks it must be Sylvie again, come to explain more, perhaps, tell him something else.

'Another one,' Janine says with a tinkle of amusement. 'She's round at the carvery.'

'Oh right, ta. Did she say what it was about? Leave a name?'

Janine shakes her head, paper-clipping a sheaf of papers. As he heads out he hears her muttering about how she isn't his 'bloody PA'.

In the carvery, there's one woman sitting in the bar area, sipping a glass of water. She sees Sam and gives him a little nod. He gets flashbacks to some of the excruciating dates he's been on since his divorce, that initial awkwardness.

As he gets closer, he recognises the face but can't quite place where from.

She half stands up to greet him, then sits back down. 'I saw you at the pub,' Tina says. 'The other night? With Martin.'

'Oh… Oh? Right, yeah.'

'Fancy a drink?' She gestures towards the bar.

'Erm, yeah, go on then.'

'I'll have a red wine,' she says and looks out of the window, towards the wooded area beyond the car park, as if there's anything to see. 'Large,' she adds, not turning her head.

Sam orders Tina's wine and the same for himself, and goes back to join her.

'How's your movie going?' Tina says, taking a long drink of her wine. The lights from a slot machine behind Sam are popping against her glass.

'Well, it's not really a movie, it's more of a…' Sam pulls himself back. 'Good, actually; it's going well. Better than I expected.'

Tina looks at him over the top of the glass, taking another sip. 'Someone bought it, have they? To put on the telly?'

'Well, not yet but…'

Tina gives a kind of smirk that Sam can't quite read.

'Remembered you said you were stopping next door. I weren't as pissed as you thought the last time I saw you, eh?'

Sam raises his glass, a mini cheers.

'Martin helping you a lot, is he?' Tina says then.

'Well, yeah, he's shown me about a bit and…' Sam snaps out of it. 'Sorry, I don't mean to be funny, but can I ask what this is about?'

Tina puts her drink down now, her previous bravado gone. She bites on the sides of her nails. 'How much do you know about him?'

'What do you mean?' Sam says. 'I just bumped into him. That's it.'

'Where? Where did you bump into him?'

Sam thinks for a moment. 'Just up at the lake. I was filming for the documentary.'

Tina shuffles forwards on her seat. She takes another slug of the wine and wipes her mouth with the back of her hand.

'He was married to my mate,' she says, her voice lowered even though there's no one around, except the barman. 'Manda.'

'Right,' Sam says. He's thinking how he doesn't want to get in the middle of a domestic, but something tells him to hear her out. She looks deadly serious now.

'So, what do you think that has to do with me, Tina?'

'They split up,' Tina says, checking around her again. 'I never really liked him, to be honest. There's something funny about him, don't you think?'

'I'm not sure that's really…'

Tina rolls her eyes. 'She told me something once, Manda. She doesn't know I'm here.'

'About Martin?' Sam says.

She nods, her mouth a hard, straight line. 'It wasn't why they split up. That was because he's a cold fish,' Tina says. 'But it wasn't that long after it happened – the girl Victoria dying – that they broke up. They'd been having a few issues.'

'OK…' Sam's mind whirrs at where this could be going.

'Anyway, she said that he came in late that night, the night she died, the girl at the lake, and that he had mud round the bottom of his jeans. He'd been out in the rain. And that in the days after he was acting "skittish".'

'Skittish?' Sam says.

'Her words,' Tina says, the drawbridge up again. 'Odd turn of phrase, I thought.'

Sam feels the hairs on the back of his neck prickle up. 'And did she go to the police?'

'No. Because they got back together after that. Limped on for another few years. You know how it is. They've split up for good now, but when I tried to raise it with her a couple of times, she pretends we never had that conversation. Says everyone suspected the blokes in their lives and I'm just getting muddled. She's a bit like that. She likes things a certain way.'

Tina knocks back a good half of her glass of wine. 'I don't get muddled, me,' she says. 'I know what she said.'

'So why haven't you gone to the police?'

'You not glad I've brought it to you?'

Sam takes a sip of his own drink. The wine creates a warm track down his throat.

'OK, then.' Tina holds a finger up. 'One: I don't trust pigs. My boy has been in bother with them and now they're always looking for ways to arrest him. When they could be spending their time looking for real criminals, like those who dump teenage girls in lakes. Two: I don't want Manda thinking I'm making trouble for her.' Tina holds up a third finger. 'Three: I want to be fair to the bloke, even if he does give me the willies. If I name names with the police, his card's marked. You come along, you're in a position to check it out, aren't you? Without his name being on some database forever if it turns out I'm talking out of my arse.'

Sam looks out at the silhouettes of the trees. In the window he can see the reflection of the bartender at the empty bar, polishing and rearranging glasses.

'You hear about people, though, don't you?' Tina presses on. 'Who insert themselves into the investigation. They get some sort of kick out of it. You don't think it's odd that he just showed up at the lake? Especially after what I'm telling you?'

'Did he know Victoria?'

'I don't bloody well know, do I? I don't see any decent reason why he should,' Tina says, slugging off the rest of her drink. 'He's hardly likely to tell me, is he?'

Sam is lost in thought, about exactly what Martin had said when he met him at the lake. How much he had given away to him.

'You're very welcome,' Tina says, huffy.

'Sorry.' Sam shakes himself out of it. 'Thanks, Tina. Thanks.'

'I trust my name'll not be attached to this when I am watching it on the telly.'

Sam takes a sip of the wine and raises the glass to Tina.

She walks out, looping a thin scarf around her neck.

CHAPTER TWENTY-SEVEN

Sylvie

I take my phone out and hover over Nathan's number. Despite everything, I just need to speak to someone who knows me, really knows me.

I hit dial with my thumb, close my eyes and wait. It's hardly one full ring until Nathan picks up.

'Sylvie?' Nathan's voice is infused with relief before he even finishes the word.

A long pause. 'I'm here,' I say.

We don't say anything else for a while, unsure of who will lead the way.

Nathan goes first. 'Where the hell are you?' he says. 'You haven't been in touch at all. You can't just do that, Sylvie. I was about to call the police.'

'I didn't know what to say to you, after that night, that row we had. You said you couldn't bear the sight of either of us, me or Victoria.'

Nathan lets out a sigh. 'Shit, sorry, I shouldn't have said that. I didn't mean it. Did I really say that?' His lovely Scottish voice.

We'd been playing with Victoria. A Sunday afternoon. Nathan joked that she didn't look much like him and he raised his eyebrows. Something shifted and it hung in the air. I was careful but my face must have given something away; a tiny flinch. That's the trouble when you get close to people, let them really get to know you. They can read even the smallest thing.

Nathan had recoiled, he was getting himself up from sitting on the floor.

'Sylvie? What's going on?' His voice was filling up with panic, a basement flooding.

I tried to arrange myself. It had come from nowhere. 'Don't be daft,' I said, but my voice sounded strained and thin. I could tell my eyes were flickering, neon signs of guilt.

'Sylvie?' Nathan's voice was more insistent. 'What the fuck is going on? Are you seeing someone else?'

'Noooo,' I said. But it sounded mocking, as if it was the most ridiculous thing in the world.

'Oh my God. You are, aren't you?'

I can still picture the look on his face. He staggered backwards as he stood up. It pains me to remember the look on his face.

'You can't just run off like that,' Nathan says now. 'And not be in touch. Where are you?' His voice is wary. 'Are you with him?'

'God, no! Don't think that. I'm at my mum's. She left me the house when she died. We obviously needed some time apart and I thought it would be as good a chance as any to sort the place out.'

'You never told me that, either.' I can tell he's shaking his head. 'You never said she left you the house.'

'I was just getting used to it myself,' I say. 'You know things were weird with me and her. And then things got weird with us and I had nowhere else to go.'

'How've you been? And Victoria?'

'You know… You?'

'Shit,' Nathan says. 'I haven't been able to sleep. I took some time off and I went back to my mum and dad's too. Cool off, you know. To think. I thought you'd be here when I got back.'

'And did you?' I say. 'Think?'

'A bit.'

'Did you tell your parents? Do they hate me now?'

'I didn't tell them, no. I just said we needed a bit of time apart.'

'Right.'

'What's his name?' Nathan says.

After a long pause, I say, 'It's Sean. His name is Sean.' It feels like the right thing to do. The truth would be worse. That I can't really remember his name.

Nathan had been away for work. Singapore. I was annoyed with him for travelling again and went to the pub with people from work. I didn't usually do that. He'd called me earlier in the day, saying the conference had gone well, that he was tired. I could hear music, laughing, glasses clinking in the background.

He said he was tired and it was stressful, a bit boring too, he wished he was at home. But I could detect a note in his voice that this wasn't really true; he just wished it was.

I didn't usually drink, but that day I just couldn't face another Friday night at home on my own.

It was a good night. One of those unplanned ones that just takes on a life of its own. One drink turned into five and ten and then who knows how many. We didn't bother eating anything; giddiness kicked in. Before I knew it, Beth and I were dancing in a nightclub in the centre of Glasgow.

The dance-floor lights revealed his face gradually, like a game-show puzzle. The memory is strobe-lit even now. It judders and pieces are missing; some have been edited in.

I stepped off the dance floor. I needed everything to stop moving. I knew he'd come over. Every time I looked across, he was staring at me, bottle tipped to his mouth.

'What's your name?' he shouted in my ear, the hairs on the back of my neck standing up.

I thought for a moment then I let myself get swept up. 'Ruby,' I said. I wanted to be someone else for the night and it wasn't hard to get into character. I was a writer, born in Manchester.

The room spun back at his flat, the edges were blurred. His bed sheets were black and there was a Mark Rothko print on the wall. When he was over me I kept seeing Nathan's face, then his again.

My body tightens even now when I remember snatches of the evening. A sharp jab of embarrassment, and something else too.

I crept out in the early morning, into my own clothes, back into my own bed and into my own life. It was easy in a way to rationalise it. Being that drunk, I hadn't been myself.

'I want to get past this, Sylv,' Nathan says, pulling me back out of that night once again.

'But what if she isn't...? Do you want to do a test to see if she's yours?'

'Is that what you want?' he says. 'If we say that she's mine, she can be. Like she was before.'

And I wonder if he's right. I think I want him to be.

'Are you alright, Sylvie? You sound really strange. I'll come and see you,' he says.

'No. I'll be home. We'll talk then. I'm going to come home. I'll come tomorrow.' Relief rushes through me at just the thought.

He exhales into the receiver. 'Thank God. Phone me or text me. I'll come and get you at the station.'

CHAPTER TWENTY-EIGHT

Sam

Before even leaving the carvery, Sam takes his phone out and opens a new text.

You about?

He sends it to Martin. The reply takes only minutes to come.

Pint? See you at the White Lion?

Sam taps his reply.

Maybe later. Fancy doing some night filming up at the lake first. See you there? Could pick your brains a bit more about Conley?

The reply bounces straight back.

OK! On my way.

Sam is surprised that, when he gets to the lake, Martin is already there, skimming stones across the water. He seems to have a knack for making them bounce.

'Alright, mate?' Martin says. He's still dressed in work clothes, his tie loosened at the collar, like someone cutting loose at the office party. He goes over to meet Sam and offers a hand with the camera, although Sam doesn't really need it. Automatically, they start to walk around the lake together.

'Thought you'd come up and get some more night filming, did you?' Martin asks. 'Few moody shots, eh?'

'Yeah. Should be heading off for a bit in the next few days. Got some stuff to do back at home,' Sam says. 'Can't live at the Travellers' Rest forever, can I? Much as I'd love to, of course.'

Sam is joking but Martin looks annoyed. 'You're heading off already?'

'Soon, like I said.'

'Bit soon to give up, isn't it?'

'I'm not giving up. I just need to take a break for a bit, take stock. Without paying for a crap hotel on top of my rent.'

Martin kicks at a stone on the ground. 'I don't see how you can be working on the documentary if you're not here.'

'Why are you so interested in this case, Martin?'

Martin looks up. 'I've told you. I lived here when it happened. It had an effect on the whole town.'

Martin runs on ahead to get in front, forcing Sam to stop, and turns to face him. He curls his lip and moulds his hair into a short-lived quiff that soon collapses.

'"Truth is like the sun. You can shut it out for a time, but it ain't going away,"' he says in a weak, lopsided Elvis impersonation.

Sam can't help but laugh, more at how surreal the moment is than Martin's impression being particularly amusing. More downright weird.

'What the hell was that?'

'Elvis said it, didn't he?' Martin says, returned to himself again now. He's walking backwards alongside Sam. 'You can't give up yet, is all I'm saying. Someone must know something and you just need to find them. I don't mean to have a go at you, sorry. I was just really excited about the work you're doing. To have someone finally care about this case, about this town.'

'I'm not giving up.' Sam tries but fails to drain the petty defensiveness out of his voice.

They stop at the picnic table again like when they first met. It's a good vantage point to get the whole of the lake in one shot.

'Have you been up here much? At night?' Sam asks, trying to sound casual.

Martin's head turns slowly. 'Me? Not really, no. Why would I?'

'Just asking,' Sam says. Martin's eyebrows crinkle up and Sam tries to weigh up whether it's exasperation or panic.

'Thought we could do a bit of filming with you, if that's alright? I mean, you know so much about the place; I think you'd actually be a good interviewee to have.' Sam pivots the camera towards Martin. Under the moonlight, he looks washed out, white skin, grey under the eyes.

'Well, I don't think I've really got much to add. I'm no connection to Victoria,' Martin says, trying to sidestep the camera's gaze, but Sam glides it along with him. 'I mean, I just offered to show you around when I saw you up here. I just don't…'

'It isn't only about Victoria though, is it? It's the era and the place and everything else, like you said, and you're perfect for that.'

Martin considers it. Before he can protest any more, Sam snaps the vice shut. 'What were you doing around the time of the murder?' He turns on the light clipped onto the camera.

Martin squints at the glare and puts his hand up to block it.

'Well, I… I wasn't doing anything.' He keeps moving and so does the camera, as if it is attached to him by string. 'I was just working and… you know, as you do. You're putting me on the spot now. It all sounds rather dull, doesn't it?'

Even in this light, Sam can detect a tightness around Martin's temples and eyes, a ripple in his voice.

'You don't remember any details? It's just most people seem to have quite specific memories. You know, like the thing where everybody knows where they were when Kennedy got shot? It's the same about that night round here, isn't it? So, where were you that night?'

'I wasn't alive when Kennedy got shot.'

'You know that isn't what I mean.' Now Sam is sure that Martin is flustered – his hand has drifted up to his hair twice before he remembers and puts it by his side again. 'I mean the night Victoria died and you know it.'

'I would have been asleep with my wife or maybe watching TV,' Martin says, a strange pitch to his voice. He speaks again then, more measured. 'Or it's possible I was working late. In fact, I think I probably was. Needed the money then. Yes, that was it.' Martin gives Sam a calm smile. 'I told you it wouldn't make very good TV. My life just isn't very exciting, I'm afraid.'

Sam won't let go now, smelling blood in the water. 'Were you ever questioned about it? I know lots of men around here were.'

Martin tries to step sideways again and stumbles over his own feet. One knee goes down on the grass. He pulls himself up again, mud up his trousers.

'Were you questioned?' Sam says again.

When Martin looks up at the camera, his hair is dishevelled, neck creased at a strange angle. 'No, I wasn't. What the hell has got into you? You're getting well off track here.' He tries to straighten his hair. 'I don't think I like where you're going with this.'

'I'm just wondering why it is you're so keen to help me out with this case,' Sam says, still filming. 'Were you out in the rain that night, Martin? Somewhere with a lot of mud?'

'I've got to go, sorry.' Martin slips again on the grass as he leaves, then speedwalks towards his car, breaking in and out of a run, looking back every few steps. Sam carries on filming him as he goes.

Sam hadn't been sure about what Tina said at the pub. She could have had her own motives. After his time working at the paper, it would be hard to surprise him about the things people would say to get one over on each other.

Perhaps he hadn't wanted to be wrong, either. He didn't know Martin well, at all. But his gut feeling about him was good, and Sam prided himself on that. It led to all the best stories and sources. And no alarms about Martin had been going off at all.

But Martin's reaction to his questions – it wasn't one of someone who had nothing to hide.

As Martin's car drives away, Sam realises his body is pulsing, his breath quick, as if he has just been running.

CHAPTER TWENTY-NINE

Sylvie

As I am putting things into my suitcase, the letter box clatters. I look out of the window and two of the children who were playing in the garden the other day, the ones who ran away, are crowded around the door, one of them crouched down, looking in through the letter box. The girl at the back sees me. She prods her friend and jumps. Both of them step back and look at me through the window. They laugh nervously before starting to go towards the steps, collecting their bikes on the way. I tap on the glass but it only hurries them up.

'Hey!' I shout after them, opening the front door, the cool air rushing in. 'What are you doing?'

The girls yelp and carry on towards the steps. One of them falls, her knee sliding along the ground. The other turns to look in horror, not knowing whether to stay and help or run and save herself from getting into trouble. I think of Michelle and the night at the lake, when we left her.

The girl on the ground starts to cry then scream. The concrete has torn her pink floral leggings at the knee and gnarled up the skin underneath too. The wound is pumping out blood and its edge is ragged and blackened.

The other girl looks up at me expectantly.

'Shit. Just wait here.'

I come back out with mum's first-aid kit and two cups of water. The girl is comforting her friend and the screaming has given way to sobbing and sniffing.

I give the injured girl one cup of water to drink and pour the other one gradually over the cut, the blood and dirt clearing away. She blinks up at me, the tears splaying her lashes out like a doll's.

'What's your name?' I say, crouching down, my knees clicking.

'Jessica.' She sniffles.

I squeeze her foot gently. 'We need to dress this wound, don't we?'

She nods as I unwrap an antiseptic wipe.

'We need to clean it first with one of these.' I open up the tissue and it unleashes a medicinal smell. Jessica shrinks backwards. The shadow of the other girl, gathered close, casts us in a gloom.

'It's going to hurt a little bit but we need to make sure it's clean, don't we?'

Jessica starts to shake her head.

'Can you be brave, Jessica?'

She steals a little glance up at me.

'Can you dab this on your knee? It will sting for a few seconds then it will be all done.'

Jessica nods, cautious, and she takes the wipe, her hand hovering over her knee. I brace myself as she goes for it and lets out a little wail, dabbing her skin a few times, then lifting the tissue away and trying to catch her breath.

I pat some cream on the wound and put a plaster on it, tapping it lightly. 'All done. Well done, Jessica.'

The colour starts to come back into her face and she pushes her hair from her eyes with clumsy, splayed hands.

'Where's the lady?' she says, pointing to the house.

'Margaret?' I follow her gaze.

Jessica shrugs and the other girl says, 'We are here to see the lady who lives in the house.'

'Why do you want to see her?' I say.

'Who are you?' Jessica asks, an edge of fear creeping into her voice.

'This is my mum's house,' I say, and she blinks in the last of the day's sun.

'Your mum?' she says, voice full of wonder, and I nod.

'Where is she?' The other little voice pipes up. 'She lets us play in the garden and now it's locked.' The girl points to the gate down the side of the house. I bolted it after I found the doll.

'The lady,' Jessica says. 'She used to leave us stuff in the garden, to find. Toys and chocolate. And now we can't get in. Is she inside? Is she poorly?'

'She went away,' I say. 'She died.'

The girls look around at each other, confusion in their faces. They fall silent.

'Now that I know who you are and that you were Mum's friends, I'll leave the gate open. I have to go soon, too, but I'll leave it open for you so you can go in and play.'

The sound of Victoria crying drifts out of the house, and the girls' eyes light up. Mum has been forgotten again already, for the time being.

'Wait here,' I say, and I bring Victoria outside. Jessica pulls herself up to standing, not putting her weight on the injured leg.

'This is baby Victoria,' I say, bending down so they can see.

The girls are transfixed, squealing. 'She's so cute. Aaaah.' Jessica takes Victoria's little hand in hers and Victoria kicks her legs in delight.

'Can we take the baby out for a walk?' Jessica says, and I stand back up straight.

'No, she's too little for that. And so are you.'

'We're not,' says the other little girl. '*Pleeeeeeeeeaaasse.* We'll bring her straight back.'

I pull Victoria closer to me, her back to the children. 'Be careful on that leg,' I say to Jessica. 'And you can play in the garden any time. Just be careful.'

The girls gather the bikes, dragging them down the steps. 'Bye-bye, baby Victoria,' they shout, waving and giggling.

As I step back inside, I see it on the mat and acidic saliva forces itself up my throat.

Another brown envelope.

This time I don't wait. I rip the envelope straight open and shove my hand inside. It's cold, metal; a thin chain. When I pull it out and hold it up, the room feels as if it spins like a funhouse. It's the gold chain with the heart-shaped locket, the one they said Victoria was missing that night, that never turned up.

My fingers are shaking but I am eventually able to turn it over – the 'VP' engraving is there like I knew it would be.

Before I wasn't sure. Now I am certain. Someone knows what happened to Victoria that night and this is a message.

I start to throw things into my bags. If I leave soon I can get back to Glasgow tonight instead of tomorrow.

CHAPTER THIRTY

Sam

At the hotel, Sam is wired. He has been watching all the footage he's captured all day. After he saw Martin at the lake last night, something almost clicked but it keeps zipping back out of view.

He watches the reconstruction video again, then closes the tab on his screen. After what Tracey said, there's a possibility it isn't accurate, but it's still burned in, even the smallest details can't be unpicked or forgotten.

On his camera, he watches the recording of Sylvie again, when she was here in the hotel room. Sam tries to avoid looking at himself on camera. He doesn't want to think about his jowls or the slowly growing gut, which always seems to look worse on film. He'd put himself in the shot to put Sylvie at ease, make her feel less like she was being interrogated. A mean trick really, but it worked.

When he's pushing Sylvie on whether she walked Victoria home that night, he is surprised at himself, at how aggressive he looks. He invaded Sylvie's personal space more than he had realised. Her knuckles are white, the duvet cover clutched tight in her fist.

Studying Sylvie's face, though, which is usually the giveaway, she looks sincere, like she's telling the truth. What Tracey said she saw, or didn't see, could be different things blurring into one to create false memories.

Sam watches the recording of Martin at the lake. That's a different story, compared to Sylvie's. Martin's face is pure panic. He definitely has something to hide. Sam watches the part back again where Martin says the Elvis quote. It still seems inappropriate and bizarre in the circumstances, but maybe that was Martin's plan; to throw Sam off, lighten the mood.

As he plays it again, a flare of recognition ignites Sam's mind for a second, and then it's gone again. Trying to get it back is like a strip light struggling to stutter on, the bulb on its way out. He's heard someone say those words before... he can hear them in his head. Not Elvis, though. The voice isn't Elvis. His mind strains. It's silent at first. Then Sam hears the phrase being said in his own voice.

And it clicks. He's seen it written down. A bumper sticker when he went to America? A T-shirt? Then, it appears. Sam reaches for his laptop, the screen gone to sleep, and wills it to wake up faster. He logs on to SomeoneMustKnow and navigates to the thread where he first found out about Victoria's case. At first nothing leaps out at him. Maybe it wasn't here. He scans through the posts, then he sees it. It isn't really part of a post at all. AaronInBetween started the thread about Victoria's murder and has regularly 'bumped' the thread to push it back up to the top of the forum. There, in AaronInBetween's signature, underneath each of his posts – *there it is.*

Truth is like the sun. You can shut it out for a time, but it ain't going away.

AaronInBetween – Here, there and everywhere.

Sam thinks about what Tina said, about people inserting themselves into the investigation.

Martin is AaronInBetween... or he at least reads Someone-MustKnow. Why has he never mentioned it?

CHAPTER THIRTY-ONE

Sylvie

The evening is getting on; I've been about to set off for ages but I keep finding one last little thing I need to do. Putting off leaving here, or putting off seeing Nathan? Soon, though, it will be too late. If I go now for the train, I can still get there today, home.

One final look around the house, the wild garden, the threadbare carpets and filthy curtains.

Standing at the bottom of the stairs, Victoria all bundled up, I look at the place where Mum fell, staring at the faded, peeling wallpaper. I turn the front door handle and cold air rushes in. It's likely the last time I'll ever be here. The finality of it pushes my breath back.

I can almost see Mum and Dad, and me, moving through the house. I think of the girls playing and the chocolates and toys Mum left for them in the garden. Stupid sentimentality kicks back in, the overwhelming feeling that I have to take something physical with me. Solid objects are indisputable; memories can't be trusted.

I run into the living room and grab the snow globe; the one with the gold glitter sand. There's one more thing too. I deliberate for a moment. Last chance.

'Two seconds, Victoria, and then we are going to see Daddy.' It already feels stilted as soon as it's out, now that I have talked to Nathan. It's a white lie, but it trips off the tongue. They start early.

I run upstairs to get the starry lamp. Victoria loves it so much. Then I can't stop myself – I have to look in Mum's room one last time. I close my eyes and think of Dad, try to take a snapshot with my mind, a memory of when I'd jump in their bed on Saturday mornings and we'd all eat toast and listen to the radio, huddled under the covers. I still have that, amongst everything else. I want to try to give Victoria that.

I can be on the train in an hour, Conley getting further and further away by the second, smaller and smaller. Soon, it will just be the past again.

Ready? *As I'll ever be.* Another of Dad's stock phrases.

I go back downstairs. I can feel myself getting lighter already. But then I feel it, like a strange hand on my shoulder… something isn't right. A bolt of shock, then a forced slow breath. The pram is empty; the breeze coming through the door. I know I didn't leave her in the living room, or on the play mat, but I look anyway.

I sweep back through the kitchen; it doesn't make sense. The house is silent. Eerily silent. I tear upstairs and around all the rooms. I look outside too.

The street is dark and it's empty. Victoria is gone.

CHAPTER THIRTY-TWO

Sam

Sam watches the door of the building, people trickling out one by one. He has been sitting in his car, lights off, for over an hour, in the business park at the edge of Conley. Just the sight of the place – with its sandstone pillars at the entrance and Scalextric-like road layout, the industrial units and bland offices – makes Sam feel heavy inside. He'd always felt lucky working at the paper; rarely resented going in. Agencies had been in touch offering him marketing or managerial work on developments like this. So far, he'd managed to stay out of their grasp, avoid real life, but for how long?

He starts to wonder if he's missed Martin, but finally he emerges into the autumn evening, manoeuvring himself into his coat.

Sam gets out of his car, slamming the door loudly. Martin looks once and then twice but tries to make it seem as though he hasn't noticed Sam. The quickening of his pace, the speed he puts his head down, give the bluff away.

Sam shouts Martin's name across the car park, but Martin just pops up his collar and breaks into a strange half-run, half-hop again, like at the lake.

'Martin!'

Martin is at his car now, fumbling with the keys in the lock.

'Aaron!' Sam shouts and Martin stops what he's doing then. 'AaronInBetween.'

Martin turns around slowly. He looks at Sam then hurries to try to get into his car, all fingers and thumbs. Sam runs over.

'I know that you're AaronInBetween on the website, Martin. On SomeoneMustKnow.'

More of Martin's co-workers are filing out from the office now.

'Will you stop shouting?' Martin hisses.

'Well, talk to me, then.'

'Get in the car,' Martin says, getting into the driving seat himself. He starts the car before Sam has a chance to put his seatbelt on and drives out of the car park. They don't speak until they reach a lay-by, where Martin pulls in. He takes the keys from the ignition. On balance, Sam unclips his seatbelt, just in case.

'What the hell are you playing at, coming to my work?'

'I needed to see you,' Sam says. 'You ignored my texts about meeting up.'

'Damn right I did after the other day. I don't know what has got into you, Sam.'

'Oh, spare me the wounded act, please. Was it you? Started the threads on SomeoneMustKnow?'

Martin pinches the top of his nose like he has a sharp headache.

'Is there something you want to tell me, Martin?'

Martin grips the steering wheel and lightly bounces his head off the centre of it a few times. The atmosphere is uneasy in the dark car. Sam repositions his feet to make sure he can get out quickly if it kicks off.

'Do you know something, Martin? About what happened to Victoria?'

Martin doesn't speak but he keeps shaking his head, more insistent.

'Will you please just stop pecking away at me like this?' Martin's breath is shallower and faster but Sam's blood is up too.

'Why did you have mud on your trousers the night she died, Martin? Why were you agitated after?'

Martin lifts his head from the steering wheel now. 'What?' He starts to breathe as if into a paper bag. 'This is getting out of hand now,' he says between gasps.

Sam looks straight ahead. He isn't falling for the panic attack routine and he wants to make sure Martin knows it. This feels like his first breakthrough. His grip is only tightening.

Martin turns his head to the side. 'You can't think that I had something to do with it? With that girl's death?'

'I think you've not been straight with me. And I'm wondering why,' Sam says. 'You've forced yourself into this investigation. I'm struggling to see why.'

Martin straightens himself up. 'You've got this all wrong.'

'So, tell me.' Sam does a mental calculation of the three moves he'd need to do to get out of the car. It's completely dark outside, there's no ambient light where they are. All Sam can see is himself and Martin reflected back.

'I was there,' Martin says, finally. 'But I never touched her.'

Sam doesn't dare to speak. Martin's gaze is pointing down into the footwell.

'I went up there to... *meet people*,' he says.

'Meet people? Meet who?'

'Just people. Please don't make me spell it out, eh? It's excruciating enough as it is.'

'I'm listening,' Sam says.

Martin's breathing is more regular again. 'I was there... waiting in the erm... well I was walking round the car park... you know, to see if anyone was around. It started to rain. Such heavy rain. And so no one came that night. In the end, I decided to just get back in the car and go home.'

'So, hang on, who were you meeting?'

'For Christ's sake, that isn't the point. It doesn't work like that. You just go up there. It was all arranged word of mouth then. Whoever turns up turns up.'

'You weren't meeting Victoria?'

Martin's face reddens. 'No, not bloody Victoria! Probably a lumpy middle-aged couple, to be honest. Jesus, do you want to hear this, or don't you?'

'Sorry, go on.'

'So, as I was leaving because of the rain, that's when I saw her. Victoria.'

The air in the car feels completely still. Sam doesn't dare speak.

'I didn't... I don't... want people to know I was up there. Why I was up there. And let's face it, there isn't really another reason I can say I was up there. Not at that time of night.'

'I see,' Sam says.

'Finally! But no one showed up that night,' Martin says. 'Because of the rain, no doubt. So I waited for a while but you know, the er... the moment had passed, so to speak. So I set off home again. And I saw her... Victoria... in the car. It wasn't the taxi, definitely not. I've seen that in the reconstruction and in the paper. It was a different car.'

'Was she alive?'

Sam's breath is held again, his chest tightening. The windows in the car are steaming up from their breathing.

'Oh yes, she was alive. She looked like she was having an argument with whoever she was with. Nothing violent. But... heated, I'd say.'

Sam tries to take it in.

'OK. So why didn't you just come to me? Tell me straight what had happened? What's all this AaronInBetween business? Lurking about on SomeoneMustKnow?'

'Fuck's sake,' Martin says. 'I feel a bit of an idiot, to be honest. I've always followed the case. And I saw Victoria's mum on the news and I had to do something but I didn't know what. But now you can see why I couldn't just come forward. I don't really want my name attached. So I thought if I got something new going on

SomeoneMustKnow about the case, maybe that would push some new information out, like it did in those cases in America. And it wouldn't matter any more that I hadn't come forward personally. But I'd still know I'd helped, that I hadn't just let it go.'

Sam stares at the sloping windscreen of the car.

'And AaronInBetween? What's that all about?'

Martin's face brightens a bit at that. 'Aaron. It's Elvis's middle name, isn't it? AaronInBetween. Get it?' He looks pleased with himself.

Sam slaps his own forehead lightly and groans.

The mood in the car darkens again. 'I'm not the only one telling porkies, am I?' Martin says.

'How do you mean?' Sam doesn't follow.

'Your man on the dirt track, following your sister in the car when you were young.' Martin puts quote marks round his words. 'That isn't true, is it?'

Sam straightens up. 'Why do you say that?'

'Just didn't ring true,' Martin says, 'Not when you said it and not now either.'

'It did happen.' Sam fidgets in the seat. He'd got carried away when he'd told Martin the story, trying to justify himself. The interest in Victoria's case had felt grubby sometimes, something to be ashamed of. Like the times he lied about reading true crime books, pretended it was something more academic or literary.

'If you say so.' Martin isn't convinced.

Sam had seen something that night, not his sister, like he'd said. The man had been there and he'd come towards Sam. He'd felt uncomfortable and he'd run away. But the car hadn't followed Sam; the man never got out. That was where the story took off on its own; that's how it went when Sam's mind had skipped ahead at the time.

'OK, I'll be straight with you,' Sam says. 'I don't have a sister. I just wanted to make you believe I care about Victoria's case and making this documentary. Because I do. I wanted you on side.'

'Well, that's better than saying something like that about a real sister, I suppose.' Martin's demeanour is friendlier again.

The heat has gone out of the atmosphere in the car, something of a truce.

After a while, Martin says, 'So, do you want to know what else I saw that night or not…? It's about the driver.'

Sam twists in his seat towards Martin, glad the spotlight is off him.

CHAPTER THIRTY-THREE

Sylvie

I want to let out a guttural scream until my throat burns or bleeds, but nothing will come. I stand in the street, a tangle of competing thoughts. I stare at my phone for where to seek help, and it stares back, blank.

Then one sharp, deep breath: a moment of clarity. The Polaroid of the lake, the doll in the pond, the locket.

I know where Victoria will be.

Hope surges at that for a second, then quickly retreats again. Who has her?

The little girls' calls: 'Can we take the baby out…?'

Everyone wants the baby: Michelle, Nathan, Judith…

All the way there, my feet feel weighted. My chest burns, lungs straining, currents of pain running up my legs. But the thought of her without me, her little face. Does she know she's in danger? Is she scared? Will the lake poison her life too?

Finally, after what feels like hours, I reach the lake. I scan the horizon but I can't focus; I'm trying to take it all in at once. It's all blurred lines. My eyes are drawn to the water, all along its unbroken surface. I try not to admit it even to myself, but I'm looking for tell-tale ripples, a blanket floating to the top… I couldn't go on.

What if I have come here and she isn't here? It could be a trick to get me out of the way, and all the while Victoria is getting further and further away.

This time I do scream; it breaks out of me of its own accord. The echoes sound like birds screeching overhead.

I have to regroup. I force myself to scan more slowly, and I see it: a shape on the bench, Victoria's blue blanket, and I start to run. It feels like I'm barely gaining any ground, stepping in glue, but soon I am in reaching distance, almost. I stretch out my hand for it, leaning down to touch it.

'I'm here, Victoria, Mummy's here.'

But the blanket is empty, as if she has vaporised in front of me; a terrible magic trick. I grab it and it unravels and catches on the wind. Her little pink rabbit falls out and lands on the ground, mud spoiling its face. The blanket still feels warm. I push it to my face and it smells of her. I breathe it in.

Victoria, though, isn't anywhere to be seen. Across the fields it's a solid, opaque black. The darkness is creeping further and further in.

I take out my phone and punch in 999. I keep missing the numbers because my hands are shaking. The three 9s stay there on the screen but I can't press the call button.

It's a trap bringing me here. The mouse's leg, the torn-off flesh. I cancel it and put my phone away again.

Someone is coming over the hill where the car park is. I narrow my eyes, force them to focus. They're holding something, cradling it.

Relief is soon swept away by dread. There is no sound. That awful space. Like when she was born. All at once, I am sorry for every time I have despaired at Victoria crying, when I have waited to go to her that fraction longer.

The person stays in silhouette for a long time, like a cut-out from a photograph. My feet drag me towards them, but as they get closer a hand juts out to warn me to stay back. And then, Victoria turns her head in her hood.

'Please give her to me. Please.'

A gesture for me to move backwards.

'Hi darling,' I say to Victoria, waving at her. No proper voice comes out, just strained air, like someone is sitting on my chest.

I keep eye contact with Victoria. Her head bobs, saliva bubbling on her lips.

'Why have you brought me here? Why are you doing this? Is this about something Sam said?'

'Don't insult my intelligence, Sylvie.'

'Why are you doing this?'

'You know why, Sylvie. I know you do. Tell me what happened to Victoria, Sylvie. I need to hear it in your own words.'

'I don't know what you mean.'

'If you want to be there for this little girl, you'll tell me. All of it, Sylvie. I need to hear from you. And I'll know if you're lying.'

CHAPTER THIRTY-FOUR

When Sylvie and Victoria emerged from Sylvie's room, the party had emptied out. Sylvie was coaxing Victoria downstairs.

Sylvie stood on the landing and put her finger on her lips. She opened her parents' bedroom door as quietly as she could. It creaked loudly anyway, but her dad didn't wake up. He was sleeping on his back, body propped up with pillows. She closed the door.

Downstairs, through the kitchen window, Sylvie watched her mum picking things up in the garden. Victoria was too drunk now and she was in one of her moods. Sylvie needed to get rid of her or get her to bed.

The music was still playing and when they went into the living room, Victoria turned it up. 'Dance Away' played out and Victoria spun and mock-pirouetted around the coffee table, pretending to sing into a half-empty wine bottle she picked up from the table. Then she took a swig from it. She couldn't walk straight, she was knocking things over. Victoria stood on the edge of the paper table-cloth, bringing a glass bowl of crisps crashing to the floor.

'Maybe you should go home,' Sylvie said. 'Or you can stay here.'

'Ugh, no thanks.'

Sylvie looked at the door. 'OK, well you could go and see Ryan. I'll walk you halfway.'

Victoria mimicked her, her face all screwed up. She relaxed it then and it smoothed out again.

'I think I should have a word with your dad before I go. Thank him for the party.'

'He's asleep.'

'Then I'll wake him up,' Victoria said, drinking from the bottle and burping.

'What is *wrong* with you tonight?'

Victoria suddenly put her hand up to her mouth and picked up the wastepaper bin. She bent over it, a slurry of liquid shooting out of her mouth. A short period of calm then another spurt. Sylvie went to her and rubbed her back. She felt sorry for her now.

She hoped this would signal the end of it, that Victoria would go home, sleep it off.

Sylvie tried to pull Victoria's hair back from her face. It was dangling into the bin, getting matted with vomit. Victoria turned her head slowly. She was still gasping for breath and her eyes were bloodshot, a string of spittle dangling from her mouth.

Her eyes were rolling in her head slightly. How much had she had? She started to stand up, steadying herself on the fireplace, wiping her mouth with her sleeve. The room smelled sweet, sickly.

'Maybe I will go in there and chat with your dad now, shall I, Sylvie?'

Sylvie heard her mum in the kitchen now, crockery clinking. The tension hovered between them.

'What is your problem with my dad?' As soon as she'd said it, she wished she hadn't asked. Victoria hadn't acted like this before. Something was wrong.

'I saw them.' Victoria got right up in Sylvie's face. Her breath smelled sugary and putrid at the same time, a blast of rhubarb and custard boiled sweets.

'I saw them, Sylvie,' she said again. 'This afternoon. He had his hand in her knickers. Upstairs in the bathroom.' Victoria spat out the word knickers, a horrible hand movement to accompany it – waggling her fingers like a dying insect struggling on its back.

She didn't say who but the realisation started to solidify in Sylvie's mind.

Victoria was slurring badly, her face white and waxy, a sheen of sweat. She looked at Sylvie to take in the impact of the blow she had delivered.

She made a gesture to move towards the door, to go upstairs. Sylvie tried to block her way but Victoria powered past her. Sylvie reached out to grab her, but Victoria yanked away, part of her nail tearing, releasing a burst of agony and anger.

Sylvie examined her finger, tears filling up her eyes. There'd be no choice but to rip the rest of it off. 'Don't you dare go up there.' Sylvie could feel the panic lurching up her body and sticking in her chest. The horror of the idea.

'Your mum,' Victoria jabbed the air, 'was with my dad!' The horrible hand movement again, a nasty little laugh. A look of panic that she was going to be sick again quickly subsided. 'It's disgusting.' Victoria retched, swallowing something down. 'Your dad is dying.'

Sylvie's heart stopped in her chest.

'Your dad is up there dying and your mother is already setting up his replacement.'

The door handle turned.

It was all in slow motion after that, a blur.

CHAPTER THIRTY-FIVE

Sylvie

Peter pulls Victoria's hood around her face to shield her from the cold wind. You feel it more up here – there's nothing to protect you. I am starting to shake, teeth chattering.

Peter. Why is he doing this? I try to fill in the gaps so I can think ahead.

My phone rings. Nathan. Peter holds his hand out, beckoning for the phone, impatient. I try to answer it first but it doesn't work. He snatches it from me and launches it into the lake. A splash, a few ripples and it's quickly under.

'I bumped into your mother in the town one day,' Peter says. 'Must've been fate because I rarely go to the shops. Judith does all that stuff. But I went in that day for some reason. The weather was nice and I wanted to be out of the house. That'll teach me.'

He lets it hang in the air then carries on. 'I saw her in the pound shop buying a load of old tat. Figures, doesn't it? She was embarrassed when she saw me. Too right, she should have been embarrassed the state she looked. But old muggins here, I was glad to see her. Victoria's anniversary was coming up, Judith was clucking around about it being in the paper. I was happy to see a friendly face. I'd missed her in a way. We always got on well, me and your mother.'

A scoffing laugh escapes from me. 'So I gathered.'

He shoots me a look of disgust. 'The thing is, I actually felt sorry for her.' His turn to scoff now. 'I felt terrible about how she'd ended up. Living like a pig. Can you imagine? It was disgusting but I felt bad! Me! So, I started going round there a bit. She wanted to get herself sorted out.'

'Were you seeing each other again?'

He laughs at that again, a horrible, hollow laugh.

'No, we were not. Aside from the fact that house made my fucking skin itch. How can anyone live like that? Aside from that, I couldn't, could I? After the last time, I always felt that maybe I was being punished. And, if it wasn't for us, she might…'

He knows.

I see my chance to get some answers of my own. 'I used to think she really went jogging, out for walks, you know. My mum. I even do it myself. Pathetic. But she was meeting you, wasn't she? All that time.'

'Well, she certainly got some exercise,' he says, an ugly curl of his lip.

'When did you start seeing each other?'

Peter doesn't answer but I can tell it's thrown him off.

I ask him again.

'It was before your dad became ill. The Christmas before. I did actually love her once, you know. I wouldn't have risked everything like that if I didn't.'

He grits his teeth, jaw set. 'I was helping her, you know, I was round there helping her clean that shit tip of a house up. My skin was crawling. But I felt sorry for her living like an old bag lady. Turns out she got what she deserved. Maybe we all do, Sylvie.'

'Victoria doesn't deserve this, does she?'

But he refuses to catch my eye and it's as if I haven't spoken.

'She thought I'd left one day, but I came back for something and I heard her on the phone, saying she needed to talk to you about Victoria, there was a journalist sniffing round.'

I think back to the voicemail she left me. I only listened to 'It's me, Sylvie…' before hitting delete.

'I walked in and her face said it all: it was pure dread. Don't know why your dad couldn't see what was going on, right under his own nose. She always was an open book, your mother.'

There's an unexpected flash of jealousy in me at that. I don't think I ever understood her; I barely scratched the surface.

I step forwards to try to take Victoria, but Peter snatches her to the side.

He goes on, seemingly talking into the air rather than to me. 'I knew something was up after that so I bided my time. Then she wrote you a letter. Poor little Sylvie, so very far away. I saw it on the dresser and I thought *hello* and I steamed it open. How very *motherly* of her to look out for you like that, eh?'

'What did it say?' Maybe there's still a way to get around this, I think. I could dig a deeper hole yet.

'When I confronted her, she was flailing around like a hooked fish. She wrote that you should sit tight and "stick to the story" if Sam came knocking. She said it would all be fine. What a loving, caring mummy.'

I wonder what else it said, the letter.

'Someone emailed the campaign website, not long after your Mum died. She said she'd only seen Victoria walking home, not you.'

I think of what Sam said in the hotel room, my mind trying to scramble ahead, losing its footing.

'And I knew for sure then that that you knew something. I couldn't let Judith see it.'

I can hear my own breath, loud and strange.

I'm surprised when he doesn't push the issue, but the change of tack is even worse. 'After, I found the locket in your room, squirrelled away like something to be ashamed of.'

I feel queasy thinking of him going through my things.

My mind is replaying what he said and a murky feeling in my stomach starts to swirl and curdle. 'After? You said after. After what...?'

'Do you know?' Peter says, his voice bright as an actor. 'Accidents on stairs kill at least two people every day in the UK. Women are more likely to fall. I heard it on the radio not long after, it was maybe even the next day. Funny thing that type of timing, isn't it? You don't think about something and then suddenly, poof, it's everywhere. There's probably a word for it, isn't there?'

I feel like I am going to be sick. Sourness in my mouth, like I can taste all that death, all that rotting.

He's supporting Victoria with just one arm now. It looks like she could fall. I have my hands out ready to spring.

'She was always quite a limited woman in her own way,' he says.

'So why did you have an affair with her then? If she was so dull in your eyes?' I can't help but stick up for her, even now.

'Because I was bored shitless, Sylvie,' he hisses. 'And so was she. She probably wasn't getting it from poor old Michael, was she, let's face it. You'll see.' He kisses the top of Victoria's head. 'Mummy will see one day, won't she? Or maybe she already has. There's no sign of Daddy, is there?'

'Were you going to leave Judith?'

'I couldn't, not after Victoria. I couldn't do that to her.'

'And before?'

'Probably not, no.' His face is a sneer. 'She didn't die straight away, you know. She was in pain for a while.'

At first I think he's talking about Victoria, but my brain catches up and I feel winded.

'Yes, I "helped" her down the stairs. Then I didn't tell anyone about it. Not going to get on your high horse about that, are you?'

I think of how long she was lying there alone, and after. How the body would have started to smell. My throat constricts and I gag.

'She took a good shove as well. She'd stacked some weight on over the years. She used to have so much pride in her appearance, didn't she? Proper little looker she was when she was younger. The noise your mum made when she landed.'

I think of that moment now, when the bone snaps.

'I thought she might go through the floor. Talk about going down like a sack of shit.'

'You killed her?' I have to hear him say it.

'An eye for an eye,' he says. 'Never was the religious type, really, but we all do Christmas, don't we, so you won't mind if I pick and choose.'

'But Victoria's death was an accident. I was there.'

His face tightens then, a straight, lipless smile. Now he knows I was there, if he didn't already.

'Please just give me the baby, Peter. We can talk, but please just give me the baby. It's nothing to do with her. Victoria wouldn't want this.'

He seems to ignore what I said, though. 'The thing is your mother didn't tell me the whole truth, but you're going to, Sylvie. And remember I will smell the stink of it if you are lying.'

CHAPTER THIRTY-SIX

Summer, 1995

Margaret came into the front room, whipping the door closed behind her.

'What's going on in here?' She sniffed the air. 'Sylvie, have you been sick?'

Victoria stifled a laugh, catching Margaret's eye.

'What the hell is going on in here, girls?' she said through her teeth.

Victoria hiccoughed and it morphed into a burp. She covered her mouth like she might be sick again, but then seemed to steady herself. 'I know what you've been up to, Mrs Preston.'

'Victoria, shut up!' Sylvie tried to read her mum's expression, gauge the reaction. She needed a way to calm the situation down.

'Your husband is dying and you... you've been fucking my dad.'

Sylvie flinched at the word, the image.

Margaret stood still for a minute, like she'd been slapped across the face. Sylvie waited for her mum to deny it, but she just looked at Victoria, her face hardening.

Victoria's voice was getting louder. 'All this time it was you, when Dad says he's working late. When they're arguing. There's a time bomb about to go off in your husband's head and you do *that* at his own weirdo death party. A funeral for someone who isn't even dead. *Yet*,' she added with extra spite.

'You don't know what you're talking about, Victoria. You've had a bit to drink. We all have. Let's get you up to bed and this will all look a lot better in the morning. Sylvie, get the camp bed and fetch her a nighty. Now.'

Victoria looked as if she was thinking about this for a moment, but then her fury was reignited. 'Nah, fuck that. Let's see what poor old Michael Armstrong has to say about it, shall we? See how he likes it. I saw you in the bathroom.'

Victoria made a sudden move to the left, like she was a football player doing a fancy move to fool the other team. She lunged for the door.

Margaret's head spun back around quickly to Sylvie. A look of blurred shock and anger twisted into her face. As quickly as Victoria had moved, Margaret stepped forwards, both her arms out. They made contact with Victoria and she went backwards.

Sylvie watched the look on Victoria's face in slow motion as she fell over the coffee table, her arms and hands flailing for something to grab on to, to break her fall. But she couldn't connect with anything. It was just empty air. There was one sharp crack, her head against the marble step of the fireplace. The CD skipped once when she hit the ground, then played on.

Victoria was splayed on the floor, one leg twisted out awkwardly to the side, an impossible position. For a moment neither Sylvie or Margaret did anything. Sylvie didn't even breathe. The silence was the worst thing. All that moved were the tethered balloons, gently floating and bobbing.

Victoria's eyes were gaping wide. She should have blinked by now.

Sylvie's thoughts skipped ahead to bright red blood pooling out all over the floor, wider and wider. But there wasn't any. It was all inside Victoria's head, pressure building up, blackening.

Margaret seemed to snap out of it. She opened the door, listened for a moment, then closed it again. Sylvie understood the noise

had not woken her dad. Nothing much did these days. He had
to be shaken most mornings. One day soon, not even that would
do it. It was unspoken between Sylvie and her parents, but deep
down she knew it.

Margaret gestured for Sylvie to stay put. She crossed the room
and put her hand on Victoria's neck. Sylvie couldn't take it in.
She couldn't be dead. Not Victoria. Not here, not like this. The
room swam.

Margaret turned back to Victoria and put her ear close to her
mouth, shaking her lightly.

Sylvie went over to the telephone table, picked up the receiver
and took a deep breath. She dialled 9, 9… but her mum jumped
up and snatched the receiver out of her hand, replacing it in the
cradle. Sylvie went to speak but no words came out. Her mum
didn't say anything either. She just stared right into Sylvie's eyes.
Something was passing between them, something was happening
that they both knew couldn't be undone.

Margaret grabbed Sylvie hard by the wrist and pulled her to the
side. Sylvie was shaking. She started to cry, almost convulse. Her
mum grabbed her by the chin and held it in position, vice-like.
'Are you listening to me, Sylvie? You need to take deep breaths
and you need to listen to me, right?'

Sylvie couldn't speak but she somehow managed to nod.

'I'm going to get the car ready and you're going to wait out in
the hall until I tell you.'

Maybe they were going to the hospital? Sylvie knew they weren't
really but she nodded, trying to persuade herself that they were.

It was a bad dream. It was all that stupid booze they'd drunk. *Why?*

She would wake up soon and Victoria would be there, like
always. They'd be topping and tailing in the bed…

Sylvie tried not to look back at Victoria, but she couldn't help
it. It was as if she was trying to understand that painful, unnatural

position. *So still.* Victoria's top had ridden up, her midriff displayed. Sylvie couldn't bear to touch her though.

Sylvie sat on the sofa and clutched her head. She tried to focus on the pattern on the carpet. Anything but Victoria. Red and gold, dark blue flowers. She looked at them so long they started to move. They shifted and swirled, kaleidoscopic.

Should she try for the phone again? They could explain, couldn't they? She was psyching herself up, but her mum came back over, putting her hands on Sylvie's shoulders. 'Sylvie, you need to breathe. *Breathe!*

Sylvie tried to speak but nothing came out.

'It's not you, Sylvie. It's all on me, but it has to be this way. We don't have any other option. Can you understand me, Sylvie?'

'*Noooo,*' Sylvie heard herself say, a low moan.

'Put these on. Get changed. And the shoes. *Now, Sylvie!*

It could almost have been an ordinary school day when Sylvie was little. Except her mum was taking the clothes and shoes off Victoria. She was yanking roughly at her jeans.

'Why?' Sylvie looked at her, blinking away tears.

Margaret was somehow remaining calm. 'Just do it, Sylvie. Please. It's under control.'

Sylvie was reminded of when she was young and she wet the bed. Her mum would come in in the night and Sylvie would wait while she changed the sheets, half asleep…

Sylvie's hands shook as she tried to remove her own clothes; she couldn't grip anything. As soon as she had loosened an item, Margaret pulled it off, bundling and rolling it up as if she were packing for a family holiday.

Sylvie pulled on the red hooded top and Margaret nodded at her to zip it up. She stepped into Victoria's Converse shoes, zombie-like, and Margaret tied the laces so tight she felt the blood throb around them. They were one size smaller than Sylvie's usual size and her toenails were squashed against her toes, digging into the flesh.

'Mum, can we please call someone? I don't want to do this.'

'I told you, it has to be this way. It has to be now.' Her mum's face was pale, all the blood drained from it. 'You need to help me, Sylvie. Can you please be calm for me?'

Sylvie thought of when she'd had an operation to remove her adenoids. This was like when she was going under the general anaesthetic. Count down from ten, they told her…

'You need to just do what I tell you, OK, Sylvie?'

Six, five, four…

Sylvie breathed in and out, a calmness coming over her. She felt like she was floating above the room, looking down on the action, rather than participating in it.

She could see her and her mum picking up Victoria's body. Margaret by the shoulders, Sylvie got the feet. Victoria only had her underwear on now. Sylvie focused on the tiny blue flowers with yellow leaves. She couldn't face panning out from the detail.

Victoria was heavier than Sylvie had expected. She wanted to tell her mum to be more gentle, but she couldn't speak.

She'd tell Victoria about her weird dream tomorrow and they would laugh about how random it was. 'You weirdo,' Victoria would say and punch her on the arm.

Sylvie and Margaret staggered flat-footed through the kitchen, into the garage.

Not in the boot, please not the boot.

The body landed in it with a dull thud. Margaret had to push Victoria's legs at an awkward angle to close the boot.

Sylvie sobbed but her mum shot her a sharp look.

'Sylvie, we have to do this. Get yourself together.'

Sylvie started to get into the car, but her mum shook her head. She pulled her back into the kitchen. The party food was still on the table, decimated. Plates with rejected sausage rolls, rogue sandwiches curling and drying at the edges. The stark strip lighting showed the make-up that had sunk deep into the grooves of Margaret's face.

'Listen to me, right? Are you taking this in, Sylvie?' She slapped Sylvie's cheek lightly.

Sylvie nodded, trance-like.

'Go to the phone box. And get a taxi to the lake. Book the taxi in the name of Victoria. Are you hearing me, Sylvie?' Her mum pushed two 20p pieces and a five-pound note into Sylvie's hand.

'You get in and you don't say anything. Nothing. You sit in the back and you look out of the window... Sylvie?'

She said it again maybe three or four times.

'Sylvie?'

Margaret spun Sylvie round and strung something cold around her – she touched it, the gold heart locket.

Sylvie shook her head but her mum's hand gripped her shoulder.

As soon as she arrived at the phone box, Sylvie couldn't remember walking there, alone. It was like she had been teleported. Her hands shook as she reached for the phone. As if on auto-pilot, she dialled the number of Victoria's house. She half-hoped that Victoria would somehow answer.

It wasn't too late, she thought. She could tell Peter and Judith what had happened, and everything would be sorted out, like it always was. But after three shrill rings of the phone in her ear she slammed the receiver down and did as her mum had said. She called the taxi and waited.

'You sure about this, love?' the taxi driver said. 'I wouldn't want my daughter up here on her own at this time of night. Or up here at all for that matter.' The rain created a film across the windscreen.

He ducked his head down so he could see out better. The road ahead was only visible in snatches, when the wiper went over.

Sylvie pressed her head to the glass and the scenery passed like a stop-motion animation. She lied to herself that maybe everything was still going to be OK. Her mum would sort it out. That's what mums do; it's what she had always done.

When they arrived at the lake, the taxi driver was about to turn around in his seat. Sylvie just pushed the five-pound note into his hand, one leg already out of the car. She didn't wait for the change. He didn't drive away for what felt like a long time, and she looked back despite herself. The glare of the headlights, full beam, made everything a white-out.

When the taxi pulled away, there was nothing for a while. Sylvie stood, panic rising, checking around her. The rain made the hairspray she'd used that morning sting her eyes and drip into her mouth, bitter-tasting.

She couldn't think straight. Maybe her mum had taken Victoria to the hospital. But why would she send Sylvie up here?

Then Margaret emerged from the darkness and pulled Sylvie into it, from the road. They walked further round the lake, Margaret's hand clamped around Sylvie's wrist.

Margaret's teeth were chattering and her hair was plastered to her face. She hopped from foot to foot on the spot, looking like a drug addict, Sylvie thought.

'Give me the clothes, Sylvie,' she said. 'And the shoes, come on. Be quick.'

Sylvie's thoughts were still tumbling. The hoody and the jeans were stuck to her and Margaret tried to drag them off her faster. The top tore, the fabric making a loud ripping noise.

'Shit, just keep going.' Sylvie was standing in just her underwear. Margaret handed her the bin liner with her dry clothes in and she put them back on. They caught and dragged on her skin from the rain.

Margaret disappeared again into the darkness. There was no sound for a while, then a faint splash. A pause, two more splashes, then nothing else. Sylvie clamped her hands to her ears anyway, pushing against them harder and harder. It was like listening to a shell and she convinced herself she could hear the sea, waves crashing.

'Get in the car. We need to go. Now.' Margaret ran on ahead and got in, flashing the lights once to show Sylvie the way. The car was parked next to the lake in the grass and the darkness. She must have got up there before Sylvie arrived in the taxi. The rain kept driving.

Sylvie was on autopilot as they sat in the car, lights off, Margaret fumbling with the keys.

'Mum, what's happening? Where's Victoria?'

'It has to be this way, Sylvie. This is for you. I am… we are only doing this for you.'

'But we could… we could have called an ambulance or Judith and Peter.'

Margaret wiped tears away from under Sylvie's eyes in swift swipes with her thumbs. She pushed Sylvie's hair back from her face. 'We can't, Sylvie. We couldn't. We wouldn't be able to explain it. They wouldn't believe us about how it happened, would they? People wouldn't look at you in the same way again, Sylvie. It would ruin your life.'

'And this won't?' Sylvie was shouting now. Margaret drove off quickly anyway.

'It would kill your father too. It would be too much. Hearing what Victoria had been saying. That can't be his last memory of us, can it?'

'Well, it's true, isn't it? Isn't it?' Sylvie's voice sounded raw, scratched.

Margaret suddenly swerved to the side, veering across the road. She brought the car to an abrupt halt, jerking Sylvie's neck forwards.

She kept her hands on the steering wheel and looked ahead, sniffing sharply every now and then.

Sylvie waited but her mum didn't deny it.

'Is he going to die? Soon?'

Margaret's face crumpled.

'Why didn't you tell me?'

'They can't fix it, Sylvie, but we don't know what's going to happen. It could be six months, even more. Your dad asked me not to tell you too much. It's what he wants. He wants you to see the best of each other before…' Margaret grabbed Sylvie's hand. Her nails were digging in, threatening to pierce the skin. There was a wildness in her eyes that Sylvie hadn't seen before. 'He needs us right now, Sylvie. He needs his family. That's why it has to be like this. I know you'll understand. You're a clever girl, you always were.'

'So, this party. Victoria said it was like a funeral but he isn't dead.' The pain in Sylvie's throat was unbearable. 'So, other people get to say goodbye but not me?'

'It isn't like that, sweetheart. It wasn't the right time for you. You're different. He wants to talk to you when you're both ready.'

They sat in calmer silence for a few minutes. There was nothing else to say. Eventually Margaret started up the car again and they pulled away.

Sylvie put her hand to her neck. The locket was still there and she wrapped her hand around it.

'We have to go back, Mum. She doesn't have her necklace. She needs it with her. She always wears it.' Sylvie reached and grabbed Margaret's hand on the wheel and the car swerved a little but Margaret didn't take her eyes off the road, speeding up.

They didn't speak for the rest of the journey. When they got in, Sylvie went upstairs, not even turning the light on. She suddenly became aware of the cool weight of the necklace against her chest and pulled it off, snapping the clasp. She shoved it into the back of her drawer, piling underwear on top of it, then got into bed in her damp clothes, shivering under the covers.

When Sylvie opened her eyes the next morning, the house was awake. A radio was talking. There was clattering in the kitchen. The sun streamed in through a crack in the curtains. Maybe it really was a bad dream. She felt a surge of hope and she clung on to it, pushing other thoughts out.

She changed into her pyjamas and rinsed her face. Sylvie was barefoot so hardly made any sound coming downstairs.

Her dad had his back to her. He was wearing an apron and was busy frying something on the hob. Her mum was crouched down, rooting for something in the cupboard under the sink. 'Silly Little Love Songs' was playing. It had been the first dance at their wedding. Her dad put the spatula and wooden spoon out to the side in time to the music, like he was in an old musical. After the way things had been in the weeks before, it was like watching a still photo suddenly come to life.

'Here she is! Sleepy head.' He turned around, egg gloop setting on the spatula he was holding. 'Just in time.' Bacon hissed and spat under the grill. 'I've made your favourite.'

He started to pile food onto the plate and toast popped in the background. The kitchen had the air of a mad science laboratory in full flow. The last thing Sylvie felt like doing was eating. But she had to. Her dad looked so pleased, warm-faced.

He turned the music off and they all sat down. Sylvie was relieved that the chaotic noises were gone. It had been making her feel even more on edge. She pushed the bacon into her mouth, aware of having to chew through the flesh, salty fat squirting out. Breathing deeply in and out of her nose slowly was the only thing that stopped her from throwing up.

Her dad smiled on as she ate. Her mum looked completely calm. The clock seemed like it was ticking more loudly than usual. She caught her mum's gaze. Her expression was mild, neutral like any other Sunday morning, but her eyes were steely, her mandible tight and clenched.

'It was such a good day yesterday, wasn't it? It was so nice to see so many old pals,' Michael said, crunching down on a piece of toast with an enthusiasm Sylvie hadn't seen in a while. Lately he'd pushed his food around his plate at teatime. He hadn't been around for breakfast very much.

'Thank you so much to my girls for organising it. It meant the world to me. Really.'

Sylvie thought she detected a crack in his voice and she froze, but he recovered himself and reached for the orange juice.

Margaret focused on her plate of food. 'Maybe we could have a run out in the car later. Over the tops or something?' she said.

Sylvie questioned again whether last night had really happened. She imagined her family sitting there at the table as figures in a doll's house.

Then the phone rang and smashed everything.

'It's Judith,' Michael shouted through.

'Slow down, Judith. What's going on?' Sylvie heard him say.

CHAPTER THIRTY-SEVEN

Sylvie

Peter stares at me, neck visibly pulsing. 'And?'

'That's it. That's the truth… Victoria. She's getting cold. She's just a baby. She shouldn't be outside like this.'

'Babies are too pampered these days. When we were young, mothers drank, smoked, we didn't have central heating. Everybody turned out just fine.' He bounces Victoria up and down. 'Most people anyway.'

His voice is calmer now, but that starts to make me more uneasy. 'All this time, you never said anything. Why? Why didn't you just say something afterwards?'

My teeth chatter. I will them to stop but it just gets worse. 'I— I couldn't. What could I say? I was caught up in it then. It was too late. I didn't know how to change it. As time went on, I felt confused about what I remembered.'

A snort of disdain. 'And what about later? After, when you were older? You were never going to say anything, were you? Even though your so-called mother is dead herself.'

I snivel, the cold making my nose run. 'I couldn't. It would have just sounded crazy. I thought about it, but no one would have believed me. They'd have thought it was all me and I was pinning it on Mum. It would have sounded worse.'

'Everything could have been different. The things Judith and I have imagined… You didn't have to put us through that.'

That makes something snap. 'If you and my mum hadn't been—'

In one sudden move, Peter reaches out to grab me with one hand and I turn to run at the same time. The neck of my jumper tears and he doesn't let go of the fabric. He bunches it tighter into his fist. Victoria looks at me like it's a game. I try to smile at her and I picture how manic and frightening I must look.

'You know she was alive, don't you?' Peter says.

The ground feels like it disappears from under me.

'Who?' I don't even want to know what he's going to say next.

'Victoria. She was alive when she went into the water. They never released that information but they told us.'

'No.'

'You could have saved her.'

'Mum wouldn't…'

'Oh, please.'

'Not if she knew.'

'You might want to think that. I bet she held her under while she begged.'

Did Mum know that? That she was alive? And she pushed her in the water anyway? A worse thought washes up then. Did I know deep down? The second two splashes. Was that when she struggled?

I feel as if I am falling in a very deep gorge. I've yet to hit the ground.

I realise Peter is looking out across the lake and I follow his gaze. A car has arrived on the other side. At first I think maybe it's the police, and relief starts to swell then quickly shrivels again. If Peter called them I might not see Victoria for a long time.

But why would he? After what he just told me.

I squint to look more closely. The outline of the car is familiar. The figure waves and I recognise the way he does it, the angle of his arm.

'Who is that?' Peter narrows his eyes too.

'It's my husband, Nathan.' I try to take another step away from him and the fabric of my jumper gives way again, the tear deepening.

Peter ignores me and looks out across the water.

Nathan looks for a while, then stops waving. He sets off around the lake towards us.

'How does he know where you are?' Peter gives me a shake, anger rising again.

'I— I don't know.' And I realise I don't. My stomach drops at that. 'But he must have gone to the house looking for me. I told him we'd been staying there. I just ran when I saw Victoria was gone. I didn't even close the door. He'll be worried.'

Peter seems more agitated then. Stupid of me to say that. He seems to realise what he's doing, then, and he lets go of me. I stumble back slightly at the release of tension. Victoria has hardly stirred, unaware of what's going on.

Peter starts scratching hard at a patch on his head. The skin soon looks raw.

I go to take Victoria from him and I expect him to struggle or snatch her away again but he releases her and I pull her to me, relief at the weight and warmth of her in my arms.

'No, no, no, this doesn't look right at all,' Peter says. 'I wanted you to know how it felt. Just a glimpse of what you've done to me and Judith. To lose your daughter. To not know where she is, what's happened to her. To think about her up here. I think about what it was like for her, you know, that night. In the pitch-black.'

'I think about that night too,' I say. 'Every day.'

Peter is still scratching his head. 'What are we going to say? To Nathan?'

'What does that matter?' I say. 'We'll just say we came for a walk or something? It doesn't matter.'

'He's seen us… And then you'll go back and play happy families? Live happily ever after? Forget all this ever happened?'

'I don't know what you want from me. We're going to go now, Peter, OK?' I start edging forwards.

'Get in the water,' Peter says, dull and distant.

'What? Peter?' I look over at Nathan and he's stopped. He's watching us.

Peter hisses through his teeth, barely moving his mouth. 'Get in the water and walk. You need to feel what it's like to be in there.'

I think about running, but with Victoria I'd be too slow. I'd risk falling. Peter takes out his phone and gets Judith's number up.

The water is icy cold when it hits me, coming up to my ankles. Peter puts the phone away again.

'Sylvie!' I hear someone shout. Nathan. His voice sounds closer now but I don't dare to look.

My head is light. I wonder if I've already passed out, if I am already under the water. In the blackness.

'*Nathan!*' I try to shout, pulling Victoria towards me. My words form small clouds in the cold air and drift away towards him.

'Keep walking, Sylvie,' Peter says.

The water is up to my thighs now, the cold running up my bones. Then it's at my waist, pouring over the top of my jeans and inside them. Solid things, too, sticking to my skin now. I'm waiting for one of the shelves to drop from beneath me. I think of the sheep's heads and dead things we heard they found in here. It feels like something scuttles across my foot but I don't know if I am imagining it. I turn back to Peter, pleading, but he nods for me to go on. He's holding his arms out now, so it looks like he's beckoning me to come back.

Soon the water will be up my body, touching Victoria.

I call for Nathan and he shouts back, 'I'm here, Sylvie.' And I start to change direction and go towards him. Trying to speed up, but the water slows me down. Something snags and catches on my feet and trips me. It's rooted hard into the bottom of the lake and I teeter, trying to disentangle myself, terrified of dropping Victoria in the lake. I right myself and try to keep my breathing steady, kissing the top of her head gently. Somehow, she doesn't seem upset or anxious. She blinks up at me, then closes her eyes again.

Peter moves along so he's level with me on the edge of the lake. 'OK, Sylvie. Come towards me and get out now.' He reaches his arms out for Victoria. I have to hand her to him or I can't climb out.

My legs are heavy when I try to get out of the lake, water sloshing off them. Peter grips my elbow, hard, and I push my weight down until I can get a footing on the side.

Peter sits on the bench slowly and gestures for me to sit next to him. Nathan is getting closer now, but he's slowed down, cautious. Peter pats the bench again. I sit down; I don't have any choice.

'We're in this together now, you and me,' he says, putting an arm around my shoulder.

'What do you mean?'

My thoughts race. How long would I get to explain to Nathan? There's so much to say, that he would need to understand. Where would I even start?

'It would break Judith, that's the thing. To know how it happened,' Peter says, putting another arm around me as if to warm me up. 'She'd blame herself, not just you and me. I'm all she has. We can't do that to her. Not now. She's been through too much already.' He strokes Victoria's cheek gently. There are thin wet tracks down his face.

I look at him in horror, but reflected back at me is his face brightening. He rubs at the top of my arms.

'I'll be watching you, Sylvie. You'll come back here regularly and you'll bring the little one to see me and Judith. That would make her happy, my Jude.'

My face prepares itself to protest. Nathan is almost here now and he breaks into a run. 'Sylvie, what's happening?'

'Why? How are you here?' I hear myself say.

'You didn't sound right on the phone so I found your mum's address. All those Christmas and birthday cards you never post. I wanted to come and pick you up. I got to the house and the door was swinging open. Your neighbour said to try here, that you often come up here. And then I was really scared.'

Peter stands up and goes towards him. 'She's alright, mate. She's just got herself a bit upset. A bit mixed up, eh, Sylvie love? She's alright now, aren't you, pet?'

'Sylvie, my God. I'm so sorry.' Nathan bends down and puts his hands on my shoulders. 'I shouldn't have let you just go like that.'

'It isn't your fault,' I say. And I think about what I'm passing on now, the next wave of ripples that will come from this. How it's changing the course of my and Nathan's life. And Victoria's.

'Thanks so much for being here,' he says to Peter, patting him on the top of his arm then putting his hand out. 'Nathan.'

Peter shakes it. 'Least I could do, mate. I've known Sylvie since she was just a girl. You're alright now, eh, love? Everything's going to be OK now, isn't it?'

I get up and I hear Peter turn to the side and say to Nathan, 'You'll have to watch her, mate. With the baby. She isn't in a good way.'

Nathan takes Victoria from me as if she's made of glass. He walks me back around the lake, arm around me but not quite touching, like he's afraid he will break me too.

CHAPTER THIRTY-EIGHT

Sylvie, two months later

Nathan rarely takes his eyes off me. He tries to avoid leaving me alone with Victoria. He's taken some 'personal leave' from work and I think of them whispering about me in his office.

He hasn't asked. No one has. Nobody has said it out loud, but it's there in the way they are around me, radiating from them even when they're not looking at me.

How could you, Sylvie? How could you consider hurting your own baby?

And I have to let them think that.

I told him that Victoria died, that being at home, Mum, had brought it all up again, put me off balance. That I'd buried it before. It was close to the truth, but not everything, of course.

Nathan wants me to talk to someone. I don't know if I can stall him any longer. His sympathy is turning to resentment. How could I not want to sort things out? I owe it to us all. If I do go, I'll have to make it all up. Or most of it. He'd finally be impressed with my creativity.

We're pulling into Conley now. My phone beeps. *Michelle.*

Are you here yet? What time shall we meet? Got some pressies for Victoria!

Over-keen, as ever, but she means well. She probably judges the least; she takes you as you are.

I kept expecting Sam to call, but I haven't heard anything from him. Judith told me that he had been knocked back for his pitch. In a strange way, there was a sting in that, that Victoria's story was rejected, not worthy or interesting enough.

We call Peter and Judith regularly. They send gifts. In return, I bring photos; we have to visit. Nathan says it's nice for me to have a connection with my hometown and with Mum. He thinks it's a way for me to heal, for us both to.

Maybe it's a small price to pay for freedom, or a version of it. To be able to stay with Victoria and watch her grow up.

Nathan squeezes my knee, looks over and smiles.

Peter and Judith come out onto the drive to meet us. Nathan and Peter shake hands. They talk about whisky and horse racing on the phone. I think Nathan swots up in advance so he can hold a conversation.

Judith has laid out tea and sandwiches already, and before I know it she has scooped Victoria out of my arms. Peter takes our coats upstairs.

When he comes back down, Nathan says, 'We're going by the house later, aren't we, babe?' It catches Peter's attention and I feel myself stiffen.

'Sylvie doesn't believe me but I've got a bee in my bonnet about the house.' Nathan puts his arm around me, squeezing the flesh. 'I know it's a bit of a state right now, but it's got real potential. I want to do it up. I'm up for the challenge, aren't I, Sylv?'

Judith is interested now, her eyes bright. 'Are you two thinking of moving back here, then?'

I say, 'We haven't thought about it,' Nathan says, 'Maybe,' at the same time, like we're in a screwball comedy film. Everyone laughs but me.

'I'll be up for helping you, lad,' Peter says. 'Sylvie told you I used to be a builder, didn't she?'

'That'd be great. Cheers, Peter.'

'We haven't decided anything yet,' I say. 'We might still sell it.'

Nathan punctures the awkwardness. 'Soooo, how was the cruise?'

'Oh, it was fantastic, Nathan.' Judith moons about the food and the entertainment and the people they met. 'It's the best time we've had in ages.'

It's nice to see her happy, enjoying life as best she can.

'Wasn't it amazing, Peter?'

'Yes, dear.' He nudges Nathan. 'It wanted to be for the price as well. Aaaaand,' Peter looks directly at me and it's like standing too close to a fire. 'We got something for you, Sylvie.'

He retrieves a paper bag from the dresser drawer and hands it to me. Something hard inside, round in shape. I pull it out, everyone's eyes on me. It's a cruise ship in a snow globe, turquoise shards suspended in the water.

'We know how much you like them.' Judith beams at me. 'Time to start your own traditions, eh? With your own little family. It was Peter that saw it.'

Judith hands round a plate of cakes. I take one and bite into it to hide my expression.

'And, now that you're all here… We've got more good news.'

'Oh, what's that?' My mind jumps ahead. *They're moving house?* Unlikely. *Renewing their vows?* Perhaps.

'Have we?' Peter says, putting his cake down.

'I haven't told you yet, either. I just found out earlier, so I thought I'd tell us all together.'

A lump of pink, sugary icing lodges itself at the back of my throat. A moment of panic at choking, then I cough hard and the cake breaks free. Nathan gives me a quizzical look.

'I mean, we weren't too sure about Sam for a bit, were we, Peter? Seemed like he wasn't really getting very far.'

Peter puts his hand on Judith's shoulder. 'What is this, love? What are you getting yourself excited about? That's over now. He did his best but he couldn't get it off the ground. Don't go upsetting yourself.'

She brushes him off. 'But this is different.'

'Is it?' Peter says.

I catch Peter's eye and he gives an almost imperceptible shake of the head. It's nothing to worry about? It's all over for me? What?

Judith reaches under the table and pulls out a newspaper. Not the same one as before, though. Newer. Peter refuses to meet my eye now, staring into the bottom of his cup.

The headline reads: 'Police appeal for mystery woman in 1990s murder case.'

It takes all my concentration not to let the crockery I'm holding crash to the floor.

'New info. Finally.' Judith fans her hand across the paper. 'Source came forwards. And guess what? Someone saw Victoria up at the lake that night in a car. Not the taxi, a different car. And the driver… it was a woman.'

The room falls silent. Nathan doesn't know what to do with himself.

I take the paper off Judith and start to scan the article. There's a picture of Sam. He's made himself part of the story now. A picture of Victoria too.

'And they're going to fund it,' Judith says. 'Sam is coming back, with a proper film crew and everything.'

I scan the article:

A group of armchair true-crime aficionados has started a crowdfunding campaign for a documentary about the death of Conley teenager Victoria Preston. The

SomeoneMustKnow project has already reached 75% of
its funding target one week after launching the appeal.

The rest of the words on the page dissolve to a blur.

Judith takes Victoria from Nathan and lifts her high over her
head, spinning her round.

CHAPTER THIRTY-NINE

Sylvie

As we pull away from Peter and Judith's, I sit silent in the car, staring out of the window.

Nathan keeps looking over at me.

I load up SomeoneMustKnow on my phone. There's a big garish button to donate to funding the documentary. Threads about Victoria's case are popping up like weeds.

The latest one is titled: 'The woman in the car'. When I click into it, they're discussing the article in the paper.

'We need to look into Victoria's mother's background, Judith,' someone writes. 'Get the information across to Sam.'

'What about female relatives?' another says. 'What can we dig up on them? Neighbours?'

It's only a matter of time before they get to Mum. And me. After they've raked over Judith's life, picked over someone else's past.

'You want me to drop you off at the supermarket, then, to meet Michelle?' Nathan says. I sense he is repeating himself.

'What'll you do?' I say.

'Might go to the house, if that's OK with you. Size a few things up.'

'OK.' And I make my mind up in an instant. 'I just want to come round with you first, to the house, and get something.'

'Just tell me where it is and I'll get it for you.'

'No, I'd rather do it myself, but thanks.'

Nathan looks at me for a moment, then gives me a 'whatever you want' shake of the head.

When we pull up, he starts getting out of the car too.

'Do you mind just waiting here with Victoria until I come out?'

I get out, open the car door and lean in to kiss Victoria, and she grins up at me.

'Sylvie, are you OK? Are we OK?'

'I'll be five minutes,' I say, and he watches me go, the car window open.

I don't go in the house, but straight into the back garden. I close the gate behind me and take out my bag, pulling out fun-size chocolate bars and scattering them in the grass for the children. It's nowhere near as long as it was now, but I hide the chocolate in the flower beds too; I place them in the rockery.

I sit on the swing seat. Nathan has cleaned it off and oiled it when we've visited one weekend. I take out my phone and then the card from my pocket and dial the number. He takes a few rings to answer.

'Hi?'

'Hi Sam, it's Sylvie.'

'Sylvie? Oh, I was going to get in touch with you. I know you don't want to talk, but I'll be using the footage I have anyway so it's in your interest to—'

'I called you, didn't I?'

'You saw the paper, then?'

I take one deep breath, then it's out. 'I want to tell you what happened. All of it. But there are conditions.'

'Go on,' he says.

'I want to get the chance to tell Judith myself, and the police if I need to, before they hear it somewhere else.'

'OK...'

'I didn't walk Victoria to the phone box that night, like you said.'

Sam breathes heavily into the phone. 'So, why did you say that you did?'

'I said that whoever your source is didn't see Victoria walking on her own. That was true.'

'I don't understand.'

'There's more as well. I want to tell my side of the story so there's no twisting it. But it has to be one shot, no edits. Tomorrow night, eight o'clock. Meet me up at the lake.'

A LETTER FROM SARAH

Thank you for choosing to read *Her Best Friend*. If you enjoyed it and want to keep up-to-date with all my latest releases, just sign up at the following link. Your email address will never be shared and you can unsubscribe at any time.

www.bookouture.com/sarah-wray

In this book, I wanted to explore our sometimes-uncomfortable interest in true crime (my own included), whether the 'truth' should always out and how the way we curate and frame the past can create many different versions of the same event. I am interested in the grey areas between guilt and innocence and how you move on, or don't, from a flashpoint moment in your life.

I hope you enjoyed Sylvie and Victoria's story and I would be very grateful if you could write a review for *Her Best Friend* too. I'd love to hear what you think, and it also helps to bring in new readers.

I love hearing from my readers – you can get in touch on my Facebook page, through Twitter, Goodreads or my website.

Thanks,
Sarah

f sarahwraywrites/
Sarah_Wray
www.sarahwraywrites.co.uk

ACKNOWLEDGEMENTS

To Keshini Naidoo at Bookouture for the encouragement, patience and ability to believe it would be alright on the night with this book when I didn't.

To Laura Longrigg at MBA Literary Agents for all her honest feedback and support.

To all my friends who have put up with my book-based hand-wringing and encouraged me to keep going.

To Patrick, Mum and Dad for never discouraging the dark side.

To my home town for all the inspiration.

And always to Leon x